Reaping the Benefits

The story is quite eccentric with its paranormal context but in fact is a pure romance at heart with a nice dose of humor. The book is written in third person, from the point of view of both protagonists, which is not common for Noyes, but it is executed perfectly. With all main elements done well, this makes an awesome read which I could easily recommend to all romance fans.

-Pin's Reviews, *goodreads*

I've read many love stories that entertain the idea of soul mates, but this one does something even more interesting. This one explores the depth of love and its ability to transcend death. This story plays with the idea that love has no limits or boundaries. Its exploration provides a unique setting for this heartfelt romantic tale. At its core it remains a romance. The love story between Jane and Morgan is tender and sweet. It's so cleverly and delightfully done; I've never read anything quite like it before. Noyes possesses the ability to see a story where others don't and turn that into something unique and captivating. She uses rich storytelling and engaging characters to enthrall and delight us.

It's fresh and original. It's everything you crave when you want to dig into a great romance. I highly recommended it.

-Deb M., *NetGalley*

I'm spectacularly smitten with Death, to be specific with E. J. Noyes' personification of death as Cici La Morte in this new and most wondrous book. Cici is not one of the main characters but she is the fulcrum about which the whole plot rotates. She simultaneously operates as a beautiful symbol of our fascination with the theme of death and loss, and as a comedic but wise Greek chorus guiding Morgan through the internal conflict threatening to tear her very soul apart. All of E. J. Noyes' previous books have had emotionally charged first-person narrative, so I was curious how her switch to writing in the third person would play out here, but it really works. Despite many lighthearted and genuinely funny moments I found that this book not only had E. J. Noyes' signature ability to make me cry, but also fascinating ideas and philosophies about grief, loss, and hope.

-Orlando J., *NetGalley*

E. J. Noyes never disappoints and this book is another added to one of my favourites. What I love about Noyes is every book is different and unique from the other which is what makes her such a special writer. The way she has me completely entrenched into the story has me wanting to read or listen to her books over and over again, it's addictive. I highly recommend the book.

-Catherine C., *NetGalley*

E. J. Noyes is an amazing writer. I have read all of her books and no two books have even a remotely similar plot. She constantly pushes herself to be a better writer. This book is no exception. This book was such a fun twist on what everyone normally thinks about life, death, and the afterlife. I loved the dialogue between the characters as well as the plot development. It was a lot of fun to read!

-Jenna F., *NetGalley*

This very unique story line turned into a beautiful story that had me experiencing a multitude of emotions, from humor to heartbreak and everything in between. The paranormal aspect works beautifully in the novel. Ms. Noyes made the supernatural aspect of the story seem like a normal part of life. The characters are well developed. The ideas of life, death, and the afterlife are handled in a manner I would have never thought about, but which works well in the book.

-Betty H., *NetGalley*

If you're looking for a lesbian romance, but with a twist of something different, I recommend *Reaping the Benefits*. It's sweet, sexy, and fun.

- *The Lesbian Review*

Wildly unique and completely unexpected, *Reaping the Benefits* wasn't a hard sell given the expertise with which the author has been able to entertain me with every book published. The letting go of reality to fall into a paranormal underworld is a most unusual backdrop for a love affair but here we are, and I enjoyed every minute of it. Despite the uniqueness of the scenery and its characters, Morgan and Jane's developing attraction eventually directs Morgan to contemplate everything. The intensity of her introspections coupled with her musings with Death is as bizarre as it is incredibly interesting. This author never fails to entertain me in the most unusual ways that leaves me ruminating over her words long after The End.

-Cathie W., *NetGalley*

Alone

E. J. Noyes is easily one of the most gifted writers pulling us into whatever world she creates making us live and feel every emotion with her characters. Definitely, loudly, vehemently recommended.

-Reviewer@Large, NetGalley

Alone is an absolutely stunning book. This book is not a 5-star, it is well above that. You don't see books like this one very often. Truly a treasure and one that will stay with you long after the final page.

-Tiff's Reviews, goodreads

For being one of my most anticipated books to read in 2019, this one sure had a lot of expectations to live up to! I can say with full authority that it met or exceeded every single hope that I had. Noyes has done it again, cementing her place as a "must-read" author. *Alone* lived up to all the hype, and is easily one of the best books of 2019!

-Bethany K., NetGalley

There are only a handful of authors that I will drop everything to read as soon as a new book comes out, and Noyes is at the top of that list. It seems no matter what Noyes writes she doesn't disappoint. I will eagerly be waiting for whatever she writes next.

-Lex Kent's Reviews, goodreads

There are only a few books out there so compelling they seem to take control of you and force you to read them as quickly as possible. You can't put them down. You just want the world to go away and leave you alone until you can finish this story. *Alone* by E. J. Noyes is that book for me. This novel is absolutely wonderful.

-Betty H., NetGalley

Not only is this easily one of the best books of 2019, but it has worked its way onto my personal all-time top 10 list. There is not one formulaic thing going on, and it's "unputdownable."

-Karen C., NetGalley

I cannot give this anything more than five stars, but damn I wish I could. I would give it 15.

-Carolyn M., NetGalley

Ask, Tell

This is a book with everything I love about top quality lesbian fiction: a fantastic romance between two wonderful women I can relate to, a location that really made me think again about something I thought I knew well, and brilliant pacing and scene-setting. I cannot recommend this novel highly enough.

-Rainbow Book Reviews

Noyes totally blew my mind from the first sentence. I went in timidly, and I came away awaiting her next release with bated breath. I really love how Noyes is able to get below the surface of the DADT legislation. She really captures the longing, the heartbreak, and especially the isolation that LGBTQ soldiers had to endure because the alternative was being deemed unfit to serve by their own government. I applaud Noyes for getting to the heart of the matter and giving a very important representation of what living and serving under this legislation truly meant for LGBTQ men and women of service.

-The Lesbian Review

E. J. Noyes was able to deliver on so many levels... This book is going to take you on a roller-coaster ride of ups and downs that you won't expect but it's so unbelievably worth it.

-Les Rêveur Reviews

Noyes clearly undertook a mammoth amount of research. I was totally engrossed. I'm not usually a reader of romance novels, but this one gripped me. The personal growth of the main character, the rich development of her fabulous best friend, Mitch, and the well-handled tension between Sabine and her love interest were all fantastic. This one definitely deserves five stars.

-CELEStial books Reviews

Turbulence

Wow... and when I say 'wow' I mean... WOW. After the author's debut novel *Ask, Tell* got to my list of best books of 2017, I was wondering if that was just a fluke. Fortunately for us lesfic readers, now it's confirmed: E. J. Noyes CAN write. Not only that, she can write different genres… Written in first person from Isabelle's point of view, the reader gets into her headspace with all her insecurities, struggles, and character traits. Alongside Isabelle, we discover Audrey's personality, her life story and, most importantly, her feelings. Throughout the book, Ms. Noyes pushes us down a roller coaster of emotions as we accompany Isabelle in her journey of self-discovery. In the process, we laugh, suffer, and enjoy the ride.

-Gaby, *goodreads*

This was hot, steamy, even a little emotional…and I loved every second of it. This book is in first person. I know some don't care for that, but it works for this book, really. Always being in Isabelle's head, not knowing for sure what Audrey was thinking, gave me almost a little suspense. I just love the way Noyes writes. I know I am fan-girling out a bit here, but her books make me happy. All other romance fans, I easily recommend this. I just hope I don't have to wait too long for another Noyes book.

-Lex Kent, *goodreads*

The entire story just flowed from the first page! E. J. Noyes did a superb job of bringing out Isabelle's and Audrey's personalities, faults, erratic emotions, and the burning passion they shared. The chemistry between both women was so palpable! I felt as though the writer drizzled every word she wrote with love, combustible desire, and intense longing.

-*The Lesbian Review*

Gold

This is Noyes' third book, and her writing just keeps getting better and better with each release. She gives us such amazing characters that are easy for anyone to relate to. And she makes them so endearing that you can't help but want them to overcome the past and move forward toward their happily ever after.

-*The Lesbian Review*

This book is exactly the way I wish romance authors would get back to writing romance. This is what I want to read. If you are a Noyes fan, get this book. If you are a romance fan, get this book. I didn't even talk about the skiing… if you are a skiing fan, get this book.

-Lex Kent, *goodreads*

If the Shoe Fits

When we pick up an E. J. Noyes book we expect intensity, characters with issues (circumstantial and/or internal), and a romance that builds believably. Considering this is Ask, Tell #3 we expected all of the above layered with epic seriousness. We were pleasantly surprised and totally floored by the humor in addition to what was already expected!

-Best Lesfic Reviews

Pas de deux

Other Bella Books by E. J. Noyes

About the Author

E. J. Noyes lives in Australia with her wife, a needy cat, aloof chickens and too many horses. When not indulging in her love of reading and writing, E. J. argues with her hair and pretends to be good at things.

Pas de deux

E. J. NOYES

BELLA
BOOKS
2021

First Bella Books Edition 2021

Editor: Cath Walker
Cover Designer: Judith Fellows

ISBN: 978-1-64247-245-5

Acknowledgments

I suppose you could say this book has been twenty-five years in the making. Though *Pas de deux* is definitely a work of fiction, the idea came to me when I was (yet again) telling the story of how my wife and I met in Pony Club and were SO not friends. You could say it was a kind of Juliet and Juliet scenario of two girls from rival riding schools, both of whom were afflicted with social awkwardness, meeting again as adults where I'd grown out of my social awkwardness and into some pretty good outrage that this person who'd been so mean and standoffish to me as a teenager had reappeared in my life. But it all worked out in the end and the real story is a pretty fun story to tell.

Epic thank-yous to Kate, who not only shared her Americanness with me at all hours of night and day, but trawled through close to 120,000 words of barely edited first-draft mush and emerged from the other side to not only tell me the story was good, but helped me make the words better.

Claire, in case you didn't know, your well-timed GIFs and encouragement always pick me up when I'm suffering a bout of Tortured Artiste™.

Christina, I don't know how you do it but your eternal optimism and seemingly casual suggestions like "Why not Rio?" turned this from a panic project to a pet project.

My eternal gratitude to Dr. Paula Williams (alphabet soup of degrees and qualifications and smart stuff after her name) who helped me make Addie sound like a real vet. Paula, not only are you the bestest equine veterinarian we know—and the Real Dewey's most favourite—but you're also an amazing friend and we're so hashtag blessed to know you. Is this day one?

Cath – every time we work together I send silent clumps of gratitude to whoever allocated you to edit my work. I'm sorry this was so wordy. And! I know I keep promising but I really am going to try harder with not using (abusing?) serial commas…

Bella Crew, you're great. Thank you.

Pheebs, I'm sure you recognise the story of how we met and our teenaged stand-offish animosity in here. This one's for you, babe, but I just made our story a little (lot) more exciting. I'm so glad it turned out that you weren't actually the mean bitch I thought you were when we were at Pony Club together.

CHAPTER ONE

Caitlyn

The Dutch voice coming through my headset hit maximum intensity. "No, stop, walk!"

My sweat and fatigue both muttered, "With pleasure" and Dewey relaxed to walk like a balloon deflating. The moment Lotte Bakker strode across the sand of her indoor arena toward us, my horse reinflated and I could feel the tense choppiness of his stride. He probably hadn't forgiven her for yesterday where she'd made us work on our transitions from piaffe to passage to piaffe over and over until I thought Dew was about to collapse or lie down in protest. He wasn't one to hold a grudge, but I was pretty sure Lotte would be at the top of his list if he had one.

A quick mane scratch and a murmured, "Good man" relaxed him again. I bent my head to wipe sweat from my face onto my polo sleeve and tried not to look as exhausted as I felt. Before arriving in Europe three weeks ago to compete in the high-level international events essential for Olympic-team selection, I'd spent years riding six or seven horses a day, on top of spending an hour in my home gym daily. My riding fitness was at its peak. But a forty-five-minute session with Lotte made me feel like I'd spent the last ten years couch-potatoing.

Lotte walked alongside us, keeping her distance from Dew's inquisitive nose. "*Caiiitttttlynnnnnn.*" Shit. When Lotte drew out your name like that you were in trouble. "Why did I make you stop?" she asked crisply.

I resisted the urge to wilt. Despite the fact I had the experience and competition results to justify my place on the shortlist for the US Olympic Dressage Team, Lotte could still make me feel like a novice equestrienne. "He's wriggling his butt. His hindquarters," I quickly corrected. Wriggling was an evasion in piaffe and Dew just being lazy—easier to wriggle than fully engage his hindquarters.

"Exactly. If you know what he is doing and you know this is incorrect, why are you allowing it to happen?"

Telling Lotte "Because I'm so exhausted I can barely sit upright" was definitely not the right course of action. Thankfully her question seemed rhetorical because she barreled on, gesturing emphatically. "He starts with a good piaffe—not great, but adequate—and then you allow him to wiggle and wobble until it looks like he is…what is that dance thing?" She paused, brightened and blurted, "Tweaking."

"I think you might mean twerking?" I ventured.

She gave my suggestion a moment's thought. "Yes. He moves his hindquarters like he is twerking. This is not how a Grand Prix dressage horse should behave. It is laziness, pure and simple." She pointed at Dew's butt. "He has so much power back here." Lotte's index finger moved to point at Dewey's head. "His problem is in here, in his mind. The piaffe work is hardest for him so he does what he can to make it easy. Logical. But never correct."

"Right."

"You let him be lazy and then all your hard work is lost. A wriggling piaffe is not a piaffe that will score nines and tens. Stop it before it happens. Hold him together. Legs legs, hands hands. Tighten that core and seat. You have the skills, both of you, now stop being so soft on him. If he does not respond, you make him respond. You do not need to be rough, we know this, but you must be consistent."

"I know."

"Good. You must always train and ride the horse in a way that sets them up to succeed. I know you are aware of this."

I wouldn't dare contradict her even if I'd thought she was wrong. Considering Lotte had won multiple Olympic and World Equestrian Games medals and was consistently at the top of the rankings during her dressage career, we were lucky she'd agreed to work with us shortlisted team members while we were in the Netherlands. I nodded. "Mhmm, yeah." Though I'd only had a handful of lessons with her, I'd learned early on that apologies were worse than not apologizing.

Lotte didn't care for apologies—she cared that you did what you were told, utilized her expertise and learned from your mistakes.

Her voice dropped to unnatural-for-her quietness. "In my years of dressage, I have *never* known a horse with this one's natural talent. You both have every skill, every movement. But this piaffe is the weakness, and we must refine it and make him want to do more. We must take you from your eighty percent scores into eighty-five-plus percent and then into ninety percent. You are on the cusp of making world records, Caitlyn. You can do this, easy. But tell me, what is a world record dressage test if you know you could have done better?" Another rhetorical question. "Now two minutes more of walk break before we tackle the piaffe again."

I let Dewey have a little rein so he could stretch his neck. Lotte was absolutely right. Dew could be lazy. The sweat trickling down my back and soaking my armpits was testament to that fact. Dewey—Midfields Adieu—adored the mental stimulation of work but wasn't as enthused by the physical exertion, especially in the piaffe where he had to sustain an elevated and collected trot basically on the spot. It wasn't so much that he was unwilling but he had a knack for trying to take the easy way, almost as if he was asking me, "Are you sure, do I really have to?" and hoping one day I'd say, "No, Dew, you don't have to do this movement perfectly, let's go back to your stall and eat a bag of licorice."

I knew sometimes I *was* too soft with him. But…he was my first Grand Prix horse, my riding partner, my goofy pal. I'd bred him, was there when he was a newborn and had spent every day of the past twelve years turning him from a gangly youngster to internationally competitive. And of my four horses, he was my unquestioned favorite. I patted him again. "We're almost done, just keep trying for me. Good boy."

"What was that?"

Shit, the headset was still live. "Nothing, sorry. Just talking to the horse."

The headset crackled with a moment of static. "He does not speak English. Show him he is a good boy by helping him do the work and then his reward is your releasing the aid, a pat and then rest and food when he is finished trying." Lotte's expression softened. "The connection you have with him is so important, but you must think equally with head and heart. You can both go to number one in the world. His walk? Perfect. Extended trot? Magnificent. And his canter pirouettes are the best I have seen, and you deserve every nine and ten you receive for them. But it is not enough to only have the talent, you must do the work."

Oh, I was doing the work. I was working my ass off to make it look like I wasn't working at all and it was starting to wear me down. I'd had no downtime in Europe and I was starting to feel the mental and physical strain. We'd landed in France to compete in Compiègne, earning first place and a respectable score of 79.800%, which I knew helped our cause of making the Olympic team.

Then we'd made the four-hour road trip to Lotte's dressage barn in Oud Gastel near Roosendaal in the Netherlands and settled into what would be our home for a month. The US Dressage Federation grant monies covered only part of my international competition costs and exchanging accommodation and Lotte's expert training for me working for her was a no-brainer. But if I made the Olympic team, the financial thing would hopefully get a little easier.

Dewey and I had two more mandatory competitions to qualify for a place on the team: the Roosendaal four-star event in one week, then the Rotterdam five-star event three weeks later. Then, if we made the final cut, it was on to the Olympics in Rio at the start of August. Not that I was counting down the days until what might be my first Olympic Games. And I was only shitting my breeches a little.

Lotte worked us hard for another twenty minutes, during which I could hear the muted approvals from the two people sitting beside the arena—Mary McDonald, the Chef d'Equipe who would manage the team, and Ian Hargrave, the team coach. When Lotte finally dismissed me, after gently scolding then effusively praising me, I thanked her, acknowledged Mary and Ian then guided Dewey toward the gate on the short end of the indoor arena.

Dakota Turner, another shortlisted rider, snarled something under her breath as she rode her imported Westphalian gelding, Pierre, past me into the arena. Pierre, his coat usually a bright white, was dark gray with sweat and foam lathered his neck. Dewey, who had no concept of social boundaries for humans or horses, thrust his head forward to say hi to Pierre who might have returned the greeting if Dakota hadn't yanked his head around and jabbed her spurs into his ribs. "Keep that mongrel away from us," she snarled as Pierre surged away with a grunt of displeasure. "Grandma Reserve," she threw over her shoulder.

I almost wanted to call after her to get some new material or make up a stupid nickname to call her, like Widdle Baby Dakota. At twenty-six, she was by far the youngest of the shortlisted riders and despite what she'd said, my thirty-seven still put me at the younger end of our team. Dressage was not ageist at all. And given my scores were the highest of everyone's, the likelihood of Dewey and I being the team's reserve pair was slim. But Dakota thought calling me Grandma Reserve was demeaning. She loved being demeaning. To me at least.

I tried to push Dakota out of my mind. She wasn't worth the brain power. Or so I tried to tell my brain. In addition to constantly trying to make out like I didn't deserve to be on the team, Dakota had started adding jibes about how uneducated I was—technically true if you went by the traditional measure of education being college—and also making fun of my supposed hick accent.

My family had moved to Tennessee for my dad's job when I was thirteen and I'd left the state at almost-eighteen to work as a *Bereiter* in a German dressage barn. I got a similar job in Florida before building my own dressage facility just outside of La Grange, Kentucky. I knew my accent was less hick and more bland American, reflective of someone who moved a lot as a kid. But according to Dakota's phone conversation with her twenty-years-her-senior Texas oil tycoon husband—which she may or may not have intended for me to hear—I sounded like a redneck. Most likely she'd Googled me and discovered my sojourn in the South and decided it was good meanness fodder.

I leaned forward to tug Dew's ear affectionately. "You're not a mongrel, and always remember you're imported too. Well, your dad was. Kind of. In a tank full of liquid nitrogen."

He snorted and shook his head, sending foamy saliva flying in every direction, including backward onto my breeches. My groom, Wren, met me on the path to the huge barn housing Lotte's box stalls. As she walked alongside she held up the video camera. "Nice," was her assessment. "Once you tightened up the piaffe it was—" Wren chef-kissed her fingers, "prime."

Wren was misnamed. The only thing she had in common with the small flitty bird was constant chatter. Chasing six-feet tall, with bright blue hair I'd never seen out of a ponytail—though she promised she was going to shave just one side of her head and have an American flag colored in if we made the Olympic team—Wren was boisterous, witty and one of the most intuitive horse people I'd ever known. I was beyond lucky to have found someone with such vast knowledge of horses who for some reason didn't enjoy competing with her own.

I unfastened my gloves. "Yeah. I'm just glad she stopped going on about it. Like, I know it's his weakest movement and I'm busting my ass to convince him to work harder at it." Smiling, I suggested, "Maybe we need a carrot on a stick."

"Maybe. Though knowing Dew he'd figure out how to cheat and get the carrot without improving the piaffe." She smiled up at me. "Guess we can't expect him to be perfect at everything."

"True."

Wren lowered her voice. "Grapevine. Lotte told Ian if he ruined the work she's done with you, she'd make sure he never coached another Olympic team." She gave me a pointed, eyebrows-raised look.

"I can totally believe she said that." A surge of excitement at both Wren's gossip and that *You know what I mean* look had the butterflies in my stomach flapping their wings. Apparently Lotte thought my selection was a sure thing. "She probably has the connections to make good on her threat. But I have to make the team first."

Wren offered a dismissive, "Semantics."

"Mmm. At any rate, all her coaching is doing wonders. And if we get to work with Ian, it'll be even better." Despite her long legs, Wren had fallen behind and I turned in the saddle to face her. Dew knew work was done and it was time for carrots and naps and was speed-walking back to the barn. "If I can just keep away from Dakota's laser eyes and razor tongue I'll be set."

I'd become pretty good at ignoring her, or faking enthusiasm and good humor on the rare occasion we had more than a one-sentence conversation. Like any sport, dressage had a mix of personalities and when I'd first started at the higher levels I'd been dismayed there were the same bitchy bitches I'd encountered in Pony Club as a teenager. And I was even more dismayed that despite my success I still felt like the shy outcast as I had all those years ago.

Wren glanced around. "Poor Pierre. Having to cart around Dakota and her four pounds of fake boobs on his back."

"Wren!" I admonished her, though I was laughing.

"What? She's gross and cruel."

I couldn't argue. Dakota really was the epitome of spoiled, stuck-up dressage queen and treated Pierre like a machine not an animal, and a machine she didn't particularly like at that. Obviously I'd never ridden Dakota's horse, but I lived firmly by the principles I'd had drilled into me from my first dressage lesson as a kid—harmony and lightness above all else, because a horse that is cowed and forced to work will never show joy for that work.

The moment I halted Dewey in the tack-up bay, he swung his head around and lipped at my right stirrup. He held it between his teeth, shaking my foot, until Wren poked his neck. "Let go, you clown," she said affectionately, taking the reins to move his head away and make him release my stirrup. It took some persuasion.

The moment Dew released me I swung down to the ground. He turned his head expectantly and I pulled off my helmet then gave him a kiss right on the black dot floating in the middle of his pink nose before wrapping my arms around his neck for a hug. "Who's my best guy? My best very sweaty guy." He nosed my back and nibbled my belt loops before I let him go.

Wren handed me the video camera then pulled the reins over Dewey's head. She worked quickly to get his bridle off, halter on and him clipped in the cross-ties. Dew played with the leads clipped to either side of his face while Wren removed his saddle. There was plenty for him to keep himself amused, but nothing to injure him. Lotte's training barn was beautifully equipped and mercifully with enough space that Dakota and I could mostly avoid one another.

A small nervous flutter started in my stomach when I thought about the equestrian facilities in Rio. Word was that construction was behind schedule and with the general vibe of crime we kept hearing about, well…I was worried. Assuming I made it, I reminded myself. But I wanted so badly to make it. I'd had international competition success, but the Olympics were different. Special. The thing I'd been thinking about almost since I'd first clambered onto a horse at the age of five.

Decades of work, sacrifice, money, and time and I'd finally made it. Well, kind of. All that was left to do was make the US Olympic Dressage Team. Then keep Dewey sound and happy, keep myself fit and healthy *and* keep our training on track so that we hit our peak in Rio.

Easy. *Gulp*.

Wren shoved at Dewey who'd drifted closer, undoubtedly hoping to get one of the carrots he knew she carried in her pockets. She obliged him. "Brandon messaged me while you were riding. The vet came out to see Antoinette and agrees it's probably arthritis. They're going to increase the frequency of her joint injections and the dosage of feed supplement. But she's still moving around and eating everything in sight so not too worried."

I set my helmet on its hook to dry out. "Sounds about what we expected."

Brandon, my other employee and also Wren's fiancée, stayed home to take care of things whenever Wren and I were away. His competence eased one stress point of this months-long stretch away which was not only full of homesickness, but financial strain. If I was home in Kentucky I'd be training local horses as well as boarding and training others. But they had all gone back to their owners, which meant no money. Not to mention I wasn't earning from coaching. And I wasn't training my own horses. Brandon would keep them in light work until I returned, but putting the brakes on their training sucked.

Wren crouched to remove Dew's protective leg bandages. "Don't forget to eat. There's leftover pasta in the fridge." Once she'd taken off all his gear, Wren would walk Dew until he'd cooled down then wash off the dried sweat, groom him, and settle him in his stall with a snack.

I sketched a salute. "Yes, boss."

Wren and I were ensconced in one of Lotte's employee cottages and we ate what we—or more accurately, Wren—could make in the cottage's tiny but functional kitchen. At her request, she did ninety percent of the cooking because I could mess up toast. We'd spent enough close-quarters time during events that we'd developed domestic-like harmony. I skirted the edge of the outdoor arena, passed the runs attached to the box stalls then continued alongside one of the fields to get to the cottage.

I'd just opened the front door when I heard Lotte yell something unintelligible at Dakota. Given how far I was from the indoor arena, and the fact we had headsets so Lotte didn't have to yell, yelling meant oops. I slipped inside before I heard anything more. Though small, the space was modern, clean and perfectly suited to Wren and me and came with a bonus cat who technically lived in the barn but had figured out pretty quickly that Wren and I were cat people. I unzipped the long brown boots I wore for everyday riding, eased them off and gave the leather a quick wipe over before storing them in their bag.

Once I'd tossed sweaty socks into the laundry and nabbed a fresh, dry polo—sponsor's name on the chest of course—and fixed my hair into a tighter, albeit still sweaty ponytail, I felt almost human. There was no point changing out of breeches because I'd be riding some of Lotte's young horses once she was done with Dakota. Lotte now bred and coached more than she rode and had jumped on the opportunity of having me around to ride for her.

While the microwave dealt with the pasta, I transferred the video of my lesson to my tablet. I studied the footage around forking up mouthfuls of food. Dewey looked as good as he'd felt, and though Lotte's hammering hadn't been pleasant at the time, I could see a definite improvement in the piaffe. Worth it. I scrolled the video back and forth and decided that after almost thirty-three years of riding, and five at the highest level of Grand Prix, I might have actually figured out this dressage gig.

The barn cat, Poffertje—or Lil' Pancake as Wren called him—sprinted through the open door and sprung onto my lap. He reminded me of Rasputin, the black and white stray who'd wandered tatty and bleeding into my barn seven years ago. I'd found him curled up in the corner of Dewey's stall, being nosed by ever-curious Dew. Multiple veterinary visits later, and Rasputin returned to Dewey's side.

Rasputin was a blessing and curse. My world-class dressage horse loved "his" cat and I let them be because Rasputin helped Dewey turn off his overactive mind when he wasn't working. But the flipside was that Dew fretted whenever we traveled without Rasputin. Case in point? The scratch on Dew's nose. Dewey was trying to reconcile the fact that Poffertje was not Rasputin and despite being a barn cat, he did not like eleven hundred pounds of Warmblood horse nosing him, nibbling him, and sniffing in his face.

Wren hopped up the steps moments after the cat had made his grand entrance. I pushed my empty plate back on the table, away from paws. "All settled?"

She rummaged in the fridge. "Yep. Also, Mary wanted me to tell you that the new team veterinarian will be here midday-ish the day after tomorrow. There'll be a meeting."

There was always a meeting. "Noted. Any word on David?"

"Last I heard this morning was he's stable but still unconscious." She opened a can of Coke and took a sip. "They're still not committing to whether he's ever going to wake up."

My stomach fell. "Damn. That really sucks. Note to self, don't ever have a massive heart attack."

"You've got that right. But the show must go on and all that."

"True. This new vet has some pretty big shoes to fill." I smiled up at Wren. "But I'm sure they'll be great."

CHAPTER TWO

Addie

I was on my way back to the practice after hours of consults—a purchase examination for a very expensive showjumper, a mysterious lameness in a dressage horse, a first vaccination for an adorable foal, diversions for an emergency colic and then a leg wound—when my work phone rang. One percent chance of it being a colleague wanting to check something, ninety-nine percent chance I was not going back for a very late lunch.

I tapped speaker. "This is Addie."

"Addie, it's Janet. Emergency call over in Pahokee. Are you free?"

Bingo. I should really open my own backyard psychic reading joint. "For you I am, any time, any place."

I could hear the smile in her voice. "Oh, you put that southern charm away, Doctor Gardner. It doesn't work on me."

"Liar. I saw that piece of cake you put in the staff room with my name on it *and* a warning for others to keep away. Admit it, you're sweet on me."

She laughed. "Maybe a little."

"I knew it! What's the case?"

"Gaping chest wound. The owner was downright hysterical but I managed to get a few details from her. Still, I'm not sure how accurate the information is. She says the mare has a massive flap of skin and maybe muscle torn off its chest, there's a lot of blood and, I quote, grossness. Consult is at eight-twenty-one Mill Road."

I ran a quick mental inventory on the contents of the numerous drawers and boxes in the back of my work truck, which had inevitably dwindled during my calls, and decided I was equipped adequately. If it was more serious than the client had said, I'd just have them take the horse and its chest wound to our equine hospital. I executed a U-turn. "Okay, on my way now. Can you call the client and tell her I'll be there in thirty minutes, max. Tell her to keep padded pressure on it if it's bleeding and if the horse will allow it, otherwise just leave it alone."

"Will do. Client's name is Charlotte. Eric vaccinated her horse a few weeks ago so she has an account with us."

There is a veterinary god. No need to collect payment after treatment. "Even better, thanks."

Pahokee lay outside the glitzy area of Wellington, Florida where I lived and worked. It never ceased to amaze that two completely different areas existed within thirty minutes of each other. Where Palm Beach and Wellington were monied, with enormous horse properties so immaculate that I would have happily lived in the barns, much of Pahokee was cropping land and the horse properties had only the most basic facilities. The area reminded me a little of my parents' farm back in Arrington, Tennessee.

I slowed to a crawl along a road that was more grass than asphalt, and peered at the letterboxes, most of which had no numbers. Situation normal when I was trying to find a new client and also rule eighty-one of Murphy's Law of Vetting. I'd almost given up hope and was about to call Janet when someone sprinted from a driveway to my right about fifty feet away. The person flailing their arms above their head to catch my attention did just that.

As I drove closer I realized it was a teenage boy making big THIS WAY gestures. He pointed at the Seth Ranger & Assoc. Veterinarians text and logo on the side of my truck, gave me a thumbs-up and directed me to an open gate and into a large field. I bounced over rutted, weedy ground to where a late-teens girl held a stocky chestnut mare with four neat white socks and a full blaze down its face. It also had a massive flap of skin and tissue that stretched almost the width of its chest and hung down at least eight inches. Nice.

This was going to be good fun. I love suturing. No sarcasm. Suturing is an artform and I am a suturing Da Vinci. I pulled on a ball cap to keep wayward strands of hair from blowing in my face. "Heya, I'm Addie. You must be Charlotte? How're you?"

"Mhmm. I am. I'm okay. Thanks," she added. Charlotte had a timid, mouse-like way about her and given the mare was standing still and appeared unfussed it seemed she was either shocky as hell, or quiet and well-mannered. Just how I liked them. Quiet and well-mannered, not shocky.

I tugged the ends of the stethoscope slung around my neck. "And who's this?"

"Smartie."

I leaned closer to study the wound and was pleased to see Smartie didn't appear to have staked herself up into the axilla which would make things more complicated. "Looks like Smartie got herself into some trouble."

"Yeah." Charlotte was doing a very good job of not looking at the bloody, gaping flap of muscle and skin, but every now and then her eyes seemed to stray traitorously and her expression would turn to grossed-out.

"Any idea what she might have gotten herself caught up on?"

"No clue. I came out to ride her and there was…" A nervous swallow. "This."

Not knowing meant the likelihood of it happening again just increased by eighty percent. Murphy's Law of Vetting rule one-oh-six. "Sure, okay. Give me a few minutes to get things set up and I'll get this all fixed up for you." I stroked the horse's neck. "You're going to feel a lot more comfortable, Smartie."

I left Charlotte talking quietly to her mare while I opened the truck canopy and fished out a clean pair of coveralls. While I squirmed into them, I gave Charlotte a rundown of what I planned. "I'll sedate her to keep her nice and still while I work, then put some sutures in to close it up, but first I'll have to give the wound a good clean to make sure there's nothing nasty in there."

"She hates needles," Charlotte blurted. "I've only had her for a few weeks. She's my first horse. She bit the other vet and then struck me when we tried to give her her first tetanus vaccine."

Oh good. "So she's not up to date with her tetanus?"

"No, well I don't really know." Her face contorted and for a moment she seemed like she might cry. "The other vet said we should give her a full course because I didn't know what vaccinations she got with the woman who owned her before. She still has two more needles to go but she *might* be up to date if her other owner was doing it. I just don't know."

Wonderful.

I dialed my compassion up a few degrees. Charlotte seemed like she was about to melt into a puddle of emotion so it was time for gentle voices and faces. "No problem, we'll just have to use a bit of Plan B and get creative. Do you have anywhere we can restrain her better?" I peered around the open, empty space. "A barn, or a solid fence?" Anywhere but in the middle of a field where eight hundred pounds of equine could pretty much do as she wanted.

"No. We only moved here last month and we're still getting everything set up."

Even better. "How is she with a twitch?"

"I've never tried one with her. She's really great, I swear, really gentle and sweet. She just really hates needles."

"Right, no problem. I'm not a big fan of needles either. Let's try the twitch first and see how we go." The two words I'd just heard—*bit* and *struck*—were not words I wanted to apply to me. I pulled the long tube with a rope loop at the end from its place of pride on the wall of the truck bay and tucked it into a leg pocket of my coveralls. Once I'd drawn up a combination of my favorite sedation cocktail for standing procedures and stuck the syringe into my left breast pocket I was set.

The mare showed no sign of aggression when I moved to her shoulder and stroked her neck. I did a quick heart rate and breathing check to make sure she wasn't going to keel over if I sedated her, then gestured to Charlotte. "Come stand over on this side with me." I carefully took a handful of Smartie's nose and slipped the twitch's thin loop of rope over it, quickly twisting the handle until the rope tightened. The mare stretched her neck, almost yanking the twitch from my hand. "Keep hold of her." I twisted the tube a few more times.

Smartie snorted a snuffly kind of sigh which led Charlotte to ask panickingly, "Is she okay?"

I grinned at her. "Perfectly. Just enjoying a shot of endorphins thanks to the pressure from the twitch. It's like gettin' a *really* good hug. On her nose." After a few seconds Smartie dropped her head, her eyes glazing over. I wished a dose of endorphins for myself was as easy as squeezing my nose.

Right, time to try the needle sedation. "I'll need you to hold the twitch for me, just move a little so you're standing behind me in case she decides to be grumpy." I uncapped the needle, stuck the cap between my teeth so I wouldn't lose it and pressed my thumb against the mare's jugular. When she didn't react, I slid the needle into the vein. Despite the natural twitch sedation, Smartie snaked her head toward us and when I grumbled at her to behave, she struck out with a foreleg, catching me on the thigh despite the fact I was well to the side. Conniving brat. That was going to bruise. I drew blood back into the syringe then pushed it forward again to administer sweet, sweet sedation.

I removed the twitch and tossed it out of the way. The mare gave us both a *Screw you* look, despite the fact I was patting her for punching me in the leg. Charlotte offered a quiet, "I'm so sorry she got you."

"No problem. Kicks and bites are a job perk." Kicks, bites, shoves, being stood on, being shit on, being covered in pus and all manner of fluids and then a hundred other unpleasant things I dealt with in my job. The pain in my thigh was just another in a long line of ouchies.

The actual wound repair went smoothly and only took an hour and a half. I put in a drain to help with swelling and took advantage of the mare's wobbly state of amenability to jab her with pain relief, tetanus antitoxin, her second tetanus vaccination which was almost due and an antibiotic.

I filled a bag with syringes and needles, leaned against the side of the truck and wrote out the dosages, which I stuck to the bottles of penicillin and a tub of oral analgesic. Given the severity of the wound, I'd decided intramuscular antibiotic injections were a better course of action than oral antibiotics, but taking into account the mare's aversion to needles, it was one of those there-is-no-good-decision decisions. "If you can build her a small run to keep her contained for a week or so that would be great. A stall would be even better if you know someone nearby who wouldn't mind putting her up in one of theirs?"

Charlotte nodded. "I'll try." After a beat she reminded me, "We're just getting everything set up here." Her embarrassment was as plain as day and I empathized because when I was a kid, I had the barest facilities and minimal gear for my borrowed horse.

"Sounds good. Otherwise she might try to bust those stitches open playing Kentucky Derby horse in this lovely large field." I smiled. "Just do whatever you can, that's all you can do."

"Mhmm. Sure."

"Okay, here's the penicillin." God help whoever has to administer that. "Thirty milliliters injected into her muscle twice a day until it's all gone. Can you get someone to help you?"

Her eyes widened. "I think me and my brother and dad can deal with it. Can you show me again? I've done some muscle injections but not many."

I ran through the process a few times and told her some tips. "I'd stick to the neck but alternate sides after each injection. If she starts to get swollen or grumpy you could try her rump, but be careful in case her butt gets bouncy." I'd been a second away from suggesting the other common injection site of the chest, when I remembered I'd just sutured a gaping wound in Smartie's chest. One point to fatigue.

"What if we really can't do it?"

"We do offer an injection service for a set fee plus travel." With nine more injections, it was going to get expensive fast. I told her just how expensive and watched her eyes widen.

"You guys sure charge a lot." It wasn't accusatory, more disbelieving, but the words stung as they always did when someone complained about fees.

I bit back my sigh. And my annoyance. "The prices are set by the owner of the practice." Standard response, though in my head I was on a soapbox shouting to all who'd listen about the fact I was just a salaried employee.

Just yesterday I'd had a new client call me a "Money hungry c-word." Though of course, he'd actually said the c-word in all its disgraceful glory. I wished I could say it was rare and unusual, but it really wasn't. I'd yet to make it through a workweek without someone dragging out the old money-hungry vet fallacy. If I made half as much money as people thought I did, I'd be living in the Bahamas, not busting my ass in rain, hail, and shine and then having clients complain about paying for my expertise.

I love my job. I love my job. I love my job. And I do. Really. The animals were fine. It was the clients who were the problem.

Charlotte's nod was slow, and I could tell by her expression that they'd be attempting the injections themselves. "Okay. I'll talk to my dad, but I think we'll have to just do it ourselves."

I arranged my face back to relaxed and interested. "No problem. Just take it easy, try to keep her calm, and you could even bribe her with food if that helps. Or make up your own twitch with some plastic pipe and thin rope or baler twine." Midway through talking my brain caught up, and I pulled out a tube that might make the process less stressful for all and added it to the bag containing the antibiotics and analgesic. "This is an oral sedative. Not quite as good as the injection I gave her but it should help. Give her that half an hour before you inject her, okay? And then there's also some phenylbutazone paste for pain and inflammation which you administer orally. I'm told it's pretty tasty so she should be fine. I've already given her some in an injection so she's covered for today. Six milliliters twice a day for the first three days, then it'll be just once a day for three days. I've written it all down."

"Okay, sure." Her eyebrows scrunched down. "So is today day one or day zero?"

"Pardon me?"

"Well if we're starting tomorrow then do we count that as the first day?"

This wasn't the first time I'd had a medication scheduling conversation like this with a client. "There is no day zero. Day zero would be yesterday. We've started today. Day one."

Charlotte's forehead wrinkled in confusion. "But it's the afternoon so it's not a full day of medication. Is this day point-five then?"

Now she was even confusing me. I held out my hand. "I'll take that stuff back, please." I stripped the stickers from the bottles and wrote out new ones with the exact days, time of day and amounts in neat block writing instead of my usual perpetually hurried scrawl. There, no room for ambiguity. "Call the practice to schedule a time to have those sutures removed, and if it's swollen, hot or is leaking gross stuff call us immediately." I glanced at Charlotte who was trying to put the horse's blanket on. Back to front. "Maybe leave the blanket off her, considering the chest strap will be right on that wound."

"Oh. Right."

I had a feeling a veterinarian was going to be back here within the week.

Back at the practice I took fifteen minutes to restock my truck, then inhaled a sandwich as I typed up my clinical notes while they were fresh in my mind. I still had an assload of paperwork, including billing for yesterday and today, a horse coming in for dental work, and another for a forelimb X-ray series. Somewhere around all that I had to do handovers with my colleague. And there was zero wiggle room to put anything off because I was flying to the Netherlands in the morning to spend a week with the shortlisted horse and rider combinations vying for a spot on the US Olympic Dressage Team.

No problem. I'd just have to bend the space-time continuum to get it all done.

I stuck my head into the nurses' office. "Does anyone know where Eric is?"

"Hospital," came a distracted voice.

"Thanks." I'd been caught out before so instead of making the trek to the barns, I picked up the phone and dialed the extension for the hospital. A tired voice answered, "This is the equine hospital. You've got Diana."

"Diana, it's Addie. Is Eric down there?"

After a pause and some muffled sounds I got an answer in the affirmative.

"Great. Can you please tell him I'm coming down to see him and not to run off before I get there?"

"Will do."

Despite me asking Diana to tell Eric I was on my way, which I was sure she had, as I approached the hospital I spotted him wandering toward the building I'd just come from. I quickened my pace. "Eric!"

He stopped on the concrete path. "Thought you weren't coming." After a beat he added a not-entirely-sincere, "Sorry."

"I called literally three minutes ago. The only way I could have gotten here faster was by teleportation." Pointing at the intensive care area of the building I said, "This way. I just need to run over this critical care case with you."

"Can't I just read your notes?"

"You can read my notes *and* listen to me tell you about the case."

"Fine," he sighed. "But I haven't eaten in five hours and I'm about to go full Hulk. Seth had me run his early morning consults again, after my night on call, and my carefully planned pancake bonanza went flying out the window."

How unsurprising. Our boss, Seth Ranger, had reached the stage in his vetting career where the unfun aspects of the game no longer appealed. And being the boss, he could simply delegate. Which he did. Usually with little regard for his staff. I offered Eric the Mars Bar from my back pocket and he practically melted with gratitude. It was worth sacrificing part of my lunch to stall his hangry Hulk-out. "I'll be quick," I promised.

The stall was set up for a mare and foal where the foal needed intensive care without the mare's interference. The mare looked up and nickered softly. I rubbed her forehead and she responded by pushing against my hand for more pats. The foal was contained in a small padded pen within the stall, which meant the mare could smell and touch it, but not pull out any of the IV, oxygen, and feeding lines or move the padded trough keeping the foal propped up to help her breathing. "Here's that premature septic foal of the Wilkerson's. Diana and Andrew will help you take her out for some time in the sun, so *please* try to do it at least a few times."

He rolled his eyes. I knew he wasn't the only one who thought I wasted far too much time and effort taking sick foals and their assorted paraphernalia out to lie in the sun. But it gave the mares sunshine and grass too, and I really think it helps the foals. After a moment, Eric gave me a head bob that I took to mean he'd think about it and try if he had time. He probably wouldn't have time, especially not with the added work caused by my nine-day absence. "Isn't this foal out of their Stakes-winning mare?"

"Sure is." Said Stakes-winning mare nickered again when her foal attempted to stretch its forelimbs out, which resulted in a head-wobbly thud back against the padded trough. I crouched and checked the lines snaking out of the filly's jugular and both nostrils were still intact then checked her heart, lung, and gut sounds. Not great, but not terrible. I'd delivered the foal myself and then in a desperate effort to save her life, wrapped her in blankets and put her tiny body on the passenger side floor of my truck with the heat blasting while I broke the speed limit to get her back to the hospital. Thirty-five days premature and septic as hell. I wasn't optimistic, but I wasn't giving up.

I stood. "The damned thing keeps trying to die on me. Money's no object, this is a million-dollar filly. Or it will be, if I can get her to an age where they can sell it. The mare's a dream, easy to milk, quiet to handle." I punched his bicep. "So don't kill her foal."

"I'll do my best. Don't kill any really expensive irreplaceable Olympic dressage horses."

"I'll try not to. And please don't forget to stop in and feed my fish. If anything here goes south you can call and I'll get back to you when I can, but if it's not urgent I'm on email." Always working, even when I wasn't working.

When I arrived home at a quarter to ten I fed my fish, apologized to them for yet another late dinner, then showered the grime from my skin and hair. Feeling clean for the first time since I'd left for work that morning, I popped a frozen meal into the microwave while I indulged in a large glass of pinot noir.

The nervousness I'd been trying to ignore about my new position on the US Dressage Team bubbled up again. A mouthful of wine helped shove it back down. Coming on board as the team veterinarian so close to the Summer Olympics was a huge boost for my career and ego, but also disruptive to the dressage squad who'd been working closely with an established veterinarian. I'd have to work extra hard to get up to speed and to a place where they trusted me.

When the team vet, David West, had suffered a massive heart attack in France last week I'd been asked to step in. At such short notice, I'd assumed that the others they'd approached had been unavailable, which was just lucky for me. My qualifications were solid and I'd been involved with dressage over the years, being the lead veterinarian at various international-standard dressage events around the country.

I needed to attend two qualifying competitions in the Netherlands at the start and end of June to get a feel for the nine horse-and-rider combinations on the shortlist as I had to assess soundness for final choice. Of course, my opinion was only one part of the selection process but my involvement could make or break a dream for someone. No pressure.

It'd taken every ounce of charm I possessed to persuade Seth that not only would this give me skills that I'd be using for his practice, but also that it was a huge publicity boost for him. He'd rubbed his sagging jowls and I could almost see cogs turning as he worked out how it'd be most advantageous to him. After making me wait an eternity, he'd agreed. But not without a grumbling dig at the fact I'd be gone for almost three weeks total in the lead-up to the Olympics, as well as all of July so I could work with the team in their training camp before we moved on to Brazil in August.

I'd packed the night before when I'd arrived home at a respectable eight p.m. so there was nothing to do now except more homework on the horses and riders. On my iPad I opened up the file that held the dossiers on my charges-to-be. Full health and training histories. As always when I looked at the files, one name stood out as if highlighted.

Caitlyn Lloyd.

I hadn't spoken to her in twenty years but I had seen her ride in person at a number of events over the past three years when I'd been on staff. She rode much the same way she had when we were teenagers—calmly confident, elegant and with skill that was almost unreal. Breathtaking. I'd had to remind myself to watch the horse, study his movement and attitude, which were things, as I told myself, relevant to my profession.

But I'd kept glancing back at Caitlyn, studying her expression, which was a mix of fierce concentration and calmness. From what I'd seen at a distance she looked much the same as she had all those years ago except she'd changed her hair from light brunette to honey-blond which made her brown eyes seem even more intense. Tall and slender with that long-legged grace so common among the dressage set, she was, in a word, hot. Really hot. The excited fluttering in my stomach was no longer from worrying about my new position but from thinking about Caitlyn.

Soon I would see the object of my first crush. The person I'd admired so much as a teen. The person who—if the pictures I'd seen when Googling just for interest's sake were correct—had certainly improved with age.

I finished my wine. Caitlyn probably wouldn't even remember me.

CHAPTER THREE

Caitlyn

In the middle of his field Dewey was enjoying a standing nap without his blankets. After the big competition in Florida almost two months ago, our intense training before leaving the States, the flight to Europe, the competition in France and then this week of training and scrutiny, I could tell he was tired.

He'd even pretended to be asleep in his stall this morning, lying flat on his side with his eyes closed when Wren and I leaned over the half-door. The promise of a piece of licorice made him crack open an eye but he hadn't moved until I'd rustled the bag. Then he'd rocketed to his feet like his butt was on fire. The guy had his priorities in order.

Even Lotte had noticed Dewey seemed sluggish during our lesson that morning and been surprisingly lenient. I didn't blame him. I was tired too and wanted nothing more than to skulk back to the cottage, shower and then nap until the end of the week. But I had a team meeting, a veterinarian to meet and then two of Lotte's young horses to ride. My nap would be nothing more than wishful thinking.

As I approached Dewey I took a few moments to gauge how he felt. I knew every part of him like I knew my own face, having watched him develop from an adorable foal to a hairy, gangly and frankly butt-ugly yearling and then into a huge, muscular Grand Prix dressage horse.

I could tell exactly how he felt by the way he held himself and right now, despite his fatigue, he was relaxed and happy. If he was happy, I was happy. "Dew!"

He raised his head, swung to face me, pricked his ears and nickered a greeting. I couldn't recall a time when he hadn't given me a vocal greeting, that throaty little sound I adored. I snapped a few photos. "Damn you're handsome."

He trotted over to the fence to meet me and I offered him a piece of licorice. Then a second piece when he gave me his *Is that really all you're giving me?* look. I was such a sucker and he knew it.

I climbed through the wooden fence, careful to avoid the electrified wire attached to the inside of the rails. Dewey frisked me, realized I didn't have anything more and dropped his nose to the grass. I leaned against his shoulder, scratching under his mane while he grazed. If there was a more relaxing place than being with Dew, I didn't know it.

Wren wandered over, eating an apple. She slipped through the fence and gave Dewey the core. "Hey. Mary's assembling the troops for this meeting. I think we're just waiting on a couple of the others."

Along with me and Dakota, seven other US riders based in Europe were on the shortlist. There was no doubt that living here would give me access to more high-level international competitions, international young-horse classes for my up-and-comers and a glut of coaches. If I hadn't worked so hard to build up my barn in Kentucky, and if I could somehow find another five million dollars, give or take, then I might have considered shifting my operation to Europe too.

I checked the time. "No problem. I should go. I heard Lotte mention she was making *Bitterballen* and *Stroopwafels* for the meeting and I do *not* want to miss them. Can you give Dew some Energy Boost with his lunch and dinner please?"

Wren nodded. "Good plan. He only tried to eat my shirt once while I was grooming him after breakfast so I know he's tired. I'll bring him in for lunch and a massage blanket session while you're in your meeting."

"Thanks. We might have to monitor him a bit more closely during these two competitions, check his energy levels. I think it's just the intensity of these lessons on top of everything else that's making him tired." Poking Dew's neck I added, "Or maybe you're just an old man."

He raised his head and snorted, as if reminding me that twelve was nowhere near old for a horse and for a Grand Prix dressage horse he was just entering his prime, where he was old enough to have the training under his belt, err…girth, while still young enough that he could potentially have another six years or more at this highest level.

Wren wiped horse snot off her shirt. "We'll keep it all on track." Her voice and expression turned soothing. "We've been here plenty of times, nothing to worry about."

No, nothing at all. Except everything.

I mhmmed in way of response, hugged Dewey around the neck then left him in Wren's capable hands so I could meet the veterinarian who would take care of Dewey for at least the next month, if not three. As I walked into the small staff room attached to Lotte's indoor arena, I scrolled through the pictures I'd just taken and picked the photo where Dew didn't have his eyes closed. It only took a few minutes to put it on Instagram and link to Twitter and Facebook.

Midfields Adieu looking as handsome as ever - #ProHorse supplements and #EquinePower feeds keep him looking and performing his best! #TwoHearts #RoadToRio #LoveNetherlands

The *Two Hearts* campaign had been started by the FEI—Fédération Equestre Internationale—the governing body of international equestrian sport, to raise awareness in the lead-up to Rio 2016, and was currently steamrolling its way around social media, mine included. Every time I added that and the *Road To Rio* hashtag to my social media posts I cringed but any interest that led to funding for the sport, which then trickled down to me, was a good thing. Without that funding from my sponsors and outside donors, it'd be almost impossible for me to compete on the international stage.

Campaigning on the European dressage competition circuit was a necessity to make the team, and these few months ran easily to mid-six figures. Not to mention the cost of losing months of coaching and horse-training revenue. Every penny helped, even if it meant I spent more time than I felt comfortable with talking about myself, posting on social media, fundraising with raffles and auctioning off things like a lesson on Dewey. Two people had purchased those one-hour sessions for a combined total of almost ten grand, which made my discomfort worth it.

Sometime this week I'd take some pictures of Dewey in his sponsor rugs and another in his custom-made saddle and bridle doing a workout. Hashtags galore. Emojis-a-plenty. Keeping everyone happy and sure they were getting bang for their buck took almost as much time as actually training and competing horses.

Dakota glanced up as I slipped into the room, set up with two groups of chairs facing each other. It was just us there so far and typically she said nothing, aggressively typing on her phone. Probably *OMG, Lloyd just arrived and is stinking up the place with her middle-classness.* She was, as usual, immaculately presented, as if the only time she went near her horse was to get on, ride and dismount. In a sport where money was king, she went above and beyond. Even her socks were designer-label, pulled to mid-calf over her breeches then disappearing into designer loafers.

I glanced down at my own socks which were a pale blue, orange, and white tartan of who-knows-what brand, and my worn and scuffed loafers. My glamour was reserved for inside the dressage arena. Just another way I sat on the fringe. High-level dressage was a big-*big*-money sport—if you couldn't access talented horses, the best coaches, good gear, and everything in between you were at a disadvantage before you'd even put a leg over a horse. The unfortunate fact was that all the natural skill and drive to succeed meant nothing if you didn't have the dollars.

The only reason I'd come as far as I had was because of hard work and dedication, the goodwill of others who'd employed me as a teenager and those who'd believed in my abilities, supplying me with top-class horses. I'd also been blessed with an enormous chunk of luck thanks to my nana's lottery tickets which, from my eighteenth birthday, she'd put in a card for me along with the message *So you can build your own barn. Save me a seat at the Olympics.* One year I'd won enough to set up my own dressage barn on eighty-four acres of prime Kentucky bluegrass, and build up my own team of horses to give my career a serious boost.

I poured a cup of coffee and dropped some of Lotte's amazing food onto a plate before settling on a seat at the end of the row. The seven other riders filtered in during the next few minutes. They were all nice enough, if not a little laconic, but we were more acquaintances than friends.

Dakota eyed the others in much the same way she always looked at me. With disdain. She saw everyone as a rival. I'd never understood the attitude because my only rival was myself. If I rode the best I could, trained my horses to the highest standard then there was nothing more I could do. I thought it was also partly jealousy—I knew she would have loved to be part of the based-in-Europe crowd, but her husband refused to live anywhere but America. Which meant I saw far more of her than I cared to during the competition season back home.

The door opened again and four people conga-lined into the space. "Sorry to keep everyone waiting," Mary said as she filled the room in her usual tornado-like fashion. Mid-fifties with steel-gray hair that

I'd never seen out of a bun and a bearing that hinted at her former riding career, Mary exuded a mix of scary-as-shit and mother hen. Thankfully, I'd managed to keep myself on the mother-hen side of her. With Mary were Ian and Ken, the team farrier who'd take care of our horse's hooves all the way through to Rio. Then there was a stranger who could only be our new veterinarian. She was about my age, dressed in heavy-duty work pants, boots, and a dark blue polo sporting the United States Dressage Federation logo. The group settled in facing us and the vet stared at me with a smile that showed a cute set of dimples, then averted her gaze when our eyes met.

I did not avert my gaze, taking the opportunity to study her while she wasn't looking my way. That smile had drawn my attention to her laughing, sensuous mouth and I had to force myself to stop staring at it. It'd been a while since I'd taken such an instant shine to someone, and the fact my libido was taking notice made me take notice. Her hair, pulled back in a ponytail, was a shade of deep rich brunette shot through with auburn and the color set off the bright brown of her eyes. I wanted her to look my way again so I could be sure they really were as unusual as they appeared. All cuteness aside, she had a sort of capability about her and not just physically. Her entire aura was that she was someone to trust—a good trait for a veterinarian.

The more I checked her out, the more familiar she seemed, but she was nobody I could place. Out of the blue, something unpleasant nudged at the back of my consciousness, something that made me oddly anxious. The anxiety came into sharp, uncomfortable focus when Mary spoke, gesturing to the woman.

"This is Doctor Addison Gardner, who is coming on board to replace Doctor West as our team veterinarian. Addison will be getting to know you and your horses in the coming weeks and will make sure all our equine athletes are in peak health come Rio. I know disruption this late in our preparation isn't ideal, but since David's health scare we've worked hard to find a competent and knowledgeable vet who will continue his excellent standards."

Her stare dared us riders to object or complain. I had no intention of doing either. Too busy freaking out.

Mary continued, "Doctor Gardner's extensive work with performance horses will ensure the highest care possible *and* she comes highly recommended by a number of top performance veterinarians. I anticipate her integration to be smooth and also extremely beneficial to our preparation."

Addison Gardner. My libido got a harsh reality check.

Shit to the power of infinity. It couldn't be, could it? I mean it wasn't exactly a common name, but still… Maybe she was actually Addison Someone Else who'd married a Gardner. But the more I looked, the more convinced I became that it was actually the girl, uh, now woman I'd known at South River Pony Club in Arrington, Tennessee over twenty years ago and who used to go by Addie, not Addison. I wiped my palms on my breeches. A flood of memory washed over me and I had to fight down a wave of panic. Lotte's delicious snacks suddenly felt very heavy in my stomach.

We hadn't been friends back then. Quite the opposite. When I'd arrived for my first Pony Club meeting as a fourteen-year-old who'd just moved to the area, Addie had been the first person I'd seen. She was doing handstands on top of the world's most patient horse while a group of laughing and cheering girls crowded around her. She'd been in with the group of rich bitches who'd been cruel and aloof in that special way teen girls had down to a fine art when I'd turned up as a newcomer to their established social circle.

The more I studied Addison, the more I wanted to slap myself for not realizing who she was. Now I knew, it was plain as day. And considering my conflicted feelings back then of being a baby gay who definitely noticed the way girls looked, and who'd spent so much time wondering how someone as cute and funny as Addie Gardner could be so damned mean, her turning up now felt like a cruel joke from the universe.

Addison leaned forward in the chair and in a low, calm voice, which still held strong hints of the South, thanked Mary then began speaking about herself. I tried to listen but my thoughts kept wandering off. One part of my brain was stuck on the sound of that butterscotch voice. Another part heard her elaborate on her qualifications—impressive, and her work to date—vast. And of course, a big part of my brain kept thinking about everything she'd said and done all those years ago. My focus snapped back to attention when she told us how much she was looking forward to getting to know us and our horses and supporting our Olympic bids. Her gaze lingered on me. She winked.

I straightened in the chair, only just stopping myself from squirming. Was she playing another mind game with me now? Should I say something about Pony Club? Or just ignore the whole thing? Or wait for her to bring it up, if at all? I *had* to talk to her, obviously, but everything that'd happened when we were teenagers played through my head at warp speed and I fought to keep calm.

She made the decision for me. After the meeting I decided to skulk back to the cottage to hide and regroup. And maybe work myself into a good panic at what the next few months held if Addison Gardner was around. I'd almost made it, the front door was in sight, when her unmistakable voice called from behind me, "Caitlyn!"

My stomach felt like it did in the lead-up to big competitions— excitement and anxiety mixing to create a flutteringly uncomfortable sensation. No option other than stop, turn around and talk to her. I mean, sure, I could have sprinted into the cottage and slammed the door but that would have been a little weird. Somewhere between her teens and now she'd developed a left-leg limp. It was barely noticeable but for someone like me who spent her life studying the way horses moved, any gait that wasn't smooth stood out. I wondered what she'd done since I'd last seen her when we were both seventeen and moving on from Pony Club to bigger and better equestrian things.

She seemed shorter than I recalled, though obviously we both could have grown. When she smiled at me, it was warm, genuine, and engaging and her eyes and nose creased with delight. And her eyes. Oh boy. I'd forgotten their exact color and up close they were even prettier—a bright golden brown, ringed with dark. She still had that air of mischievousness about her, an almost casual irreverence as if she was always on the verge of either telling or playing a joke. I'd been on the receiving end of both.

Thirty-seven-year-old Caitlyn's libido woke from where it'd fled in panic to come back and take notice. A lot of notice. Fourteen-year-old Caitlyn poked Current Caitlyn in the butt and reminded her that Addison wasn't a nice person. Or, at least she hadn't been when I'd known her all those years ago.

Still smiling, Addison held out her hand and her handshake was firm and warm. She held on for a second longer than for a normal meeting of acquaintances. "Caitlyn Lloyd. We meet again. You've done well for yourself, putting South River Pony Club on the map."

"Addison. Thank you. It's…surprising to see you again." I cleared my throat, fighting to contain my upset inner teen. "So, um, you're a vet?"

She grinned, which made her cheeks dimple, which turned some of the fluttering in my stomach from nervousness to excitement. "Nah, I was just wandering around the Netherlands, saw some horses and thought I'd pop my head in. Seems they really need a hand, because Mary grabbed me and asked if I could take care of some dressage horses." At my apparently stunned expression, she smiled and offered something less facetious but still with that cheeky, teasing grin. "Yes, I'm a veterinarian. And obviously now the veterinarian for the US Olympic Dressage Team. I, uh, have actually been the vet at a bunch of events in the States where you've competed but thankfully I've never had to see you. Not because I didn't want to," she hastened to add. "But, you know, vets at competitions are for when things go bad."

"Really? I've never seen your name in any of the fine print about organizing committees and whatnot."

"Mhmm. They only ever use initials, not full names in those things." Her smile had a touch of eye roll in it. "Dr. A. Gardner. Probably so they think it's Andrew, not Addie. Yay, misogyny."

"That's great. Really great. Not misogyny but you being a vet. I didn't know you'd gone to vet school." I fought down a blush at the realization that as a kid I hadn't really thought of her as having any sort of intellect. "Do I call you Doctor Gardner?"

"If you like, but that's just a waste of syllables. Addie is fine. I kept telling Mary that only my parents use my full name, but she sure is a stickler for protocol. Addison just makes me feel like I'm in trouble."

"Sure. Addie it is. Just like old times." I made a vague, helpless gesture as I stated the obvious. "So, we're going to be working together."

"That we are. Who would have thought it, way back in the Pony Club days, that we'd be horsing together again all these years later." Her smile was brilliant, as if the two of us interacting was the best thing she'd done all year.

"Yeah…who would have thought it," I parroted. The part of my brain that I rarely let loose, the part that acted before thinking, somehow squirmed free to blurt, "Maybe I should just jump in the water trough now to save you the trouble of shoving me into it later."

The smile faded until confusion was plainly painted on her face. "I'm sorry, pardon me?"

"Don't you remember that?" I remembered the humiliation like it was yesterday. "I could put manure in my helmet too if you'd really like to reminisce."

Her forehead wrinkled and I could see her working to make the connections. When she finally spoke, the words were exaggeratedly slow as if she wanted to be sure I really got them. "Okay, sure. But I'm not really sure what you're gettin' at."

Addie's deliberate obtuseness made another thing I rarely let loose flare—my, admittedly mild, temper. "No? You need a little reminder?

I'm talking about how you and your group of minions made my life hell at Pony Club."

Her eyebrows shot up. "I'm sorry, I really don't know what—"

"Seriously, it's fine." Hello, liar. "Just thought I'd clear the air." I folded defensive arms over my chest.

"Right…" she drawled. Her expression was still one of absolute disconnection, and I wondered if she'd repressed everything she'd done or watched others do. Her face softened. "Clearly, I really don't remember things the way you do." Addie paused, as if trying to decide whether or not to say more. "What I do remember is trying to impress everyone. And I sure as heck never had a group of minions. Not sure where you got that idea. I *was* a minion, a piece of crap to that group really."

I untucked a hand to sketch a dismissive wave. "Mhmm, okay then, sure."

Addie's eyes widened. "Caitlyn, look. I'm sorry, I really am, if something I did upset you. I wish I could offer an explanation or help you work through whatever you're talking about, but I can't because all I remember is all of us doing stupid shit to everyone else."

"Stupid shit?" My voice cracked up embarrassingly. "You and your group of bitchy bitches bullied the shit out of me for three years."

Addie's voice broke as she exclaimed, "Bullied? Hey, no…that's not—" She cut herself off and her expression made it clear she was really thinking about it, trying to put the pieces together. But she couldn't, that much was also clear. She blinked rapidly. "Is now really the time to be talking about this?"

I made myself stand tall, knowing I would feel stronger for it. But instead, it made me feel as if I was looking down on her. And that felt almost as horrible as the feeling of childhood inadequacy that'd been my constant companion back then, and which had made a poorly timed reappearance now. "Is there a better time?"

Addie mumbled something that sounded like, "How 'bout never?" After a slow inhalation she said, "I really think you and I have very different experiences and recollections of that time." She raised both hands, palms up. "Despite appearances, I wasn't part of that group, not really." Her voice dropped and took on a fierce intensity. "And I definitely don't think I was a bully. I was…well, awkward and socially inept doesn't even scratch the surface of what I was. Remember how I was the poor kid riding a borrowed horse in a group of girls who had endless money?"

I had no answer for that, because I didn't remember anything like that. All of my memories were tuned to *What Addie Did*, not *Who Addie Was*. I shrugged in response.

"Caitlyn, I don't know what else I can say except another sorry, and to point out that sometimes people change drastically from teenagers to close to forty-years-old. I'm not trying to make excuses or diminish something you *obviously* have strong feelings about but it's been twenty years since Pony Club so please excuse me if I don't recall every word I ever spoke to you." It came out a little snappish and more than a little defensive.

I responded with my own snappy and defensive, "Fine."

She rubbed the bridge of her nose and when she spoke it was calmer, almost resigned. "Look, I'm here to make sure your horse is performing at his best. I'm damned good at my job and my appointment comes with the full support of the US Dressage Federation. They trust me and trust what I can do for the team. So maybe you need to find a way to work past your little bout of teen angst." She squared her shoulders and smiled, though it was one of those tight, forced *I'm trying not to say bad things* smiles. "I'm here to help, regardless of what you think happened in our past." She turned around and walked back toward Lotte's barn.

What I *thought* happened in our past? What the hell? Someone was delusional and it sure as hell wasn't me. "Hey!" I called at her back, and when she stopped and turned to face me, I demanded, "Why *did* you push me into the water at the clubhouse sleepover?" Possibly the most pointless thing I could have asked at that moment, but apparently now was the time to get stuck on pointless details.

Addie threw both hands up in a gesture that was pure exasperation, then spun around and kept walking away.

CHAPTER FOUR

Addie

Half an hour after my conversation with Caitlyn my frustration still lingered, leaving my body tight and tense. Frustration around horses, especially highly strung performance horses, was just asking for bad behavior and I decided to settle myself with a walk around the fences enclosing the lush green fields. Being out of sorts with jetlag and hours cramped in a plane seat may have played a part in how I'd reacted, and I hoped some fresh air would settle me. The conversation had struck a nerve I didn't even know I had and as I walked, I tried to figure out how I'd managed to be on such a different wavelength to Caitlyn.

Bullying?

What. The. Actual. Fuck?

Sure, we hadn't exactly been BFFs or BFs...or even Fs at Pony Club, but it wasn't for lack of me trying. I'd tried so hard to get her to talk to me, to like me, to want to be my friend, and for years had been met by a cool wall of no thank you. Everyone at the club teased and joked and played pranks back then, and I couldn't understand why she was taking it so personally and seemed to have such a vendetta against me now. Didn't she realize I was so awed by her incredible natural riding talent and her quiet wit and confidence and oh my goodness those legs and her smile and—

That teenage Addie who had a massive crush on Caitlyn wilted at the thought that she'd gotten it so wrong. No matter. Kids had stupid thoughts and said stupid things all the time. I was an adult now with a very respectable career that only looked to get more respectable, not the poor kid begging and borrowing gear to attend Pony Club and trying to get the rich girls to like me so they wouldn't tease me.

Most importantly, I had a job to do. I shook myself off, squared my shoulders, then collected my equipment from my rental and made my way back to the barn. In my years of vetting I'd learned there were many ways to approach problems, including combative clients, and given this situation, antagonism on my part was only going to create a hostile environment. Hostility in the lead-up to the Olympics was counter-productive, so I'd be polite and friendly, ignore any barbs slung my way and forget that I used to dream about kissing Caitlyn Lloyd.

The moment I entered the barn I spotted Caitlyn in the laneway outside one of the box stalls. With her was a tall, blue-haired woman and a huge bay horse who I knew was Dewey. I looked at a lot of horseflesh every day and appearances tended to be low on the list of things I appreciated, which started with horses that don't kick or bite me. But I had to admit he was one of the most stunning horses I'd ever seen. He was huge—a solid and muscular 16.3 hands high, which meant that at five-foot-seven I'd barely be able to see over his back. I crossed my fingers that he was amenable because working with recalcitrant equines sucked. Working with large recalcitrant equines could be a dangerous nightmare.

The rich dark dappled brown of his coat was set off by a thick black mane and tail, and one fore and both hindlimbs were white with stockings that went halfway up his legs. The other forelimb had an odd not-sock—a slash of white slanted across the lower part of the limb. His head was a refined, elegant shape with a thin white blaze down his face leading to a pink nose that spilled over his right nostril. From photos, I knew he had a little black dot floating in the pink of his nose that just begged to be poked with a forefinger. Dewey's ears pricked as he turned his head to watch my approach, and I swear those soft brown eyes lit up with curious excitement.

I set my bag against the outer stall wall and rapped my knuckles on the wood. "Knock knock."

The two women turned to face me. The blue-haired one had a pleasant, welcoming expression. Caitlyn, on the other hand, was guarded, bordering on unfriendly. Given the conversation earlier, I hadn't expected a hug but I had hoped for at least fake politeness. We clearly had different recollections of Pony Club. My time back then had been spent balancing my crush on her, keeping my school and horse lives separate, and trying to fit in while being socially awkward *and* the poorest member of the club. Which the rich girls never let me forget. Going along with their antics, being a goofball and sometimes verbal whipping girl for that crowd had always felt like a small price to pay for not feeling like a total outcast.

I slapped on my friendliest smile. "Hi." I directed my gaze to the person I didn't know. "I'm Addie Gardner, the new team veterinarian."

The return smile was broad and warm, as was her voice. "Wren." She waved. "Caitlyn's groom extraordinaire."

"Nice to meet you." I cleared my throat and turned my focus to Caitlyn. "Do you and Dewey have an hour for me?"

Dewey apparently did, if the way he kept trying to stretch his nose out to touch me was any indication. Caitlyn, on the other hand, seemed as if the thirty seconds she'd already allowed me were too many. Her mouth held a distinctly tight line and her brown eyes narrowed as she studied me. Over the years, whenever I'd thought of her—which was admittedly a fair amount—I'd always remembered those eyes as luminous. Now they felt like a bucket of cold water. After a long moment of staring at me like I was here to euthanize her horse, she gave me a flat, "Why? I'm busy. I have to ride Lotte's horses this afternoon."

I held up my iPad. "I just want to get some basic information, take photos of normal limbs, collect resting vitals and whatnot so I have baseline stats to go on. I'd also like to video his normal trot-up so I know his gait. I have David's information and I know you've already been over some of this with him, but I like to get my own feel for things." Silence hung thickly, and in an attempt to fill it I added, "I'll be doing it for all the equine athletes."

The suspicious expression eased to a kind of resigned wariness. "Sure."

Wren backed up. "If you don't need me, I'm going to grab lunch." At Caitlyn's nod, which was admittedly delayed, Wren said, "I'll be back in an hour or so."

Amid an uncomfortable silence, I ran through a dozen openers and discarded each one. Out of desperation, I looked around, hoping for inspiration. At the back of the stall, a large laminated picture of a tuxedo-coat cat had been fastened with zip ties to the vertical bars that made up the top half. I pointed. "That's Rasputin right? Dewey's feline best friend?"

Surprise flashed over Caitlyn's face. "Yes. How'd you know that?"

"I follow your social media accounts. The cat door in Dewey's stall back home is adorable." Shit. I hadn't meant to let slip the fact I was one of her followers. Before the conversation could move into awkward territory at that revelation, I turned slightly to the side and started scratching Dewey's chest. He curled his head around to bump my shoulder with his nose and I felt the unmistakable sensation of him playing with the back of my shirt. I'd read interviews where Caitlyn spoke about what a quirky, affectionate, and personable horse he was, and it seemed she was right on the money. I stroked his face then gestured at the bare stalls either side of Dewey's. "He doesn't like other horses?"

"He likes them *too* much. We've learned that having him pulling blankets over the eyes of an expensive Warmblood doesn't endear him to people, so he has to be on his own like a social outcast whenever we can get the space. Big competitions are a nightmare, I usually have to request a stallion box with extra-high walls."

"So that's where the arrogance comes from? He's always put with the stallions so he thinks he's one too?"

Her eyebrows shot up and I thought I saw the ghost of a smile. A small win. "Could be. Most likely it's just him. He knows he's the best horse in my barn."

"And half of one of the best teams in the world too," I pointed out.

She flushed, as if the idea of being so good, of nipping at the heels of the top horse and rider combinations on the Grand Prix circuit was embarrassing for her. "I'm just lucky to have him."

I murmured my agreement and placed my tablet down on top of my bag so I could settle my stethoscope in my ears. "Could you hold him still please?"

Caitlyn kept him from nuzzling me as I checked his heart and lung and gut sounds. "I'll just take his temperature." To Dewey I apologized, "Sorry, pal. The thermometer's been in my pocket so at least it'll be warm." All his vitals were normal and I recorded each one in his file, then backed up a few steps. "Can you take him out closer to the entrance where the light's good so I can get some clear body and limb shots?"

She did as I asked and held him while I first studied his general condition and muscling—excellent and with no noticeable evidence of overuse on one side or body part indicating he was compensating due to pain. Not that I would have expected anything of the sort with an elite athlete. I took photos of his body, all four limbs from multiple angles, as well as his hooves. Then I videoed as Caitlyn trotted him away from me in a straight line and back again, simulating what was required at competitions to check the horses were sound to compete, which he was. The whole time, I sensed defiance from Caitlyn, as if she was daring me to find something wrong with the horse.

I couldn't. "He's gorgeous. Tell me about him."

Her expression softened instantly, as if a switch had flipped. "What do you want to know?"

"Everything." Dewey was clearly key to getting her to open up to me so we could have a good working relationship. Yeah, that's it, a good working relationship.

The corner of her mouth twitched. "That's heading into dangerous ground. I could talk about him all day."

"Then do." I really did need to know everything I could about him, even what she felt innocuous. More than that, I hoped if we had some easy conversation about something she clearly loved, the ice between us might crack. I knew it was too much at this stage to hope for it to break.

"He naps at least twice during the day, lying down flat on his side like he's dead to the world, in the sun if he can. If he can get something in his mouth to play with it, he will and he'll probably ruin it in the process. He always leaves part of his dinner hay to eat during the night. He'll turn himself inside out to get a treat from you. And he's missing Rasputin so he's been a bit more unsettled in the stalls than usual when he's generally pretty chilled out, not spooky or tense even when we go away."

I paused my frantic typing. "Have you thought about a blanket with the cat's scent on it and bringin' it whenever you're away from home?"

"We did once but he spent the whole time in the stall with it in his mouth, shaking it and spooking the horses around him. Plus we didn't want him to get any ideas when he went home to the real Rasputin."

I laughed. "Ah, yeah. Probably best you don't then. You bred him, right?"

She nodded. "Mhmm. His sire is Farewell Three, and his dam is Antoinette. I'm not sure if you remember Antoinette from Pony Club?"

"I do remember her," I said evenly. She should know that I would remember that horse. The mare was gorgeous, German-bred, with talent and attitude in equal measure.

"She was injured and had to be retired, so I decided to breed from her." Her nose wrinkled adorably and for a moment I forgot her earlier hostility. "I made plans and saved, and now I have Dewey."

"Has he ever had any major health issues or lameness?"

"No lameness except for a couple of hoof abscesses over the years. Uh, he *was* three weeks premature."

"From premature to this massive guy?"

Another small smile. "Yeah. I think that's why he's such a human addict, all that attention in the first few months. I'm just lucky he didn't go the other way and turn into a resentful horse because of all the treatment. And lucky that I went to check on Antoinette that night. He'd just been born I think, the cord was still attached. He wasn't breathing properly so I was trying to get him up on his chest to get the fluid out of his airways. It felt like forever but finally he sneezed gunk all over me and took a breath."

"Wow. That must have been intense."

"It was. And expensive." She grinned and swatted at Dewey, who'd started nibbling her belt. "He owes me an Olympic medal."

Laughing I agreed, "That he does."

Her expression changed to confused consternation, as if she couldn't decide what to do or say. After a while, she quietly asked, "So um, where are you working? Are you still living in Tennessee? Do you still ride?"

I smothered my surprise at her casual interest. "Nope to Tennessee and nope to riding. I did my DVM degree at Colorado State, then someone pulled some strings so I could do some time in big vet practices in England and Germany. Then I moved on to California and later, Kentucky. Now I'm in Florida. Wellington. It's mostly racehorses, eventers, dressage horses and showjumpers. Basically a lot of highly strung horseflesh. But there's enough cheeky kids' ponies and amateur riders with sweet horses to give me some balance." I tapped the screen and scrolled to the next group of questions.

"Oh. I hadn't realized you'd left Tennessee."

I stared at her, trying to decipher what she wasn't saying. "Well, no, why would you?" When she didn't answer, not that I'd really expected one to my rhetorical question, I plowed on. "What feed supplements would you bring to Rio if you're selected?"

She apparently knew why I was asking, and the annoyance in her answer was barely disguised. "David already cleared them." Caitlyn folded her arms over her breasts. "I've never had my horses or myself test positive for a banned substance and I sure as hell am not going to start now."

"Sure, no problem and I'm obviously not accusing you of anything. But I'll still need to see the list and give you permission to first, bring them into the country and second, use them."

Her jaw bunched. She straightened and the change in posture gave her a distinctively superior air. But I didn't feel inferior at all. I'd spent most of my life having people looking down at me, from my parents to my childhood peers, professors and fellow students at college, and now even my boss and some clients. I stood as impassively as I could and waited for her to respond.

All she ground out was, "Why?" Being antagonistic over something as simple as telling me a supplement that'd already been okayed by the previous vet seemed ridiculous.

"It's my professional reputation on the line as well as potentially yours. I don't care if the head dressage steward himself gave you permission to take a supplement into Brazil. I have a duty of care not only to the team but to myself and I refuse to sign off on something that I haven't sighted." Six months ago, David West sent a proposed packing list of medications and supplies to the USDF who then forwarded the list to Brazilian authorities for approval. Mercifully, everything was okayed but if I treated a horse I'd have to inventory every single item used and adhere to strict paperwork standards. Smuggling vet drugs in Brazil was apparently a real issue. I kept eye contact with her. "It's your call."

Dewey nudged her shoulder, nibbled her polo shirt and she waved him away absently. "Not now, Dewbles," she murmured.

The interaction seemed to soften her and I tried for a slightly softer tone myself. "If you could just send me the list of supplements by the end of the week then I can check they're all okay and put my signature against them on my list. That's all." Smiling, I reminded her, "Here to help, okay?"

She nodded. "Okay."

I exhaled slowly, softly, so it didn't come out like a rush of relieved air. "What are his favorite treats?"

"Why do you want to know that?"

"Because I find it easier to do my job when they associate the woman with the pokey needles for blood draws and thermometer for their butt as someone who also brings treats."

"Oh, right. Um, licorice and peppermints. Plus the usual, carrots and apples."

"Ah, a sweet tooth, Master Dewey." I lowered my voice and leaned into him. "A man after my own heart. I'm partial to peppermints myself."

He pushed his nose toward me, and I just had to kiss it. He responded with a nudge and a huff-sniff in my face. I pushed him away before he could get nibbly, and it was only then that I realized what I'd done. "Sorry. I should have asked you. I just can't resist when someone sticks a kissable nose like that in my face."

For the first time she seemed relaxed and almost open. "No problem. I get it. I'm addicted to kissing his nose too."

I cleared my throat. "If you don't mind, I'd like to have a chat with your regular veterinarian, just to see if there's anything I need to know. And to open up a line of communication in case I need to consult with them." I glanced up to find her watching me intently. "If that's okay?"

"Sure. It's usually Teresa Warren at LakeVets in La Grange."

I didn't bother hiding my surprise. Or relief. "Really? I was in vet school with her. She's a great veterinarian. And a friend." That should make things a whole lot easier, considering Teresa and I were in contact every few months about tough cases, frustrating clients and also personal life stuff as a way to get some distance from the constant work stress. She'd never mentioned Caitlyn which boded well. "You two are in great hands."

"That she is. And yes we are."

"When you have a moment, could you please email LakeVets and let them know it's okay to release details to me?"

Another nod. "Sure. What will you want?"

"Everything from the last two years, perhaps three if there's something in there that makes me want to look closer."

"I'll let her know."

"Thanks." I finished my notes and saved Dewey's file. "Right, I think we're pretty much done here." I offered her a card from my back pocket. "If there's anything you need or anything else you think of, feel free to call or email me. Of course I'll be at Roosendaal and then come back again for Rotterdam."

She took the card carefully, like someone who thought I had cooties. "You're not staying here the whole time?"

"'Fraid not. I have to head back to the States between the two events." Because Seth had bitched so much about me being away I'd contorted myself to move between the two countries. "But I'll be with the team twenty-four-seven after the final selection is made."

"Sure. Sounds good." She almost sounded genuine.

I rubbed Dewey's face. "He really is adorable. And such a good guy."

Caitlyn smiled like I'd just given her the gift of life. "Yeah, he is."

We were making progress. Note to self: remember Dewey is the center of her universe. I bent to put my iPad in my bag. "Don't forget to send me that supplement list so I can look it over."

Her smiling mouth tightened into something resembling a scowl. "Fine."

I bit back my sigh. Scratch that previous thought. Progress is back to square one. I almost tried to walk things back, to soften it, to rewind thirty seconds where I'd thought she might be able to be civil. Just as quickly, I decided her issue with me was her problem, not mine. I was going to stick to polite and professional, and just do my job.

And if she wanted me to do it well, then she could come on board.

CHAPTER FIVE

Caitlyn

As with most big competitions, we had a few days on-site prior to our first test for the horses to settle and acclimate to the arenas and do our soundness check. Den Goubergh, the site of the Roosendaal competition, had excellent facilities for horses and humans, and Dew had settled perfectly into his temporary accommodation. We'd passed the trot up with flying colors, he'd had his arena acclimation ride and not batted an eyelid and everything seemed on track for a good competition. That said, I would have been happier if not for the thorn in my sock that was Addie Gardner.

To say things between us were awkward would be an understatement. She seemed to be everywhere and the fact I had to interact with her made me close up tighter than a clam. Whenever I looked at her, some stupid part of my brain insisted on showing me a replay of the times she'd teased me, been mean to me or played some prank on me when we were kids. Yet, despite my impersonation of someone with a vocabulary of just twenty words, Addie appeared unconcerned and almost too friendly. And Dew adored her, which made the whole thing even more uncomfortable.

Wren, who had a radar for drama, seemed to have made it her personal mission to find out everything about me and Addie and Pony

Club. Persistence was my groom's middle name, and she was totally unphased by my refusals to answer. Given I was still trying to wrap my head around the whole thing, which included going over and over events from my teen years, I simply had no answers for her. Because I didn't even know how I really felt.

We were staying in Lotte's deluxe horse truck, which had bunk beds as well as a small bathroom and kitchen, and each night when I came in for dinner I was treated to Wren's Twenty Questions. The night before the competition began, I collapsed into a chair at the table to watch Wren cooking and when she started up again, I just…caved. I had no idea if I was worn down by her persistence, was having a lapse in concentration or if I just wanted to get it off my chest. "Seriously, it's nothing. We did Pony Club together for a few years and had some stupid teen stuff going on. I never expected to see her again and it's thrown me for a bit of a loop, that's all."

Wren's head snapped up and I caught a flash of manic grin. "Aha! I knew it! Come on. Spill. Obviously you two have history. I've never seen your hackles go up like that with anyone. Not even post-breakup Elin encounters. I actually thought you were going to snarl at Addie. Not to mention you've looked like a mannequin every time you've spoken to her since, like you just don't know what to say. Were you guys teen besties who had a massive falling out?"

"That's because I *don't* know what to say to her. We weren't friends, okay?" My laugh sounded dry and nervous. "Quite the opposite. And now some part of me reverts to an insecure teenager, right when I need all the confidence I can muster." I leaned down to unzip my boots and pull them off. "It's freaking me out a little, and all that panic and insecurity is putting me in full lizard brain." Freaking me out a little was the understatement of the month. Knowing that someone from so long ago, someone who shouldn't affect me *could* affect me was frustrating.

Plus, Addie's refusal to acknowledge what she'd done and then to act as if everything was peachy just pissed me off. But as usual with any annoyance, I found it hard to keep a firm grip on it, and Addie's quiet jokes and easy manner were loosening my grip further, leaving me in some weird uncertain space. Not that I wanted to be bitchy, because I wasn't a bitch, but I felt like I should show some respect to teen-me who'd suffered and not just roll over like a puppy promised a belly rub.

"Hmmm. Well, she doesn't seem freaked out at all." Her tone was almost teasingly sing-song.

"What do you mean?"

"Caitlyn," my groom sighed. "Don't play dumb, not with me. If I see it with Addie then there's no way you don't."

See…what? "I really don't know what you're talking about," I said honestly.

Wren's response was exaggeratedly slow. "She looks at you like you're her ex that she's still hung up on and utterly heartbroken over."

I almost choked on what she'd said, and my own response was a spluttering, "What? No way. That's absurd. There was never anything between us except teenaged animosity." The idea of Addie Gardner and *that* was totally ridiculous. "I think maybe you need your eyes checked."

"Mhmmmmm." The facetious agreement spanned three octaves up then back down. "Sure thing, boss."

I stared at her. Wren turned away and rummaged in the small fridge wedged under a counter. Apparently she'd decided she'd said all she needed to.

For now.

The quiet lasted another two minutes before she dove in again, over the sound of chopping. "She's cute. If I was inclined that way, and single, I might ask her out. She has the most incredible eyes. And those dimples? Adorable."

"I suppose you're right," I conceded. Though it wasn't so much a concession as an agreement because Addie Gardner *was* cute. There was no denying that. But I couldn't show Wren all my cards. She'd get insufferably smug. Insufferably-er smug-er. And given everything that sat alongside Addie's cuteness, I didn't want to get into an argument with Wren about why I wasn't jumping the vet's bones.

"Course I'm right. And she's hilarious. And fun. We had a great chat."

Feeling an odd defensiveness prickling my skin, I asked, "How'd you know that? And when did you have this great chat?"

"Yesterday afternoon. She's talking to all the grooms, wants to get our opinions, like, eyes on the ground type stuff." Wren let out a particularly loud exhalation. "The relief is real, Caitlyn. Flying with the horses can be pretty boring if you don't have someone good to talk to. I love Dew, but he's a shitty conversationalist." Everyone spoke as if us making the team was a done deal. Realistically I knew we probably would, unless a disaster befell us, and that confidence helped. But also…superstition. If I thought about it, it wouldn't happen.

I fought the urge to cross my arms over my chest. "It's settled then. You and Addie can have all the fun chats you want to." I didn't mean it to, but the statement came out dry and defensive. Interesting.

Wren's reply was a cheerful, "I plan to."

"Great."

"It sure is." After a few seconds, she reached over and poked my arm. "Come on, grumble-butt. What's up?"

"Just thinking." I scrambled for an answer that wouldn't give away what I was really feeling. "I'd have liked to try out the new Freestyle music a few more times before maybe doing it in Rio." Shit. In my haste to pretend I wasn't thinking about Addie I'd totally just jinxed myself.

Unlike the Olympics where we would potentially ride three different tests—the Grand Prix, then if we scored high enough, the Grand Prix Special and then if we made the cut after the Special we would ride the individual medal-deciding Grand Prix Freestyle—these two remaining competitions only had the Grand Prix and Special. Our *Frozen*-themed Freestyle soundtrack had been a hit at the Florida competitions in January and March, but the more ears and reactions I got the better. Dew always responded better to crowd engagement and if I had a better idea of what to expect, I could hype him or chill him accordingly.

"I'm sure it'll be great," Wren soothed. "Your choreography always scores top marks and only a sadist wouldn't like a *Frozen* Freestyle."

I grinned. "We all know dressage is full of sadists…"

When I walked Dewey out of the arena after my Grand Prix I was ninety-nine-point-eight percent pleased and zero-point-two percent pissed. The scoreboard held the results from each of the judges positioned at their specific letters around the arena and then my total score of 79.630%. I would have been happier with a score over eighty, but I'd been tentative with my extended trot work because Dew had felt a little tighter than usual and I didn't want to push and risk ruining his naturally good rhythm.

I scratched his neck underneath his braids. "You were fabulous, Dew. Pity about the rider."

He snorted and I couldn't tell if he was agreeing with me, or just relieved it was carrot time. Dew loved the atmosphere of big shows, but also loved his downtime. I waved at the spectators in the stands on all four sides, then waved with both hands when a contingent from somewhere started whooping. At least the audience was happy.

Waiting by the gate was Wren and the head honchos of the team. Wren's expression said it all. Hell yes. She kept silent as we walked back to the stalls, her naturally long stride just keeping pace with Dew. Ian and Mary had to work to keep up and while Mary chattered the whole way, Ian was his usual quietly restrained self, nodding and occasionally murmuring, "Good, good."

Mary beamed up at me. "That ride is worthy of a place."

And I just kept nodding along as I rode out of the melee to where I could dismount. Ian and Mary melted away, back to the team officials' area to watch Dakota who was scheduled to ride three after me. I leaned down and hugged Dew around the neck, then swung to the ground. Wren pulled the reins over his head, then ran my right stirrup up while I did the left and then loosened the girth. Her head popped over Dew's neck. "I can see it on your face. Need I ask?"

Shrugging, I pulled my helmet off and smoothed my hair, checking it was still in a tight bun at the back. Cameras were everywhere, ready to document the competition for every equestrian publication on the planet, which meant I not only had to look presentable but I had to look pleased, not annoyed with myself. I clipped the strap of my helmet together and hooked it over my arm so I could pull off my white gloves. "Could have done more with the extended trot work but he felt a bit tight. Didn't want to risk it. Now I feel like I should have gone all out."

"You're in first place," Wren said dryly. She didn't need to say anything more—we'd worked together long enough that the unspoken was just as known as the spoken.

"For now," I countered, trying not to make it sound like I was sulking. "There's practically a whole class to ride after me."

"Caitlyn." My name was a sigh. "Perspective. The scores from your qualifying competitions thus far are more than enough to secure you a place on the team."

"You're right. I know." I let go of my self-flagellation. In the scheme of things, the score was fine. My Inner Caitlyn piped up to remind me that I was only competing against myself, that my goal was to improve our training and our scores. And if that stacked up to beat other people and secure us a place on the team—great. I grabbed Dewey's face and kissed him on the nose. Camera shutters clicked behind me. He pricked his ears at the sound and more shutters went off. Narcissist.

By the time Dewey had cooled down and been settled back into his stall to eat the rest of his day away it was almost eleven a.m. I'd removed my tails and boots but remained mostly dressed to ride in case I was required to attend the prize-giving ceremony. Wren had left to socialize and inhale the latest gossip from the other grooms. Once I'd studied the video of my test three times I went to watch the rest of the riders.

I was still in first place, though Dakota was chasing my heels on 77.071%, and the few combinations who I knew could beat me were yet to ride. I stared at my name and score. It was a good score and when compared to my main competition in Rio it would see me get a medal. If I got to Rio. Don't jinx it. I found myself a semi-secluded spot in a back corner of the stands and settled in to watch. There were some good rides, a couple of great ones, and some that I knew the riders would rather forget.

My skin prickled when the announcer's voice over the loudspeaker introduced the final combination of Lynn Bergler from Great Britain riding Marionette. The Jensen family had previously owned that horse before they'd sold her to Lynn for the tidy sum of eighty thousand dollars. I'd thought the price was a little low given the horse's breeding, temperament, trainability, paces, and prospect as a broodmare.

And I was only a little bitter. The Jensens had given me the ride on Marionette when the mare was a hot, uncooperative green-broken three-year-old. I'd figured out what made her tick, turned her attitude around, then taken her through the ranks and turned her into a seriously competitive Grand Prix prospect. That is, until four years ago when the Jensens had abruptly informed me that they'd been offered a sum they couldn't refuse and I lost the ride.

Given it was the second time they'd sold a horse out from under me, I'd decided to never take on one of their horses again, even if they did breed the best dressage Warmbloods in the States. Such was the nature of top-level competition—the unspoken rule was every horse has a price.

Except Dew.

I'd rather never ride Grand Prix again than see the horse I'd bred and trained and been with nearly every day of his life owned and competed by someone else.

Lynn had done well with Marionette and it was a respectable test. But not quite enough. After her final salute, I turned away from the arena to double check the final scoreboard. Time to grab my horse and get dressed again for the prize presentation. I accepted congratulations and well-wishes on my way to the stalls and when I finally got there after ten minutes of conversational detours, Wren and Addie were outside Dewey's stall, engaged in an animated conversation while Dew tried to get involved.

Wren's laugh echoed through the space, followed by a lower belly laugh. Addie's. I hadn't heard her laugh like that since…well, way back then. She looked up at my approach, flashed me a smile, then touched Wren's shoulder. "I'll catch you both later to check on Dewey."

I tried to make my smile as bright as hers and knew I'd fallen short by a few hundred megawatts. "Sounds great."

Once she'd left, I turned to Wren who'd resumed wrapping Dew's legs in blindingly white bandages ready for the presentation. "Are you two best pals now or something?" The question sounded oddly defensive, and I couldn't figure out what was up with my tone.

"What do you mean?" She glanced over her shoulder.

"Cozy chats, all that touching."

Wren snorted a laugh. "Have you blinkered yourself or something?" Her tone was pure incredulity. "She touches *everyone* while she's talking, Caitlyn. She's like Brandon, Mr. Never Still Hands himself." Wren stared. "How haven't you noticed that?"

"Probably because…because she's only been around for a few days and we haven't engaged in any deep and meaningful casual touch conversations?" Did Addie used to be like that? I had no idea.

"Right." She finished the last bandage and stood. "Have you watched the video of the test?"

"Mhmm."

"You want to talk about the ride?" Wren gestured for me to raise my chin so she could straighten the diamante bar through the stock tie at my neck.

"Tomorrow." I made myself smile as I checked my hair was presentation-ready. "After I've ridden the Special. Then I'll either need to gloat or grieve."

It was very nearly grieve.

Dressage isn't just doing the movements well but knowing how to ride a competitive test which means preparing and riding accurately to the markers. I was so focused on what came next that I let Dewey down. As we came around the top of the arena in collected canter, Dew's attention wavered at some commotion in the stands. My fault. I was so intent on the impending transition to collected trot then going all out in the extended trot to make up for those I didn't quite nail the day before, that for a few seconds I forgot the most important thing. My horse.

He fumbled the transition to collected trot and I thought it was completely lost. Mercifully, his focus snapped back to me at my outside rein half-halt reminder and he placed all his trust in me, forgot about the noise and gave me everything. He floated down the long side of the arena like he was trying to win a competition for biggest and best extended trot. If I'd messed up during our piaffe, where Dew was less able to recover from mistakes, then I would have ended up somewhere in the middle of the rankings instead of lining up at the end of the day next to one of my teammates, Beau, to collect my second-place sash and prize money.

After posing for a million photos, engaging in some quick media interviews and talking to a few of the competitors who'd stuck around for the presentation, I snuck back to the truck and changed into comfortable jeans and a sponsor logo-laden polo. While Wren prepped Dewey for the drive back to Lotte's, I packed up the truck. And thought. And then thought some more. We were in a great position. My horse was sound and fit. My scores were the highest of everyone on the shortlist. Dew had felt great. I'd felt great. We had another competition down, and one big one to go. Then maybe one big *big* one after that. And shit, what if—

The nervousness building in the pit of my stomach made me feel sick. Closing my eyes, I leaned my forehead against the exterior of the truck. "Nobody's going to die, nobody's going to go bankrupt, nobody is going to run you out of the dressage scene," I whispered to myself. "Do your best, be as prepared as you can be and that's all you can do." Right. Easy. I opened my eyes and stared down at the churned-up-by-hooves grass below my feet.

A quiet Tennessee drawl asked, "D'you make a habit of talking to yourself?"

Trying to act as if Addie hadn't just startled the shit out of me and sparked my irrational annoyance, I stepped away from the truck. "Only on special occasions." I side-eyed her. "Shouldn't you be working?"

Her eyebrows shot up. "Direct. I'm all done here. I've already checked your horse out. With Wren present," she clarified quickly. "And given there's only a handful of my charges here today, it's not as hectic as you might think. Plus everyone but you and Beau have left for the day." Addie moved in beside me, leaning against the open side door of the truck.

Only five of us had chosen to ride this competition, the others having already completed one of the qualifying competitions in Compiègne late last month. The only compulsory event for selection was Rotterdam at the end of the month, where the entire shortlisted team would be jostling for one of the four key or one reserve positions. I'd decided to ride both of the two non-compulsory qualifying events to make sure that I had as many good scores under my belt as I could fit.

"Right. Great." After a moment I added, "Sorry. You're right, that came out a lot blunter than I'd meant it to."

"How did you mean it to come out?"

"I—" Frowning, I thought about it. Now she'd turned the directness on me and I had no idea how to respond. "I'm actually not sure. Not like that." I tried for small talk. "What have you been doing today?"

She smiled, and her response was slow as if the answer was obvious. "My job." She touched my forearm then yanked her hand back as if my skin had burned her. Wren's "She touches everyone" echoed in my head. Addie's shoulders did a slow rise and fall and when she spoke again it was a one-eighty topic turnaround. "You okay? You seemed a bit...freaked out?"

Surprised by the softness of the question and her genuine and obvious interest, I answered truthfully. "I am. Both okay and freaked out." Smiling, I said, "Just overthinking things, that's all." I debated if I should elaborate and after a moment, confessed, "There's a lot of balls to juggle at the moment."

"Ah yes. I know that feeling." Addie folded her arms over her breasts. "You know that saying about juggling life stuff, and trying to keep a lot of balls up in the air? It's all about knowing which ones are plastic and can be dropped, and which are fragile glass and should be kept off the ground."

With a rueful smile I said, "Unfortunately, at the moment, all of them are glass."

Her answering smile was slow. "In that case, I've every confidence you're going to keep each of them in the air." She cleared her throat, swallowing as if her mouth was dry and she couldn't talk. "Dewey gets my tick of approval—vitals normal and no heat in any of his limbs. I'm off to see the other horses who uh, didn't have to stay for the prize presentation and then I'm headin' back to the States."

"Oh. Right." I'd have expected to feel relieved that she was leaving. But I felt...nothing.

"I'll be back here in a little over two weeks. I've talked to the veterinary practice Lotte usually has come to do her work and thank the Lord they speak fabulous English, right? I know you have their contact details for emergencies but if there's anything that feels weird or out of place don't hesitate to contact me at any hour." She paused and added a quiet, "Or if you just want to chat."

"Sure. I mean I hope I *don't* have to talk to you before you're back." Realizing how it sounded, despite it being an old joke, I added a hasty, "Of course because that means there's something wrong with Dew."

Addie leaned closer for a conspiratorial, "Of course." She pushed away from the truck. "Well then. I guess I'll see you just before Rotterdam?"

"That you will."

"Great. Okay then. Take care. Uh, bye." With a shy wave she walked away, and I could hear her muttering something as she went.

I exhaled a long breath. Despite my panic when she'd arrived, the conversation had been perfectly natural. Nice even. Maybe I could set the past aside and be a normal person around Addie. Enthusiastic back pats for me. Rational Caitlyn jumped onto the soapbox to speechify about how a comfortable, friendly relationship between the two of us would make the next few months easier.

But there was friendly, and then there was the weird nervous feeling when I was around her. Like I was a teenager all over again and wanting someone's approval. Wanting someone to notice me. Wanting someone to like me. I knew myself well enough to realize this dual-sided emotion was partly my teenaged self reflecting all of that past angst back at me, and partly the fact that I knew I was physically attracted to her. Hell, anyone who liked women would probably be attracted to her. But given our history, it was more than a little confusing.

And I so did *not* need confusing right now.

I almost laughed at myself. In front of me was the very definition of confusing. So what could I do about it? I had zero answers. But somewhere inside was curiosity. There was something about this Addie who was so different to the Addie I'd known. Which Addie was the real one? The right one?

I had no answer to that question either.

CHAPTER SIX

Addie

Caitlyn had cleared her veterinarian to talk to me, and I'd adjusted my flights to make a stop in Kentucky instead of taking the free day at home to sort out my jetlag. I hadn't seen my friend Teresa in over six months and probably wouldn't see her for another six the way things were going, so it seemed a perfect opportunity to catch up. Besides, these conversations were always better in person, even if you weren't talking to a friend.

When she'd said she'd be spending the afternoon in clinic doing paperwork I'd laughed. "Yeah sure, until an emergency comes up."

Teresa was emphatic. "Nope, not at all. Two half days a week for paperwork, no exceptions. We've got enough vets on staff that the work is always covered." She'd exhaled. "This place is like the fucking unicorn of vet practices. I'm never leaving. Even if the pay isn't as good as other places, it's so worth my mental health."

Unicorn of vet practices indeed. I couldn't even imagine what it would be like to have a few hours of genuinely uninterrupted time at work. Most days I did my paperwork during my lunch break, or once I was technically off work but still in the office, and sometimes even when I got home because Seth believed in cramming as much into his vets' schedules as he could. His was one of the practices that paid in the top twenty percent of vet salaries nationwide and he probably thought that entitled him to wring as much out of us as he could.

My first impression of LakeVets was comfort. My second impression was competency. When I stepped into the reception area—which smelled as all veterinary surgeries did of disinfectant layered over the top of animal scents—and asked for Dr. Warren, the receptionist flashed me a wide, genuine smile. "I'm sure she's out back, I'll just go check. And who should I say is here for her?"

"Addie Gardner. She's expecting me. I'm a friend."

I wouldn't have thought it possible, but the smile grew wider. "Wonderful! I'll be right back." It seemed that friends visiting you at work was a fun thing at LakeVets, unlike at my workplace.

Teresa burst in less than a minute later, her arms spread wide and her face alight with her brilliant smile. She crashed into me, absorbing me in a tight hug. "Dang, girl, you look good. Tired, but good."

I held her at arm's length. "Have you looked in a mirror lately? I'm pretty sure you only had two bags under each eye, not four, the last time I saw you."

"You're hilarious. And you try incubating a human." She rubbed her stomach. "Five more months. Feels like an eternity."

Squeezing her shoulders, I told her, "I'm pretty sure it's only going to get worse."

"Yeah, well, I've had plenty of practice with on-calls so I'm sure I'll be fine with the waking up for feeding and crying. And that's just for me. Who knows what the baby will want." She winked, hugged me again, then dragged me off with a "Thanks, Kendall!" thrown over her shoulder at the receptionist.

As we wandered through the building, Teresa gestured left and right, never slowing as she rattled off, "Offices and shared space for eating and hiding from clients, lab, small animal surgery, and then just through there is small animal accommodation."

The more I saw, the more impressed I became. Though not brand new, the practice was clean, large, and well laid out. All the equipment was modern, and I couldn't see anything I'd have wished for that they didn't have. Even a standing MRI machine which Seth refused to buy, deeming it an unnecessary waste of money, despite its diagnostic mastery. I lovingly touched the edge of the screen and murmured, "One day I'll get to use one of you."

The more I saw the more I felt gratitude that Teresa had such a great workspace. And a childish kind of jealousy that I didn't. Everyone was friendly and cheerful, despite obviously being in the middle of work and by the time we'd left the examination area I felt like I'd made ten friends. We paused in a huge treatment room with three crushes to restrain horses and I leaned against the wall. "What's happening here while you're off having a kid?"

"I'll be stepping back from hands-on equine stuff soon, then dusting off my small animal medicine until I can't work anymore. A locum is going to step in and try to fill my shoes. Try." She flashed a beatific smile.

"Good thing your head's so big, otherwise you'd have trouble balancing that baby belly."

"Need a big head for my big brain." She pointed to the back of a tall, rake-thin man dressed in bright pink scrubs and studying digital X-rays on a laptop. "Come meet my boss."

I knew who her boss was. Emmett Lake, the proprietor of LakeVets, was something of a legend in my profession. He was on nearly every veterinary board imaginable, reviewed journal papers for fun and was rumored to actually be a nice guy into good medicine rather than just making money.

Teresa dragged me over to Emmett who turned at the intrusion, eyes lighting up when he saw Teresa. His gaze fell to me, the look of excitement only dimming fractionally. Teresa gestured between me and her boss. "Emmett, meet Addie Gardner, my bestest of friends from college and, dare I say it, a veterinarian of greater skill than even I. Addie, this is my boss and an all-around scoundrel, Emmett Lake."

Emmett had a roguish, mad-scientist look about him as if he was about to tell you he'd just discovered the cure for colic and then crack a dad joke all in the same breath. His voice was a surprisingly high tenor and I detected a trace of East Coast when he dipped his head and said, "The pleasure is all mine." He offered his hand and I took it.

"Likewise. I've just been given the tour. Your practice is very impressive."

Emmett was obviously pleased by the compliment. "Why thank you." He closed the laptop and leaned back against the stainless steel table. "Gardner...I read your paper on using bone marrow stem cells to treat superficial digital flexor tendon strains. Very impressive. You really think it's worth the trouble to obtain marrow stem cells to treat an injury that's usually managed traditionally with anti-inflammatories, rest, and physical therapy?"

I couldn't tell if he was baiting me or disagreed and wanted to have discourse on the matter. I would have liked to look at Teresa but sensed that it might be taken as discomfort or weakness. It was neither—I just wanted to see if my friend could give me any clues as to whether her boss always jumped right in like this less than a minute after meeting someone.

Regardless, I'd spent years researching and doing trials and I stood behind my data. "Yessir, I do. And I agree with your assessment regarding traditional therapies. When appropriate," I added with a smile. "But eighty percent of my work is performance horses— eventers, showjumpers, dressage horses, racehorses. Those animals are people's livelihoods, their enjoyment, and leisure and they demand the best level of care and innovative options to keep their horses sound. As do my pleasure riding clients too, of course."

A bushy white eyebrow shot up. "Then this is about your ego, not providing a high level of care?"

Laughing quietly I said, "Don't we all have egos? This is good science, sir, and my therapy does provide a high level of care. The theory and practice behind it, as well as the number of people citing it and now using the method, back that up."

"You stand by your knowledge, even when an old bastard like me challenges it. I like that. And I absolutely agree." He clapped me on the shoulder, and his expression turned manic, like he'd caught me in a practical joke. "We've been using the protocol with great success in some of our clients' performance horses and we've even managed to find ways to bring the costs down a little without impacting our bottom line. Happy clients always come back, and they bring their wallets with them." His chuckle was deep and genuinely amused.

Anxiety I hadn't even realized I'd been holding let go, leaving a wave of adrenaline in its wake. Apparently my brain thought Emmett Lake's opinion was super important. I fought to stop myself from grinning like a fool. "Yessir, I agree."

His expression turned serious. "You're taking care of our Dewey, and Caitlyn?"

"I am, yes."

"I'm sure you know how special that horse is, as is his owner. We're so proud to have one of our own out there on the world stage."

I caught Teresa's smiling eye-roll and got the feeling that Emmett talked about Caitlyn and Dewey a lot. "Well, they've certainly earned their place."

"That they have. Right, I've got to head out and castrate a bunch of unruly colts." He offered his hand again, his face relaxing back into the slightly amused expression he'd been wearing at our introduction. "You take care now and take good care of our team in Rio."

I shook his hand firmly. "Thank you, sir. I'll do my best." Oof, that was cringeworthy. Why not just fall to the floor to genuflect?

He walked away whistling Darth Vader's Theme from *Star Wars*, but he made it sound so jaunty that it was amusing rather than ominous. Teresa turned to me like someone had slowed her to half speed, her expression pure *Well look at you, pal*. "You sure impressed him."

"Really? Didn't seem like it. Seemed more like him poking at me to find weak points in my armor. Or something."

"Trust me, he's impressed. I've seen him talk to more equine vets than I can count on all my digits ten times over and I think that's the first time he's ever brought up any research papers with anyone." She grinned. "And you calling him *sir* every three seconds didn't hurt your cause."

I blew out a breath. "I can't help it. He's a legend, and in the face of legends I still revert to a scared little vet student. And what cause do I have that's now not hurt?"

"He's an absolute teddy bear." Her blue-gray eyes widened. "And the cause of having someone like Emmett Lake thinking you're brilliant."

"Mmm. Good to know. And how'd he know about that paper? He doesn't review for that journal."

"He knew about it because I showed him and told him my super clever friend wrote it."

"Super clever?" I nudged her. "Aww, you really like me."

"Maybe a little. Come on, you can buy me a second lunch and we'll go over Dewey's case history. And then you can tell me all about how much you hate your workplace."

"I don't hate my workplace," I answered automatically and not entirely truthfully.

Her cheek pat was level-ten condescending. "Sure thing, Addie. Sure thing."

Teresa brought her laptop to the small café across the street from LakeVets and we settled next to each other in a booth that looked back on the Kentucky bluegrass fields behind the surgery. I had coffee, Teresa decaf tea with a side of grumbling about limiting caffeine. While we waited for food she emailed me Dewey's file and then brought up his history.

After a sip of excellent coffee I asked, "Anything I should worry about?"

"Nah. There's nothing much here really, just routine stuff. We medicate his joints as a precaution but he's never had a significant lameness. He's on a daily gastro-health supplement but routine scoping never shows gastric or pyloric ulcers. It's just to support him while he's in high-stress environments. He's a wonderful horse, so easy to work with, and Caitlyn and Wren take wonderful care of him."

"Yeah I got that impression. Did an exam and all he did was try to hug me."

"Sounds like him." Teresa smiled up at the waitress delivering our lunch. She dove right in and after a huge forkful of pasta salad, said, "Caitlyn Lloyd is a dream client. Never argues, follows treatment plans to the letter, always wants to discuss and be involved, doesn't bullshit when I ask her what's going on. And always pays her bills in full and on time. If every client was like her, I'd be a happy woman."

I hmmed, and Teresa kept on rambling, "She always gives me a cold or hot drink depending on the weather, her horses are well-behaved and she's always ready when I turn up, even if I'm late. Her facilities are immaculate. She's an incredible equestrienne and also just a damned nice person."

"Damned nice?" I almost choked on my turkey sandwich. "Yeah, I didn't really get that vibe from her. At all."

"What vibe did you get?"

"Hostility mostly."

She swallowed her mouthful to snap a defensive, "What do you mean, hostility? Are you socially deficient? If you can't get along with Caitlyn Lloyd, you can't get along with anyone."

Time to come clean. "She and I have, um, history."

Teresa's fork clattered to the plate. "Fuck, Addie. Did you sleep with her and break her sweet little heart?"

"What? No! Of course not." Though I'd loved to have done the former and then very much *not* break her heart. "How or when would I have done that?"

She shrugged. "I don't know. Sometime. What is it then?"

"We were at Pony Club together when we were teenagers, way back when I used to ride the horses, not treat them. That's all. We… weren't friends." But I hadn't thought we were mortal enemies as she'd seemed to.

"No? Interesting. Well, I'm glad you didn't hurt her, she got enough of that from her ex-girlfriend."

It took me a moment to register what Teresa had said and when I did, my heart did a little stutter step that was a simultaneous *oh fuuuck* and *oh yesss*. "Wait, she's queer?"

"Uh, yeah." She may as well have said *Duh*. "World's oldest news. Don't you follow equestrian sport news at all?"

"Not really." But clearly I should have been. "Dressage Divas are a small percentage of my client base and my spare readin' time is either vet journals or smutty romances."

"You are the worst lesbian I know. Aren't you all supposed to have some built-in sonar system to find all the other ladies who like ladies?"

"Radar and it's called gaydar and mine has always been faulty." And apparently that fault was inbuilt from my teen years.

"She was dating Elin Nygaard, the Danish Grand Prix rider, for almost two years until Elin broke up with her right before the World Equestrian Games in 2014. Huge deal, rumors everywhere that Elin had been cheating. Caitlyn said nothing about the whole thing, then went out there and wiped the floor with all the other riders. In the press conference afterward she very graciously thanked everyone who'd supported her and had the most incredible underhanded dig at Elin. No names mentioned of course."

"Of course," I said dryly.

"It was wonderful, and also hilarious because she's *so* shy but just got this steely kind of fuck-you vibe about her when she basically told the world Elin Nygaard could go screw herself."

"Shy? Really?" Frowning I considered that. "I don't remember her being shy at all."

"You went to Pony Club with her and you don't remember her being shy? Addie, excuse my cliché, but do you live under a rock? On a scale of introversion being zero and extroversion being ten, I think she'd barely make a three."

"It was over twenty years ago. Some days I don't even recall the demeanor of someone I spoke to yesterday." I ran desperately through my memories, trying to find this *shy* that Teresa was talking about. I remembered confident, cool, and aloof but not shy.

"Mm, I know that feeling. Look, Caitlyn Lloyd is amazing and that's all there is to it. Elin's horse died of massive impaction colic about six months after the WEG. It was bad, like fuck being the surgeon on that case kind of bad. And Caitlyn made the sweetest tribute post about it. I have no idea how she just rises above all the shit that happens on the dressage circuit. She's like cream floating to the top."

Cream. Interesting visual. "Does this Caitlyn Lloyd Fan Club that you're clearly the president of have membership badges or is it just a secret handshake kind of deal?"

Teresa snorted out a laugh. "Very funny. Seriously though, you really should pay attention to the dressage-circuit gossip. It's amazing what you can find out, even if half of it isn't true," she said cheerfully.

"And now that you're going to be immersed in that world, don't you think you should keep up with all of the trash talk?" There was undisguised teasing in her voice.

"I'll take that under advisement." We both knew I had no intention of doing anything of the sort. I was allergic to backstabbing and gossip.

"Come on. What's this really about? I honestly don't know anyone who Caitlyn Lloyd isn't friendly with. She doesn't even say bad things about that bitch trying to make the team, what's her name…" Her nose wrinkled.

"Dakota Turner?"

"Yeah! That's her. Never met her but the grapevine gossip is enough to say I don't want to. But I've never heard Caitlyn say anything nasty about anyone on the circuit."

I glanced around to make sure nobody was nearby, but still kept my voice low. "Yeah, Dakota is a bitch. And I've only spent a tiny amount of time with her. Entitlement doesn't even begin to cover it."

"Right. So tell me, if Caitlyn is friendly with even nasty people then why are you so special as to earn her ire? Ire that I really can't even imagine."

"I actually don't really know." I backtracked. "Welllll, I do because she basically told me why she thinks I'm a shit, but I don't get it." I blew out a long breath. "She said—" I paused and rethought what I was about to say. The difference in the way we viewed how we'd acted toward one another during that time didn't change the fact events had occurred. I *had* teased her when we were kids at Pony Club, but not in a way I'd thought cruel. "Look, I was a workin' class nobody trying to not be the bottom of the trash heap in a place where money was king. And the things I did and said weren't taken how I'd thought they were. She thinks I'm a bullying bitch."

Teresa laughed so long and loud I wondered if she was about to pass out. "You? A bully? Now that's something else I really can't imagine."

"What can I say? I was an awkward little queer kid who didn't know how to talk to girls, especially one who I…admired. You know, like that stupid saying? He pulls your hair because he likes you." Shit. I really hadn't meant to admit that. I bit my lower lip to stop myself from making any more admissions.

Teresa was silent for an eternity and I braced myself for a teasing barrage. Instead, she quietly asked, "And do you still admire her?" I could almost hear the air quotes on the word admire.

"I thought I did. Mostly I'm just confused because it's clear we are on separate pages about Pony Club. Separate pages in different books."

I sighed. "I was really looking forward to seeing her again, seeing if we could maybe be friends. But that's total pipe-dream territory now. She seems to think I'm still some mean, idiotic fourteen-year-old who's about to hide her saddle or something. Nothing I do is going to make her see I'm an adult and have almost grown past my socially awkward phase and that I behaved like that idiot back then because I had a huge moony teen crush on her." Have a huge crush on her, I corrected in my head. Despite Caitlyn's coolness, I was still attracted to her. Old ideals were damned hard to shake.

"Then maybe it's time you figured out how to tell her why you behaved the way you did. Without the hair pulling."

"I never actually pulled her hair."

"No?" Teresa's laugh was short and full of mirth. "Well you never know, maybe that's her kink now. This is the time for you to get your shit together and get over your childhood baggage."

"I don't have baggage," I said instantly and perhaps a little petulantly.

"Everyone has baggage. Granted, yours always seemed less fucked up than everyone else's."

"Okay fine, of course I have baggage but I don't have baggage about my time at Pony Club with Caitlyn Lloyd." Even if she did.

"Good. Then talk to her, like really talk to her. Make the effort. I promise it'll be worth it." She stole a sip of my coffee. "If for no other reason than you guys need to get along or it's going to add a whole other level of stress to an already stressed-as-fuck situation."

I grunted, then mumbled my answer. "I'll try."

CHAPTER SEVEN

Caitlyn

I found Wren in the tack room, chunky headphones over her ears, dancing as she cleaned a saddle. Leaning in the door, I waved to get her attention. She grinned, wiped her hands on the towel draped over a saddle stand and looped the headphones around her neck. "What's up?"

"Do you have some time to help me with a thing?"

"Of course." She capped the bottle of leather dressing. "What are we doing?"

"I have to do those Dewey autographs, and some idiots on the Instagram post said that I was just going to do it myself and pretend the horse painted them."

Wren snorted. "Ha! As if you'd ever do that."

"Right?" Dewey's engaging persona and playfulness was a gift from the money-raising gods. "So I'm going to video it and show them all it really is him. Then I might get another fifteen takers if I put up another autograph auction." Every dime helped, even if it meant constantly putting myself in the public eye and opening myself up to ridiculous criticism. I was willing to bet none of the other USDF members had ever had to do anything like an auction to raise money for their campaigns, because every one of them was independently wealthy or from family money. I had enough cash for rainy days, to keep my barn running and my career chugging along, but it wasn't enough on its own.

"Probably will," Wren agreed.

"Could you grab the artist for me please while I change?" Even fun activities required shout-outs to my sponsors. "I'll do it at the cottage so we're not in the way here."

"Sure."

When I'd finished dressing in jeans and sponsor-laden clothing Wren and Dewey were outside the cottage. She'd taken off his blankets and groomed him, and he looked every inch the camera-ready horse. Wren stared at the clothesline with pegs ready to hang each piece of artwork, the table I'd set up with a pot of green paint and one of those huge thick-handled kiddie paintbrushes, and the metal baking tray into which I'd poured black paint for Dew to stamp a shoe print onto each of the heavy ten-by-twelve cards before he decorated them with the green paint.

Wren was trying to dissuade Dew from sticking his nose into everything. "This is gonna get messy," she sing-songed.

"Tell me about it."

Dew nickered at me, then stretched his head forward to receive a treat, straining at the end of the lead. I gave him a carrot then tied him to the porch railing. He immediately started nibbling Lotte's flowers.

I lightly slapped his shoulder. "Can you *not* do that?" I tugged his head up and faced Wren. "So I was thinking if you could just follow whatever we're doing, me going back and forth with him and the table and the clothesline, and I'll try to edit it into one of those cool fast-motion time-lapse looking things."

"Sounds great. You going to add a funky soundtrack?"

"Mhmm. The *Three Stooges* would be appropriate, or maybe "Flight of the Bumblebee" to reflect what's going on inside Dewey's brain. I'll try to keep the bending over in front of the camera to a minimum."

"I bet Add—" My groom's lips parted then slammed back together again. "You know what, never mind. Let's make a movie."

I eyed her and decided to let her slip go.

My plan was to do each of the fifteen cards with a Dew shoeprint, hang them to dry, then start from the first one and get Dewey to add his paint flair to them. If offered, he would hold anything not edible in his mouth and usually had to give it a shake for good measure. If my plan went to plan, I could hold the cards close to the brush and get some of the paint on each one. Then he could have a piece of licorice after each piece of artwork was done which should entice him to keep "painting." The possibility for disaster and hilarity were equally high.

I positioned myself at Dew's head and gently pulled his halter to make him face forward. "All right, are we ready?"

"Let's do it." Wren held up the video camera. "Three, two, one... aaaaction!"

I flashed a wide smile. "Hi, I'm Caitlyn Lloyd and this here is my partner in crime—Midfields Adieu, AKA Dewey." Dew nudged my shoulder. I nudged him back. "We've been doing a little fundraising to support our bid to make the US Dressage Team for Rio 2016, which is in fifty-six days!"

Dewey, apparently bored with my thirty seconds of talking and not paying him attention, started nibbling my ponytail then my polo collar. Laughing at his whisker tickles, I pushed him away. "One of the items we offered was personalized artwork made by Dewey himself, and we thought you guys might like to see how the next Michelangelo creates his masterpieces."

Ever the cooperative and attention-loving horse, Dewey treated the whole thing as a game. Within an hour I had fifteen hilarious paintings made by a horse, paint in places I didn't want paint, and hopefully some good footage that I could edit into something fun. And Dewey was now twenty-five percent licorice.

"Aaaand cut," Wren yelled.

I leaned against Dew's shoulder, relieved that I could finally switch off. Introvert battery status? Close to empty. "Great, thanks so much for helping."

"No problem. FYI, you have paint...like, everywhere," she observed as I moved everything out of Dewey's mouth range.

"I know." I poked Dew's cheek. "Yet somehow, he's managed to keep himself clean." I wiped my hands on some paper towel then took the camera from Wren. "Time to clean up and do some editing I suppose."

"And time for me to get back to making leather things shiny. Call me if you can't figure out how to edit." She untied Dewey. "I'll take care of this one."

"Thanks. And I'm not a total Luddite you know."

"I'll remind you of that when you can't get the music on your phone to download again. It's your turn to cook dinner, by the way." She couldn't quite hide her alarm.

"Fear not, your tastebuds are safe. I'm already planning on just ordering something. I've got that video chat Q and A thing with

Dressage Daily tonight so I need to prepare. Nightmare fuel," I mumbled. But I'd agreed to it because it was good publicity and as I kept broken-record chanting to myself—publicity translated to funding.

Wren was aware of my aversion to social interaction, even online, and she laughed quietly. "I know, but you'll be fine." As she led Dew away, she called back over her shoulder, "Just pretend they're all naked." Then she said something under her breath that I didn't quite catch.

I laughed my way through editing and compressing the video to five zoomy minutes, added a zany song over the top then posted it to all my social media accounts. By the time I'd been out to say goodnight to Dewey and had dinner, the video had become one of my most popular. It had brought in more likes, comments, and shares than even the ones of my winning rides at the WEG in Normandy and the adorable video of Rasputin balancing on Dewey's back while Dew got up from a lying-down nap, that I'd captioned *Next Team USA Vaulting Member?*

Most importantly, I now had over fifty new customers wanting to purchase their very own Dewey autograph. More work, more stress, but that extra ten-thousand-ish dollars would set us up for part of next year's competition season at home. I wanted nothing more than to relax, but it was time for more social media interaction. I took a few minutes to review the notes I'd been sent by the journalist and noted the questions were straightforward, but not easy. It was never easy.

Just before seven, I checked that I looked presentable and logged on to the live chat where I smiled and joked with the host, answered her questions and those asked by the virtual attendees for an hour and a half—everything from "How do I make my horse canter on the correct lead?" to "Why can't I sit on my horse's medium trot?" to "How do you get your horses looking so great?"

I mentioned my sponsors at every opportunity, explained my background, which they probably already knew, talked about my coaches, my vet team, my employees, everyone here readying us for Olympic selection and smiled so much my cheeks hurt. When I was finally done, I thanked everyone profusely for joining the chat, slapped my laptop closed then practically sprinted into the kitchen to make a drink.

Less than a minute after I'd collapsed on the couch, an unknown FaceTime caller request interrupted my book, dark chocolate and ice-cold vodka. Probably a telemarketer. The moment I twigged that the number had a Florida area code was the same moment I twigged that I knew someone in Florida. Plus, telemarketers didn't really go for FaceTime. I swiped to answer and a familiar face popped into view. My stomach did a funny little drop. "Hello."

"Caitlyn, it's Addie. Gardner?" There was an unmistakable edge of fatigue in her voice, making her twang even twangier. She laughed and added, "Sorry, you probably guessed that by my face."

"Yeah, I did." Her face with the interior of a car as backdrop.

"Right. I'm sorry to call so late there but I meant to call you first thing this mornin', then mid-mornin', then at lunch and well, I'm sure you get the idea. And also sorry for the FaceTime, but I'm always better face-to-face."

"No problem, and that explains the unknown number. I thought you were someone trying to sell me something."

There was an awkward pause before another laugh broke the silence. "I might still try. Just a quick call. First up, I wanted to let you know that I've spoken with Teresa Warren and I now have all of Dewey's history. Everything looks fabulous and I don't anticipate anything underlying that might cause issues going forward."

"Great. I mean I know he doesn't have any issues but I'm glad you're satisfied now too." Though I tried to sound neutral, it definitely came out a little accusatory and I hoped she didn't catch the edge in my tone.

If she did, she did a good job of hiding it. "I am satisfied. I—" Her forehead furrowed as she leaned closer to the screen. "Something with a twist?"

I held up the ice-filled glass, which she'd apparently seen. "Vodka." Addie's expression of confusion made me ask, "What?"

"Nothing. Just thinking about how good that would be right now." The question came out before I could stop it. "Rough day?"

She smiled tightly. "It has indeed been a day." A dismissive wave. "No matter. In a few hours I'll be on the couch myself with a glass and a fistful of chocolate."

It was right on my tongue to ask her about her day, about why it'd been so obviously shit. But that felt like crossing a boundary. So I said nothing, just slowly raised my chocolate until it was in view.

Addie burst into laughter. "I feel like we're living in a parallel universe. Only you're a few hours in front of me."

"It does feel a little like that."

"Enjoy it." She sobered, clearing her throat. "There's nothin' else going on you think I should know about?"

"Not since I saw you six days ago, no."

Her expression turned sheepish. "Right. Of course."

"And I did agree I'd call or email if there was anything going on here that you should know about. I'm a woman of my word." It came out teasing, though I hadn't consciously intended it to.

"You did." Addie jumped at the unmistakable loud sound of a phone ringing. She disappeared out of view for a moment before popping back. "I have to go. Work's on the other phone. Talk soon, take care." I caught a flash of panic before she said a hasty goodbye and the screen went blank.

I stared at the phone for a few long moments. Even though I'd promised myself that I was going to shove my teenager problems out of the way so we could work together, the call had left me feeling off balance. Probably me adjusting my thought processes to Nice Addie. That was it. Couldn't be anything else.

Wren strolled into the room and dropped onto the other couch with all the gangly uncoordinated grace of a newborn foal. "Are you talking to yourself?"

I dropped my phone onto the couch. "That was Addie. Doctor Gardner. Addie."

She made an encouraging gesture. "Pick just one name, you can do it."

I gave her a middle finger along with, "Addie."

"Ah. Is everything okay?"

"Mhmm." I dragged my legs up onto the couch and tucked them underneath me. "She was just letting me know she's talked to Teresa about Dew. How's Brandon?"

"I think he's enjoying being a bachelor again. The house probably looks like a tornado went through it, but you know the barn will be spotless." She smiled the slightly spaced-out smile she always did when mentioning him. "Everyone and everything is fine."

"Yeah, he messaged me earlier. With pictures."

"Not surprised." Wren changed position so she lay on the couch with her too-long legs slung over the arm. "Seriously though, what's going on with you and the esteemed Doctor Gardner?"

"Nothing's going on," I said immediately.

"Sure," she drawled. "Then why did you look like you'd just spoken to your idol when I walked in?"

"Did I?"

"You did."

I took a few moments to think about how to phrase my answer. All I managed was, "I guess she's easy to talk to."

"That she is. And I can see that *but* just resting on the tip of your tongue."

I took the bait. "But…I'm trying to figure out if I hallucinated those Pony Club years, or what's going on now. I just don't know. She's not the way I remember her at all and I'm finding that weird and hard to reconcile."

"People grow up, Caitlyn. Sad fact of life. How exactly did she use to tease you?"

"Usual teenager stuff. Hiding my gear, tossing dried manure at me, calling me Lesbo Lloyd." Among other things.

Wren barely contained her laughter. "To be fair, you are Lesbo Lloyd."

"Obviously, but being called that as a teenager was mortifying and, on top of everything else that crowd put me through, it was awful."

"Did she do those things to anyone else?"

"Some of it." After a pause I admitted, "Everyone got called stupid names."

Nodding slowly, Wren mused, "Right." After a long pause she sat up and dropped her feet to the floor. "I can understand how you'd be hurt by that as a kid and holding on to stuff like that is totally normal. And if Addie had come to you now and thrown manure at you and hidden Dew's bridle then yeah, totally permissable to punch her or whatever. But she didn't."

"No, she didn't," I agreed. "See my dilemma? Teen me is stuck on the past and current me thinks she's actually nice, and knowledgeable and…cute."

Wren nodded slowly, a few stray mhmm's escaping as she did. "You know, when you first hired Brandon, I thought he was nice to look at but an absolute idiot. I couldn't stand him and I was so grumpy that you'd subjected me to this fool."

I laughed at the mental image. There was Wren's Way and then there was the wrong way, and though I'd hired Brandon as a highly knowledgeable horseman and very capable rider, there'd definitely been friction when he'd first started out. "What changed your mind?"

"I actually don't know. He was so weird around me all the time, like he'd either act like I was some beacon of equine knowledge to be tiptoed around, or just talk utter nonsense to the point I thought maybe he was a few fries short of a Happy Meal. Turns out he was nervous because he thought I was hot." Grinning, she affected an overly casual shrug. "He's right of course. Once he settled down and started acting like himself, I realized what a great guy he is and how perfectly suited we are and it all kinda just fell into place. I just had to give him a chance to show me who he really is."

I raised my glass to her. "I'm glad you came around."

"Me too. And if I'd never had that lightning-bolt realization then I wouldn't be as happy as I am now. Sometimes you have to get rid of shitty old ideals to make way for the new, better ones."

CHAPTER EIGHT

Addie

Being startled awake by my work phone was the worst way I could think of to wake up during an on-call night, especially at…2:13 a.m. Bah. Thanks to muscle memory I'd answered the call, which was sure to be a drag-me-out-of-bed emergency, before my eyes were fully open. "Equine after hours, this is Doctor Addie Gardner."

A high-pitched voice demanded, "Who is this?"

I…just said, didn't I? I tried again and made sure to enunciate very, very slowly. "Doctor. Addie. Gardner. You've called the equine after hours number of Seth Ranger and Associates Veterinary Practice."

"Yes, I know that. My horse is colicking. I need you to come out right now."

"Okay, sure. And who am I speaking to? Can you give me some information about the horse and colic?"

"Margaret. He's been colicking on and off all day."

He's been colicking all day and you only decided to call a vet in the small hours. People… I pushed the bedcovers off. "Sure, and where is the horse?"

"Lying in his stall."

No problem, Margaret. I'll just work my ass off for the most basic information so I can come and help you. "I mean, where are you located? What is the address? A suburb? Street?" Any damned thing that might help me?

"I'm in Alva."

I pulled the bedcovers back on. "Unfortunately that's outside of our coverage area." Waaay outside our after-hours coverage and barely inside our regular hours service zone. "Have you tried calling Dr. Sam Kenwick in Clewiston?"

"Not answering his phone."

It seemed Sam's frustrating client intuition was better than mine. "Okay, you could also try Muce Veterinary Services and LaBelle Vets who both service your district and offer after-hours."

"They're both busy with other emergencies."

"Right. Sure. If you'd like to bring the horse into our equine hospital in Wellington then I can treat it there."

"No, I can't do that. Can't you just come and collect it and take it back to your hospital?"

Sure thing, Margaret. And why don't I just pay your bill for you too? "No, I'm afraid I can't. As I said, we don't service your area and we also don't provide transportation services." Call it emotional fatigue or whatever but I *almost* broke one of the rules and offered her advice over the phone. Given I didn't know this woman, or her horse, or the reason behind this colic, I thankfully caught myself and snapped my mouth shut.

"Well you're not very helpful, are you?" Silence.

I didn't need to look at the screen to know she'd ended the call.

I covered my face with my pillow and yelled into it. It would have been nice to say that people speaking to me like that was an anomaly, but it wasn't. After settling my pillow back under my head, I fought to push aside the annoyance from someone treating me like I was an idiot. Despite my best attempt, frustration hummed through me and I knew there was no way I was going to fall back to sleep without switching my brain over to non-work.

My personal phone would be somewhere under the covers where it always migrated after I'd inevitably fall asleep reading on it, and after a minute of blind fumbling I found it down near my knee. Nothing newsworthy so I switched to social media. Caitlyn had posted a new video two days ago titled *The Artiste at Work*.

I didn't think, I just clicked. Within minutes I was laughing. The whole thing was hilarious, from the Dewey-interrupted intro to his adorable painting efforts and Caitlyn's valiant attempts to keep paint off herself, all wrapped up in a fast-forwarded, funny soundtracked package. By the time I was done, the frustration left over from the phone call had all but dissipated.

I clicked a *like* reaction and after a moment of debate, added a comment. *How much for one of these masterpieces?*

Within ten minutes Caitlyn had responded. *For everyone else, $200. For you, $300.* She'd added a tongue poking emoji.

Laughing, I liked her comment then started the video again. A text interrupted my viewing and I stared at the name at the top of my screen until the notification disappeared. Caitlyn Lloyd. I swiped to check the message. *Why aren't you asleep?*

On-call client related insomnia.

Damn. After a few seconds another message landed. *Try to get some sleep?*

I ignored the excitement of texting with her to quickly type out *Will do.*

The interaction was so simple but her apparent concern left me feeling kinda floaty, almost dreamy. Only sorta-awake and full of comfortable, smooshy Caitlyn vibes, I made a decision. Not only was I going to keep up my polite and professional demeanor, even if she didn't respond in kind, but I was going to go a step further. I was going to accept that as a teenager I hadn't behaved in a way to foster friendship with her, or in a way that actually conveyed my feelings, and I'd own up to it, apologize to Caitlyn and hope for the best. Clean slate and all that.

The café next to work was a godsend for coffee and as was usual for mornings after nights on call, breakfast too. After the lovely Margaret's phone call, I'd had another call just after three thirty a.m. to a difficult foaling and had had to utilize my spare set of clothes and the shower at work. I took my breakfast into the office I shared with Eric, pulled the door mostly closed and called Teresa.

Given an equine veterinarian's workload, I'd expected to just leave a message and wait for her to call me in a few days at some odd time, which in normal-people land was bizarre but in vet land was perfectly normal. But she answered with her usual chirpy, "Addie! To what do I owe this pleasure?" In the background was a rumbly truck engine and a hip-hop song which gave away the fact she was driving between consults. "Talking to you twice in two weeks? I am truly hashtag blessed."

"Missed the sound of your voice." I spun my chair around so I could prop my feet on the trash can. My lower back grumbled at me for slouching. I ignored it. Relieving the ache in my leg was more important than a grousing spine.

"Truth be told, I'm surprised to hear from you again so soon. Thought you'd be up to your eyeballs with work and that sweet Olympics gig of yours."

"Oh, I am, don't you worry. This may be the last few minutes of free time I have until the end of August so thought I'd make the most of it. As for my Olympics gig, that's why I'm calling. I took your advice and called Caitlyn to let her know I'd spoken to you."

Teresa's response was slow and careful, as if praising an idiot. "That's great, Addie. I'm so proud of you. But I was actually talking about you two discussing things unrelated to equines."

"Like what? Everything between us is related to equines."

"And how are you enjoying that relationship?"

"Just fine because that's my job, remember? USDF veterinarian? Horses? And there is no *relationship*."

"Right. Sounds to me like you wish there was."

"No comment." I had plenty of comments, but none I wanted to verbalize.

"I hope reality falls out of a tree and hits you in the head so you get a clue." The engine sound cut off. "Now, as much as I love hearing about your failed attempts at socialization, I have a hot date with a hoof abscess."

"Yummy. Nothing like pus to brighten your day. And nope, that was it."

"All right then. And for the second time, talk to Caitlyn about something not horses. Try asking her a question like, I don't know… what do you like to do when you're not riding?"

"Thanks for the tip, Ms. Social Interaction Monitor."

"You'll thank me later."

Talking to Caitlyn about something other than horses wasn't necessary. As long as we could have a civil conversation, I'd call that a win. I didn't need to know what her favorite food was and what kind of underwear she preferred. On second thought… That was an idea to think about later.

I'd barely finished my breakfast when Seth barged in, pulled out Eric's chair and thumped down. Never a fan of preamble, it still stung when he came right out with a blunt, "I've had a client complaint. About you," he added, as if there was any doubt.

My heart fell out of the sole of my boots. Unfortunately, complaints weren't rare and also fortunately, they were spread around among all of us. But it never felt nice. I tried not to look too panicked. "Who is it?"

"Heidi Fletcher."

"Oh. The broken forelimb two days ago?" What her complaint could be was beyond me.

"That's the one. She's alleging you euthanized her horse."

"There's no allegation about it. I did euthanize it. There was no other option because it'd shattered its cannon bone, which I could tell without X-ray because it was dangling in the air, blowing in the breeze and hangin' on by skin and tendon only type stuff."

"I know."

"I also told her that this injury was not really recoverable, and unless the horse was a highly valuable breeding prospect and the owner had a large budget and the time and facilities to rehabilitate, the humane option was euthanasia."

"Right!" A meaty forefinger was thrust in my direction. "She's taken offense to the fact you used the term 'highly valuable' and the insinuation that her horse was not."

"It's not. I know what she paid for it and I could count the digits in that sum on one hand if you cut two of my fingers off." I sighed. "Highly valuable in monetary terms and highly valuable in emotional terms are two completely different things. She barely manages to pay her vet bills, Seth, and those are just the routine things. Even if I'd thought it was treatable, which it absolutely would *not* have been, she would never have agreed to it because it would've cost too damned much."

"Sure, I know, but I have to follow these things up."

His detachment made it clear he wasn't really listening to my side of things, and my runaway annoyance jumped the tracks and took off. "It was a twenty-year-old horse in poor condition. And given she admitted that she only checks in on her horses every few days, *and* the maggoty condition of the open wound which tells me clearly that the horse had been hobbling around that fucking paddock with a fucking broken leg for at least two days, maybe I should report her to the SPCA for cruelty and neglect." It'd been all I could do when I'd arrived and examined the leg to not let loose with my temper and a bout of tears.

"You'll do no such thing. What you *will* do is call Mrs. Fletcher and smooth this over so she gives up on her frivolous idea of lodging a complaint with the AVMA."

I had to close my gaping mouth before he started making stupid comments about fish out of water. "There are zero grounds for an official complaint, she's just trying to shift blame. They'd laugh her out of the room. Are you going to back me up on this? I'll send you my case notes and you can see for yourself, including the pictures. Even a vet student in their first week would reach the same conclusion. Hell, a non-vet would have."

"Call the client first. Smooth things over with her. Then we'll talk." He stood. "And make sure she knows the bill is due."

"You have a debt collection person, Seth, and it's not me," I ground out through clamped molars. It was as if he was trying to make my life as hellish as possible. Oh hi, Mrs. Fletcher, can we talk about your neglect and me putting your horse to sleep and by the way my boss wants you to know you owe him money.

"Just do it."

As he ambled out of my office it took everything I had not to throw something at the back of his head. An email notification on my personal phone pinged and I picked it up. Fuck you, Seth, I'm checking my personal emails at work.

Wren Robertson
Desperate snack food favor

Hey Addie!

Sorry to hijack your email address but Caitlyn stuck your business card to the fridge and she knows anything left out in the house is fair game. All fine here but I have a HUGE favor to ask and standard disclaimer that OF COURSE you can decline (but I'll be super sad).

When you come back to the Netherlands can you please bring some Reese's Cups, Hershey's, Cinnamon Bears, Starburst, Tootsie Rolls…anything! My fiancée is terrified of the process of shipping stuff internationally and we've totally run out over here. We're sad, deprived bunnies, relegated to eating nothing but Haribo things. Obviously I'll reimburse you for the sugar and your time.

Eternally hopeful and forever in your debt.
Wren

Laughing, I wrote back.

Done. No need to pay, consider it my contribution to the US Olympic dream. I will arrive laden with sweet and chocolatey goods.
Addie

It took barely five minutes for her to reply to my reply.

Marry me. Thank you! You've saved my sanity. For real, who wants high quality European stuff when you've grown up on American sugar? Caitlyn loves Blow Pops. Just in case you were curious. See you soon! Wren :)

Caitlyn loves Blow Pops. Huh. Who woulda thought? Seemed some things hadn't changed at all. They'd sold them at the Pony Club concession stand and she'd buy one every lunchtime, and then I'd see her with the stick hanging out the side of her mouth as she was leaving. I pulled up the packing list on my phone and alongside sugar-free peppermint Life Savers (for Dewey) I added everything Wren had asked for with Caitlyn's Blow Pops at the top of the list.

I spent most of my day out on calls and had rushed lunch and some paperwork in between emergencies. Five p.m. had come and gone. As had six p.m. I finally finished all my consult case history and billing for the day a little before seven and decided it was time to get the heck out of Dodge. The quietness of the surgery was deceiving and I snuck around like a cat burglar, hoping nobody would grab me to call someone, check or treat something. I was almost successful. When I was halfway to my car, Diana ran an intercept from my right side. "Addie! Sorry, do you have a minute?"

I cringed, and bit my tongue on saying, "Not really, no, not at all." A shower, glass of wine, movie, and bed were calling my name. And I really needed to clean my fish tank. But I knew none of the nurses would ask for a hand when they knew I was long past done for the day unless it was desperate. "Sure. What's up?"

"That colic-surgery stallion of Will's in stall eight has hit his head on something, fuck knows what, and his forehead is gushing blood. Everyone's out on late calls, in the middle of something delicate, or gone for the day and I can't get near the bastard. Every time I open the door, he tries to savage me. He's managed to get his muzzle off." She grinned and fluttered her eyelashes at me. "You *are* the stallion whisperer."

I told my shower and movie to hold on for an hour and then I'd be right with them and nodded in weary agreement at Diana's request. "No problem. Can you grab a wound dressing kit and a staple kit and I'll meet you at the stall? And grab him some feed as bribery because I'm going to have to use the jab stick."

The idea of climbing into a confined space with a large and obviously unhappy stallion was low on my list of things I wanted to do, and drugs on the end of a pokey-pole would mean I could sedate him from a nice, safe distance. In an ideal world we'd have a few extra hands on deck to help, but I'd learned in my first few months working at this practice that it was far from an ideal world.

I prepared my favorite drug cocktail for this exact situation then stuffed a couple of other syringes in my pockets, just in case, and wandered down the aisle toward stall eight. When I saw the stallion lunging at Diana over the lower stall door, sending a spray of blood flying from his forehead, I backtracked to increase the dose I was going to stick into him.

Stallion whisperer or no, the huge Thoroughbred still managed to get his teeth into my shoulder and tried to go for my face before I poked him in the neck to sedate the living shit out of him. Perhaps a little too much sedation if the short time it took for him to wobble and drop to the ground was any indication. Ah well, that's why the drug company had invented a reversal agent.

I peered over the lower stall door and snorted out a laugh. The horse looked like he'd been out for a night with the boys and fallen up a set of stairs, with legs everywhere and neck extended so his head rested at an awkward angle on the wall. Thankfully our stalls were padded, because I was pretty sure this was a valuable breeding stallion and trying to explain that I'd broken it would likely get me fired or sued. Probably both. Breeding stallion or no, my professional opinion was that he'd be a much nicer horse if someone removed a pound or so from between his hind legs.

It took barely any time to palpate his skull for obvious fractures—nothing indicated—then clean and staple the massive laceration on his forehead. The only obvious thing to have caused the injury was the automatic waterer in the corner but even then it was plastic, not metal, and he would have had to contort himself to make the injury. Horses.

Once finished, I put his muzzle back on, administered the antidote for the tranquilizer and got the hell out of the stall before he came to. Diana's groveling gratitude made me feel marginally better about my huge bruise, missing skin and certain hematoma. She rushed off with a final flurry of thanks and a facetious, "Thanks, Danger Mouse!"

I pulled the collar of my shirt away to examine the damage. Yikes. That needed ice. Which would have to wait until I got home. Home. Yes. While I'd been busy my needs had shifted to bath, book, and bourbon. I gently rubbed the lump in a futile attempt to stop it hurting so damned much and found myself thinking of Dewey who'd stood completely still while I'd been checking him out. If every one of my patients was as amenable as him, I'd be one happy veterinarian. Dewey certainly didn't need a muzzle, but muzzling Caitlyn to stop her acerbic tongue might come in handy. I chastised myself. That was a little unfair, runaway brain. Since our initial meeting she'd been cordial, if not a little cool, and certainly not muzzle-worthy.

As I made my exit from the equine hospital, Seth popped his head out of the scanning room. "Addie, come look at these scans and tell me what you think. I'm just back from Lear's Racing Stables. Two-year-old colt in training with suspensory branch desmitis. I'm thinking of doing biologic therapy tomorrow, then extracorporeal shockwave therapy in a few weeks."

I watched my bath-book-bourbon grow wings and fly away.

When I finally made it home at nine p.m. after being subjected to yet another of Seth's *I know you're off shift but I want to discuss an in-depth treatment plan and come and look at this horse and oh what do you think of this* sessions I was too tired to do anything more than eat a banana before taking a closed-eyed shower and crawling under the covers to attempt sleep. I wonder what he'd have done if I'd told him I had plans and really had to get out of there. Probably laughed.

I suspected he was trying to wring as much work out of me before I skipped off merrily—his phrasing—to play with world-class dressage horses for a few months. I knew he knew that wasn't what I'd be doing at all, and was making light of it to downplay the importance and make me feel like shit for abandoning my post. A post he'd given me permission to abandon because he knew what good publicity it would be for his practice.

I'd been working at Seth Ranger and Associates for over six years, and while there'd always been the vibe that we were lucky to work there and should just take what was dished out—unfortunately not unusual in my profession—the animosity and indifference had definitely ramped up in the last three or four years. Not a great way to foster a happy workplace. But I loved the work and my salary was *really* good, which not only helped with my college debt but my remnant childhood unease about not having much money. It'd become a case of sticking with the devil I knew.

Even if the devil was an asshole six days out of seven.

CHAPTER NINE

Caitlyn

One of Lotte's clients had left Douglas, who I'd been calling Dougie—a four-year-old green-broken stallion by the champion Grand Prix stallion, Damon Hill—at Lotte's barn for me to try out. I loved everything about Damon Hill and his son seemed like an excellent example of the bloodline. Like his father, Dougie was quite small but had a huge presence and big expressive paces that made him feel like he filled the arena, and he was willing and enthusiastic without being out-of-control hot.

I made a mental note to do some more math once I'd dismounted. Technically I could afford to purchase him on my own and there was always the prospect of keeping him as a breeding stallion, which after some Big Tour wins would bring in a nice sum every year. But his price tag would seriously dent my rainy-day savings.

Or I could put forward a proposal to one of my major sponsors to syndicate the horse and have either just me and them as co-owners, or possibly add a third equal party. The arrangement wasn't unusual at high levels of equestrian sport, and it was actually rarer to find international-class riders who owned their mounts outright than it was for them to be riding someone else's horses.

Even a split percentage of revenue from Dougie's service fees would help cover running costs during my leaner months away competing, though working out competition and breeding arrangements for stallions could be a nightmare. Especially when there were multiple parties.

If I got Dougie, then I would have a sure thing to take Dew's place, especially if my young horse, Dirk, continued on his current path of being too anxious in high stress situations, in which case he'd be sold to someone less competitive than me. My whole life was made up of uncertain *ifs* which I did my best to make certain.

Hopefully I could keep Dew sound and happy for the next four years ready for Tokyo 2020 which would be his second, and last, Olympic Games. After years at the highest level of competition, it became more difficult to keep horses physically and mentally sound. Then, if my Small Tour horse, Dimity, stopped being so marey and opinionated she might move up to the Big Tour.

If...if...if...

If I didn't stop thinking about the future when I should be concentrating on the present, I was going to have a meltdown. I could see Wren bringing Dew in from his field for his afternoon session with the massage blanket, and made a transition down from Dougie's naturally balanced canter to his expressive rhythmical trot. We did a loose cool-down trot around the arena, while I asked him to stretch his head and neck down and relax through the back while keeping steady rein contact.

A direction change, more long-and-loose trot before I brought him back to walk. Dougie spotted a gremlin in the field to our right and spooked. It was such a minor spook that it barely rated on my spook-o-meter and I laughed, patted him, then kept on doing what we were doing. There was such a fine line between flamboyance and a look-at-me quality, versus too tense and looky to be able to compete at high levels. Dew, bless him, had enough of each to make him the perfect Grand Prix horse. And it seemed Dougie did too.

Wren and a couple of the other grooms had arranged to meet in town for dinner and once we were done for the day I'd waved her off and told her to have a great time. An evening by myself was just what I needed. While I was ruining dinner, I called Mom for my weekly Skype chat and just as I was about to give up and try again later she answered with her typically drawn out, "Hellloooo."

"Hi, Mom. Sorry I didn't call earlier. How're you and Dad?"

"It's fine, I know you've got stuff going on." She laughed. "We're all fine. How're you doing, Caity?" She was the only one, thankfully, who called me that.

"I'm good. Busy with the usual stuff. We're driving to Rotterdam the day after tomorrow. First day of competition is Thursday."

"And how are you feeling about things?"

"Good. Excited." I added a handful of diced green pepper to my creation and jumped back when the pan hissed at me. Hastily, I turned down the heat. Oil burns were not a great way to start an Olympic campaign. Potential Olympic campaign. "Some nerves brewing, but nothing big or unusual." And I knew they'd disappear the moment I sat astride Dewey.

"Good. Now, turn that heat down, Caity, I can hear you burning your dinner. Have you added garlic? You always forget to add garlic."

"Carbon is good for you. And it's not burning, it's…sizzling. And yes, I have added garlic." Have added…about to add because I forgot and you just reminded me…same thing. I sidestepped to the fridge for the jar and dropped half a teaspoon into the pan.

"Hmm." That one sound conveyed all her maternal disbelief and disappointment that my culinary skills were basically nonexistent. "Let me guess, dinner is whatever vegetables are wilting in your crisper, tofu and rice."

"Close. I ran out of tofu and haven't managed to get to the store." Staring into the pan at my bland dinner, I conceded that perhaps I should have donated these vegetables to Lotte's neighbor's pigs and just eaten takeout.

"What about all those recipe books I've sent you? And the sport nutritionist's ideas? Hundreds of recipes just waiting for you to try."

"I have them. Somewhere. At home which is nowhere near here. And yes I know I could look online, but all the recipe books in the world aren't going to help someone with zero cooking ability, Mom. It's like a language I just can't learn no matter how hard I try. I'm a one-trick pony and cooking ain't my trick. Even those cooking classes you paid for didn't help much. Cooking Maestro Caitlyn is a ship that sailed long ago. And it sank. In flames."

The fact my mother didn't argue or try to placate me was both comfortingly familiar and a little insulting. "At least they'll feed you well in the athlete's village."

"True." Those brewing nerves fluttered in my stomach at the idea. "So you won't have to worry about my dietary needs for those few weeks. Assuming we make the team," I clarified.

Mom, master of emotion, obviously picked up on the slight quaver in my voice. "I'm sure you'll be just fine. You always are. I'm so proud of you, always have been. And remember that the results don't matter.

All that matters is you do your best and act in the spirit of good sportsmanship, just like they taught you at Pony Club. I know you'll do both and that's enough for your dad and me."

We both knew there was far more than that at stake, but I loved her simplistic attitude. I rummaged for cutlery. "Speaking of Pony Club. Do you remember a girl called Addie Gardner from the South River Pony Club when we moved down to Tennessee?"

"Name's familiar but I can't get a face."

"She used to ride that chestnut gelding with all the white, looked similar to Antoinette. Reddish brown hair, really unusual light brown eyes, dimples. I think she was about my height back then but now she's a bit shorter." I realized my description was bordering on waffling and clamped my lips closed on saying more.

"Ohhhh, right. Yes, I remember now. The *poor* girl."

"Mom!"

"What? The family was poor, and by her mother's own admission too, Caity. Not that we were exceedingly wealthy either, mind you, but I know the Gardners struggled. I was friendly with her mom. You know we all used to sit around and gossip while you kids were off being equestriennes."

"Really? But Addie was in with the bitchy crowd." The rich bitchy crowd. Given how cruel and rude they were to those deemed not good enough, I found it unfathomable that someone without money would be allowed in their ranks. "They all went to an elite school, were a super-tight group and there's no way they'd let her be in their crowd if she wasn't rolling in it. I don't believe it."

"Well you should believe it. And I know for certain that Addie was not at that school. Don't you recall we gave Addie and her horse a ride to competitions a couple times because they didn't have a trailer or even a car that was capable of towing a rented trailer?"

That, I did recall. I hadn't questioned why at the time, just assumed something was wrong with their car or trailer. Being horrified at having to share the car with Addie, I hadn't delved into the reason behind it. But now I thought about it, I couldn't actually remember the experience at all, how she'd behaved, if we'd talked. She'd probably been mean, which was why I'd wiped the memory. Or...perhaps it had been totally inoffensive. I wished I could remember. "Why'd we give her a ride?"

"Because it was the right thing to do for someone who needed help." The explanation had come out matter-of-factly and also with a steely edge as if daring me to express an opinion that conflicted with Mom's good manners. "They were totally reliant on others. I don't even think they owned the horse, and I know her mom worked a second job to help pay for its upkeep. I also know Addie used to spend all the time she wasn't on that horse or doing schoolwork, either babysitting or doing odd jobs to get money so she could help out. Her mom always gave me gas money and also usually a cake or something to say thank you. Good people. Kind people."

"That's nice of them," I said vaguely. Apparently there was a lot going on behind the scenes that I'd never known. Another dot point to add to the list of things that maybe weren't as I'd thought they were. I was starting to feel a little like my teen years had existed in a separate dimension. And if my mom had things happening under my nose, what about everyone else? What about Addie?

"It was. So why'd you bring up Addie?"

"Turns out she's our new team vet. We've been seeing a little of each other and will be spending a fair bit of time together until…I come home. Whenever that is."

Mom's squeal of delight was genuine. "Well isn't that nice. Just goes to show how you can make anything of yourselves if you try." She paused for a dramatic beat. "Must be nice to have a familiar face around. Were you two friends back then?" The question was slow, as if she already knew the answer and was leading me.

"Not really no. Not at all." I felt like a whiny idiot when I said, "That group she used to hang out with were all mean to me, remember?"

"As I recall, you were all horrible to one another. Typical teenage girls, mean and catty and forever playing pranks. Do you remember when you and your friend stole all my food color dye to paint a girl's horse with a rainbow right across his belly? She was in tears because she thought it'd stain all his white fur."

Gray, and hair. Smiling, I agreed, "I do remember that."

"Mhmm, and as I recall, she was not at all impressed."

"It shampooed right out, Mom. It was totally harmless."

"Didn't seem that way to her."

I turned off the buzzing rice cooker. "Is there something you want to say to me? You know I'm not good at reading between the lines, and you've got *that* voice." Thankfully my psychologist mother rarely turned her professional gaze to me. Or at least not to my face. But she did insist I have another psych's professional eye on me while I was growing up chasing dreams.

"All I'm saying is sometimes people misconstrue other people's actions. I know everyone used to think you were snooty and aloof because you're so shy. Did you consider how you might have come across to Addie? Now I'm not saying whatever she did to you when you were kids was mean or not. What I am saying is maybe you looked at it in a different way to what was intended. And maybe you should look at the reasons behind why you might do that."

I was still and silent for so long that Mom prompted me with a, "Caity? You still there? Did this danged call drop out? I still see you. Blasted technology."

"I'm here. Just thinking."

"Good. Think away. It's good for you. But not too much. Just the right amount is good."

Well that's not cryptic at all. "Noted."

"Do you recall when you and Addie rode that *pas de deux*?" She mangled the French. "Quite the performance. You worked so hard together on getting your choreography and music just right, and your horses were so perfectly matched. I'm not sure I've ever seen two kids so happy."

"I remember." We'd been put together because our horses were so similar. After a few moments to drag my memories back, I admitted, "It was fun."

"Mmm, thought so. So maybe it's not all as you remember it. Oh! I have to go. Patrice is here, we're going to the movies. Be safe, call me when you can, give Dewey a pat from me and say hi to Wren. Love you."

"Will do and love you too."

Over dinner, my mom's advice circled around and around my head. Of course, that led to me thinking about my conversations with Addie. I had to admit that she really was nothing like she had been. And the more I thought about it, the more stupid I felt. Who was the same as they were twenty years ago?

Objectively, I could also say Wren was right when she'd said Addie was cute. And funny. She was sweet, and kind to Dew and aside from that initial meeting where she'd seemed startled into forgetting to be polite, she'd been nothing *but* polite. Everything pointed to her being a decent person now.

So, I could hold on to childish idiocy, or move on. I trusted her, because she was an appointed team veterinarian and clearly more than capable. But more than that, setting all the professional stuff aside, I had to admit I felt comfortable with her. Or more accurately, comfortable leaving the welfare of probably the most important thing in my life in her hands if need be. But was I comfortable enough to set aside twenty years of background grudge?

I poured myself a small glass of red and took it and a few squares of chocolate into the living room with my iPad. A few years ago I'd digitized the three full photo albums of horse pictures taken with the camera Nana had given me for my thirteenth birthday, and saved them in the Cloud. Most of the photos were just repetitious shots of horses grazing, tied up with tack on or pictures taken by friends with most of me or the horse not actually in the picture. The albums also held photos my mom had taken during Pony Club meetings, rallies, and competitions. Riding, receiving ribbons and trophies, falling off.

One photo caught my eye. A picture of Addie and me riding the *pas de deux*. I'd always been so focused on myself that I'd never paid much attention to how other Pony Club members rode, but in this photo she looked as if she belonged on a horse. Our horses' strides were completely in sync, both of us polished to perfection. She had a massive smile on her face, and when I zoomed in, I noticed we were both side-eyeing one another. Interesting. It should have been such a standout moment in my early riding career but I couldn't recall any details, this "working so hard together" that Mom had mentioned.

There was another image that made me pause. The picture was a candid shot of the club members during one of our monthly meetings. In the foreground, sitting on the concrete bleachers in front of the clubhouse were Addie and the Elites. They were hamming for the camera, holding up cans of Coke and burgers. Except for Addie. Her smile was tight, expression one of forced mirth. Instead of Coke she had a plastic reusable water bottle and in her other hand was a sandwich wrapped in tinfoil. On her knee was a fun-size Mars Bar.

Just to Addie's left and a row down I sat with my head bowed. Hair escaping my ponytail, a smudge of dirt on the knee of my jodhpurs, my boots polished mirror bright. On my lap was an unopened sandwich—PB&J undoubtedly—and a half-eaten banana. I zoomed in, trying to remember the girls' names, and failing. As I stared at the picture, it suddenly dawned on me that Addie wasn't actually looking at the camera, or even her friends.

She was looking at me.

CHAPTER TEN

Addie

I'd spent most of the flight to the Netherlands doing up client billing and clinical notes ready to send back to the work servers the moment I had wi-fi, and when I landed after multiple flight legs was hit by the wave of suppressed fatigue. Fatigue was my near-constant companion but this was some next level shit.

I collected my rental car and checked into the same apartment three miles from Lotte Bakker's place and just over a mile from my new favorite Netherlands café. After a longing look at the bed, I showered, chugged an energy drink and jumped back in the car to go see Caitlyn. And Dewey. Oh, and Dakota and Pierre too. Right.

I'd meet up with the other seven riders and horses who were based in Europe when everyone came together at Rotterdam tomorrow. Thankfully it was only two horses to check straight up because I was weirdly foggy for someone who was conditioned to being awake for inhumane stretches of time and at bizarre hours.

On my way to the barn my eye was caught by someone riding a very flashy liver chestnut with a delicate, dished head marked with a distinctive thick, off-center stripe running down its face. Though obviously young and inexperienced, the horse was one of the most eye catching I'd seen. Even more eye catching was Caitlyn. If I hadn't recognized her by the long brown, instead of the usual competition black, boots she always wore when schooling horses I would have known her riding style anywhere. She just always looked so…natural. She really could get on anything and make it look easy, as if the moment she put a leg over a horse she was made complete.

The horse's ears followed me as I walked past but I said nothing to distract him or Caitlyn, though I would have loved the distraction from my imminent meetup with Dakota Turner and her dour groom, Eleanor. I still couldn't figure out if that was just Eleanor, or if spending years around Dakota had made her that way. At least they had the horse ready for me, and both were perfectly polite.

Pierre was the picture of health and despite having apparently banged his knee two days prior, I saw no sign of it. Dakota was losing her mind as if he'd fractured something. I spent twenty minutes reassuring her that I wanted her to compete, and of course Pierre's welfare was my highest concern, and yes I was indeed as good as everyone said I was, and based on my expert opinion he really didn't need the knee imaged to confirm what my eyes and hands already knew.

Wren had passed by Pierre's stall a few times on her way around the barn to do whatever she was doing, making funny faces behind Dakota's back with each pass. But now that I wanted to talk to her, she was nowhere to be found. I wandered down the laneway looking for either her or Caitlyn. Lotte's barn was set up so that the horses' stalls were in a different area to where they were tacked up, groomed, and washed down to help them separate work from rest.

I found Caitlyn with the liver chestnut tied up in the cross-ties while she groomed and chattered to the horse. The horse noticed me well before Caitlyn did, and rather than risk startling her by suddenly appearing in her line of vision, I waited until she'd stepped back to exchange brushes to clear my throat. Her attention snapped to me in an instant. Her smile was quick. "Hey. I wasn't expecting you until later." She pressed her lips together like words were trying to escape and she was doing everything short of clapping a hand over her mouth to stop it.

"You should enjoy me being early while you can. We vets know what everyone says about veterinarians always being late."

"True. I'll bask in your timeliness." Caitlyn's study of me was intense. "How are you?"

"Tired." I offered a weary grin. "Jetlag, really not a fan."

"You look it." Her mouth fell open and she hastened to backpedal. "I mean, just like…"

Laughing, I said, "It's fine. I'm sure I look like shit on a stick. But you watch out once I've had some sleep. I'll be cute as heck."

I'd meant it just to tease and assure her that I didn't mind her comment about me looking tired. But her expression made me do a double take. She looked...interested. Interesting. Even more interesting was her quiet, "I'm sure you will."

Though I wanted nothing more than to jump right into that, it really wasn't the time or place. I tried to contain my smile to ask, "Who's this?"

"Dynamite Romance, also known as Douglas. Despite Lotte's disapproving stare, I've been calling him Dougie because he's just so damned cute."

"He sure is." I checked Dougie's mood, which seemed more than amenable, and scratched along his shoulder. "What's his breeding?"

"By Damon Hill, out of a Fürst Romancier mare."

I whistled. "Nice. Let me guess...Lotte wants you to train him up be an international Grand Prix superstar?"

Laughing, she said, "Not quite. He belongs to a client of hers who wants to sell him, so she's left him here for a week for me to play with. And I'm trying to decide if I can afford him on my own, or if it's worth going into a partnership to own him, or if I even want the hassle of competing a breeding stallion." When Dougie nuzzled her, she patted his chest. "Yes yes, I'm sure you'd love being a breeding stallion." She turned to me. "I think I'm being swayed by the fact he'd fit right in with all my other D-named horses. Dewey, Dimity, and Dirk."

Given his overall demeanor, the news that the horse was an entire male was surprising. "He's a stallion?" I bent to confirm. Yep, he sure was.

"Mhmm. A very well-behaved one, except sometimes when we're around other horses he gets a little boisterous and has to be reminded to pay attention to the human." She smiled. "He's young and still figuring himself out and how to be polite in society. Never thought I'd get attached to a stallion, but from the short time I've spent with him, I'm in love." Caitlyn lowered her voice, leaning close to me. "Don't tell Dewey."

I pretended to zip my lips. "Secret is safe with me. I think there's room in all of us to change our mind or find room to love more than one thing."

Her gaze seemed overly measured. "True."

The mood hadn't exactly grown heavy, but there was a definite shift in the vibe between us. Time for subject change. "Did anything exciting happen while I was away?"

"Poffertje finally let Dewey sniff him for more than a microsecond, so that was a huge moment in the life of Dew."

"I can imagine. Do you think it'll happen again or is it a one-time deal?"

Caitlyn made a so-so gesture. "Conflicting answers. If you asked Dew he'd say absolutely it'll happen again, but I'm pretty sure Poffertje wasn't a fan of being licked."

"Noted." It took all I had not to make the inappropriate comment that'd jumped into my brain at her statement about licking. To further distract my juvenile brain, I pulled out a resealable bag full of candy. Dougie's ears pricked at the sound. "Here, I got you something. Blame Wren," I added when Caitlyn's expression turned suspicious.

When she realized what was in the bag, she laughed. "Blow Pops." She shook her head, still laughing quietly. "My secret weakness. Thank you."

Her obvious pleasure gave me a dose of the warm and fuzzies. "Well come find me if you need someone to help you eat them all."

She was already unwrapping one. "Will do."

After checking out Dewey and spending almost three hours in a logistics meeting with Mary and Ian, it was pushing seven p.m. Though I was almost wilting with fatigue and jetlag, going back to my apartment now would be a mistake. I knew the moment I stumbled through the door I'd be showered and in bed within ten minutes and going to sleep this early was not going to reset my body clock to Netherlands time.

Hidden behind the barn was an area with some bench seats, a neat garden and cute metal buckets filled with sand for those who needed a nicotine fix. It seemed the perfect place to sit and chill. Though it wasn't hot, it was surprisingly humid, and I felt damp and uncomfortable. Suck it up, Buttercup. This is nothing compared to what it's going to be like in Brazil. I popped some gum in my mouth and sat on the grass with my back against the outer wall of the building so I could stretch out my legs.

Blessed moment of relaxation. I was used to having very little time to decompress during workdays and had become an expert at not only quickly switching off but making the most of limited quiet time. The next few months were going to be make or break for my potential career as a USDF vet, and the weight of possibility would have been crushing if I let myself dwell on how I could screw it up. So I didn't let myself dwell. This was no different to other jobs—do the job well, keep your paperwork in order, don't be an arrogant dick.

I entered today's clinical notes on my tablet. I was happy with the fitness of the horses but the timelines for each event leading up to, and then for the Olympics themselves, didn't leave much wiggle room. If anything went wrong I'd be fighting the clock to get things right.

Someone came around the corner of the building and I pulled in my legs to avoid tripping them as they passed. Caitlyn. Her expression was both cautious and pleased. The pleased part pleased me. She fidgeted with her phone. "I thought I saw you sneak out here."

"Caught me. Is everythin' okay in there?" I shuffled away from the wall, readying to stand. If I kept sitting, staring up at her, I was going to stare at things I shouldn't.

"All fine, no dramas at all. Just…" She smiled, an entirely forced and too-bright smile as if she had suddenly changed her mind about something. "Do you mind some company?"

As if I'd say no. "Not at all." I settled back and gestured for her to sit.

She sank to the ground beside me, pushing herself backward until she rested against the building in a pose similar to mine. I expected her to move sideways once she realized just how close we were, but she didn't. Caitlyn drew her knees up. "I thought you'd be asleep by now."

"I'm trying to keep myself awake a little longer to get my circadian rhythms in line, and I know the moment I see a bed my resolve will crumble."

"Ah. Of course." She gestured at me, and then the garden. "Do you make a habit of sitting outside barns at night?"

"Sure do. I quit smoking almost ten years ago, but I can't give up my love of lurking in the shadows of barns to brood." Smiling, I peered at her. "Smoking always felt like a good way to unpack difficult cases, but eventually I got sick of being an outcast standing fifty feet away so I wouldn't accidentally start a fire in a barn. So now it's gum chewing. It works almost as well as a cigarette. Almost."

"You brooding? I don't see it."

I leaned in, lowering my voice to conspiratorial. "I'll have you know I'm very mysterious."

There was a long pause until she eventually murmured, "Actually, that's true." She cleared her throat. "I still feel like I don't know you. I didn't know you back then, only what I thought I knew, and I don't know you now." The words rushed out, as if she was unsure or wanted to get them out before she changed her mind.

"And you want to know?" I ventured.

There was no pause this time. "Yes."

This felt perhaps too intimate, but she'd started the carousel and the polite thing would be for me to stay on it. "What exactly do you want to know?" Or more importantly, why did she want to know? The obvious explanation for her curiosity was that she was interested in me in some capacity. Professional? Personal? I let myself hope it was the latter. A little bit of hope never killed anybody, and her manner had definitely softened enough for me to feel like friendship wasn't entirely off the table.

"Whatever you want to tell me," she said quietly.

Personal it is. I had to subdue my excitement so I could answer calmly. Perhaps unwisely, I blurted the first things that came to mind. "I keep my red wine in the fridge, hate it at room temperature. I *love* folding laundry, like it's probably one of the most soothing monotonous things for me, aside from cooking. I love the sound of ice cubes cracking in drinks. I cheat at cards and boardgames which I accept is sneaky and shitty and makes me a bad person." I sucked in a breath. "You asked if I still rode and when I said no, I obviously neglected to say why. Fear. I haven't been on a horse since my last competition, right before I was due to start college, which ended in a horrendously broken leg and also made my first few months of college pretty shitty."

Caitlyn peered down at my legs. "I wondered about the limp but I didn't know how to ask. I mean it's not hugely noticeable." After a beat she added, "But I noticed."

She noticed. That thought echoed in my head. I laughed, nudging her with my elbow. "Saying hey, Addie, what's up with the limp would have been a good start. You can ask me anything you want. I might not always have an answer, but you can ask."

"I'll remember that next time I'm curious about you."

Next time she was curious about me. The thought that she'd been curious at all made my stomach do a funny little twist. "Did you… want to know more?"

"Yes," she whispered.

"I cry every time I watch *Steel Magnolias*, like a full ugly cry. I'm a bed sprawler. I'm allergic to dogs which makes my job interesting because there's always dogs and I really like them. I suck the salt off pistachio shells, which I acknowledge is a little gross. And I still have the spare ball cap you gave me from your car that day your mama gave me and Buddy a ride to the dressage day and I'd forgotten a cap." I felt the heat in my cheeks at that last admission which felt like the most personal of everything I'd told her.

Caitlyn was silent, slowly nodding as if thinking through everything I'd told her. After an embarrassment-laced eternity she said, "Okay. There's a lot to unpack there." She shifted so she faced me. "You really still have that cap?"

"I do."

"Why? I'd totally forgotten I'd even given it to you."

More embarrassment curled through me. "Because I didn't want to toss it. It was yours and I felt weird about returning it, but I didn't know how to bring it up. And you never asked for it back so I figured you didn't want something that I'd worn."

"Not the case at all," she murmured.

"Do you want it now? Well not *now* now but when we get back to the States? I can ship it to you."

Caitlyn's smile was warm. "No. It's yours. I don't even remember what cap it was."

"New York Giants," I said immediately.

"Ah, my favorite team." She touched my left leg, just below my knee. "Will you tell me about the accident?"

The fingers remained on my leg and I stared at that hand, studied the shape of it, the taper of her fingers. I knew that hand, those fingers, would be strong yet gentle and capable of the softest nuance all at once. "I'd decided to do a one-day event at the last moment, just a last-minute kind of thing because I'd arranged to give Buddy back to his owners. They were going to sell him and had promised to give me a portion of the price for all the work I'd done with him over the past six or so years. I begged a ride to the event with another family. Our dressage test went really well and I was sitting in second place." I smiled. "Must have been all that time I'd spent watching you ride your tests."

"Must have been," she echoed teasingly.

"Uh, there'd been some rain through the week, and most of the morning too. I was at the tail end of the competitors to ride cross-country and the footing on takeoffs and landings was muddy as heck. Buddy slipped coming into the eighth jump, this huge thick log spread. He righted himself and then just kind of hit the front part and flipped over the jump. He landed on top of the back log and crushed my leg underneath him, spooked himself I guess, then got up and galloped off but my foot was stuck in the stirrup. I'm not sure if it was him landing on it, or being dragged that broke my leg." I shrugged. "Probably a combination of both. He was totally okay though."

Caitlyn looked utterly horrified and not a little nauseated. "Fuck. That's just...fuck."

Nodding I agreed, "I think fuck just about sums it up. Compound fractures of my tibia and fibula, along with a displaced fracture of my ankle. I saw the scans after. The fractures were so comminuted that the X-rays looked like a bunch of scattered broken sticks. If I was a horse, I would have been taken out back and shot. Luckily I was still on my mom's insurance because there were a lot of surgeries and PT. It's fine now, but I just haven't ever found the guts to get back up on a horse." Frowning, I mused, "I think if I still rode, thinking about it and talking about it would be upsetting or frightening but instead, it's kind of just this blank space."

"I'm pretty sure if I'd ever had an accident like that I probably wouldn't want to ride again either."

Smiling, I disagreed, "Ah, but I doubt you ever would have that kind of accident. You were always far better at sticking on horses than me. At any rate, college helped. I already knew riding would be put on the backburner once I was at school, so it was easier to distance myself from it."

"Mmm. You can always hop on Dew if you want. He's so safe I've had kids ride him. It's amazing what parents will spend to let their kids ride a trained Grand Prix horse."

"I might take you up on that one day. If I find my courage."

"I'm sure you will. I always remember you as being the first to jump into anything at Pony Club. Like that time they taught us vaulting and polo."

I laughed. "That was before I realized I don't bounce as well as I used to."

Caitlyn's hand slid to my thigh. Her fingers stroked my leg, an unconscious sort of movement as if offering comfort. She repeated the movement, then paused and tensed beside me. The hand on my leg went totally still. "I'm sorry."

"You don't need to be. I'm not." Sensing her confusion, I decided to tease. "Must be all the time you've been spending with tactile ol' me."

"Must be." She exhaled and the fingers started moving again, tentatively as if she was either worried or wanted to really take her time to study the structure of my leg. "I...might check on Dew then go find some leftovers for dinner. Then I think it's bed for me too."

The mere mention of sleep had me suppressing a yawn. "Good plan. I'm used to going for long blocks of time without sleep but over twenty-four hours being switched on is a little too much for even me."

"You didn't sleep on the plane?" Caitlyn stood and offered me a hand.

"Nope. I had to do some paperwork that I didn't finish before I left. And I'm still trying to equilibrate, move from being one type of vet to another. I need a day to get my brain into gear, forget about all the shit going on in my workplace and focus on this job and all its specific requirements."

As we approached Dewey's stall she asked, "What's going on in your workplace?"

Slow clap, Addie. I had no idea what was wrong with me, or what siren call her voice was that constantly made me forget to censor myself around her. "Work stuff. The usual batches of unpleasant clients, workplace politics and a boss whose passive-aggressive comments about me being away for so long are less passive and more aggressive."

"Really? But you do such a great job here with us." Dewey's head rocketed over the lower half-door at our approach. Caitlyn offered him something from her pocket then pushed him backward so we could enter his stall.

"I'm trying." I pushed my hand underneath Dewey's neck blanket and scratched his mane, and he reacted with a lip curling head bob of enjoyment. "This guy seems happy enough with me." Dew turned his head to nuzzle my arm in the equine version of *Thanks for the scratch, let me reciprocate.*

"We all are," she said. As if regretting what'd just come out of her mouth, she backed away and started checking the feed and water buckets.

Something had obviously spooked her and turned her from relaxed and chatty to twitchy and anxious. "Do you ever get nervous? About riding I mean."

"Mhmm, of course. Not while I'm actually riding though. When I'm on his back, everything just feels like it's meant to be." She snorted. "Sorry, that came out like an inspirational quote."

"No, I get it." I leaned against the wall, deliberately keeping myself out of her space. Dewey, having frisked us both for treats again and coming up short, returned to his hay in the corner.

"Why do you ask?"

"Just thinking about my own anxiety with my short-lived career in horse competitions." I grinned. "I used to get so nervous before and even during that I felt like puking or peeing, or both."

Caitlyn took two steps forward, bringing her back into my personal space. "I remember feeling like that as a kid. But everything felt so much bigger when I was younger, beyond me and my control. My anxiety isn't about me or Dewey. It's about everything else. Everyone else," she admitted in a small voice.

"What d'you mean?"

"External expectations can be a crushing weight. I have so much to worry about all the time and that doesn't even take into account the actual riding and training part of my job." It seemed as if she regretted blurting out her inner thoughts, and I hoped she felt comfortable enough with me to know that not only did I want to know these private things, but that she could trust me to hold them close and keep them secret.

"That makes total sense. I get it. I empathize. Expectation was where most of my anxiety came from in Pony Club. Because I knew that it was costing my parents money they didn't really have or want to spend, and I'd begged rides to the competitions so I always felt like I had to do well to prove that I wasn't ungrateful." My smile felt rueful. "And I rarely did well."

"My mom reminded me of something yesterday." She paused. "Do you remember when we rode that *pas de deux*?"

I exhaled. "Yes, I remember. All of it." When Caitlyn had asked me if I remembered Antoinette, my surprise that she didn't recall we'd ridden a competitive class as a partnership had felt smothering, as if I remembered every moment where it seemed she'd remembered nothing.

"Why did you agree to it if things between us weren't..." Her forehead wrinkled. "Friendly?"

"Because it was you," I said matter-of-factly. My voice dropped until it sounded soft and wistful. "You know our first-place trophies? Mine sits on my bookshelf where I can see it every day. I remember how hard we worked on choreographing it all, choosing music, how it felt to ride next to you and feel like we were so in sync with each other. I remember how for those few hours every week when you met me at the Pony Club to practice I felt like I could just be me without the others in the way of me wanting to be your friend."

The edges of her mouth turned down. "I'd forgotten that part. I've been so focused on the other stuff that it never occurred to me to think of times that were just normal."

"Normal." I nodded slowly. "That about sums it up. Those tiny moments made me feel like maybe you didn't actually dislike me as much as I thought you did." I had to force back unexpected tears.

"I didn't dislike you. I just didn't like the way you—" She cut herself off. Shaking her head, Caitlyn tried again. "I have a proposition for you. Two really."

My eyebrows jumped up. "Really? And what would those be exactly?"

"First, I'd like to move on from that time in Pony Club. It doesn't matter now. And it's not helpful to what we're trying to do here."

I felt like someone had released a pressure valve, and tried not to seem as relieved as I felt. "I'd like that too. Very much. But, I do want you to know that I'm sorry for how I was, how I treated you and made you feel when I was being a shit. I don't know how to explain the nuances of my teen self's behavior now, but if I could just say that what I was trying to say back then wasn't coming out the way I meant for it to come out, at all."

"Noted. And thank you." She smiled shyly. "Consider your apology accepted."

A chunk of the tension I'd been holding on to since we'd met broke off and fell away. "Thanks. And the second thing?"

Caitlyn exhaled the word. "Friendship."

"Friendship," I mused, trying to sound relaxed and casual though my heart was pounding like a jackhammer at the possibility. "I think I'd like that even more."

CHAPTER ELEVEN

Caitlyn

Poor Wren had caught a cold that turned from mild discomfort and sniffling and sneezing to a raging head cold. She'd been staying away from me as much as possible, which, considering the close quarters of our truck accommodation, was no easy feat and had been mumbling that now would be the time my usually robust immune system couldn't hold out as it usually did. She was insufferable, shooing me away whenever I came within five feet of her, telling me to sanitize my hands and even going as far as wearing a bandanna around her nose and mouth. I'd never seen her this paranoid about me getting sick, though to be fair we'd never been in the lead-up to Olympic selection, but her behavior was starting to fray my nerves.

As for Addie… She and I were not quite ships in the night, but close. There'd been a sort of softness about our interactions, as if she felt less guarded talking to me, and I wondered if it was her, me, or our agreement on friendship. But given our general busyness, the only time I really spoke to her was during Dew's morning and evening checkups and those conversations were strictly professional. Still, even if we weren't talking, I'd often find her nearby like she'd materialized from nowhere. Having her quietly going about her business in the background and knowing she was there lent a solid comfort to a time tinged with uncertainty.

The morning of my first test in Rotterdam, the Grand Prix, Wren had dialed herself down from a ten to an eight-point-five and was borderline bearable. I'd drawn late morning in the riding order, which suited me and Dew perfectly. It would give him time to settle after breakfast—God help us all if he didn't feel he'd had a fair go at eating—then be prepped for our test without rushing. While Wren dealt with Dew over at the huge complex holding the stalls, I put on some music and had my usual chill-out dance party in the truck before getting dressed.

White breeches with my lucky belt, lucky rainbow socks and long black boots polished to a high shine, spurs set just right with straps tucked, my shirt and stock tie with the diamante bar pin in it. I shrugged into my Team USA tails, smoothed my sky-blue with red-bound collar and carefully buttoned myself up. After a quick glance in the mirror to make sure my makeup was spot on—as in it would make sure the judges could see I had a face but wouldn't look like I was wearing any makeup—I spritzed my hair and bun with hairspray and left the truck with my helmet and gloves tucked under my arm.

As I walked, I pulled down the tongues of the sky-blue vest under the tails so they sat perfectly over my belt buckle. When I came close to where Wren held Dewey, I could see she'd pinned a piece of paper to her shirt that proclaimed in thick block lettering I HAVE A COLD. Oh for crying out loud.

I put my helmet on. "Bit close there aren't you, Typhoid Mary?"

"I'm not breathing, not even behind my safety mask. Five-feet perimeter!" Wren was the epitome of pathetic, blocked-up discomfort.

"You're holding my horse. I kind of need to be where he is. That's what dressage is about. A person rides a horse." I looked Dew over as I pulled on my white gloves, carefully seating my fingers. "He looks amazing as always." My tack gleamed and Dew shone with health—his dappled coat so glossy I could have checked my makeup in it, his mane divided into ten perfect button braids, and his thick tail fluffed. I gave everything a quick once-over. Though I trusted Wren completely, checking the saddle and the two bits in Dew's mouth was more a superstition than anything. "Okay, I'm ready."

Wren made no move to help me mount nor did she move when, exasperated, I told her I'd just mount myself. She cleared her throat. "No, you can't do that. Maybe we could grab Mary or Ian? They're over at the warm-up arena. Or just nab someone to help." She looked around. Then around again. "Um…"

I was not going to ask someone to do something my groom was perfectly capable of doing, especially not Mary or Ian right before a test when their energy would clash with mine. "Wren," I sighed, stuffing my annoyance into a corner. "I need to get on him. Now. A cold isn't going to kill me." Not that I wanted one, but I was fairly confident that if I got hers it wouldn't be the end of the world.

"It might. I've been sanitizing everything, but…" she trailed off, a shrug ending the sentence for her.

"Have you Lysol-ed my horse?"

"No," she mumbled. "Couldn't find any." The creases at the corners of her eyes told me she was smiling behind her mask. Seemed the cold hadn't squashed all her humor.

Addie appeared out of nowhere. "I must strongly advise against spraying anything resembling Lysol on a horse." Her smile reached her eyes as she studied Wren who was still keeping her distance—no easy feat given she was holding the thing I needed to mount. "What's this? A standoff? That bandanna makes you look like a bandit, Wren."

I poked Wren with the end of my whip. "She won't let me mount my horse on my own, nor will she straighten my stock tie and pin or give me a boost because she thinks she's going to give me her plague."

"Ah. That wouldn't be great." Addie's gaze slid over my body before coming back to meet my eyes, which felt as wide as plates at her blatant checking out. When she realized she'd been caught, her eyes matched mine for size. Addie cleared her throat. "For many reasons."

"Exactly," Wren agreed.

Addie looked from Wren to me. "Is there anythin' I can do to help?"

"Yes," Wren said at the same time I said, "No thanks."

I threw my hands up. "Don't mind me, you two. I'm just here to ride the horse."

"We won't," Addie said cheerfully.

Wren reached into her fanny pack and extracted a cloth which she held out to Addie. "Can you please make sure the stock tie and pin aren't crooked, then do boot clean and hoist her up?"

"Yes, boss." Addie took the cloth and tucked it into her back pocket.

I followed the progress of the cloth. Purely to make sure she hadn't dropped it. Most definitely not to look at the part of her anatomy against which that back pocket rested. She really did have a great butt, and now that we were certified friends, I could totally think that. Right? "I *can* mount him myself," I argued. Remember me? The rider? "No, you can't," Wren rebutted. She meant in a general sense, not literally. Obviously I could get on my horse alone and without a mounting block. But it went against the routine, and the routine was king. Superstition was real. Just ask my lucky socks, lucky belt, lucky gloves and lucky…pretty much everything really.

Now was really not the time to argue, or go against our routine, so I gave in. Addie stepped in close and I raised my chin for the stock tie and bar pin check. As she tugged and fluffed the fabric, I watched her intense concentration, as if this simple task was the most important thing she'd do all day. She was so close I could see the laugh lines around her eyes, relaxed now but just waiting to crease with mirth.

Her fingers stilled and she glanced up to find me watching her. "All set," she murmured. After taking a backward step, she turned to Wren. "Does that pass?"

"Perfect." Wren took a small object from her pocket and after pumping hand sanitizer into a palm and cleaning the tiny device, offered it to me. "Earpiece."

I stared. "Seriously. Did you really just sanitize the earpiece?"

Addie's expression was an eyebrows-raised *Don't question the crazy* look. I settled the earpiece in my ear, ready for Ian's instruction during my warm-up. "Can I go ride now?"

Wren, apparently satisfied, nodded. "Now if you can hoist her up, Addie, I'll be forever in your debt."

Addie snapped a salute, though it seemed more teasing of Wren's dictatorship than serious obedience. "Done. Who knew all those years at Pony Club giving leg-ups would pay off? I've been waiting for this moment to shine for twenty-something years."

When I positioned myself to mount, bending my left leg back, Addie moved behind me. She wiped the sole of my boot, then with both hands on my left shin hoisted me as I jumped into the saddle. As I settled my tails over the back of the saddle, Addie polished my boots with surprising efficiency, then gave me and Dew a once-over, wiping nonexistent dirt from his shoulder.

"I won't wish you luck. You don't need it." Her expression relaxed, as if she'd just thought of something pleasant. "So…have a great ride. I'll be watching."

"Thanks," I murmured.

Wren triple-checked us then made her typical thumbs-up as she echoed Addie's, "Have a great ride."

I gathered both sets of reins, threading them through my fingers. "Will do."

As I rode away I heard Wren ask Addie, "Want a job?"

Dew and I threw everything we had into the test, and when I rode out of the arena to a score of 81.717% my elation was sky high. Just one more test like that and I'd be seeing Caitlyn Lloyd and Midfields Adieu on the list for the US Olympic Dressage Team. I searched the crowd for familiar faces and spotted Mary and Wren standing with Ian. Camera shutters went off all around me, and I waved to the crowd, patted my horse and kept looking at faces, hoping to see one in particular.

Disappointment colored my jubilation when I realized Addie was nowhere to be seen. I had to head slap mentally to remind myself that she was probably working with the other horses right now, not watching me ride. I felt like a kid upset that a parent hadn't shown up for an important event, and the conflicting emotion dampened my excitement. Dew, having apparently picked up on my mood, took the opportunity to spook at absolutely nothing and only years of reflexes saved me from hitting the dirt. That was going to make a great photo.

Once Wren had taken care of Dewey, I sent her to take a nap in the truck. Her groveling gratitude was all the proof I needed that my usually stoic groom really felt like shit and needed to rest up. I checked Dew was settled and eating his small snack, waiting on the chance we'd have to ride again for a presentation, then went back to watch the other US riders. Dakota and Pierre had an excellent test and I made sure to raise my hands to clap loudly as she exited the arena. I nearly fell over dead when Dakota smiled at me. An actual genuine smile. Could it be that we might reach some sort of truce this century?

Mary and Ian had long melted away and I tried to relax in the stands while watching the remaining tests. A few riders and shy fans came up to talk to me, and I signed pictures and posed for a few photos during the breaks. Given those yet to ride, my placing seemed assured and I decided it was time to go rouse Wren. Maybe I'd take a quick look around to see if I could find our team vet to…make sure all was in order. That's it, nothing more.

I'd just stepped outside when my phone vibrated. Addie's name on the screen sent an immediate roll of warm pleasure through me. Interesting. That was a step up from before and also definitely something to unpack later. "Hey. What's up? I was wondering where you were."

"Caitlyn, can you come to the stalls, please? Immediately? There's a slight situation here." She didn't sound panicked exactly, but there was a definite edge to her voice that sent my pleasure at having her call me into serious anxiety territory.

"What's wrong? Is Dew okay?" I was already jogging toward the stalls, having to slow to a walk every time I came near a horse. Which was frequently.

"He's fine, but he's causing a bit of an uproar and I can't get hold of Wren."

"Wren and her head cold are taking a nap. And what do you mean, uproar?"

"Hard to explain. He's perfectly fine, promise, but I could really use your help if you could make it fast?"

I had to strain to hear her over the bizarre sound in the background. It sounded like an odd and constant wibble-wibble-wibble. "What's that sound?"

"That, is Rasputin."

The moment she said it, I knew exactly what had happened. Oh no. My horse was such a dweeb. I showed my competitor's ID to the security guards and jogged down the path toward the stabling complex. As I drew near, the first thing I noticed was Dakota and Pierre on the gravel outside the stalls. The gelding was whirling in circles, eyes wide and nostrils flaring as he snorted and danced away from the entrance. Inside was the unmistakable sound of horses freaking out—snorting, panicked whinnying, bodies hitting things. My heart fell as I rushed inside.

The next thing I noticed was Dewey. The idiot had somehow managed to break the zip ties and pull the laminated picture of Rasputin from between the vertical bars of his stall and was walking around the space, shaking it back and forth. Well that explained the wobble-board sound. Of course, *of course* my horse would be the one playing the fool. I groaned.

Addie was in the stall with Dewey and I could see the glee in his eyes as he played keep-away. The moment I opened the lower door she turned to me, her shoulders dropping. "Thank God," she exhaled. "I've been tryin' to get it off him but he won't let me near him. I can get close, but as soon as I go to grab it, he's off. And he's *really* tall when he puts his head up."

"Of course you can't get it, that's part of the game." I knew because I'd played the *I have something and if you want it come get it off me but hahaha you can't catch me or reach my head* game with Dewey for twelve years. I tried to ignore multiple instances of hundreds of thousands of Euros worth of massive dressage horses, some of which were Olympic hopefuls, potentially damaging some very expensive part of themselves as they lost their shit in the stalls around me.

Rustling the bag of licorice I'd snatched from the bucket outside Dewey's stall immediately grabbed his attention. He dropped the picture to the shavings and practically lunged at me in his haste to get a treat. I grabbed the blanket strap under his chin to stop him from getting hold of the picture again, and with my free hand extracted a piece of licorice. The moment Dewey stopped playing with his toy, the three horses around him deflated. Only the occasional loud snort gave away the fact that moments earlier they'd been convinced a monster was going to eat them. I glanced over my shoulder. "If you hold him, I'll get his cat picture."

"Deal." Addie and I swapped places and she accidentally captured my fingers as she took hold of Dew.

When I was sure she had a solid grip, I let him go, retrieved the slobbery laminated poster and dropped it over the stall door when Dewey went to grab it again. "This is why you can't have nice things," I told him and when he gave me a mournful look, I added, "Don't give me that face. It's your own fault."

Addie unlocked her phone and slipped out of the stall. I followed her as she peered into the stalls around us, where the rest of the USA horses were housed, and held out a hand to them until they came forward for a tentative sniff. "Mary, can you contact the team and get them to come and check on their horses? There's been a…spooking incident in the stalls and I'd like to do an examination of each and trot them up to be sure there's no lameness. Caitlyn and Dakota are already here. Hmm? Not that I know of." She paused, eyeing me, and I could see a smile pulling at the edges of her mouth. "No, the item causing the issue has been removed. Great. Thanks. Bye."

I covered my face with my hand. "Oh God. Why couldn't I have a normal horse instead of a weirdo?"

Addie touched my back, her fingers tapping a slow rhythm that made my skin tingle. "Normal horses are boring. His quirkiness is part of what makes him so talented. And adorable."

Her attempt to make me feel better was cut short by Dakota dragging Pierre toward us. Pierre resisted with every fiber of his body, the whites of his eyes showing as he tried to make it clear he did *not* want to come anywhere near the bogeyman. Dakota swore at him and threw the lead rope at her groom, who immediately started calming the horse. Dakota strode directly up to me. Oh joy, I could not wait for whatever vitriol was about to come my way. So much for our minor truce.

With hands on her hips she stuck out her breasts until she was practically pushing me away with mammary tissue—not as pleasant as I generally found that activity. Her expression was pure rage, and her voice ice when she snarled, "Are you and that horse of yours mentally deficient?"

I was about to answer with a facetious, "It's highly probable" which I knew would infuriate her more, when Addie interjected, "Actually, a high playfulness quotient, problem-solving abilities and an inability to tolerate boredom like Dewey displays are all indicative of a very high intellect. I believe those things are part of what makes him such a talented Grand Prix horse."

Dakota straightened, her expression turning to steel. It was an expression I knew well. It was her *Who do you think you are, peasant?* look. Addie didn't flinch, didn't look away. If anything, she seemed more composed, more in control. Dakota spat out one word. "Talented?"

"Yes," Addie agreed. "Very."

Dakota's face contorted as her mouth worked open and closed. Clearly, Addie challenging her had drained her of the ability to respond. She snatched the lead from her groom again, gesturing wildly at Dewey, to the displeasure of Pierre who threw his head up to avoid her flailing hand. "That mongrel isn't worth a fraction of any of the other team horses. Pierre could have done a tendon spooking like that. You're lucky I was holding him and he wasn't in a stall where he could have gone right through the wall. I'll sue your hick ass if he's hurt himself. This—" She thrust a forefinger at the gelding's face, and when Pierre flinched she yanked hard on his lead, making him flinch again. "—is the most talented and expensive horse on the team."

Ouch, poor Pierre. I felt like slapping Dakota's hands. If I were Pierre, I'd have channeled some fight response or something and taken a chunk out of her. But he seemed so cowed that he just took what she dished up. And she was such a goddamned liar. Her aggregate scores over the last three years were right in the middle of the group's. She was as delusional as she was nasty.

Addie stepped away from my side, both hands out in the ultimate gesture of placation. "Pierre is clearly still upset, so why don't you take him outside where he can calm down and I can finish my exam, then I'll give him a once-over."

Dakota whirled around, followed by horse and groom, both of whom seemed reluctant. I didn't blame either of them. I could still hear her derisive snarling. Dew nudged my shoulder as if to say, "Didja see what I did, Mom?"

Really not the time to be flaunting your weirdness, Dew. I pushed him away as Addie bent to close the bottom bolt on the lower door. Once she'd straightened, I asked, "Is all that true? About the boredom and playfulness quotient and stuff?"

Her smile was mischievous. "How the hell should I know? I'm a veterinarian, not an animal psychologist."

"Sneak. You didn't say anything about my intellect," I murmured.

"Didn't I? Hmm. You're right." She grinned and backed away. "Now if you'll excuse me, I need to check the most important horse on the US Dressage Team." Addie glanced at Dewey who stood with his head over the half-door, studying us with bright, curious eyes. "He's fine."

I laughed when she winked at me. "Yeah, he is. Pleased with himself too, I can tell."

"It was really funny, if you discount all the potential disasters." She touched my forearm. "Your ride was utterly brilliant. Sorry I had to rush off and couldn't tell you right after. And sorry I have to rush off now." After a gentle squeeze of my arm, Addie walked off, calling after Dakota to please stop lunging her horse around and around and raising his heart rate.

I collapsed back against the stall door and watched Addie walking away, until I caught myself and realized I'd been staring. More than just staring. Her ass really was— Yes. Wow. Good job, Obvious Luster. That casual contact from moments earlier had my skin buzzing. The touch had indeed been casual, simply getting my attention or reinforcing her point or…something. Something that wasn't an indication of anything more.

But I'd wanted it to be, and the disconnect between my feelings and what was actually happening was confusing. Not only confusing but also *really* badly timed. And a flat-out all-round bad idea. How could two busy people who lived in different states ever find time for anything more than friendship?

Dewey nudged me again, this time to remind me I wasn't paying him enough attention. I poked his cheek. "Do you know the trouble you've caused? As if Dakota needed any more reason to hate me."

He snuffled around my pockets, apparently not caring about anything more than getting another treat. I kissed his nose. "You really think I'm going to give you more after what you did?"

Dew snuffed me again, this time doing his adorable huff-blow thing into my cheek. I was such a sucker. I gave him another piece of licorice, kissed the side of his nose again then slipped away before any of my teammates coming to check on their horses saw me.

CHAPTER TWELVE

Addie

The morning after the five-day competition in Rotterdam, I engaged in my Netherlands pre-work ritual where I pretended to workout then went to the café for amazing coffee and breakfast. The two activities of half-hearted exercise and a huge breakfast totally canceled each other out. A few mornings, I'd seen Caitlyn running through the village but had felt too self-conscious to call out to her.

That was weird because things between us had been noticeably easier as we navigated our new friendship. Our interactions were light, but also somewhat shallow. I hated the light and shallow. I wanted to dive deeply into her, to learn as much about her as I could. I wanted her to share things with me.

I ordered and settled at a corner table of the quiet café overlooking a busy street to catch up with the world. Nothing exciting in the news, and just the usual work emails. Once I was done with breakfast I'd have to rush off for a meeting with Mary, Ian, and video-conferenced team selectors where we'd finalize the team for Rio. I was certain I knew who it would be—the performances left little doubt—and my job was to tell them if I was happy with the horses' soundness. I already knew I'd be spoiling the chances for one of their choices.

Midway through my eggs, bacon, toast, and an incredible avocado salsa type thing that I really had to learn how to make, the slow creak of the café's door pulled my attention away from my plate.

Caitlyn. Shit.

Despite that newly found ease, I bent my head, trying to shrink in my seat. This meeting outside our defined roles as vet and rider made me uneasy, as if it might break the rules of our friendship which up until this point had always had horses as a buffer. She ordered at the counter, then stood against the wall and stared at her phone. I stared at my food and tried valiantly not to stare at her.

I wasn't doing very well with the not staring, and the game was up when Caitlyn glanced up at her name being called and spotted me on one of my sneaky peeks. A slow, knowing smile followed a second after and once she'd collected her coffee and a croissant, she zigzagged her way through empty tables to me. She went with the old faithful, "Mind if I join you?"

"Of course not." I pulled out the seat to my left. "The more the merrier." Dumb dumb dumb.

She set her food and coffee down, then shed her light runner's jacket and hung it over the back of the chair. "So this is where you disappear to once you're around the corner. I've seen you running a few mornings but didn't want to interrupt."

"Oh, I don't run. I jog. Slowly. With lots of walk breaks."

A quick smile. "Ah. My apologies."

"You're forgiven. Day off today? You're not usually here."

"No, I'm not. And yes, it is a day off." She leaned back in the chair, twisting until she sat sideways to cross her legs. "No work for Dew today, then light work tomorrow, and then…who knows." She sipped her coffee before carefully breaking off a piece of croissant and popping it in her mouth.

She'd placed second and third in her classes at Rotterdam, and across the board, her qualifying scores were the highest of any on the shortlist. In my mind, she was a sure thing. But it wasn't my place to tell her. So I went to my own personal old faithful. Change the subject. "The food here is really good," I said inanely. "I've been coming here for almost all my meals."

"You don't cook much?" Laughing, she held up both hands. "No judgment, I've screwed up boiling a pot of water."

"Back home I try, really I do. Nearly every weekend I'm not working, or on my days off after on-calls I swear I'm going to make up a batch of wholesome meals like some fatigued, frazzled Julia Child and freeze them for later. Then I usually fall asleep on the couch before midday." I gestured to my plate. "Plus eating here is better than my usual plain eggs breakfast or sandwich and a Mars Bar lunch."

"I think I remember you always having that for lunch at Pony Club too." When I nodded my confirmation around a mouthful of avocado salsa, she asked, "Nothing's changed?"

"Not a bit."

Caitlyn's face held an odd expression and I took a few moments to study her, to decipher it. Part shy, part expectant and most surprisingly—really interested. Not that I was keeping tally, but this was the second time I'd been the recipient of that look of interest from her. When she realized I was watching her, she flushed and asked, "You like your routine, huh?"

"I really do. Sometimes it's the only constant in a day that's always full of surprises. It helps," I added quietly, now utterly embarrassed by what I was saying yet unable to stop myself from sharing these stupid things.

"I totally get wanting some continuity in your life. I'm the same." She shrugged. "Which makes things like being away at competitions or overseas tricky because I have to adapt both myself and Dew. And you know how well horses adapt to change." Caitlyn scrunched her face up, as if trying to convey exactly how much horses loathed their routines being messed with. "Probably why we're all so superstitious."

"That explains your lucky rainbow socks."

Her eyebrows shot up. "How do you know about my lucky socks?"

"I'm observant and I figured there had to be a reason, other than a broken washing machine, for you wearing the same socks for every test."

Caitlyn held up both hands. "In my defense they aren't actually the same pair. I have a bunch that are the same pattern and I do wear a clean pair every time."

"Ahhh. Then it's really just superstition-lite?"

Her laugh was sudden, loud, and rich. "Something like that." She tore another piece from her croissant but instead of eating it, asked, "What else have you noticed? About my competition habits that is." The question was phrased in such a way that it felt a little too personal. A little too leading. And I didn't care.

I took a few moments to think about my answer. Like our chat outside Lotte's barn, she'd opened up the space to be personal and it was up to me if I ran with it. If both of us were willing, then what was wrong with changing our dynamic again? "I notice the way you touch the American flag on the saddlecloth before you mount, like you're worried the embroidery has somehow moved. I notice how when you're warming up you make room for everyone, even when they forget the arena rules and don't give you the same courtesy. I notice how you thank every person who's volunteered and comes to tell you it's your time, or the arena staff who let you into and out of the competition arena." I bit my lower lip but the admission came out anyway. "And I notice the way you always look in the direction of the competitor's area when you come out of the arena."

"I'm looking for you," she admitted quietly, and I knew from the way she'd said it that she knew I'd already suspected as much.

"And I'm watching you." Smiling, I added, "Before I have to run off to do something else that is."

She said nothing. But there was staring. I took the opportunity of silence to finish my breakfast and a quick check of my watch told me I should really leave. "I'm sorry, but I need to head off. Important meeting this morning."

"Oh? How important?" The question had a lilting sing-songiness about it, making it obvious she knew which meeting I was referring to.

"On a scale of one to ten? About a nine-point-five."

"So you're pretty important yourself, being involved in such a meeting?"

"Mhmm. I'm a very big deal."

"That you are," she agreed. Caitlyn finished her croissant then used a forefinger to collect crumbs. And I had a sudden mental image of leaning in and pressing my fingertips to the plate to collect those crumbs for her. Of course in this mental image she'd suck my fingers, which was a very nice thought but not entirely appropriate. Caitlyn pushed her chair back. "Mind some company on the walk back?" Her gaze spent a second on my mouth before making its way back to make eye contact with me.

My voice was embarrassingly squeaky when I said, "Not at all."

We both stood. I nearly fell over. Ninety percent of the time she was around me, she wore breeches which, being skin-tight, left little to my already overactive imagination. But tiny workout shorts were something else entirely. Something incredible. The ache of wanting her was so sudden it felt like a gut punch and I had to turn around and pretend I was checking something to stop my gawping. I could imagine those legs, wrapped around me and had to close my eyes to force the image out.

"You okay?" she asked.

"Mhmm. Just making sure I didn't drop anythin'." I turned back to her and zipped my jacket.

We'd taken barely ten steps outside when she said, "So after talking to my mom recently, I was reminiscing and looking through old photos from Pony Club."

Relieved for the chance to shift brain gears, I said, "Oh? I'd love to see some if you don't mind. I don't really think I have any from then."

"Sure." She fished out her phone and handed it to me.

Displayed on the screen were the members of the Pony Club, hanging out on the steps of the clubhouse. I could pick us out easily but found myself struggling to recall the names of the other girls. I let out a short laugh. "See? My sandwich and a Mars Bar." Studying the photo, I hoped she hadn't seen what was plainly obvious—that I was staring moonily at her.

"Mhmm, that was one of the first things I noticed."

Oh shit. Yeah, she'd totally realized I was acting like the lovesick teen I'd been. I cleared my throat. "So, listen. I've been thinking a lot about things since we, uh…reconnected. I want you to know that I really *am* sorry for the way I behaved in Pony Club."

"You don't need to apologize again and again. I know you are. I see that in the way you act with me now." She blew out a shaky breath. "And I'm sorry about my reactions earlier this month. They weren't particularly rational but there's obviously still an insecure kid inside me somewhere."

"It's okay. Let's make a deal—no more apologies, from either of us."

"Deal." She glanced at me. "Do you remember stuff from back then? You and me?"

"I remember every interaction I had with you," I murmured.

"I thought I did too, but I'm starting to realize I may have forgotten a few things or blown stuff out of proportion. Like what was probably harmless teasing and joking felt like cruelty and bullying back then."

"I think everything feels larger than life when you're young. I know it did for me. And I feel like a shit for having made you feel humiliated and upset. Sorry, that was almost an apology."

She grinned. "Almost. I know it was dumb because it wasn't just me it happened to, but…it *was* hurtful. And I couldn't understand why *you*, because I didn't think I'd done anything to you at all that would have warranted that. It was confusing, that's all." Her eyes were wide, almost fearful, as if she expected me to tell her I just really didn't like her back then.

Truth or not quite truth? If I didn't tell her the truth now then everything that came after this for us would be meaningless. But the truth was frightening and forward and could jeopardize our tentative foundations. I wanted to tell her the reason, let it out into the world, but the implications of that truth made my stomach feel like it wanted to leap out of my throat.

After my overly long silence, Caitlyn murmured, "You don't want to say?"

"I do, it's just…" Exhaling, I took a chance and let it all out in a rush. "I did it because I was a queer kid with a huge crush on you. Not just how you looked, but everything about you from how you rode to your voice. I wanted you to notice me. It's as simple as that. But you didn't, and I couldn't figure out if it was just because I sucked or maybe you weren't picking up what I was trying to say." I laughed quietly. "Which we know now I wasn't actually saying clearly."

"So you were mean to me because you liked me?" She didn't seem alarmed or bothered. The opposite really, and the quiet hopefulness of her realization made me feel like the air between us was humming. "I had no idea you were even into girls. Women," she quickly corrected herself.

I tried not to hyperventilate my response. "I am and yes, pretty much. I told you before that I was socially awkward. I guess when I tried talking to you and you never really engaged with me, my teen brain thought it was time to go next level."

She grabbed my hand and pulled me to a stop. "I'm shy, Addie. Painfully shy. I don't think I talked to anyone back then unless I was forced to. People usually think I'm cool or aloof or even mean, but it's the exact opposite. Conversations with people I don't know are really hard and when you add some teen awkwardness to it? It's a recipe for disaster."

"I get that," I said, trying not to sound as manic as I felt about her admission. "Shit, how easy things would be if people could manage actual conversations with one another."

Caitlyn's response was a rueful, "Yeah. I should have just told you I thought you were cute and asked why you were being mean."

She. Thought. I. Was. Cute.

I ignored the excited flip-flopping of my stomach and began walking again, relieved when Caitlyn fell in beside me, closer than before. "See above with the awkwardness and crushing on you." Telling her had made me feel both light and heavy—getting it off my chest felt wonderful, but memories weighed me down. "So there it is. I wasn't intentionally trying to make you feel like shit. I was just a scared little queer kid who was trying to hide and pretend they weren't queer in a place where being queer was going to get me nothing but an ass-kicking. I was trying to figure myself out and I didn't know what to do about it or the way I felt about you."

"An actual ass-kicking?"

"Pretty much." I offered her a wry smile. "I was born and raised in 'God Hates Fags' country, Caitlyn, and my father used that saying like he used butter on his bread. His neck is as red as the state I was born in. If you can think of every stereotype about a closed-minded southern man, he's it." I thrust my chest out and adopted a gruff voice with my drawl dialed up to ten. "Why you wan'a horse, why you need to go to college, why d'you think you're better'n us?" I raised both hands, palms up, having no answer to any of those rhetorical questions.

"What did you do?"

"Hid myself," I said instantly. "I was a lesbian living under his roof and having to hide myself every second of every day until I could go somewhere where people didn't think that someone like me was hateful. My life back then was a Venn diagram that never felt right. Hiding my sexuality. Trying to fit in at Pony Club. Then there was school where I had actual friends and did really well. And I was terrified of you, this person I was so into, seeing how…little and insignificant I was."

"I never thought you were little or insignificant. I really had no idea," she quietly said. "It never twigged *that* could be the reason."

My eyebrows shot up. "Of course you didn't. I don't think anyone did really. It was all just stupid childhood fantasy." I reached out, then rethought the movement and drew my hand back. "Being a kid is hard. Being a queer kid in that environment? No fucking thank you. I never told my parents, never intended to either, just thought I'd quietly disengage from all that hate when I was old enough. But they found out."

Caitlyn's response was a quiet, "How?"

"Decided to make a surprise trip to visit me at college. Saw me kissing my girlfriend. Made a scene. All very drama-movie moment of course because not only was I a disgusting queer but they'd spent good money to come see me. My dad tried to tell me I was no longer welcome to the Gardner name. And my indignant outrage being what it was, I told him he could go fuck himself and that he was lucky I was going to keep it because me being Doctor Gardner, DVM was probably the only bit of decency that name would ever have." My grin felt incongruous. "Then I did a very clichéd spin around and flounced off."

She lightly touched my shoulder. "I'm so sorry you didn't have support."

"Thanks." I tucked my hands into my pockets. "The worst part is I don't think he was a bad dad before that. I mean, he grumbled about me riding, but he paid for things I needed even if they were secondhand or cheap versions, and he took a cut in the income from the horses boarding in our fields so I could ride one of them for free. It's kind of hard to reconcile the two fathers sometimes." I cleared my throat. "Mama's okay, well more like she's tolerable about it. We exist in this kind of mutually accepted silence on the matter. We talk every few months for about three minutes and I get birthday and Christmas gifts shipped to me with generic I-hope-you're-well messages but that's it."

"Shit," Caitlyn breathed. "I mean my parents didn't exactly throw me a rainbow parade but it didn't take them long to realize that this was how it was and who I am and they came on board pretty quickly with the 'We love you and want you to be happy.' I'm sorry your parents didn't act the way they should have."

"Thanks. It's fine, really. Less people to buy gifts for at Christmas." I exhaled. "So yeah. That's my big bad secret. Sorry, it got kinda heavy there for a minute."

Caitlyn's eyebrows furrowed, and I could feel the tension of her trying to work through feelings. "I appreciate you being honest. I won't lie, being hated by the Elites wasn't nice and as much as I tried not to let it bug me, it really did. Insecurity is dumb."

I gripped her hand, squeezing to emphasize my point. "They hated you for the same reason Dakota is such a bitch to you now. Because they're jealous of you. Of your talent. Of how you can get on any horse and make it look so easy when they are handed best horses around and they *still* can't get a tune out of them. I wasn't an Elite and I *never* hated you. Not by a long shot."

"I kind of wish I'd known the real you back then, not the you I had in my head." Her smile, though tentative, was still genuine. "Assuming she's just a younger version of who you are now?"

"Pretty much. Young me was a little dumber for sure, the way I approached you being the prime example of that. But a lot of time has passed since then, Caitlyn. And there's plenty more time in the future if you'd like to try the way things should have been when we were kids."

She didn't hesitate. "I think I would like that, yes. We've already got friendship, right?"

"Right."

"That's a pretty good starting point I think."

A starting point for what exactly… I'd had so many years of this physical crush, but now I was also discovering there was an emotional and intellectual side to her that only strengthened my desire. Rather than ask her to elaborate, I said, "I agree."

Caitlyn slowed to a stop at our intersection and glanced down at our hands. Her expression felt like mine—surprise that after I'd grabbed her hand earlier neither of us had let go. She carefully disengaged and cleared her throat. "Well, this is where I leave you. I guess I'll see you after your meeting?"

"That you will." I checked my phone. "Nobody has called in a panic about their horses so my day is already off to a great start."

Her slow smile and the soft intimacy of her response left me with absolutely no doubt as to what she meant when she said, "Mine too."

CHAPTER THIRTEEN

Caitlyn

As Mary closed the folder, her expression was both satisfied and sympathetic. "Thanks, everyone. We'll send out an official USDF statement in a few minutes so it will go live when everyone in the States is waking up. Please refrain from announcing anything publicly until then. Those of you selected for the team need to have their measurements for uniforms to me by next Wednesday." She glanced around the group of assembled riders. "I know I speak on behalf of the selectors when I say we're so proud to have had such a group of talent from which to have chosen our Olympic team, and we look forward to supporting all of you throughout your careers."

As the management team left the room, Addie deliberately avoided my gaze, though to be fair she'd avoided everyone's except Mary's and Ian's during the announcement. Probably for the best. I'd noticed the rider whose horse had been declared unsound to compete throwing more than a few glares in Addie's direction. I understood their frustration and upset—to have come so far and not make it because of that would be devastating. But she'd made the right call.

I took a few moments to collect myself and exchange words with the rest of the riders, then slipped out the door. The grooms had formed a huddle outside and they all split apart when the door opened.

Wren pointedly stared after the management team who were talking quietly as they walked away, then back to me. After a gesture of pure exasperation, she blurted, "Well?"

I blew out a long breath and felt a chunk of the tension I'd cultivated over the last few months exit along with the air. "Time to brush up on your Portuguese. We're going to Brazil."

Wren threw victorious arms in the air. "Fuck yes! I knew it!" She dropped her arms and her voice. "And our friend?"

I glanced at Dakota who stood fifteen feet away with her back to us. "She's coming too."

* * *

Ken arrived to change Dewey's shoes the next morning, followed closely by Lotte's farrier, Marcus, who'd graciously agreed to share some of his larger equipment. I knew Addie was around, having seen her car, and when she wandered into the barn with a mug in one hand and her iPad tucked under her arm, I felt a tingle of excitement.

She greeted both men then came toward me, deflecting Dewey's interest in her coffee with a carrot pulled from her back pocket. Her smile was warm, friendly, and added some interesting tummy flutters. The touch of her fingertips on my arm was light and all too brief. "Mornin'. And congratulations on making the team."

I fought down a blush. "Thanks."

Before I could introduce the two men to each other, Ken said hi to me and Addie then went straight over to Marcus's truck to introduce himself. As he strapped on protective leather chaps, Ken began discussing hoof knives and medicated hoof dressings like he and Marcus had been pals for years.

"Farrier's Club," Addie murmured, leaning close. "Super-secret society, almost as hard to crack as the Chiropractor's Club. I've infiltrated both and I've almost managed to get into the Acupuncturist's Club. Almost." She offered me a wink then sidestepped away to talk to the farriers. Marcus stood by while Ken picked up Dewey's right foreleg to study his hoof. In typical no-nonsense farrier fashion, he got to work removing the four shoes while we watched on. Addie pulled her sunglasses from her head and threaded them into the neck of her polo.

I followed the progress of her sunglasses. Lucky lenses. Staring at the eyewear, I said, "Probably not a great place to put those, unless you want to donate them to Dewey's toybox." Dewey was already straining against the cross-ties. The sunglasses were an obvious toy if you were a horse with a low boredom threshold, and he was trying to nose Addie's breasts. Not before me, pal.

Oh shit.

Now *that* was an unwelcome thought in a sea of unexpected thoughts. My cheeks flamed as I tried to push down the excitement tingling through me.

Smiling in a way that made me feel like she knew exactly what I was thinking, Addie indicated Dew's bare feet waiting to be trimmed and shaped. "I should probably pay attention to this." With a light squeeze of my forearm, she left me standing at Dew's head while she moved to the portable forge on an extendable arm at the back of Marcus's truck which would heat the new set of shoes so they could be shaped to perfectly fit Dew's manicured hooves.

I rubbed my arm where she'd touched me.

With the roar of the gas furnace in the background I watched Addie as she discussed biomechanics, hoof and limb angles and the like with the two men. She lacked the arrogance of some veterinarians, but she seemed confident in her knowledge and that her opinion mattered. Did she have this confidence as a kid?

Watching Addie didn't answer my question. All it really did was give me more questions. About myself as well as her. She glanced up and caught me staring. She stared right back and after a few moments, she smiled, cheeks dimpling. My return smile was automatic. Addie's wink was so quick it might have been imagined, then she returned to her note taking.

Once done with Dewey, Ken threw me a double thumbs-up. "He's all set. I'll see you both in Rio."

"Thanks so much. And sorry again about the teeth marks in your belt."

He grinned. "It happens."

Dewey thanked Ken for his nice neat feet and new shoes by snorting in his face.

Addie walked beside me as I led Dewey back to his stall where he'd have a snack before some time out in the field. "No Wren today?"

"She's online shopping for—" I air quoted. "Rio-appropriate clothing. She's insanely superstitious about things, as you may have guessed from her not allowing me to mount Dew on my own. According to her logic, bringing clothes for Brazil's climate would mean we wouldn't be selected."

"Gotcha." She offered a bright smile. "Not that I think there was any doubt about you guys making the team."

"Mmm, well it's all done now and it's time to relax. Or freak out about all the prep we need to do."

"Right," Addie mused. "I'm sure it'll all be fine, and remember we're here to help you guys in any way you need."

My libido brain helpfully piped up with, "I can think of one way you could help me." Okay, that was enough. I was going to kick Wren out of the cottage to go have dinner with the other grooms tonight so I could spend a little time with myself. I cleared my throat. "Team selection and Olympics glory aside, at least we'll get to spend some more time together, working on that friendship thing."

For the first time since we'd reconnected, Addie blushed. Her head snapped back down to concentrate on her iPad and after a few long, silent moments, she glanced up again. "I really like the way that sounds." She lightly touched my forearm again, just the barest brush of fingertips on my skin but it sent a rush of goose bumps coursing up my arm.

I stared down, marveling that something so innocent could be so affecting. "You always touch me," I mumbled, aware of how dumb and obvious it sounded.

Addie backed up a few steps, well out of touching range. "I'm so sorry. I touch everyone," she added quickly. "It's just a habit, something that happens without thought."

"Everyone?" I had seen how tactile she was with Wren and for some reason the thought that I wasn't special somehow was oddly disappointing.

She deflated. "Well, not really everyone. Just people I'm comfortable with. I try really hard around clients and stuff to stay out of reach, otherwise it's weird. And I've tried not to with you. I'm sorry if it's made you uncomfortable. I know it's not appropriate." Addie laughed. "Though I think maybe we've already stepped over that particular line. It's just…it's…being comfortable. Around you." Addie indicated a circle around herself with both arms. "Okay. This is my space, which is outside of your personal space, and I'm going to stick to it."

I stepped into that circle. "I'm not uncomfortable at all. Far from it. And I'm happy to have you in my space."

Dewey, the master of comedic timing, nudged me hard in the back, sending me flying forward. I scrabbled for something to grab and finding nothing, fell against Addie who had no time to do anything but grab me until we were pressed front on in an awkward, yet admittedly nice, embrace.

Awkwardness aside, the hug felt natural, comfortable, and I had a quick flash of what it might be like to do it again. And anything that might follow on from a hug... The feeling that rolled through me was a beefed-up version of that pleasant tingle from before.

"Really uncool, Dew," I mumbled once I'd managed to extricate myself from Addie's arms. The moment I was free, I wanted to do whatever the opposite of extricate was.

Addie on the other hand seemed totally unconcerned by our impromptu cuddle. "Does he do that often?" The question came out rough and croaky, and made me think she wasn't as unaffected as she appeared.

"Only when no one's paying attention to him. I'm sure you've noticed how much he loves people and he just doesn't grasp the concept that humans can't spend every minute interacting with him." I flicked the thick muscle of his neck and received an attempt at mouthing my belt in response. "In addition to thinking he's the center of the universe, he's also a huge narcissist. Have you seen him when he hears a camera shutter go off? It's like he turns into a Vogue model."

"Well if I was as good lookin' as— uh, him, I'd probably have a touch of narcissism too." Addie cleared her throat and pulled a small bag of peppermint Life Savers from a pocket. She gave one to Dewey, who crunched it enthusiastically while nudging her for another, then popped one in her own mouth.

I shook my head when she offered me one, as she did every time she gave Dew a peppermint. "Hold up a minute." I fished my phone from my pocket. "Do you mind if I take a photo?"

"Of course not."

Laughing, I amended, "A photo that will be on my social media page."

Addie grinned. "Same answer."

"Great. And sorry, but trying to keep everyone happy and engaged is kind of a constant job."

"I get it. Now how do you want me?"

"Exactly as you are," I said, and could hear an underlying wistfulness that I hoped she didn't catch. For crying out loud. When did I turn into a romance sap?

Addie leaned against Dewey's neck, smiling hugely as she held up the bag of peppermints and the thermometer that was always in her breast pocket. I clicked my tongue until Dew's ears flicked forward, then snapped the photo. "Thanks."

"My pleasure."

I tried to ignore the nuance of that statement and wrote out a quick social media post.

The US Dressage Team veterinarian Dr. Addie Gardner making sure Midfields Adieu is at his best, with a treat to make the not nice stuff better.

I added my usual hashtags then linked the picture to my social media accounts. While I'd been playing publicity person, Addie had started playing with Dew who was trying his hardest to get her fingers into his mouth. I knew she'd figured out by now that he wasn't bitey so much as mouthy so I didn't feel my usual need to defend him and tell someone he was just playing around. She seemed oblivious to my scrutiny.

Dew's ears were pricked, his eyes bright as Addie kept twinkling her fingers against his lower lip. She let him win a few, sacrificing slobbery fingers to keep him happy. She'd poke his nose, wobble his lower lip, gently pinch some of his nose and then laugh when he managed to lip at her fingers. My horse was happy as a clam, playing one of his favorite games with a willing and enthusiastic participant.

Addie laughed. "Ah! You got me. I need my fingers back, please. Yep, you got 'em! Now you don't. Nope. Nope. Yep!" She laughed again, the sound rich and filling the space. She had an amazing laugh, loud and unashamed, as if laughing were like oxygen for her. Addie offered Dewey another Life Saver. "Last one. Sugar free or not, nobody needs that many peppermints." She fished another one from the bag, popped it into her mouth then kissed the side of his nose. Addie seemed to finally register that I was watching, and turned to me, leaning against Dewey's shoulder. "He's such a hilarious goofball. Like you can tell that he's just having such a great time and there's no malice in him at all."

"Nope, not a bit. There's very few people he's met that he didn't like, but he really adores you."

"I am pretty adorable." That grin again, cheeky and dimpled, made my stomach tighten.

My automatic response fell from my mouth. "That you are." The moment I said those three words, I wanted to clap my hand over my mouth, scrabble in the air to take them back. Not because they weren't true, but because I was afraid to let her hear my confession.

The grin turned to a slow smile of pleasure. "How about another selfie?"

"For your social media?"

"I don't really use social media, except to see what other people are doing." She winked. "This one is for me." Addie positioned herself on the other side of Dewey, holding her phone out.

Dew nudged it with his nose and as he smeared Dew-snot on the screen, I shuffled in on his other side. Addie ducked under his neck, popping up barely two inches from me. "My arm's too short. Can you take it?"

"Sure." I managed to ignore the thud of my heart in response to her proximity. Addie ducked back to the other side and leaned in to kiss the side of Dewey's nose while I did the same on my side. Dew yawned—oh the boredom of being photographed—and I quickly snapped some photos.

Dewey raised his head and moved away to make friends with his hay feeder, leaving Addie and I in the same position but without a horse between us. I turned my head slowly, simultaneously hoping I wasn't going to bump into her mouth and then being disappointed when I didn't. My heart hammered and my mouth was so dry I wouldn't have been able to speak, even if I'd been able to think of what to say.

"This is like *Lady and the Tramp*," Addie blurted. "But with a horse instead of spaghetti."

"*Lady and the Tramp?*" I raised my eyebrows. "And which one am I?"

She exhaled a shaky laugh and backed up so we weren't inches from each other. But she was still so close I could smell the peppermint. Still so close that all it would take was the slightest movement and I could press my lips to hers, kiss her long and deep until we were both gasping for air. The corners of Addie's mouth turned up. "That's a question that doesn't have a correct answer, so I'm pleading the fifth." There was a hint of pink dusting her cheeks and neck.

I moved forward into the space Dew had vacated. "Really? No witty pun or comeback?" The low husky intimacy of my voice didn't surprise me at all. What did surprise me was the sudden intensity of my feelings.

Addie's eyes widened and I heard the crunch as she bit the peppermint. Dew's ears pricked and he abandoned his hay to snuffle her neck. Lucky. Addie pushed him away and I could see her nervous swallow. After an eternity she said, "No. I can't think of anything to say."

"I can think of plenty I want to say to you," I murmured, reaching for her. She didn't resist when I pulled her toward me.

But she did hesitate. "Caitlyn, about what I said yesterday morning. That admission. I don't want it to make things weird between us."

"Weird how?"

"Like an expectation, you know like oh hey we're both into ladies and here we are together…"

"No? What if I'm okay with an expectation?" This was so not a good idea. Actually, it was a great idea but perhaps not in our current location. I glanced around, noting nobody was around and that we also had a horse to shield us from outside view.

Her eyes went wide. "Oh. Well in that case…"

If we were quick, we could— I dismissed the idea. I didn't want to be quick. I wanted to be indulgent. Addie stood utterly still, eyes locked with mine, and her expression of want and acceptance broke the last of my resolve. I couldn't help myself, I had to touch her. She didn't move when I brought my hand up to touch her face, lightly stroking my fingertips along the line of her jaw. She didn't move when my thumb brushed the edge of her mouth.

But she did move when Wren's voice boomed from behind us. "Hey, that's where you are." I damned well moved too, cursing Wren under my breath as Addie and I jumped apart. My groom had the worst timing. She leaned over the stall door, her gaze moving between both of us. "Sorry, was I interrupting a…consult?" The question was sly, knowing, and she had her teeth in her lower lip as if forcibly restraining herself from saying anything further. Judging by the lip twitching, she was barely restraining a manic grin.

Addie's composure was admirable. She offered a smooth, "Not at all. I'm all done." She turned to me, her expression its usual calm, friendly one but with an underlying helplessness. "Hooves look great. No heat in any limbs and vitals are spot on as usual. He gets an A-plus."

All I could do was nod and mumble, "Great, thanks."

"I'll catch you both later." Addie slipped out of the stall, and Wren slipped in.

The moment she'd latched lower half-door, Wren spun around. "Holy shit. You two looked like you were about to devour each other."

"Mmm. Thanks for the interruption by the way."

Both hands came up, and her face melted from manic to conciliatory. "I'm *so* sorry, I'd already spoken before I realized I was interrupting whatever that was."

"I don't know what it was. I don't know what's going on. If anything actually is." It'd happened so quickly, been so unexpected that I hadn't thought. Just acted.

"Seems to me like something is going on. And anyone with eyes who's paying attention to you two would agree."

"Great. So it's totally obvious that I'm—" I broke off, not even knowing what I was, aside from acting like someone with a very neglected libido. "How can I go from being totally not friends to wanting to jump her bones?"

"Because Addie is great? And you're allowed to change your mind, Caitlyn. There's no rule stating that you gotta hang on to feelings just because you think you should."

I knew there was nothing wrong with upending long held notions, but this all felt sudden and confusing. "I know that. But why and how? Because she's nice to my horse and nice to me, all of a sudden I want us to be…" I trailed off, not even knowing exactly what I wanted to happen between us.

"Well why not? Isn't that as good a reason as any?" She leaned against the stall wall. "What are you holding on to? Has she apologized for back then?"

"Yes, and I believe her, and I think I've let it all go. I just don't need this right now."

"Friendship?"

"No. I mean yes. I mean it's just—" After a long pause I mumbled, "My stupid libido. She's *super* cute, all right? She's fun and funny and I like the way I feel when I'm around her, but the timing is awful and even if it wasn't I have no idea how we could sustain anything back home." Because of course my brain had gone there—I wasn't the fling type and the idea of me and Addie just having some fun and saying see you later wasn't something that interested me. "We live in different states and are both so ridiculously busy we barely manage our lives now. I need to put a lid on this or I'm going to lose all my focus because of a woman."

"You have the best focus of anyone I know. I don't think an attraction is going to get in the way of anything." The panic I felt at her use of *attraction* apparently wasn't as hidden as I'd have liked it to be. Wren laughed. "Yes, Caitlyn. Attraction. I've been watching you two make googly eyes at each other for weeks now. *And* I have never seen you so relaxed with someone so quickly."

"I have no idea what you're talking about," I said airily and not at all convincingly.

"Right." Wren sighed. "You two are either completely oblivious or just masters of trying to ignore the fucking obvious."

CHAPTER FOURTEEN

Addie

The whole team of riders, horses, grooms, management, and me had moved to a dressage-competition facility in Den Bosch, an hour outside of Rotterdam, for four weeks of training and team cohesion stuff before we left for Brazil. The venue was set up for long-term accommodation with small modular cabins in a row beside the horse stalls for those of us who didn't have huge horse trucks with living quarters that rivaled a four-star hotel.

My cabin was closest to the stalls, which was both a blessing and a curse. Blessing—close to the things I had to check on at all hours. Curse—everyone passed by on their way to the horses, and some of them didn't know the meaning of "Let the vet have an hour off the clock unless your horse is injured or dying."

While the others rarely troubled me and the only time I saw them was during my daily checks, Dakota Turner had quickly become the most demanding member of the team, stretching both my personal and professional patience to its limits. Not only did she manage to find me when I was working with other horses, but she'd developed a habit of knocking on my door to impart her opinions.

By the start of the third week everyone had settled in, the horses were working well and I'd managed to control my rampant thoughts about Caitlyn so they only occupied about twenty percent of my waking hours. Most of that twenty percent was thinking about our very-almost-a-kiss. How she'd pulled me toward her. The way she'd cupped my face, the slow caress of her thumb over my lips. And, of course, what might have happened if we hadn't been interrupted. That thought had kept me awake every night since it'd happened and if my soft arousal each morning was any indication—I'd probably been dreaming about it too.

The team had a meeting that didn't require my attendance, so with nothing on the agenda for the afternoon, I drove into town to do some shopping. Thanks to Google I'd found the two stores I wanted: a boutique to buy a dress and a pet supplies store. The last thing I'd expected to need in the Netherlands were either of those two things, but here we were.

The dress was for a team dinner at some fancy restaurant before we left for Rio, which I would have loved to have known about earlier so I could have packed a suitable outfit. Scrolling through various websites, I'd picked two dresses I thought might suit and sent a quick email to the boutique asking nicely if they'd hold them in my size. I was in the door and out again with a dress, clutch, jewelry and pair of matching shoes in twenty minutes. If only all clothes shopping was so easy. The pet store visit was just as smooth, and even after stopping for groceries and wine I was back at the dressage facility in less than two hours.

Judging by the people exiting the building, my timing was perfect. Caitlyn was heading toward the stalls, her face a mask of concentration. When she spotted me pulling bags from the car, she came over right away. "Hey. I wondered where you were."

"Hey yourself. I had some errands to run. How's everything?"

"All fine, just getting the dos and don'ts for Rio." With a smile she added, "There are a lot of don'ts."

"Oh? I might need you to be my Rio mentor then if you've now got all the inside information. Far more interestin' than reading my vet's information packet."

"Consider yourself mentored." Caitlyn pointed a thumb behind herself, in the direction of the stalls. "I'm just going to check Dewey. We think he's spiraled deep into cat withdrawals without Poffertje. With any luck some super friendly stray will come along and he can have a pal." She grinned. "It would be super irresponsible to go pick up a cat from a shelter for him, right?"

"Super irresponsible," I echoed.

"You want to come with me to break the news of no cat to him?"

"I can do better than that." I fumbled with the bags until I found the right one. "Here."

Caitlyn took the bag, holding it up as if she could see through the paper. "What's this?"

"A gift."

"Oh, thank you. I wasn't expecting anything." She dipped her hand into the bag and withdrew a dog toy. Her eyebrows creased together as she studied the item. "Um, thanks. It's...great." The forced politeness of her reaction was adorable.

Time to put her out of her misery. "It's not actually for you." I took it from her, tugging the rubber handles at both ends of the black and white cat. Or cat-ish. Given the toy was made of rubber, the shape was a little indeterminate. "It's for Dewey. Apparently robust enough to withstand even the chewiest of dog jaws, and no fluff or anything to cause trouble. Big enough that he can't swallow it, and no squeaker inside to cause a noise complaint. Perfect toy for a bored equine. I mean it's not a real cat, obviously but I thought it might be a decent stand-in."

Caitlyn laughed. "Well now I feel really stupid." She turned the toy over in her hands. "So you went out shopping, and you thought of us?"

"I did. Just a little something I thought Dewey might like. Wren mentioned yesterday he's started trying to get hold of the blanket buckles at his chest while in his stall, so I thought a toy might help keep that mouth busy when it doesn't have bits in it."

"That's so sweet and thoughtful. I love that you got Dew something. He's going to love it. He loves anything he's allowed to put in his mouth," she added, as if sensing I was about to ask how she knew.

"Great. Anything that keeps him happy makes me happy."

"Same," Caitlyn said quietly. Her expression turned inward for a moment before she seemed to remember I was there. She smiled, but it was an automatic kind of smile, as if her brain had triggered a cue for *Social interaction, smile*!

I touched her arm and felt the muscle tense under my hand. "What is it?"

"I..." She paused, swiped her tongue along her lower lip. "Uh, should probably go give this to him."

"No problem."

Caitlyn held up the cat. "Thanks for this. I'll let you know how it goes." She walked away, swinging the cat by a handle. I stared after her for a few moments then turned back to my shopping haul.

Dakota's knock and call of, "Addison?" at seven p.m. while I was preparing dinner added another straw to my metaphorical camel's back. I cringed internally at the sound of my full name. She was the only rider who did it and I had no idea why the shortened version, which I'd cheerfully and repeatedly said she could call me, was so offensive to her.

I opened the door a crack, not wanting her to see into my personal space which was admittedly a mess of partially unpacked clothes, folders and laptop resting on top of my unmade bed, tablet beside the stove and yet-to-be-washed dishes. In the dim light I could see she was, as usual, fully made up and dressed not in riding gear, but as if she were about to hit the clubs.

I offered a friendly, "Hi." Nothing more, nothing less. It was up to her to tell me why she needed me.

"Addison," she said again. "Can you please check Pierre's temperature? I'm not sure the previous reading was correct."

The previous reading taken less than an hour ago that was abso-fucking-lutely perfect? "There's nothing indicated and I see no need to check it again, and so soon. If you're concerned about his earlier perfectly normal temperature reading, then maybe you or Eleanor could take another and if it's anything outside the range of ninety-nine to one-hundred-one-point-five, then I'll be in his stall faster than you can say fever."

"But—"

"Dakota, there's no real reason to take the temperature of a horse that's displayed no signs of illness and again, had a perfectly normal temperature reading less than an hour ago."

She pouted at me and I was sure she thought the expression would change my mind. It did anything but. "Yes but Pierre is—"

"One of five horses under my care who are all equally important. Including the reserve," I added when she opened her mouth to give what I knew was a spiel about Pierre, The Only Horse On The Planet Who Mattered. A few nights ago she'd been on a call outside the stalls, which meant I'd overheard her mouthing off about the other three core horse and rider combinations, as well as the reserve horse and rider combo.

All the combinations absolutely deserved to be on the team but it burned to say they were all *equal*. Technically, I supposed they were equal. But the biased, and also realistic, part of me knew Dewey and Caitlyn outshone the rest of the team like she was a supernova and they were dying stars. But despite how I felt about Caitlyn, I wouldn't let anything skew my treatment of the other horses who weren't Dewey. Just because I had a raging crush on Caitlyn and wanted nothing more than to spend all of my time with her didn't mean the horses should get anything less than the best.

Dakota still hadn't responded. I raised my eyebrows at her and when she still didn't answer, smiled and said, "If you'll excuse me, I'm in the middle of cooking dinner. If you get a reading outside those limits I just mentioned, come back and I'll come right out and see him."

She offered a grudging, "Sure." She really was a caricature of the spoiled rich girl used to getting everything she asked for the moment she asked for it.

"Great. I'll see you in the morning." Because I was certain if she bothered checking the horse's temperature, it would be perfectly fine.

The knock at my door at a quarter to eight interrupted me washing up, which wasn't exactly a bad thing, but still set my pissed-off gauge to seven out of ten. What in the everlovin' name of Christ could Dakota Turner possibly want from me now? I was all for caution. All for covering all the bases. But given how long I'd been vetting, and the time I'd spent with these horses, I knew the only thing wrong with Pierre was his rider.

Calm blue oceans. Kittens. Dirty martinis. I threw middle fingers at the closed door in a childish attempt to make myself feel better then flung the door open, smoothing my expression to one of calm tranquility. I'd had oodles of practice at forcing my face to wear an expression that wasn't how I was feeling.

The person on my doorstep was definitely not Dakota.

Caitlyn offered a shy smile along with an awkward wave. "Hey. Sorry to interrupt your evening."

"You're not interrupting at all." Before my brain engaged, I blurted, "I thought you weren't you. I gave you double birds from behind the door. Sorry."

Her eyebrows bounced upward. "Oh. Well, I'm sure whoever you meant the middle fingers for deserved them." The shy smile turned sly. "So who was it?"

I hedged. "I probably shouldn't say." Dakota. Dakota. Dakota.

She studied me, her expression calm and watchful the way it got when she was turning something over before she spoke. It made me feel like she was somehow pulling the answer out of my head, and I tried to look as neutral as possible, not like a veterinarian who had an annoying client. The corners of her mouth edged up in a cheeky smile.

Caitlyn leaned in so she was inches away and whispered, "I'm pretty sure there's only one person around here who inspires that kind of response. Does your problem rhyme with Takota Durner?"

I let out a breath that sounded like a gurgly kind of choking sound. "Can I plead vet-client confidentiality?"

"You can, but your expression says everything." She leaned against the exterior wall, arms folded over her breasts. "It's fine. I've known her for a while and, yeah...I'm sorry for your pain." She grinned. "But it'll be over after Rio and then you never have to think about her again. Until maybe the World Equestrian Games."

"I hope so," I mumbled. "I'm just trying to give everyone the same treatment, keep everyone on the team happy and their horses healthy, but it seems she thinks team is spelled with *me*."

"T-E-M-E?" Caitlyn laughed. "Sounds right."

"Look, could we just forget I said anything about it?" I sounded like a strangled goat. "Total professionalism fail."

"You didn't say anything, not really. I prodded until you answered."

"True. But still." I cleared my throat. "You wanna come in?"

"Please. I didn't come here to admire the paint job." She peered at the wall. "Though it's quite nice."

Laughing, I ushered her inside. Her seeing my mess didn't bother me as it would for anyone else visiting. "How're you and Wren coping in the truck?"

"It's fine. We're used to sharing small living spaces when we're competing, though she keeps making noises about how much she's going to enjoy some personal space in Rio."

"If either of you ever want some time apart then feel free to use this place. I'm not in here much, too busy working." I grinned. "You riders are busting my butt."

"I'm pretty sure your butt's fine." She leaned backward as if checking. "Mhmm, it sure is. And sorry to keep you busy. If it's any consolation, we're all busy."

I fought down a blush at the butt-check. "It's fine, seriously. I was teasing. This kind of work is a five-star vacation."

"Ah, so you should be thanking me."

Laughing, I said, "I suppose I should." I indicated she should take a seat wherever she could find a spot.

She declined my offer of a drink and settled on the two-seater, shuffling to the side to make room for me. Everything in this space was cozy and comfortable, but tiny, and no matter how I sat on the couch we were right in each other's space. After a few moments of deliberation, I gave up trying to arrange myself and just sat comfortably. "You do get some downtime, right? Have you been out exploring? I've seen a little of the country, but I'd love to come back sometime to take a real vacation."

She nodded. "Yeah I do get breaks, like five minutes here and there, but I've never been one for vacations or sightseeing so it doesn't bother me."

"No? Why not?"

"Time mostly." Shrugging, Caitlyn added, "And sitting on a beach or at some fancy resort drinking by myself doesn't hold much appeal. I think I spend enough time away to trick my brain into thinking I'm vacationing. Plus there's always horses back home needing to be trained which gives me a dose of the guilts thinking about taking time off. I'm sure I'm the only one who's not going to hang around for the closing ceremony."

"Really? I thought you were a certified introvert so shouldn't a vacation alone appeal?"

Thankfully she seemed to have taken it in the joking manner I'd tried for, smiling as she answered, "Introvert, yes. Hermit, no. I make my employees take time off but when it comes to me I just can't do it. Feel too guilty."

"I feel guilty about days off doing nothing after I've had a weekend on call," I blurted in a clumsy attempt to maybe make her feel more at ease. "But I'm usually so wrecked I can't do anything but sleep and lounge around the house, despite my self-assurances that I'm definitely going to do housework, or cook, or learn a language or something." I touched her shoulder, relieved when she didn't recoil, and considered leaving my hand there. After a moment more of consideration, I pulled it away. "I think we do what we need to in order to live in a way that's comfortable."

"I suppose you're right." She shuffled backward on the couch and crossed her legs.

I peeked at those legs. Mmm and hmm. "So, what can I do for you? Given I checked on Sir Dewey two hours ago, and he was happily swinging that poor rubber cat around, I have to assume you're not here to chat about him."

"No, I'm not. And yeah, he's fine. We're all fine." Despite the verbal acknowledgment, she didn't seem fine exactly. Not un-fine, but…on edge.

"Hey," I murmured. "What's up? Are you really okay?"

"Yeah. I am, really," she added at my raised eyebrows. "I'm okay, but confused," Caitlyn clarified.

Clearly she wanted to discuss this confusion, so I didn't hesitate to ask, "How so?"

Her fingers played with the hem of her tee, twisting it around, picking at it. After a long pause she said, "I'm starting to feel like I've missed out on a lot in my pursuit of a dressage career. In my personal life, that is. I've *never* had that feeling before and it's kind of freaking me out feeling it now. I know where it's come from, but it doesn't make sense when you and I aren't even, you know. Together."

"Feeling what exactly?" I knew what I felt—a crushy kind of physical, mental, and emotional attraction with a healthy dose of lust on top. And I was sure she felt something along those lines.

Caitlyn wilted like a kid asked to stand up and read their assignment in front of the class. "Don't you know? Do I really have to try to find words for...this?" Her expression was pure *Help a gal out.*

She looked so adorably panicked and so earnest that the fun-loving part of me wanted to tease and draw her discomfort out. Just like I would have done as a kid. Just the way that'd upset her then. I shoved that idea aside and went full adult. "Words for what seems to me to be a strong mutual attraction developing between us?"

She exhaled. "Right. I think those are the words."

I smiled, trying to seem casual. "There's no pressure here, Caitlyn. No expectations, just seeing what's happening, right? I mean, we haven't even kissed. All this...whatever it is we're feeling could end up being a no-physical-attraction dud."

"That's a good point," Caitlyn murmured. She moved so quickly I would have been startled if I wasn't already in the "A kiss is happening very soon FOR SURE" mindset. Her hands moved to my waist, pulling me toward her. She lingered, her thumbs gently massaging my waist and as our eyes locked, she dipped her head to brush her nose against mine. Barely a heartbeat passed, and she kissed me. No hesitation. Soft at first, quiet and calm, as though testing if we fit together.

I knew we fit. I'd felt it the moment her lips had brushed mine as a sort of acceptance or rightness or whatever the hell people called it. It didn't matter what it was called, I just knew that kissing Caitlyn, having her hands stroking up and down my sides, my hands cupping her jaw made my pulse race and my stomach flutter and my...you get the picture. Along with the pleasurable sensation of a damned good kiss was an unexpected rush of emotion that we'd found this place together, finally.

There was a sweet tentativeness about her and I mustered all of my self-control to keep from pulling her on top of me, taking over and deepening the kiss. As much as I wanted to stroke my tongue against hers, to open my mouth and let her in, I also wanted Caitlyn to lead. My feelings had been simmering for over twenty years and I was certain of them. I needed her to be certain too.

The gentle, unhurried kiss built like kindling taking its time to light. Slow, slow and then fast. She groaned and I felt her lips part. I paused, waiting a heartbeat until the tip of her tongue slid over my lower lip. Felt like certainty to me. I clutched handfuls of her top, holding her close as her tongue lightly explored and found mine. If I'd realized this was what my first kiss with Caitlyn would be like, I probably would have made a move twenty-something years ago.

She smiled against my lips, then murmured, "It's really not a dud."

"Nope." After a shaky inhalation I felt somewhat composed. Or at least composed enough to ask, "What do we do about this not-dud then?"

Her answer was to kiss me again. And again. And again.

CHAPTER FIFTEEN

Caitlyn

After almost four intensive weeks, I felt like Dewey and I were set to peak at the Olympics with both our training and fitness. The other team members were similarly on target, with the exception of Dakota and Pierre who, at the start of the week, had troughed with their canter pirouettes. Pierre had been refusing to perform the movement and instead of pirouettes he got tighter and tighter in the back and neck and then stopped dead in the arena, despite Dakota and Ian's best efforts.

And Addie and I...well, we were existing in a kind of state that was neither peaking or troughing. Between riding, workouts, countless team meetings, uniform fittings, and managing my social media I barely had time to eat and sleep, let alone find time to spend time alone with Addie. She looked frazzled most days, and with trying to figure out if Pierre's training issues were physical, she was as busy as me. The fact we were both busy, that *that* was the reason we were struggling to find time and not that she regretted our quiet admission of our attraction to one another and our not-so-quiet kiss, made me feel better.

We'd still managed to find occasional moments to talk, or just hang out somewhere semi-private for ten minutes where she'd help me work on the stash of Blow Pops. Sometimes, but not sometimes enough, we checked again to make sure our attraction wasn't a dud and always found mutual agreement that nope, it was real. Addie kissed like kissing me was the most important thing in the world—a slow soft balance of lips and tongue, hands on my hips with fingers massaging, or on my face gently caressing. And every time we parted, she'd make the same sound of regret and satisfaction rolled into a moany sigh that made my stomach muscles tighten.

More than anything it felt like we were tiptoeing around, trying to find some neutral territory where we weren't three seconds from a hot make-out session. But with every passing day, the tiptoeing felt more and more like stomping. Something seemed inevitable but I had no idea what that something would be. I knew what I wanted it to be—the obvious progression to intimacy—but what might come after that was equal parts terrifying and exciting. After an eternity of consideration, I weighed up my fears and decided intimacy and all that came after was far preferable to no intimacy.

If I could make it through the final team dinner tonight then I might suggest we spend some time alone together afterward. The compulsory weekly team-bonding dinners had mostly had the desired effect. As much as Dakota could be called a team player that is. Dressage was an odd sport, where the definition of team results was actually your individual results counting toward your country's team tally. That mindset often made team cohesion tricky.

The first three dinners had been at small local restaurants, and this fourth and final one before we flew to Brazil in two days was somewhere fancy. I hoped the one good dress and heels I'd packed almost two months ago were suitable for fine dining. Mary ordered cars for us all and I'd heard them leave one by one as I readied myself and panicked about my dress, my makeup, my hair and if Addie would like what I was wearing. All those important things.

Wren finally told me to get on with it and herded me into the car. She jumped out as soon as it was stationary, mumbling something about needing a drink or five. The moment my feet were on the sidewalk I noticed Addie exiting the car in front.

Oh boy.

Her black cocktail dress looked like it'd been painted on. It dipped tastefully low to show a hint of cleavage that had me desperate to see the rest and clung to a body full of delicious curves. Instead of being up in its usual ponytail or braid, her hair fell loose almost to her shoulders in a shiny, straight curtain of red-brown. If I hadn't spent so long staring at her over the past few months, I may not have recognized her.

She turned slowly to face me and I saw the subtle movement of her head as she looked me up and down before she walked over. "Hey."

"Wow," I blurted before my brain caught up. I almost said more but thankfully managed to catch myself before I started drooling and blathering.

Her eyes went wide. "What?"

"You look absolutely incredible. Different. I mean good different. Great different. Really great different. So great." Okay, so I hadn't managed the not blathering.

"Oh, phew. I thought you were about to tell me I'd forgotten to zip my dress. Actually, wait a second." Her hand went to the left side of her ribs. "Nope, I don't need an adult to help me."

My eyes followed the hand checking just beside her breast. "Not at all. Just took me by surprise, that's all." She smelled incredible, like flowers and spice and it took every bit of willpower not to lean in and lightly brush my nose along her neck to inhale the scent of her.

Her mouth quirked knowingly. "Ah yes. You don't recognize me out of dirty boots and pants and covered in assorted horse grime, with my hair going in a hundred directions."

"Pretty much that, yes," I admitted. "Sorry. I just didn't realize you liked…" I couldn't figure out how to describe what I saw, so opted for a vague gesture.

Her dimples flashed. "Wearing clean clothes? Being freshly showered? Smelling like something other than horse shit, horse sweat and basically every equine fluid imaginable mixed with human sweat?"

All of that yes, not that any of it bothered me, but I couldn't articulate. I cleared my throat and managed, "Dresses."

"Ahh." The grin relaxed into a slow smile. "I do. If you stick around, you might find I like a lot of things you wouldn't expect. And probably a few things you would."

"Well, I love surprises and this is definitely one of the better ones." My gaze wandered downward. Who knew that underneath her usual attire of cargo pants and polo shirt was *that* body. And those legs. The scars from her cross-country accident were faded but still obvious and I paused a moment to take them in. Then my attention wandered. Heels. Maybe three-inch if her almost-equal height was any indication. And they did things to her legs that made my stomach twist with both nervousness and excitement. My libido, which had been cruising along happily with her dressed in everyday work clothes, jumped in a rocket ship and went skyward.

"Glad to hear it," she murmured. "And how are you? Sorry, I forgot my manners. Too busy losin' my mind over how incredible you look." That indulgent gaze, as if she were committing me to memory, made my skin feel as if it were on fire.

"I know the feeling." After a long, slow inhalation I felt controlled enough to continue, "And I'm great. Do we really have to do this? Now I just want to find a cozy restaurant somewhere and have dinner with only you." And then plenty of things afterward that were not safe to verbalize unless I wanted to skip dinner altogether.

"That would be my Plan A too, but unfortunately we're stuck with Plan B—make eyes at each other all night and hope nobody notices." She grinned. "Well, nobody but Wren who apparently notices everything if her sly looks and offhanded comments are any indication."

"Does that bother you? Is *us* a problem? I mean, pretty much everyone on the Big Tour circuit is either hooking up with someone else on the circuit or legally attached to them." I smiled wryly. "Except me."

"No, us isn't a problem. It is the opposite of a problem. And technically I'm part of the circuit, so I'm sorry to say you're no special snowflake, just hookin' up like everyone else."

"We're not hooking up," I pointed out, and saying it aloud made me realize just how much I wanted it to not be the case.

"No," Addie mused. "We aren't. Yet…" Then as if she hadn't just said something that had my skin tingling, she took my elbow and turned me toward the restaurant door. "Ready for some team bonding?"

"As I'll ever be. Which isn't very much."

"No?" Addie's smile was naughty, which did nothing for the excitement fluttering around my body. "Well I'm very into bond… ing."

I tried for a *Did you really have to say that now?* expression but had the feeling I just looked helpless.

Dakota's approach was to flirt outrageously with Addie, despite the fact Addie wasn't inviting it, and Dakota was married to her much-older-than-her oil-tycoon husband as she liked to tell everyone regularly. I wondered if she thought she and her horse might receive some sort of preferential treatment as a result of said flirting. Wren had been wrangled into a seat at the other end of the table, leaving me sandwiched between Mary and Ian like some goody-two-shoes sitting with the teachers. Never great at small talk or idle chat, I tried to keep my face from falling into resting-bitch face, which was its unfortunate default expression when I was trying hard to pay attention.

Addie, seated directly opposite, glanced my way occasionally in between being her usual friendly self with those around her. She managed to be interactive and friendly yet gave Dakota no leeway with her flirting. A fact Dakota didn't seem to recognize if her constant attempts were any indication. Every now and then Addie would catch my eye, and either wink or make an expression that was clearly *Can you believe this woman?*

Yes, Addie. I certainly can believe that woman.

The others talked mostly among themselves and Ian. That left me to a riveting conversation with a tipsy Mary. I lost count of how often she whispered that I shouldn't tell the others but I was their big hope for an individual medal. Thanks, Mary, because that doesn't add to my pile of pressure *at all*… I'd employed my nod, smile, and murmured "I'll do my best" routine for the third time when something cool touched my calf.

I almost jerked my leg away until I realized it was Addie. Or rather the incredibly sexy heel attached to Addie's foot. Her look was deliberately innocent, and having clearly confirmed that her foot had met its intended target, she kept sliding it up and down my calf. The whole time her foot caressed my leg, she kept up a conversation that bounced between Dakota and the others around her. Talent.

With one elbow propped on the table she played with her drop earring, ran a forefinger along her jaw…down her neck…across her collarbone. I gulped a mouthful of wine and managed to avert my eyes before I embarrassed myself. I managed to keep them averted for about five seconds, before they were pulled back to her blatant display of sexuality. A rush of heat ran down my spine and spread outward at the sensation of her foot sliding up and under my dress to caress the soft skin just above my knee. Ahem.

If it wasn't pre-dessert and still impolite to bail I probably would have shot Addie a very pointed look and politely made my excuses. Stupid social conventions. For now it was more small talk paired with excellent food and wine. I supposed it could have been worse. I could have been sitting next to Dakota.

Once the last plates had been cleared, the group relaxed into drinking mode and plans were being made to check out some of the local bars. Mary reminded everyone of their obligations, and our flights to Brazil the day after tomorrow. It probably would have been more effective and less hypocritical if not for the bottle of Moët she'd consumed.

By the time it seemed things might finally move on around nine thirty p.m. I was still mostly sober, and watching everyone get drunker had become tedious. But Addie was still at the table and I was not leaving before she did. Or without her, a little part of my brain helpfully added.

Addie's quiet, "Excuse me" cut through the white noise of chatter. She stood, gave me a look, then walked off in the direction of the ladies' room. I watched her departure, admired the sensual roll of her hips as she made her way through the restaurant, and hoped fervently that my face didn't look as hot as it felt.

After a minute, I excused myself too, ignoring Wren's arm flick as I passed her. Only one stall of the bathroom was occupied, by Addie obviously, and the moment the bathroom door had closed behind me I felt a sudden wave of uncertainty. What if I was mistaking all this for my own wishful, lustful thinking? What if here and now was all she wanted?

Feeling conspicuous about just standing around in the ladies' room, I washed my hands while studying myself in the mirror. A pang of anxiety flared, that familiar kind that always came whenever I thought about romance, intimacy, sharing myself with someone. The anxiety fueled by the fear that I wouldn't ever be enough, that they'd realize my selfish priorities left little room for anything or anyone else.

The toilet flushed and the door behind me opened, and I raised my eyes to find Addie and that dress in the mirror. Her smile was slow, her gaze sliding lazily downward to check out things below my waist.

I turned. "Enjoying all the attention from Dakota?"

"Not at all." She gently pushed into my personal space and washed her hands. "It's not attention from the person I want." After a pause, she smiled at me, her expression both knowing and incredulous. "Are you jealous?"

"No," I said immediately. "I'm amused."

"Good. There's nothing to be jealous about." Her voice was a low, lazy drawl that made me think of honey trickling from a spoon. "Because I don't want her. Not at all."

Excitement pushed that anxiety aside and I fought to moderate my voice so it didn't sound rushed and squeaky. "Who do you want?"

"You *really* have to ask me that?" She took a step forward until we were toe to toe. One of Addie's arms snaked around my waist, holding me in place.

"No. I just want to hear you say it." Needed to hear it and have it out in the world where I'd know it to be true.

"You, Caitlyn. It's only ever been you." Addie's fingertip traced the bare skin of my chest, dipping lower until it skimmed the neckline of my dress. "The day we saw each other again for the first time since Pony Club, you asked me why I'd pushed you into the water trough." She smiled. "I realized just now that I never answered you."

"You didn't? Honestly I'd forgotten I'd asked that. So," I prompted. "Why did you do it?"

"Because I wanted to see your boobs through your clinging wet shirt."

"I see. And did you see what you wanted to?"

"Yes."

"And did you like what you saw?"

"Yes."

I stepped even closer until out bodies lightly touched. "I'd imagine they've filled out a little since then."

Addie's tongue flashed out to swipe over her lower lip. "They have," she whispered, those two words a hoarse, strained admission. "Quite a lot and quite well in fact."

"Would you like to see them again?" My boldness surprised me. Normally I'd have waited for the other woman to make the move, never pushing until I was entirely sure of the answer. But her undisguised want not only made me certain and pushed away all my fear, but had my insides turning liquid with need.

"I would, very much. But this time I don't want it to be sneaky." Addie drew a finger along my collarbone. "I want you to show me."

I sucked in a sharp breath. The implication of the words, that delicate knowing touch, hit me like a freight train. Then Addie's lips were on mine, a furious, possessive kiss that stole my breath. A teasing tongue, the gentlest nip of teeth. Some distantly rational part of me recognized we were in a bathroom where anyone could walk in, and that doing what I most wanted wasn't a good idea. But that thought wasn't enough to make me want to stop. I pulled Addie into the stall furthest from the sink and locked the door, but before I could do anything, she'd spun me around and pushed me backward. A thigh slid between mine and her body pressed me to the wall. I clutched her back, groaning as she sucked my neck.

Addie stilled. "Too far?" she whispered.

"Not far enough." I leaned in and kissed her again, slicking my tongue along her lower lip.

She opened her mouth to me and for a second I didn't know what to do. My whole life was about reading nuance, feeling for things that weren't visible, understanding rhythm and balance. But right now I was utterly lost. Luckily, Addie knew exactly how to lead. She drew me in, stroked my tongue with hers and kissed me so deeply I felt like I was falling.

Addie pulled away first, inhaling a sharp breath that didn't help to steady her voice. "I think we should go."

I nodded my agreement, unable to find words with all the thoughts and sensations flooding me.

The two words she spoke made me quiver. "Where to?"

"Unless you want to have sex on a very narrow bunk bed and risk Wren bursting in at any time, it'll have to be your place."

"Narrow bunk, yes. Interruption, no. I want you all to myself until the morning."

I had to swallow before I could answer, "Good. Then take me to bed."

CHAPTER SIXTEEN

Addie

Thankfully nobody batted an eyelid when Caitlyn and I made our excuses and slipped out in the middle of post-dinner drinks. Actually, Dakota did, but it was more of a drunk eyelash fluttering in my direction than an *I know you're sneaking away to have sex* look. Wren's pointed look, however, was just that—a smug, sly nod coupled with a knowing wink at both Caitlyn and me.

The moment we'd rounded the corner out of sight, Caitlyn took my hand. She twined our fingers together, her grip firm as if she was afraid I'd disappear and yet at the same time there was softness in the touch. Caitlyn pulled me to a stop at the host stand and had a quick conversation with the young woman about ordering a car.

We were silent as we exited the restaurant and she let her fingers carry a conversation for her. The way she kept moving her thumb along mine and the gentle squeeze of her fingertips made my nerves tingle, and by the time we were standing on the sidewalk I felt entirely undone.

Caitlyn peered down the street. "Car should be here in five minutes. Too long," she murmured.

"You can do a lot in five minutes..."

"Yes, you can," she agreed. Leaning in, she whispered against my ear, "Unfortunately, what I want to do to you might get us arrested for public indecency." Her hand slid down my back, stopping just above my ass.

My body was still humming from our kiss in the bathroom and this touch, her casual words, sent a shudder down my spine. "If you're trying to stop us doing things that might get us arrested, then maybe we shouldn't touch. It'll only lead to…things." I backed up a step and stayed there until the car arrived.

Caitlyn and I sat at opposite ends of the rear seat and in the dim light I could barely make out her expression. I stared out the window as we drove, trying and failing to grasp the thoughts zinging around my brain. I'd been thinking about taking Caitlyn to bed for so long and now that it was on my doorstep, I realized anxiety was knocking as well.

The light from the small office at the far end of the box stalls was on—there were two horse-savvy security guards on night watch—and one of them peeked out the door as we walked past. Apparently satisfied he knew who we were, he waved and popped back inside.

"Do you want to look in on Dewey?" I asked. I really didn't want to delay, but I also knew where Caitlyn's priorities lay.

She glanced at the dark building. "It's fine. But thanks. They haven't called to say anything's amiss and Wren will check him when she comes home."

Caitlyn stood behind me on the tiny porch as I searched through my clutch for the key. And searched. And searched. The anxiety of being unable to find what I needed coupled with the press of her against my back and the barely-there touch of her lips on my neck and shoulders had my hands trembling, and I couldn't focus on the basic task. When her hands wandered down my stomach, I decided I'd better do something about finding the key before this got completely out of hand. I snatched a handful of stuff from the bag. Phew. "Got it," I said inanely.

"Good," she said. Then a longer kiss to my neck as I pushed the key into the lock. "I was about to give the security guys a peep show," Caitlyn mumbled against my skin.

It was all I could do to open the door and usher her inside. I locked the door again and when I turned around Caitlyn was a breath away from me. "Are we really doing this?" she quietly asked.

"Yes, I think we are. If you're sure." I paused to give her every opportunity to tell me she didn't want this, that she wanted to slow down and back up a step. She did anything but. Gripping my hip with one hand and my arm with the other, she pulled me to her and kissed me. My anxiety fled, replaced by excitement as she let me know just how much she wanted *this*.

If I'd thought she was hungry before, she was ravenous now. She was a little taller than me, but not stronger and she let out a squeak of surprise when I pushed her backward until she was against the wall. The bed was too far away—we could get there later. Right now I just had to have her. I knelt and pushed her dress up to mid-thigh, kissing my way up her leg until I was too impeded by fabric to go any higher. Her breathing rasped out, loud and erratic, and a restless hand tangled in my hair.

Caitlyn helped me yank down her panties, kicking them away before pulling my hands to her skin. If my grip on her thighs was too rough and my mouth too hungry, she didn't tell me to stop. Instead, she kept urging me on with barely coherent words and frantic hands. Her leg was slung over my shoulder, the heel of her shoe digging into my back as I slicked my tongue through her heat. She was completely bare of hair and the sensation of smooth, warm skin against my lips made my stomach tighten with need.

Caitlyn's breathing hitched and grew shallow as I sucked her clit, and she took a fistful of my hair, guiding me to press my mouth more firmly against her. I took my time exploring her, tasting her and with every sweep of tongue and touch of lips her muscles grew tighter, her breathing even shallower. She exhaled a disjointed, gasping, "I—yes, that's…yes…there."

I tried desperately to focus on her pleasure, on giving her what she wanted and not the torturous pressure between my thighs. The problem, of course, was that Caitlyn's quivering and moaning had my arousal building until it was hard to concentrate on the delicious woman I had in my mouth. Her head hit the wall with a soft thud and she hissed out something that was either pain or pleasure. The flood of wet heat in my mouth reassured me it wasn't the former. The grip on my hair tightened.

"Mercy," she begged. "Please."

I wiped my mouth on her inner thigh and couldn't help going back to place a lingering kiss against her wetness. She twitched and pushed me away, exhaling a moan. I stood, but before I could press my body to hers, she placed a hand on my shoulder to keep me in place. Caitlyn's grin was pure devil as she reached behind to unzip her dress and unfasten her bra. She pulled the garments from her shoulders and let them fall, leaving her utterly naked.

Caitlyn unclothed left me incoherent. I managed a kind of squeaky gurgle then a moany kind of gasp which she thankfully seemed to take for what I was trying to say, which was something along the lines of "You're gorgeous, I'm speechless." Her mouth turned upward in knowing smile as I let my eyes wander.

She was long and lean, supple and muscular from so many hours on horses, with endless legs, small firm breasts and a wondrous landscape of curves and swells. She had an intoxicating combination of confidence and an obvious vulnerability, as if she truly didn't understand just how much I wanted her. Just looking at her had my stomach quivering with anticipation, my skin goose pimpling.

Caitlyn toed out of her heels which brought us almost eye-level. "Now," she murmured, "I believe I said take me to bed, not to the wall."

"Okay." I had to swallow and after an eternity of trying to find something sexy, something clever, got out a husky and not-at-all-clever, "I want you to sit on my face."

Her mouth quirked. "Oh really? I thought maybe you could sit on mine." The tip of her forefinger traced a line from the base of my throat to my navel. "It's been a while since you've...ridden anything, hasn't it?"

I sucked in a sharp breath at the sensation of that same finger moving lower until it moved under my dress and, through the fabric of my panties, brushed over my clit. I stated the obvious. "That's not what I meant."

"No?" She pushed fabric aside and slipped lower, teasing me before coming back up to slide over my clit again with slow, deliberate strokes. Her touch was that perfect pressure of firm yet light that sent heat rolling through me. "Still, I think you should go first." A firmer stroke, a second finger teasing my entrance. "I've been thinking about tasting you, about you coming in my mouth all night, *and* you've already had your mouth on me, so I think it's only fair that now I get what I want."

It took every ounce of willpower to not melt into a puddle of helplessness. This dynamic was exciting, intoxicating—commanding Caitlyn was sexy as hell and it was all I could do to not spread my legs and beg her to fuck me senseless. But I wanted it to last, wanted to draw out our pleasure for as long as I could, which honestly probably wasn't going to be that long. I nodded. "One condition."

"What's that?"

"No more puns about riding." I nuzzled her neck. "I don't want to think about horses, or work or anything except making you come until the sun comes up."

"Deal." Caitlyn took my chin in a gentle grip, turned my face back to her and kissed me with such intensity I thought my knees would give out. I fumbled with the zip under my armpit until she took over. Caitlyn unzipped my dress, her knuckles brushing over my ribs, which sent me into a paroxysm of squirms. She stilled her hands. "Ticklish?"

"Mhmm. Very." My abdominals tensed, waiting for her to take advantage of the information.

Instead, she gave me a teasing smile. "Oh, I could have so much fun with that." Before I could answer she dipped her head and resumed our knee-weakening kiss. As we kissed, Caitlyn unfastened my bra, then apparently deciding it was too much effort at that moment to break contact to remove my clothing properly, pulled straps and fabric from my shoulders, then reached down to yank the dress up over my hips so I could slide my panties down. Her hands came up to cup my bare breasts, fingers teasing my nipples as her tongue slid against mine with languid pleasure.

I managed to grip her hips and pull her to the bed, and she twisted us so she fell on her back with me on top of her. My dress was still bunched around my hips, and the sight of Caitlyn trying frantically to wrest it up and off sent a shudder of desire rippling through me. She was always so controlled, so calm, and this desperate side of her was so damned sexy.

"Wait, just wait," I murmured, gently pushing her hands away. I managed to remove my dress and she lay on her back, legs twisting restlessly in the sheets as I settled astride her hips.

I took a moment to just look. To indulge. As I studied the exquisite naked form in front of me, Caitlyn's hands slid to my ass, pulling me forward until I lay on top of her. Our foreplay was intense and consuming, playful and passionate, and with every touch and kiss and look and gasped-out word my arousal grew until it felt unbearable. She found the spots that made me beg her to linger there a little longer. I found the spots that made her twitch and moan. When I was clumsy, she was certain. When she fumbled, my touch was steady and sure.

Caitlyn guided me up her body until I was straddling her shoulders, then pulled me down to her face. The first touch of her tongue was a light flick against my clit that sent a pulse of desire through me. My bed had no headboard and with nothing to grab, I had to press my hands against the wall for balance. My thighs trembled as Caitlyn's lips closed around me, sucking until I thought I might collapse. The touch of her lips and tongue were light as her hands roamed my torso and deliberately avoided my ticklish places. She teased my nipples, stroked up and down my back, and throughout it all she kept up her unrelenting attention to my clit.

Both hands slid down my back, over my ass and then disappeared from my body. A moment later I felt her gasp against me and the unmistakable jerk of her body underneath mine, and I knew exactly what she was doing. I reached backward, trying to find her hands. "Don't you dare touch yourself," I gasped, pulling one hand up to kiss her palm. "That climax is mine." I sucked her fingers into my mouth, tasting her for as long as I dared before pressing that hand against my breast and using her fingers to tease my nipple. She groaned against me, sending ripples of heat down my legs. Caitlyn's other hand slid upward to grip my ass, holding me against her mouth.

Her tongue was slow and soft, building my climax languorously, and at another time I would have begged her to keep at that sweet torture. But I couldn't stand it, couldn't wait. "Just a little harder, faster...please."

Both tempo and speed changed so suddenly that the climax hovering just out of reach jumped away in fright. Groaning with frustration and the burning arousal that just wasn't...quite...there, I offered a helpless suggestion. "Maybe a little less harder and faster?"

Her laughter was so sudden and unexpected that I burst into giggles with her. Until she kept laughing while trying to keep her tongue on my clit and her mouth on my labia. The vibration against me brought my climax speed-walking back. "Keep that laughter up," I mumbled, "and I'm going to come in your mouth."

She said something I didn't quite catch, but the way she'd said it made me think that was exactly what she wanted. Caitlyn eased back, tongue and lips working together until I built to a breaking point. Wanting to keep the sensation going, I tried to hold on just a little longer. But I made the mistake of looking down at her. Our eyes met and I had a moment of such intense connection that my orgasm rose swift and hard. I fell forward, catching myself against the wall as she carried me through my climax with a soft, warm tongue and gentle hands.

The burning heat came back to a slow simmer and I clumsily disengaged myself, trying not to kneel on her arm. Caitlyn didn't help one bit, her mouth exploring the insides of my thighs as I tried to move away so I could do what I most desired. When I'd finally extricated myself, I lay full length on top of her and almost immediately she lifted her hips to press herself against me. The slippery arousal against my thigh left me with no doubt as to what she desired. Sliding my hand between us, I found her heat and the landmark I most wanted. Her clit was swollen and when I circled it with my fingers she buried her face in my shoulder, her teeth grazing my skin.

Caitlyn stayed there, pressing open-mouthed kisses to my shoulder and neck, lightly sucking, occasionally biting as I played against her. The fact she was enjoying it was obvious. But equally obvious was the fact that she wasn't going to climax any time soon with what I was doing. I tried different pressure, different movement, different spots but still felt as if I wasn't quite hitting the mark. The more time passed, the more I realized I just wasn't getting it, wasn't getting what she wanted, and the uncertainty made me self-conscious, which made me miss the mark even more.

I paused, inhaling a shaky breath. "Okay. Time out." Kissing her, I let my tongue speak for me, hinting at what I wanted. "Maybe…" Caitlyn bit down lightly on my lower lip. Game on.

I kissed my way down her neck, sucked her collarbone, played my tongue over her nipples. They were so delicious that I lingered for a while longer before I traced my tongue down the center of her stomach and over the soft bare skin above her clit. Caitlyn gripped my wrist, her nails digging into skin as she lifted her hips up to meet me. I waited for a heartbeat before I took her in my mouth again. Caitlyn spread her legs wider, inviting me in, and I accepted. Settling an arm under her thigh I pulled her closer to me as I revisited the landscapes I'd briefly touristed before. She was intoxicating and I was drunk on the taste and scent of her.

Caitlyn fumbled her hand over my shoulder, partway down my bicep. "I want…I want…"

I raised my hand to find hers. "What is it?"

She took my hand and briefly guided my fingers to my lips before she brought that hand down between her legs. Caitlyn's fingers curled over the back of mine, pressing my fingers against her entrance. I bit back a moan. "You want me to fuck you?"

She managed a jerky nod and when I slid inside her she tightened around me. Her vocalization was a frantic, begging, "Oh my God, yes, yes."

When she asked me for more and harder I gave it to her. When she asked me to keep licking her, keep fucking her, just like that, don't stop…there, please, I followed her until I felt the unmistakable clench and flutter around my fingers. Caitlyn had a hand over her mouth but it did little to muffle the sounds of her orgasm. Her other hand moved erratically over her torso, over my head and neck until she stopped twitching, and relaxed into the bed. She reached for my hand again, kissed the side of my thumb, my palm, each fingertip.

I rested my head against her thigh and tried to fight the overwhelming rush of emotion. It felt like I'd been pulled apart and put back together again, made better somehow, even though I hadn't felt broken before. I buried my face in the soft, smooth skin of her inner thigh and tried not to cry.

We lay like that for some time until I'd recovered my faculties and lost some of that desperate arousal that'd been making me dumb with desire. Some of. I moved back up the bed to lie beside her and slung my leg over hers, reaching to cover us with the sheet. Caitlyn gripped my hip and pulled me closer and we stayed pressed together, just being with each other. She broke the easy silence first. "So was it everything your teen self imagined?"

I laughed. "Oh no no. I don't think I ever imagined anything quite like *that* when I was a kid. My imaginings were more chaste kisses and cuddles. Maybe a butt grope if I was feeling naughty." I kissed her exposed shoulder, her neck. "I was *not* sexually precocious at all. I think my head would have exploded if I'd imagined anything like what we just did."

Caitlyn propped herself up on an elbow. "You never read any women-loving-women books as a kid?"

"Oh shit, no. Nooo. I wouldn't have even known where to find that stuff, and bringing that into my house? Big no way." I traced my fingers up and down her side. "Probably would have given me an unrealistic expectation anyway."

"How so?"

"Have you ever noticed in books and movies there's never any fumbling or nervousness or people taking time to climax because they can't quite get in sync?"

"I have noticed that." She raised an eyebrow at me, and her question came out mock-haughty. "What are you saying?"

Dammit. "I…never mind."

"Uh-uh, no way, you can't slip away that easily. Ve haf vays of makink you talk!" One hand slid up my thigh, over my hip and along my side.

I tensed. "You wouldn't."

"Why wouldn't I?" Her fingers played over my ribs—not roughly enough to make me freak out at an imminent tickle attack, but still enough to make me desperate to get away. I squirmed and jolted and laughed and squealed and tried to get free of her fingers. The moment

I'd flipped onto my back she took the opportunity to pin me to the bed with her thighs on either side of my hips and her hands lightly holding my wrists to the bed.

"I surrender," I panted.

Caitlyn stopped instantly and flashed me an angelic smile. "Good. You were saying?"

She had me. I cleared my throat. "I'm sayin' that we got there in the end and it was magnificent. But I was embarrassingly clumsy and I sure hope you'll give me another chance."

"You weren't clumsy, far from it." Caitlyn dipped her head, hovering a whisper away from my lips. "But I thought you'd never ask."

CHAPTER SEVENTEEN

Caitlyn

When my phone chimed its normal alarm at five thirty a.m. I leaned over the bed and fumbled for my purse, which I thought had landed around there when we'd been frantically undressing last night. Last night. A slow roll of excitement at the memory made my stomach turn over. My phone wasn't by the bed, and it was then I realized I'd left my purse on the coffee table. I untangled myself from limbs and sheets and tried to get my bearings in an unfamiliar space in the early morning light.

"S'that?" Addie mumbled. The bed shifted and a more coherent question of, "What time is it?"

I silenced the alarm. "Five thirty."

"Mmph, early. Too early for you to be riding. Are you leaving before your carriage turns into a pumpkin?"

I laughed. "Not quite, but I do have to get back to the truck."

"Why? Nooo, come back to bed."

I gave in and slipped back under the covers. Just for a few minutes. "Because I'm obsessed with taking my contraceptive at the same every day for maximum effectiveness and minimum horror."

"Oh." Addie pressed herself to my back, her skin warm and soft. She leaned in close and kissed the side of my neck, my jaw. Her voice was low and amused. "I'm not sure if you know this, but you don't have

to worry about that with me. I promise you're okay after you and I…"
She gently sucked my neck. "You know."

Laughing I rolled over and pushed her until she fell backward to
the bed with me on top of her. I dragged the sheet up to cover us.
"Ha-ha. I might not be a super-smart veterinarian but I *am* aware of
the basics of reproduction. I spend a large chunk of my life in front of
crowds wearing skin-tight white breeches and trying to avoid camel
toe. Add a period and you have a potential match made in hell. So I
choose no periods, thank you very much."

"Mmm. Sounds reasonable." Addie snuggled into me, her face
against my neck. She kissed my skin, lingering to brush her lips along
my jaw. "Is an alarm gonna go off in the middle of the night in Brazil
when you're in bed with me while you're adjusting your pill time? Just
so I can be prepared and tell myself I haven't just had a call for a sick
horse and need to spring out of bed."

In Brazil…when you're in bed with me. The implications of
sleeping with her again rushed toward me at a million miles an hour.
So many pros but also, so many cons. Her wandering hands and lips
weren't helping my objectivity. A knock at the door stopped me before
I could say anything.

Addie scrambled from underneath me. "Just a minute!" she called.

I had a few seconds to admire her and all that I'd had hours to
enjoy last night—the soft fullness of her breasts, the tight curve of her
ass and her womanly shape blending with hints of muscle—before she
snatched a robe from the hook outside the bathroom door. I didn't
know whether to hide under the covers, in the tiny bathroom or just
sink to the floor and hope whoever was at the door didn't see me. After
a moment's deliberation I pulled the covers over myself and sat up. I
wasn't ashamed and I wasn't going to hide.

The knocking got louder and more obnoxiously insistent and
Addie's muttered, "Dammit" was quickly followed by, "I'm coming!"

The moment Addie opened the door, a familiar voice laughingly
said, "I am so sorry to have interrupted that."

"Wren," Addie breathed. She carefully kept the door just open and
herself angled in such a way that wouldn't allow anyone to see into her
cabin. "Thank God, I thought you were— Never mind."

Wren laughed. "You're safe." She passed a bag through the door.
"Thought I'd drop off some clothes so Caitlyn doesn't have to skulk
back to the truck in last night's dress and risk everyone knowing what
you two got up to last night." Wren's hand snuck through the gap,
waving cheerily. "Morning, boss. See you soon."

Once the door had closed again, I threw the covers back and swung my legs to the floor. "Oh my God. It hadn't even occurred to me about getting back this morning."

Addie set the bag on the end of the bed. "You sure won the groom lottery."

"I really did. She's more like a sister or friend than an employee." Wren was even so attuned to my routine that at the top of the bag was a small package. I popped a pill into my mouth and collected last night's clothing from the floor.

Addie watched me for a few seconds before quietly asking, "You want coffee or breakfast?"

"I really shouldn't, but thanks. I'm up now and I have stuff to do, and—" I flailed desperately for more truths because I really didn't want to go. But staying now would just make it even harder for me to leave her. "I need to pack up, clean the truck so it's ready to hand back and make sure Dew's ready for his big trip tomorrow." Tomorrow. When we would go to Brazil. For the Olympics. The thought filled my stomach with the good kind of excited fluttering.

I'd been trying so hard not to focus on that part of what we were doing, to just act like we were preparing for any big competition, but now that we were about to leave I could allow myself some of that excitement where it wouldn't get in the way of things. Once we arrived in Rio I would have to set aside everything except what I was about to do. Which meant setting *this* aside too. The thought turned some of my excitement into dread.

Addie's nod was thoughtful. "Mmm, true. I guess I should do some work too. Kinda got a big event coming up." Her eyes wandered lazily over my body as if absorbing parts of me into her consciousness. "I gotta say, you gettin' dressed again is criminal."

"Sorry about that." I shrugged into a top and Addie stepped forward to pull my hair carefully up through the neckline. After fumbling for a while to get my hair in order—no mean feat given my general dishevelment after last night—I gave up and just wrapped it around itself in an impersonation of a bun and hoped it'd stay for the walk back to my truck.

Addie nabbed a hair tie from the coffee table. "Here."

"Thanks." I secured my hair, then stuffed last night's clothes, heels and purse into Wren's bag. "So…"

"So," Addie echoed, tucking her hands into the pockets of her robe. "I'll just come out and say it. Last night, early this morning was incredible. And I recognize that the timing right now is shit, but I'm up for more of that, and more of us getting to know one another."

"The timing really is shit," I agreed. Then I said something stupid. "Maybe sleeping together was a mistake."

Her eyebrows peaked. "A mistake?"

"Not a mistake," I amended quickly. "Just maybe not the right time."

Addie bit her lip, grinned. "Even if it was a mistake, I'm happy to make the same mistake again."

"Addie…" I said quietly. "You're right, it was incredible. But I *really* don't need the very tempting distraction of you right now. This is the biggest moment of my life, one I've sacrificed a lot for, one that others have sacrificed and supported me for. And if I mess it up because I'm too busy sneaking off with you, or thinking about sneaking off, then I let everyone down—my family, my sponsors, everyone who donated money so I could get here, my coaches, Dewey and myself."

Her expression relaxed into understanding. "Okay, I totally get what you're sayin' and I respect that and I'm on board. But what about after when the Olympics are done and we're back in the States?"

"What about it?" The question sounded snider than I'd meant it to, and I forced myself to soften my tone. "You work in Florida. I'm based in Kentucky. I can't pack up my whole operation to start over somewhere else. And if I ever did decide to move my base it would be to Europe so I didn't have to spend months away from home to compete on the international circuit. Long distance sucks and especially with both our workloads I don't see how we're ever going to find time to spend together. I mean, I spend six or more hours a day on a horse, another few hours coaching others, and the rest is paperwork and sleep. And you're an equine vet who works ridiculously long hours. It's not like I can fly down for a weekend and skip training or competing. And if you ever came to Kentucky, well I might be able to fit you in for some quality time between eleven and eleven thirty p.m. if I can manage to stay awake." I exhaled, trying to calm myself. "And despite what happened last night, I'm really not the casual fling type."

"Do you regret it?" The hurt in Addie's voice was unmistakable and also surprising.

So I lied, just a little. "No, I don't." I regretted it not for the reasons Addie might think, but because it was a tease, a small glimpse of something I could have but never would. Something that would only hurt me in the end.

"Good. Because I certainly do not." She sat on the tiny two-seater couch and pulled me down beside her. "I'm willing to do whatever it takes to see if we could turn this into something more permanent."

"I know you will, and I want to say I will too. But I've realized long distance isn't my thing. My last girlfriend lived in Europe and I saw her three months of the year while I was there for the European circuit. Even then it could barely be classed as dating. More like sex whenever we were in the same city and could find time." And considering who she was sleeping with when we *weren't* in the same city, and maybe even when we were, the idea of opening myself up to cheating because of distance again felt like ice water thrown in my face.

"I don't think Kentucky to Florida is really long distance, Caitlyn. If I have to take a short flight every weekend that I'm free to come see you then I'll do it."

"You say that now…"

Addie's eyes fluttered closed as she inhaled a long breath. "Okay. Maybe now isn't the time to talk about it, and maybe we can come back to it once everything's settled. But I want you to know that's my position on the matter."

"Noted. And yes, later is a good idea." I bit my lower lip. "Are you upset?"

"No. I'm not. Because I'm sure we can make this work somehow."

She sounded so convinced, so unwavering that my building anxiety stopped in its tracks. "I'm glad, because I don't want this to be an issue between us."

"Then we won't allow it to become an issue. Simple." Addie's smile made it clear she knew it wasn't that simple. But neither of us took it further. She kissed the tip of my nose. "This nose is a very kissable nose. Better than Dewey's even."

"Wow. Now that's a compliment. Is that all you find kissable about me?" It came out kind of coy, but she didn't seem to mind.

"If you'll recall last night, I think you'll realize I find everything about you kissable." She confirmed with a gentle brush of lips against mine.

I did recall, and the recollection made my skin hot. I opened my mouth to her and allowed myself a few moments to indulge until reality intruded. After what felt like the world's most unsatisfactorily short kiss, I peeled myself away and only just managed to swallow my groan of frustration. I stood. "I have to go. For real this time."

"Sure thing. I'll see you later today." Addie stood too and made an awkward move toward me, then shuffled backward. A shy laugh burst out. "Sorry, I was just about to hug you until I realized it's kinda weird."

My answer was to hug her. Her arms snuck around my waist and she pressed herself full length to me, which really didn't help my needing-to-leave conviction. I kissed her forehead then extracted myself. "Not weird, hugs are great. I'll catch you later."

I detoured to check on Dewey who was happily eating breakfast but accepted a carrot from the bucket on the floor outside his stall, then backtracked past Addie's cabin and kept walking to the truck. The door was unlocked and the moment I climbed the stairs into the living area I smelled coffee. Bless you, Wren. My groom sat at the table, long legs stretched out instead of being squeezed underneath. I stepped over them. "Morning."

Her face was impressively neutral. "Good morning. I left the bagels out for you."

"Thanks." I tossed the bag of clothes onto the lower bunk bed and tried not to think about the look in Addie's eyes as I'd been undressing last night. I'd poured coffee, popped a bagel into the toaster and peeled a banana when Wren cracked.

Her question was a casual, "You scratched the itch, huh?"

"Mmm. Well, sort of." I broke off a piece of banana. "But you know how sometimes you scratch and instead of soothing it, it just gets itchier and itchier?" Then you could either stop scratching and ignore the itch or keep scratching until you'd made a raw weeping wound. I wasn't stupid enough to think that sleeping with Addie would miraculously shut my libido up, but I had hoped it would at least make it be quiet for a few hours.

"Oh shit."

"Yeahhh, that about sums up my thought about it."

"What are you going to do?"

"No idea. We talked about it, about the timing of it all, and then… all the other stuff, like distance and the fact we're two women with ridiculously busy lives."

"And?" Wren prompted.

"And nothing. I'm about to embark on the most important time of my career. I can't think about shit like maybe dating Addie, if we could even figure out how to make a distance relationship work."

"Dating. Relationship. Hmm. Can I say something?"

I made a sweeping gesture. "You're going to regardless of what I say, so go right ahead."

"I get that the timing is awful, but I've never seen you so relaxed or happy. And it's because of her. If there's ever a time to be relaxed and happy, it's now. Everything else can be dealt with later. For now, why not just enjoy it and the obvious benefits." With a wink, she added, "Relaxation is never a bad thing."

"You mean while riding, right?"

She gave me a mock-innocent look. "Of course."

I took my time finishing my banana. "I just don't want to lose focus."

"I get that. But, Caitlyn, your focus is insane. It's literally part of your job description. I know how well you can compartmentalize. Why would Addie be any different to any other thing you've had to put aside or block out or ignore in prep or during a competition?"

Wren's reasoning was solid but Addie wasn't an ordinary distraction. I shrugged, unable to find the words.

Wren stood and tossed my just-popped bagel onto a plate, which she set in front of me with the jar of peanut butter. "Finish your breakfast. We need to go over the packing for Rio."

* * *

When we arrived at Amsterdam airport at three p.m. the next day, Wren and I were subjected to a maze of ID checks and confirmation that the horse in the truck had markings and a brand that matched the one they had on file. Once they were satisfied Dew was Dew, we were allowed to drive up to the huge facility where he would spend a few hours relaxing in a box stall before being put into his jet stall and loaded next to his travel partner for the flight.

Addie and the two nominated grooms—Wren and Eleanor—would be on the dedicated flight transporting the horses to Brazil and the rest of us would follow later that evening. Once Wren had parked I waited for the hiss of the airbrakes before I spoke. "Let's make sure everything's on schedule before we get him out. He can stay in the truck and relax in the air-conditioning."

Wren stretched, squeaking as her fingertips hit the interior roof of the truck. "Good plan."

Dewey's plane was being made ready, and the huge cargo facility buzzed with people and the sounds of world-class horses calling out to one another. I wandered the corridor until I spotted Addie in the stall with Pierre, her stethoscope in her ears as she listened to his gut sounds. I knew my appearance hadn't gone unnoticed, but Addie didn't acknowledge me except for a quick smile, before she moved the stethoscope to another spot on Pierre's belly. Technically, Dakota didn't acknowledge me either, unless you counted a withering look as acknowledgment. From her, it was.

I summoned my courage and said a quiet, "Hello, Dakota. Pierre looks great." Looking great and wearing a brand-new blanket, halter and shipping bandages. A prickle of self-consciousness poked me in the back. Dew's travel gear was a few years old now but everything was clean and functional. My sponsors would have provided new gear if I'd asked, but why would I?

We were about the same height, and I knew she hated not being able to literally look down at me as I'd seen her to do others. She seemed taken aback that I'd spoken to her, and after a long pause, which I suspected was merely for effect, she muttered a grudging, "Thank you."

That was about the extent of our small-talk repertoire. I backed up a few steps to wait for Addie to finish with Pierre. She twitched his blanket back into position then smiled at me. "I'll be right with you. Give me ten?"

"Will do." Feeling foolish for interrupting, I slipped away to unload Dew and put him in a stall.

The moment Dewey walked down the ramp out of the truck, he raised his head to look around, ears swiveling back and forth as he took in the surroundings. Apparently satisfied that it was just another thing he'd done heaps of times before, he frisked Wren for treats. She gave him a carrot then led him into the building to find the stall labeled with his name. I followed behind, carrying a bucket of carrots and nets of hay for the flight. The moment Dew was let loose in the stall, he dropped to his knees, folded to the ground and rolled, groaning in pleasure.

Once he'd stood and shaken himself off, as if shaking off the truck ride, I unbuckled the straps at his chest, then removed his blanket to make it easier for Addie to examine him. I placed it neatly with the rest of his belongings that would travel with him on the plane. The cabin was climate-controlled so the horses didn't need blankets when they flew—just sheepskin-padded halters and thick protective bandages on their legs. I had to fight the urge to check, uh, re-re-recheck that he had everything he needed.

Wren and I groomed him while we waited and after fifteen minutes or so Addie wandered over. She had a clipboard tucked under one arm and an iPad in that hand, and in the other she juggled a small briefcase and her ever-present vet bag. She glanced at Wren then did a double take. Laughing, she said, "Great hair."

Wren grinned and stroked the clipped side of her head where she had, as promised months ago, had an American flag colored into the now-peroxided undercut. "Thanks."

Addie slipped into the stall, dropped her things at a safe distance from Dewey and reached up to stroke his face. "Hello, big guy." Addie planted a smacking kiss on Dewey's nose, then pushed him away when he snuffled her cheek. "He good to fly?"

"Sure is," I answered. "He's got more frequent flyer miles than me."

"Ah, well maybe someday he'll take me as an add-on to his membership and we can go to the beach somewhere."

The image of Addie in a bikini waltzed merrily into my head. I didn't mean for it to happen, but a weird little gurgle squeak escaped my mouth. Wren glanced at me then snorted. I rearranged my features into something I hoped didn't convey that a very sexy image was still stuck in my head and cleared my throat. "He spends his whole life in a sand arena, he'd probably pick something that didn't resemble work."

Addie smiled, ignoring the Wren and Caitlyn Comedy Hour. "Fair enough. I'm partial to skiing too if he wants to take me to Japan or something." She winked and tapped a few things on her phone before shoving it back into her butt pocket. "I'll get some vitals, do a bunch of paperwork and physical checks and stuff, we'll stick his identification tags on everything, and then he can chill and eat before we load him up. As can both of you." She looked between Wren and me. "Could I have his passport please?"

"I'll grab it," Wren said, handing me Dew's lead. "My bad, I should have brought it with me." Her demeanor was a little too forced and I wondered if she hadn't deliberately forgotten the document to give herself an excuse to leave.

Addie waited until Wren had gone before she spoke. "You good?"

"Mhmm. Healthy as a…horse."

Addie grinned and I had to keep my eyes up instead of staring at those adorable dimples. Stupid libido. She pulled the stethoscope from around her neck. "You're a laugh riot. That's not what I meant."

"I know. But I'm good, thanks."

She touched my arm, let her fingers linger, then pulled away. "Let's get this health check and paperwork started so we can be on our way."

Wren had returned midway through Dewey's exam to deliver his passport, then melted away again mumbling something about moving the truck so it wasn't in the way. She gave me a pointed look, which made absolutely no sense. Did she want me to move the truck?

Dewey's vitals were spot on, and he was deemed fit and ready to fly. I hung around, trying not to watch Addie too obviously as she filled in paperwork. She took a photo of his passport then put it inside her briefcase. The moment she'd straightened up again, she quietly asked, "Seriously, how're you feeling? You can tell me." The question was so unexpected and asked so gently and with such genuine interest that my brain froze.

Before I could answer, Dakota flung her arms over the lower stall door. Sigh. "Addison! When are they loading the horses?"

Addie turned away from me. "In three hours, which is right on schedule."

"I can't see the loading conveyors anywhere."

"Probably because they're not needed for another three hours, which is right on schedule."

Dakota flounced away, griping loudly to…absolutely nobody because the only people around were Addie and me. Though I was sure Dakota knew that organizing equipment to load the horses into the plane was the responsibility of the cargo company and airport staff and not Addie's job, it was just like her to pile something on anyone she thought she could grind down. "Is she always like that to you?" My question came out tightly around clenched teeth.

Smiling as if she knew what I was implying, Addie asked, "Like what?"

I flipped a wayward clump of Dewey's mane back to the right side. "Like a raging stuck-up bitch with a superiority complex?"

"Oh, yeah, pretty much." Her eyes were saucer-sized. "Or not. Not at all. Ignore me. I said nothing."

"No need to." I sighed. "We all know the Dakota hates Caitlyn story. It just pisses me off that she's like that with you."

"She's just trying to assert her dominance. It doesn't bother me. And I've told you before, she's nasty because she's jealous of you," Addie insisted quietly. "Caitlyn, being around you, watching you ride is like being around a supernova. It's intense, electric." Her expression was soft, almost reverent, and it made my chest tighten. She softly caressed my face. "Nobody compares. Not even close."

CHAPTER EIGHTEEN

Addie

My main impression of Rio was not as hot as I'd thought it would be, but humid as heck. The Dressage, Showjumping and Three-Day Eventing Teams each had a dedicated vet, and thinking about the other two disciplines made me grateful I was a dressage vet. I felt sorry for the eventing horses who would have to gallop for ten minutes and almost six kilometers across country over a set of forty-five formidable jumps, as well as perform a dressage test and a showjumping round. I was going to have to be on the ball to manage heat stress in my dressage horses but the eventing vet was going to have to deal with some serious heat exhaustion after the cross-country phase.

The flight to Brazil had been as smooth as I could have hoped, with all the equines behaving like the seasoned flyers they were. I'd managed to cut my mooning-over-Caitlyn time down to just a few hours, scattered into minutes here and there between making sure the horses were traveling well.

I wouldn't have had nearly as easy a time, or anywhere near as much fun, if not for Wren who was not only knowledgeable and capable but an amusing and witty person with whom to spend eleven hours in a tin can. A tin can that was made more for the comfort of equines than humans. She made me play endless games of I Spy, somehow managing to find more words beginning with H than I'd thought possible for such an enclosed space, and then laughing when I guessed Horse, Hay, Halter—wrongly—every time. Apparently Hideously Dry Skin, Horrible Uncomfortable Seat and Help I Need More Leg Room were perfectly acceptable items for the game.

Eleanor was friendly enough whenever I spoke to her but didn't go out of her way to interact with anyone, even when invited to join in. But she was calm and competent which was good enough for me.

I had mixed feelings about arriving in Rio—an understandable excitement for what we were about to undertake, churned up with some serious nerves about my role in the whole thing, layered with wanting Caitlyn to have a great time and an excellent competition. If I'd been able to separate work from the Olympic experience then I'm sure I would have been zinging about like a sugar-hopped-up kid but for now, I felt a little overwhelmed.

I'd been looking around the facilities for about ten minutes when the US Dressage Team horses' trucks rolled into the Deodoro Horse Complex a little after nine thirty a.m. Caitlyn and the other riders weren't due for a little while yet and I had no idea if she'd drop her things at the athlete's village or come straight to see Dewey. Knowing Caitlyn, it'd be Dewey first, herself second.

Eleanor and Wren helped the transport staff unload all our horses and settle them in with some feed and water, and Wren wasted no time hanging an American flag on the side of Dewey's stall where he couldn't reach it. They'd taken away his picture of Rasputin, and on the lower stall wall out of reach was the usual laminated page that listed his name, country, owner, groom, veterinarian and a few notes for the team of roving volunteer veterinarians. Also listed were phone numbers for everyone associated with the horse, just in case.

I took my time checking each information sheet—Caitlyn Lloyd and Midfields Adieu (Dewey), Beau Dennison and Gallantoro (Grub), Dakota Turner and Pursuit of Perfection (Pierre), Jesse Waldorf and AGP Solar Flare (Sunny) and our reserve team of Simone Lane and Fürst Dream (Freddo). Satisfied everything was in order, I decided to explore.

Though my office wasn't quite ready, the equestrian complex was impressive and the quality of facilities eased my anxiety. State of the art and with roomy, airy box stalls, a fully equipped equine hospital and laboratory with all the bells and whistles, the veterinary staff had access to everything we could want. Being inside a military compound meant security was excellent but as I found out, there was a flipside. There was always a flipside.

Caitlyn arrived in a whirlwind just after midday, clearly having come straight from the airport, and rushed into the Team USA cabin equipped with PT equipment, beanbags for chill time, a kitchenette and fridge, and most importantly—air-conditioning. "How is he?" was the first thing she asked and when I assured her that he was fine, the obvious worry about her equine partner deflated and she asked, "And how are you?"

"Delightful. You can leave your bags here. Everyone else has." I saved my report, checked she'd collected her competitor's ID lanyard, without which she wouldn't be going anywhere and guided her toward the building housing the horses. "Come on, I'll show you where the stalls are. Last I checked about twenty minutes ago, Wren was in with Dewey. Phone signal is a bit weird and intermittent but I'm told they're bringing in some equipment to help boost it."

"That explains the radio silence. I've been calling her since I cleared customs."

I touched her shoulder. "All is well, I don't think he's taken his nose out of the hay feeder since we put him in his stall. But listen, I've had word that the military within the barracks, just over there—" I pointed, "—are going to be shooting. We've tried to get them to just…not do that, given the circumstances, but it's a no-go. 'They are military, therefore they practice their marksmanship' was the basic reply to our request."

"Shooting what?"

"Targets presumably." I widened my eyes. "Hopefully. But just a heads-up that there's going to be random gunfire so we can prepare for freak-outs. Mary and Ian will probably call a meeting to let the team know the situation. Nobody is in danger of gettin' shot," I hastily added. "But this is an active military facility and they're adamant that the show goes on as normal, even during the Olympics."

She deflated, hand on her stomach. "Oh thank God. I'd thought you were about to tell me Dew's shoes hadn't made it to Brazil or his feed supplements had been confiscated or something equally as horrifying." Caitlyn shrugged. "No big deal. We're used to it." At my raised eyebrows she clarified, "My neighbor likes to shoot clay pigeons. The horses get used to it pretty fast and Dewey isn't worried about gunshots. Sheep, on the other hand are a different story. Terrified."

Grinning, I said, "Good to know. I'll try to make sure no sheep sneak into the arena." The visual of huge Dewey galloping away from a tiny sheep was pretty funny. Horses were scared of the weirdest things. I touched her arm, let my fingers linger, wanted to let them linger for even longer. "Now I've delivered you safely, I have to get back to my paperwork. Sorry."

"No problem." She raised her hand as if to touch my face, then dropped it again. After a quick look around, she took my hand instead. "I have to find Mary and the officials and who knows who else. Then I have meetings and things like that. I'll catch up with you later?"

If I could learn to not melt into a puddle whenever she touched me that would be really great. I managed a breathless, "You bet."

Later never really eventuated. Caitlyn had been caught up in whatever the athletes were doing and when I wasn't checking out the veterinary facilities, meeting other vets and making sure all the feed was correct, I was basically glued to the stalls. Thankfully the horses were eating and drinking and seemed happy in the boxes that would be their homes for the next two weeks.

Me on the other hand? I felt like I'd been hit by a jumbo jet. Jetlag plus excitement plus nerves equaled some serious ass dragging. Given all my charges seemed okay it was time to go find my apartment and sleep. My messages to Caitlyn kept failing and after five attempts I gave up. If she'd had anything serious to talk to me about then she would have surely found me—there were only so many places I could be. I collected my gear from the team cabin, closed the door and checked that the numerical lock had clicked shut.

My fatigue was overwhelming, and I tried to tell myself to get used to it because it wasn't going to go away any time soon. I'd be run off my feet making sure all the equine athletes were in top form, health-wise. Depending on the schedules for non-competition-day training and competition-day preparation I'd have to juggle my time among the groups—riders, grooms, owners and personal coaches—who'd come along as well.

Then there was the team farrier and physiotherapist, plus Mary and Ian who I sensed might have viewpoints opposing mine over any clinical issues. My job was to ensure every horse was in top form leading into the competition, and if I had to butt heads then I had to butt heads. Deep down I knew that all this work meant there would be very little time for Caitlyn and me to spend together. Just when it was starting to feel like that was a very good idea.

I made one last round of all my horses and said goodnight to the few grooms still there. Being close to ten p.m. they were right on the edge of the curfew when they'd be asked to leave and the security crew would take over. As I approached Dewey's stall Wren beckoned me over. She looped her headphones around her neck. "Have you spoken to Caitlyn?"

"Earlier this afternoon, yeah."

"Right. She was looking for you but had to go and was trying to message to let you know but the phones here are so fucked up. She asked me to tell you, if I saw you, that she's sorry but she had to call her mom and then go back to her room and die of jetlag. Said she'd find you first thing in the morning when she didn't feel subhuman."

"Ah. I know that feeling."

Wren looked me up and down. "So it would seem."

"You sayin' I look like shit?"

She grinned. "I am."

I matched her grin, though mine felt wearier than hers. "I feel like it, truth be told. You finishing up here?"

"Yeah, just making sure he's comfortable for the night."

Dewey abandoned his hay and came over to insert himself between me and Wren, leaning over the lower stall door to nibble my shirt and check for treats. I rubbed his face. "Sorry, pal. I'm all out." He kept frisking me until he hit my ribs. That was it. The tickly zone was a no-go zone. Giggling and squirming, I pushed him away and received a mopey look in response.

Wren pushed Dewey's chest to back him up a few steps. "You're ticklish? Well that explains a few things," she mumbled.

"Like what?"

Wren's head snapped up. "Never mind."

"Oh no. You can't do that, drop a hint then run away like that. It's against the rules of...of..."

"Of what?"

"Of not leaving me hanging."

"Fine. Just this once." She leaned in, mouth twitching like she was biting back a smile. "You guys are *not* quiet, and that's all I'm going to say."

"Ohhh Christ on a cracker. Really? Goddamn."

Wren gave me a maternal shoulder pat. "Fear not. It was only me who walked past after dinner the other night. I'm a twenty-nine-year-old grandma, so I came home while the others stayed and drank some more. I wanted to check on Dewster before bed, that's all."

I knew I was bright red and tried desperately to push aside the embarrassment. "I have not been this mortified since vet school when I tried to do a rectal pregnancy test on a steer."

"Why? Only someone right outside would have heard you guys uh, having a great time. There's no rules against it, as I'm sure you know. So what's the issue?"

I liked Wren, I trusted her and I knew Caitlyn did too. But I didn't want to spill my intimate feelings to her. Though I really didn't have anyone who I could confide in, except Teresa. Even then, our relationship tending to be mostly work-related with the personal sprinkled sporadically throughout. "Timing, mostly." That was the easiest answer.

"It's not like you guys have a static immovable timeline though, right? The Olympics don't go forever."

No, but Caitlyn's dressage lifestyle and commitments did apparently. I made a hmm-ing sound of noncommittal "Yeah I hear ya."

Wren poked my bicep. "For the record, you guys are so adorable. Especially when you're both trying to pretend you don't just want to jump each other."

I wilted. "Great. Is it that obvious?" I'd thought I'd been doing a semi-decent job of not looking like some lovestruck teenager every time I came within a hundred feet of Caitlyn.

"Only to people like me who spend most of their time gauging the moods of Caitlyn and Dewey. That's my job, as is keeping them calm and happy." Wren dropped an arm onto the lower half-door and leaned into it. "Looks like you've taken over that second part for me."

I bit my lower lip. "Really?"

She nodded. "This might sound a bit bodyguard-ish, but just give her time to get used to the idea of someone wanting her and wanting her exactly as she is." Wren glanced around. "Elin Nygaard fucked her over big time and Caitlyn isn't the sort of person who just moves on from that. But for the first time since it happened, I can see she wants to."

"I want to, too."

"Good start. If you're serious then know that she's not going to just lie down and accept these feelings. She's going to fight it like a bronc being saddled for the first time. Fear is a powerful motivator, especially for someone like Caitlyn who spends so much of her life suppressing fear and anxiety so horses don't sense it."

"Are you saying she's going to bite me?"

Wren grinned. "No more than she already has." The grin faded. "But her fear of being hurt again is huge, and she doesn't have many people she'll show that fear to. Every now and then it breaks out and makes her act in ways she normally wouldn't. I've seen it happen before and my gut says it's going to happen again."

"I don't want to hurt her. I just want the chance to—" I cut myself off before I blurted something that shouldn't be blurted to Wren.

But it seemed Wren knew, despite my silence. She leveled a calm look at me. "I know. Which means you have to show her that and show her in whatever way you have to."

Apparently she'd said all she felt she needed to because I got a, "Catch you tomorrow" before she settled her headphones back over her ears.

I nodded, hiked my bags up onto my shoulders and wandered off to find one of the cars to take me to my apartment.

If Caitlyn and I could just keep spending time together, sex or no sex—though sex was always preferable—then maybe subconsciously when the time came to make a choice about where we went from here, it would all slot into place for a wonderful *yes*. I knew it was a sideways approach. But Caitlyn's fears and my desire...need, yeah, okay, desperation to be with her were at odds with each other. So all I had to do was show her that I wanted her beyond the bedroom. How hard could it be?

CHAPTER NINETEEN

Caitlyn

I'd spent my second morning in Rio making sure I knew where everything was around the equestrian complex, checking the arena surfaces with the other riders and nailing down training schedules and arena familiarization times. I'd also taken a peek at the eventing cross-country course and the huge, technical jumps confirmed that I'd made the right choice as a teenager when I'd decided I liked jumping, but nowhere near as much as the nuance and intricacy of dressage.

Along the back of the building housing the box stalls were tiny modular offices allocated to the veterinarians and management teams. Time to find Addie. The modulars were arranged alphabetically by country, which meant I had to wander along the entire length to find the USA's office at the end of the row. The humming air conditioners added to the general noise and busyness vibe.

I peeked inside the window and noticed the small office was indeed occupied. Addie answered within seconds of my knock and her welcoming smile made my skin heat up even more than the temperature. She pulled the door wide open and a blissful rush of cool air escaped. "Hey, you. Come on in."

"Sorry to intrude. I just wanted to see how you were getting on. And…I'm bored." There wasn't much to do until the team started training this afternoon and though I loved being with Dewey, staring at a horse eating wasn't very exciting.

"No intrusion at all," Addie assured me as she closed the door. "I've been meaning to find you after not finding you yesterday but time's kinda run away from me."

"It's fine." I peered around. The space was mostly taken by a huge desk that had papers and lists spread across the surface along with her ever-present tablet and a laptop. A walkie-talkie with the volume turned down low made constant noise, and she had two phones and some vet equipment taking up the rest of the table space. They'd provided a sink and fixings for tea and coffee as well as a tiny fridge jammed into one corner. The whole impression was claustrophobically cozy. "So, you finally got your own office."

Addie cleared papers into a neat stack and pulled out the second chair for me. "I sure did. They were having problems with the AC yesterday that they had to sort out before letting us in. The best part is Mary's already told me the room is all mine. You know how she is about being with y'all all the time."

I sure did. "Could be worse. It's kind of like having a mom and a teacher and a boss around all at once."

"True." Addie dropped into the other chair and brought her feet up onto an overturned milk crate. "I'm sorry I missed you last night. Wren gave me your message."

"It's fine, and I'm sorry I bailed. I tried to hang on but just got flattened around seven. Passed out almost as soon as I found my room."

"What's the athlete's village like?"

"Cozy. Great food. I'm rooming with Simone. Apparently Team USA got one of the better buildings so we have both hot and not-brown water as well as beds, and there's no exposed wiring so I guess that's a win? But it's hectic, like there's this party atmosphere simmering underneath all the competitiveness. There are so many socks on doorknobs it looks like laundry day and I've seen more bare skin in the halls than I care to."

She arched an eyebrow. "Interesting. I'd heard rumors that the Olympics is the best time for hookin' up."

"Based on what I've seen already, it's no rumor."

Both Addie's eyebrows bounced up and it looked like she was only just managing to keep herself from saying something innuendo-laden. She made a tactful subject change. "FYI, I'm on call twenty-four-seven so if you need to reach me you can call my usual number, and also this local number." She passed me a card. "Or page me on channel three with anyone around here holding a walkie-talkie if you need anything."

"Anything?"

Laughing, she amended, "Anything relating to your horse's wellbeing. I believe it was you who said you needed to concentrate on this Olympic thing." Her voice grew serious. "And you do. You're absolutely right. As much as I'd love to have you in my apartment for a few hours every night, you need to focus."

"I don't want that." At the hurt expression that flashed over her face, I clarified, "I want to stay all night, every night. But what I want, and what's practical are at different ends of the scale."

Her face relaxed into relief. "I know that feeling well."

"Buuuut, I'll be done by the end of Monday the fifteenth, assuming we make the Freestyle."

"You *will* make the Freestyle," Addie interjected.

"Mmm. Either way, I'll be elated or despondent and I'll need to be congratulated or consoled. You up to the task?"

"You need to ask?" she murmured, the words a quiet husky question that promised something delicious later.

"No," I mused. "I don't think I do."

The look Addie gave me was pure hunger and leaving her like that was both delicious tease and painful torture. But given what we'd just agreed, or re-agreed, now was not the time. She had work, and it was almost time for me to give Dewey his first Rio workout to loosen him up after his travel and start acclimating him. "I should let you get back to it, and I have to go watch the team ride before it's my turn. Maybe I'll see you later."

Addie laughed. "I'd say there's a very high chance of that." She glanced at the uncovered window, and apparently came to the same conclusion that I had. Zero privacy. Even for something as innocent as kissing. Of course the trouble with us was that innocent kissing tended to lead quickly into other things. Under the table she touched my knee. "I'll be around the stalls once everyone's done with their training sessions. Maybe we could have dinner one night or something? Even if we're not…you know, I'd still like to see you, talk to you away from dressage-dressage-dressage."

"I'd like that." I stood and pushed the chair back under the table. "I'll sneak you into the athlete's village, or we can hit up the concession stands and have popcorn and ice cream or find ourselves a food truck somewhere."

"You speak my language."

"Good to know." I allowed myself a quick squeeze of her hand, then left her to her work while I went to train my horse.

Despite the heat and humidity, Dew seemed settled and was eating and drinking as normal. More and more horses were arriving, turning the place into a seething mass of people and horses that somehow seemed organized in its chaos. I'd watched Dakota and Beau ride, then left to grab Dewey for our session. The team had decided to utilize the air-conditioned indoor arena, but it seemed everyone else had the same idea and after ten minutes of trying not to bump into other horses I decided it was just wasting time and indicated to Ian that I was going out to one of the eucalypt-lined outdoor arenas.

Within minutes I was dripping and Dew was a lather of sweat foam on his neck where the reins touched him. After twenty minutes I decided he'd had enough and brought him back to a walk. I desperately wanted to wipe the sweat trickling down my face but knew I'd just have more there immediately.

Ian's voice through my earpiece sounded tinny. "He looked fine for what we're trying to do today which is just suppleness and acclimation."

Wren met me to open the arena gate after I'd given Dew a ten-minute cool-down walk. "He looked a little flat," she said.

He'd felt more than *a little* flat. A niggle of worry took root. I knew we weren't in a unique situation—all the horses had to acclimate—but what if we couldn't get him comfortable in the heat? I dismounted and we led him straight to the hose-down area to strip off his tack and bandages. Wren wasted no time getting him hosed off then scraping the hot water from him and hosing him down again.

I collected three baggies of ice from one of the many dispensers beside the hose-down bays and after wrapping each baggie in a towel, placed one behind his ears and hoped he wouldn't drop his head. After positioning myself against his chest I reached around to press a baggie into each of his armpits. Or…forelegpits. The added benefit was that Dewey's third cold shower was also my cold shower. The looks he was giving us clearly said the tropics were not for him.

It didn't seem like we were alone. Every horse seemed to be struggling with the heat, and the forecast until the end of the competition was for much the same with a few cooler days of respite. Addie arrived a few minutes after we'd settled Dew back into his stall, and she looked not unlike Dewey had after the ride—sweaty and puffing. I'd spotted her rushing around from one place to the next and being waylaid by people before zinging off again. She looked so utterly beat I wanted to hug her. She leaned over the lower half-door. "How was your ride?"

"Hot. Sunny."

"Yeah, I'm hearing that from a lot of people." She offered a weary smile and pulled her tablet from her satchel. "How's the Dewmeister?"

"He definitely struggled a bit during the ride but he seems back to normal after a few cold showers, and some time with ice and the cooling fans by the arena."

"Good. I'll check his temperature, heart rate and breathing later. No point now because they could still be skewed by his workout. I'd like to increase the electrolytes in all the horses' feeds to make sure they're putting back what they're sweating out and to ensure they're hydrating."

"Already done."

"Of course you have." She smiled as she typed something into the tablet. "Okay, I have to jet. I'll be back later to check on you guys. Stay cool."

"You too," I called after her.

After feeding Dewey Wren had left to grab herself an early dinner with a few other grooms, and I'd stopped in to say goodnight to Dew before heading back to the athlete's village to eat, shower, and sleep. When I hugged him around the neck and pressed my cheek into his bulk, he curled his neck around until his head was against my back in his version of a hug. And in true Dew fashion, I felt his nibble on my belt loops. "Hey!" I reached back to swat at him. "None of that."

Addie appeared and slung her arms over the lower half-door. Though her fatigue was obvious in the lines and shadows of her face, her smile for us was still brilliant. "You all done for the day?"

"Sure am. You?"

"Mhmm. Just trying to figure out if I can be bothered eating dinner or if I'm just gonna go collapse into bed."

"Same."

Dewey submitted to another tight hug and me smooching his nose while murmuring, "Sleep tight, rest well, see you in the morning, love love love you. Wren will come see you before bedtime." I gave him the last carrot and submitted to a body check to satisfy him that I wasn't hiding treats before he moved back to his hay feeder in the corner.

Addie had clearly been watching us and when I faced her, her eyebrows slowly rose. "What about mine?"

I brushed hay from my breeches. "What about your what? You want a carrot?"

She leaned closer and spoke in a voice too low for anyone else to hear. "My kiss."

I kept my voice equally low. "You want me to kiss you right here? In front of everyone?"

Her dimples made a brief appearance. "Well it's not really *every*one. Just Dewey. And he's more interested in food than us."

When I blew her a kiss, Addie's hand shot out as if catching a fly and she pressed her fist against her mouth. It took me a moment to figure it out. "Did you just…eat my kiss? If you're going to do that then I'm not going to blow you any more kisses."

"What? No! I was putting it on my lips." She mimed the same movement again. "See? Like your blown kiss onto my lips? Look, I'm sorry. I've never had such a great kiss blown at me before. I panicked."

"Evidently," I said dryly.

Before I could reach over to unlock the door, Addie had opened it for me. She took a small backward step but was still firmly within my bubble of personal space. Rather than ask her to move, I slipped past her, being sure to brush against her as I passed.

"Cruel," she complained as she closed and locked the stall door.

She probably wouldn't be saying that in a minute. "Come with me."

Addie followed me through the laneways, bumping into my back when I stopped dead outside the ladies' dressing room. A quick peek confirmed the space was empty and I dragged her inside. My intent had been to press her against the door because she made the hottest sound when I maneuvered her body how I wanted it, but also to provide a barrier in case anyone tried to interrupt us. But Addie gripped my hips and spun me around, doing exactly what I'd intended to do to her.

My breath whooshed out as my back hit the door, then Addie took what little I had left with a kiss that was almost frightening in its intensity. When I opened my mouth, her tongue met mine. A soft stroke. A gentle suck. The warm fullness of her mouth invited me deeper and when Addie bit my lower lip, my simmering excitement went to full boil. Nestled alongside was another sensation that was just as intense, and ten times as frightening.

Need.

Not the frantic kind that came with desire. But the softer, more in-tune kind of need where being near her immediately soothed and settled me. That kind of need was dangerous. Addie broke away from the kiss first, pulling back just enough so that we were no longer kissing, but our foreheads touched. She clutched the front of my polo. "I feel like kissing in bathrooms is kind of our thing."

I was almost afraid to ask her to clarify. "And is our thing a good thing or bad thing?"

"A little of both. Kissing is always good. Bathrooms, not so much."
She pulled away, but not before kissing me again.

She made me so weak. Made me forget everything I kept telling
myself I shouldn't do. I could tell myself that I was just getting caught up
in the Olympic moment, that all the hype and excitement permeating
the air around me was filling my lungs. But I knew that wasn't really it.
I'd found something, *someone* who made me feel more in two months
than I had in two years, and I was drunk with the sensation of finally
being seen. I ran my palms up and down her arms. "How tired are you
exactly?"

"You know, suddenly not so much. You wanna go?"

"Yes." Tangling my fingers in Addie's hair, I pushed her head back
to expose the tantalizing skin of her neck. I kissed my way to her ear,
sucked the lobe. "But I don't want to put a sock on the doorknob. Your
place."

"Done. But first, my shower. I'm forty percent dirt and sweat right
now."

"Only if you let me join you."

Her expression blanked for a moment before it turned serious and
her voice turned softly intimate. "I would never say no to you joining
me for anything, Caitlyn."

There was none of the first-time awkwardness and no preamble.
The moment her apartment door closed behind us we undressed each
other as if we'd done it a hundred times before, only breaking from
kisses when the necessity to free ourselves from a garment absolutely
required it. We left clothing by the door, near the kitchen, outside
the bathroom. Addie bent to bury her face in my breasts, light lips
exploring skin before moving to claim first one nipple then the other.

She pulled me into her shower and pushed me against the wall, the
cool tile against my skin contrasting with the heat of her pressed to my
back. She sucked my neck, one hand reaching to stroke up and down
my belly as she fumbled to start the water with the other. The arctic
blast made us both jump and I took the opportunity to twist around to
face her as she moved away to adjust the temperature. There. Better.
I pulled her against me, tangled a hand in her hair and kissed her. She
met me as she did every time we kissed—with passion, enthusiasm,
and a hint of shyness.

Addie straddled my thigh, one hand hooked under my ass and the
other cupping my breast. She drove her thigh against me every time
she slid herself against my skin. Glorious, wet friction. Her face was

pressed to my shoulder, teeth grazing my skin as we rocked against each other. The sensations built into a slow roll of pleasure that I knew was going to peak soon if she kept up that steady roll of her hips. Apparently I wasn't the only one thinking that.

"Okay, time out," Addie gasped. "Shower first, then sex."

"What about sex in the shower?"

She offered a sheepish smile. "Tried it, love it, but I really can't balance properly on a slippery surface and a concussion isn't on my agenda tonight."

I reached for the soap and quickly started lathering myself, trying to ignore the warning bells of arousal as I washed between my legs. "Then you'd better hurry up because I find myself a little short on patience right now." Once I was done, Addie made no move to take the soap from me and her expression made it clear what she wanted. I obliged, running a hand down the center of her breasts. "Stand still."

She tried valiantly, and almost managed but her ticklishness got the better of her when I washed under an arm and moved down over her breasts to her torso. "Uncle," she begged and I complied with her request for mercy, moving my hand downward to linger against her pubic hair. Her expression was pure *Are you kidding me, that's not mercy.*

"Spread your legs for me," I murmured and when she leaned back against the wall and did as I asked, I washed her, lingered as long as I dared. Addie's breathing hitched and I covered her moan with a kiss, kept kissing her as I played through her folds.

Her response was a shaky, "That doesn't feel like soap."

"It is definitely soap. It's also my finger." I slid my forefinger upward over her clit, then back down again.

Addie shuddered. "Screw this. That's clean enough." She snatched the showerhead from its cradle and rinsed herself at lighting speed. Dammit. I hadn't realized it was a detachable showerhead. Next time…

The moment she'd finished, her mouth was on mine, tongue demanding entry. She managed to shut off the water, open the shower door and pull me toward her bedroom without our lips breaking contact. Still wet, we fell onto the bed in a tangle of slippery limbs and furious kisses. Addie straddled me, pinning my hands with a loose grip to the bed as she sat up.

Her eyes roamed over my body for such long, silent moments that I started to squirm. "What?"

"You," she said simply. "You're gorgeous." A flush started at her cheeks and worked its way to her ears and down her neck. "Sorry. I just made things weird, didn't I?"

"You made things the opposite of weird."

She'd made it intimate, intensely so. I'd known desire from other women. Lust. Need. Want. All of those things. But the way she looked at me made me feel as if she wanted me on more than just a superficial sexual level. And that want made me feel stripped bare. Addie lowered herself onto me, twisting us to lie side by side and we kissed slowly as our hands roamed and rediscovered.

A silent, mutual understanding seemed to move between us and our hands slid between thighs. She parted me as I slid my fingers through her folds, and when I felt her familiar slippery heat, fresh arousal flooded me. We moved together, slow…fast…frantic…soft, and the whole time our mouths remained within a whisper of each other.

Addie's unerring fingers slid against me, drove softly inside me, brought me closer and closer to the edge until I felt the unmistakable heat spread through my body. I tried to keep up, tried not to be selfish and leave her behind, but as I felt myself move closer and closer to climax I lost all my control. She rocked her hips against my still and selfish hand, and with her teasing fingers, her kisses, her sweat-slick body, brought me to the brink. I fought it, tried to hold it until I could focus again on her pleasure, but Addie was having none of that. As if she knew exactly what I felt, she murmured, "Let go."

Those knowing fingers stroked my walls as her thumb worked lightly at my clit until I couldn't hold back anymore. My climax started as a slow roll of warmth then burst into a bonfire of heat as I came. She exhaled a grunt when I unconsciously bit her lip, then inhaled as I sucked the pain I'd just created.

Addie kept kissing me as soft, sensual arousal suffused me. It took me a while to move out of dumbstruck orgasm brain so I could get right on the very important issue of her climax. I rolled her onto her back and pressed myself to her side, and when my fingers slipped over her wetness, she gasped and let out a helpless, "Please." She cupped the back of my neck, pulling me in for a kiss. I stroked her, loving the way she shuddered against me, loving how she begged me to not stop, to keep doing that, until she cried out her pleasure. Her climax was glorious and her vocalization loud and unashamed. Addie buried her face into my neck and I could feel the air moving across my skin as she tried to catch her breath.

I ran my fingers over the sweat-slick skin of her back. "Sorry," I mumbled. "I just couldn't wait."

She grinned lazily. "Lesson number seventeen in Caitlyn and Addie go to bed? Never apologize for enjoying yourself, for wanting more." Addie's kiss was long and slow. "Listening to the sound of you coming is enough to set me off."

"Yes, ma'am."

Laughing, she flicked my hip. "Nooo, not ma'am. Do you remember how Mrs. Spicer made us call her that during lessons at Pony Club?" Her mock shudder was elaborate.

"Then what should I call you?" I could think of a few things but the fear of verbalizing those deep dark desires kept my words inside.

Her response took almost a minute to emerge and when it did, it was barely above a whisper. "One day, maybe, whenever I mean, in the future I…think I'd like you to call me your partner."

Though I'd been thinking something along those exact lines, I couldn't think of what to say. "Addie, I—"

She pulled the sheet over herself as if desperate to cover up, to smother what she'd just said. "Forget about it, it was…never mind." She kissed me as if afraid of what I might say. But she didn't know that if given the chance, I would tell her I wanted that too. I wanted it even as I feared it, even as I knew we couldn't make it work. Not with the way our lives were now.

This thing we were doing ran contrary to everything I'd been telling myself. All the constant justification of my denial, all that I'd worked so hard for, all that being with her could jeopardize, fell away the moment she touched me. When she kissed me, I forgot my self-righteous speeches about not losing sight of the big picture. When she looked at me with that intense, knowing gaze, the part of me that longed for someone to *see* me rejoiced.

In the past few months I'd thought more about my life than I ever had. And it boiled down to one notion. What was all this ass busting for without someone to share it with, really? What was success if I went home to an empty house? But now was the worst time to find all those feelings. Now was the time to concentrate on the thing I'd worked nearly my whole life for.

But Wren was absolutely right—not that I needed her to confirm what I felt so clearly myself—having Addie with me soothed my anxieties, made me relaxed, made me feel normal in a time that was abnormal. So I just needed to find the balance. I had to.

CHAPTER TWENTY

Addie

Caitlyn had taken a car back to the athlete's village just before eleven p.m. and after hours of patchy insomnia I decided there was no point in hanging around my apartment thinking about her and waiting until it was time to get to work, so I showered and dressed to head over to Deodoro early. Earlier than everyone else including the grooms who were usually there first for six a.m. feeding, stall cleaning and taking their charges for a walk to let them stretch their legs.

"Sorry, everyone, it's thermometer time!" I peered over the first stall and found Dewey still lying down. "Laaaazy." I opened the half-doors, securing the top one in the open position and locked the lower door behind me. Dewey didn't get up. A mental alarm bell chimed softly. I knew he was big on naps, but he always got to his feet and came rushing over to anyone who came into his stall. Still, he'd had a busy few months and a huge climate adjustment, and it was understandable he'd want to chill out.

I collected his halter from the hook outside his stall and slipped it onto his head. Dewey snuffled at my leg but that was it. No nuzzling, no grabbing my pants. Alarm bell number two. I knelt and lifted his top lip to check his gums. Paler than they should have been but slippery enough to make me happy that he wasn't dehydrated. Pressing a thumb into his gums usually yielded a quick capillary response and an attempt to grab my fingers. I got neither. I slipped my hand under the neck of his blanket on the left side to check his hydration by pinching the skin of his neck and was satisfied with its recoil.

He was alert and vaguely interested in what I was doing, but he wasn't *Dewey*. I checked the levels in his feed and water buckets. Water, half-empty—good. Feed, still had a few handfuls in the bottom of the feeder, which was probably him sifting out the extra salt and electrolytes—not great. Hay, mostly gone—okay.

"Come on, buddy. Time to get up." I gave him a nudge in the butt and received a *Do you mind?* look in response. After another butt nudge and a tug at his lead, Dewey stretched his forelegs out and with a quiet groan, tried to stand. He made another attempt and finally got to his feet, standing with his head and neck low and at an odd angle as if he was having issues with his balance. Oh fuck. With my phone wedged under my chin I called Caitlyn. No answer.

I left a message, then tried Wren who answered on the second ring with, "Yeah yeah, I'm coming. Tell him to cool his jets, breakfast is on the way."

"Yeah I don't think he's worried about breakfast. He had trouble gettin' up." I unwrapped my stethoscope from around my neck. "And—"

Her breathing picked up and her answer was a rushed, "Be there in a minute."

Dewey stood quietly with his head and neck still held low while we waited for Wren, who came skidding to a stop outside his stall. Dewey raised his head a few inches and let out a half-hearted nicker as Wren opened the door. "What's going on, my man?" she asked Dewey as she took the lead from me. The next question was directed at me. "What's up?"

"Not sure. Could be nothing. But, he's just…quiet. He had balance issues while trying to get up, and he's not keen on raising his head."

Wren studied him for a moment. "Yeah, you're right. Is Caitlyn coming?"

"Left her a message. You got him? Just going to get some vitals." While I waited for the thermometer to do its thing I ran through some possibilities. It was the same feed he'd been eating for months. He'd drunk enough water for me to be happy. Fatigue was highly likely, but the neck stiffness…ehhh it didn't quite tally. Travel sickness was unlikely given he'd never suffered it before, but not outside the realm of possibility. Early colic. Low-grade infection. A virus. Reaction to something in the environment. Attention seeking.

The thermometer's insistent beep interrupted my thoughts. Upper normal limits but not alarming. His heart rate was mildly elevated but not enough to really worry me. Respiration was a little fast but again not worryingly so, and his gut sounds were okay.

So I had a bunch of clinical signs that weren't exactly normal, but also not enough to cause panic, and nothing diagnosable yet. I crouched by his head and recorded all the vitals, as well as general observations. If this was a normal horse at home then I would give him a shot of phenylbutazone to bring his temperature down and make him more comfortable. But this was a horse about to embark on an Olympic campaign and bute was a prohibited substance.

Still crouching, I asked Wren, "Can you go pick him a handful of fresh grass please?" Often horses with mild colic would pick at forage while ignoring the richer bulk feeds and it was a very sick horse who would ignore fresh grass. Dewey rested his nose against my shoulder as I typed, blowing soft breaths against my neck. I stroked his face. "I know, pal. We'll figure it out and get you feeling better."

Dewey ate Wren's fresh grass, but only when she offered it near his mouth. The moment she moved it away from his easy reach, he refused to follow. Luckily the feed and water weren't set up high or he would have had had issues accessing them overnight. I pulled a carrot from my pocket, broke it in half and held it right under his mouth for him, relieved when he ate both halves.

My phone rang. The panic in Caitlyn's voice was sharp and raw, rising higher and higher in pitch as she spoke. "I'm on my way. What's wrong with him?"

"I'm not sure. He's got a very mild temperature, is moving stiffly with his neck, but nothing else is standing out other than he just seems not himself."

"Is Wren there?" Caitlyn sounded as if she were running and about to burst into tears.

"She is. Dewey's okay, Caitlyn. I promise he's not about to keel over." Okay was relative. "We're taking care of him 'til you get here."

"I'm almost there." Then I was listening to the sound of nothing.

I clutched the phone to my chest. Okay okay, think. What could it be? Time to look at everything that doesn't seem right, aside from neck stiffness. I glanced at Wren whose alarmed expression probably mirrored mine. "Let's get that blanket off him."

We worked at opposite ends to remove his blanket and Dewey's discomfort was unmistakable when he tried to turn around to nuzzle Wren as she fiddled with the straps under his belly. He huffed out a little groan. Wren stopped dead, then moved to his head, murmuring to him. Dew nosed her, but it was with far less enthusiasm than his usual snuffling. I felt like crying at his obvious discomfort.

Caitlyn burst into the stall and Dewey nickered quietly at her. She rushed to him, hands moving over him as she demanded of me, "What's going on? What's wrong with him?"

"I don't know, and I don't know aside from the fact he seems to have a sore neck. I don't know the cause just yet. I'm about to do a full examination."

She stroked Dewey's face as she murmured tearful things under her breath to him. Wren pulled the blanket from him and slung it over the lower half-door. The moment I'd moved up to his head, the reason for the neck stiffness became abundantly clear. The blanket had covered spongy edema the size of a small melon on the right side behind his jaw, and welts spread down along his neck and up over his cheek. When I palpated the area, Dewey flinched the moment my gentle fingers touched the hot, swollen skin.

From behind me, Caitlyn said, "That's swollen, right?"

"Mhmm, yeah. And hot." My differential diagnosis just narrowed to localized trauma or an insect bite. We were getting somewhere. I kept examining the site and without turning around said, "Can one of you please carefully pick up his blanket again. Look inside it, around the head part on the right side specifically and see if there's any bugs like ants or bees or spiders in there."

I checked his airways and breathing and within a minute Caitlyn had come back, offering me the rug for examination. "There's a bee," she said, voice choked. "A huge one. It's all caught up in the rug binding and squashed."

I looked where she indicated. "Then it looks like he was stung by a bee." I closed my eyes and for a few moments gave in to my adrenaline. When I opened my eyes I felt calmer, and my focus had sharpened. I turned, my words directed at both her and Wren, who had a look of panicked and trying not to seem it. "First things first, I need to get him to the equine hospital. I'm going to have the trailer brought around for him."

"Okay," Caitlyn whispered. "I'm just…he just seems so…not him." She exhaled shakily. "Okay, anything you have to do then do it. I just need you to make him feel better."

"I know. And I will. I promise I won't let you guys down." She started when I touched her arm. "Caitlyn, look. As soon as Dewey is comfortable we need to talk to Mary because if I have to treat him using a prohibited substance with a long detection time then I'm sorry, but obviously he can't compete."

Caitlyn slid down the wall of the stall like her legs had just quit on her. She drew her knees up and wrapped both arms around them, bending her head to rest her cheek against the top of her knees. "I know. But can't we…try something else?" She looked as if saying the words disgusted her.

"Of course we'll try *if* that's an option. I know the stakes as well as you do." I quietly cleared my throat, hoping to shift the lump of upset sitting there. I looked at Wren who was pointedly not looking at us. I was stuck between two things, and I knew right then that my professional priority was going to butt up against my personal one. "But my focus is his welfare. You know I'll do everything I can to get him well, and ready and able to work but I can't guarantee anything other than that I'll try."

She nodded, her eyes cast downward.

"Look at me." When she finally raised her chin to make eye contact with me, I crouched down and took her face in my hands. "I'm going to do everything I can to get him better." I had to inhale a long breath before I told her the rest of my truth. "But I really do need you to be prepared for the fact I might not be able to treat him in a way that allows you to compete. I'm sorry that it may mean things don't work out as you want them to, but his wellbeing is my priority. Do you understand what I'm saying?"

"I know and yeah, I get it," she said flatly.

I offered her a tissue from my pocket, though what I most wanted to do was gently wipe the tears away. Caitlyn wiped her eyes then took the hand I offered. Once she'd stood I gave her a quick side-on hug. "Come on. We need to get him to the hospital and we'll go from there."

Dewey was settled in a hospital stall with icepacks strapped to his swelling while I waited on rushed lab results, went over and over his notes and kept a close eye on him to ensure this wasn't affecting his breathing. He was stable—his signs weren't progressing but neither were they resolving, which meant I had to intervene.

I'd left a voice mail for Teresa with all the details, along with an urgent request that she call me, and she did within five minutes of my frantic message. She dispensed with formality and jumped right in. "Fuck me, Addie, what's going on down there? Bees? Are you fucking serious?"

"Unfortunately, yes. I don't suppose this has happened to him before and you've magically treated him with something that's not on the banned substances list and he got better in hours?"

"No," she said quietly.

I scrubbed a hand over my face. "Goddammit. Caitlyn's due to ride her first test on Thursday. That's…six days away and if he's going to compete, everything needs to be totally cleared by then. Preferably days earlier." If I wanted to be fully comfortable with sending him out to compete I'd have to use a controlled substance that would not only resolve all his signs, but clear through his system in three days maximum. It wasn't just paranoia about positive samples—I needed to ensure he had time to recover and train adequately before his first test.

"Have you got labs back yet?"

"Nope. Still waiting. I mean…talk about rocks and hard places. I'm too goddamned scared to give him anything just yet."

"You're going to have to make the call, my friend. That's your job. His welfare above everything else."

"I know. I'll do that, obviously." I blew out a long breath, turning to check there was nobody in earshot. "But it's gotten complicated."

"Complicated how?"

"Let's just say Caitlyn Lloyd and I have been doing a whole lot more than just talking as you'd suggested."

There was such a long silence that I began to squirm with embarrassment. Finally Teresa spoke. "Wow. Just…wow. And yay. That is something we are going to talk about as soon as you get Dewey's treatment figured out."

"Yeah. I just don't know what to do. He's comfortable enough and settled." Another call notification cut in. Caitlyn. "I gotta go, I'll call back." I swapped calls. "Caitlyn—"

"How is he?" she demanded. "Is he okay?"

"Looks goofy, but he's doing okay."

"Can I see him?"

"Sorry, but no. Not yet."

Silence.

"Hello? Caitlyn?"

Nothing. She'd hung up.

A member of security arrived minutes later to tell me she was there and demanding to see me. I made sure everything was okay with Dew then peeked out of the door to find her looking as if she was working up a good head of steam and a flood of tears all at once. I closed the door behind me. "Hey. I know this is hard but he's comfortable, I've spoken to Teresa and I'm just about to figure out how to treat him. I'm taking good care of him, I swear." I reached for her hand, not caring who might see, and was stunned when she pulled back.

Both her arms came up to fold over her chest as she asked again, "Can I see him?"

I fought to keep myself neutral as I repeated myself. "Sorry, no." At her look of disbelief I added, "It's their policy, not mine, to ensure biosecurity and so things don't get crowded in here. If it were up to me you'd be in there as much as you want. Honey, he's comfortable and stable and I'm working on multiple treatment plans. I just need to talk to a few people first to make sure I'm covering all bases."

"Shouldn't you be talking to me?"

"I am talking to you," I said calmly.

"Doesn't feel like it."

I'd had enough experience with distraught clients, plain nasty clients and everything in between to recognize that this was anxiety and stress talking. Still, it hurt. I tried for some levity. "Are we doing some weird reversion to Pony Club thing, or did I miss the memo about it being ice queen day?"

Her mouth fell open. "Are you really joking right now?"

"No, I'm—" I bit back the words. Getting into an argument now, or even a discussion that wasn't directly related to Dewey's care was counterproductive. "I'm doing my job. So if you'll excuse me, I'm going to get back to that. I'll call you the moment I have a plan."

Caitlyn's mouth fell open, and as she closed it, her jaw hardened. She looked upset. She looked angry. But worst of all? She looked as if I'd betrayed her. After a hard stare, she turned away from me and walked off.

The worst part was that I couldn't think about that right now. I had to set aside Caitlyn's distress, despite the fact I was the obvious target for it, because I knew it probably wasn't really about me. My priority was figuring out what drugs I could use to make her horse better. I slipped back into Dew's stall and checked the ice packs were still covering the swelling. He nuzzled my arm. I stroked his face. "At least you still like me."

I had two options. Option one was go hard and hit him with everything to get him well fast, including banned competition substances—Olympics be damned. Or, option two which was treat him conservatively with a controlled substance that had a detection time under three days to allow a safe margin and hope it worked so he could compete and not return a positive test.

Option one meant no Olympics for Dewey and Caitlyn. Option two ran the risk of the treatment not working, which meant I'd have to go with option one anyway. My armpits felt damp and I had a sudden sick feeling that I had no idea what I was doing. I closed my eyes and leaned my forehead against Dew's shoulder. I *did* know what I was doing. This was my job, to know these things and act in a way that ensured the welfare of the horses under my care and the best possible result to enable them to compete.

I pulled out my phone and opened up my veterinary drugs app again to resume checking and cross-checking the drugs I wanted to use against the official FEI guidelines. Once I'd checked that, I'd get confirmation from Mary and clearance from every on-site veterinarian I could find to confirm I should and could treat the horse with my chosen drugs.

Dexamethasone, a corticosteroid to relieve inflammation and reduce swelling. Detection time of forty-eight hours. Sold. Now to find an antihistamine.

CHAPTER TWENTY-ONE

Caitlyn

We had a plan.

With my permission, Addie had started Dew on a drug regime that she'd called her soft option—the thing that would allow us to compete. We'd discussed not only the drug clearance times, but the fact I needed as much time as possible for Dew to train and finish acclimating. Everyone agreed with this approach. But if Dew didn't start responding in a way she was happy with by tomorrow midday then she would have to move to her hard option using banned substances or controlled substances with a long detection time, which meant my shot at the Olympics was over.

Because I wasn't allowed to see him, Addie had sent me photos of Dew chilling out after she'd given him the drugs. The fact she'd gone out of her way to keep me informed made me feel worse for being so harsh with her. A bee sting obviously wasn't going to be fatal and if we were home I'd have been upset about Dewey's discomfort but able to deal with it. But we *weren't* home, and we didn't have endless time or options up our sleeve to get him better. The consequences of us being unable to resolve the issue loomed over me. Maybe everything we'd worked for would be for nothing.

I'd been called into an emergency meeting with Mary, Ian, and Simone, our reserve rider. The gist of the meeting was if Dewey wasn't okay then the reserve horse and rider combo would take my place. Because Olympic qualification was for the combination of horse plus rider, we couldn't just swap out one or the other—not that I'd have wanted that for anyone, including myself. We would have to nominate the change of horse-rider combination by Tuesday, the day before the first day of Grand Prix, at the latest. I could see my whole life's ambition crumbling around me and there was nothing I could do except sit there and listen.

And I felt like such a horrible person for even thinking about all of this when Dew was unwell. But the thoughts niggled and niggled and I couldn't get rid of them. Simone was quiet, speaking only when addressed. I had no idea how she felt about the whole thing. If it were me, I'd feel simultaneously like shit that something had happened to one of the horses and elated that I might have a chance to ride.

Mary wrapped up the meeting. "We'll keep an eye on the situation with Dewey, how he recovers and trains over the next four days, then make a decision on Tuesday." She eyed Simone. "Keep training as if you're competing Thursday."

My stomach fell to my boots and I fought to look normal instead of like I wanted to fall to the floor and bawl. I knew exactly what Mary wasn't saying. Even if Dew recovered and I was riding him, if it didn't look like he could be competitive then the reserve would take our place. Mary continued, still talking to Simone, "You've been allocated main arena familiarization with Freddo this afternoon."

That was supposed to be the slot for me and Dewey. I spoke up. "But what about arena familiarization for Dew?"

Mary's face gave nothing away, nor did her voice. "We'll figure that out when we're more certain and he feels better." She picked up her phone and stood. "That's all for now. Stay in contact."

I rushed out of that room and away from the sour taste of disappointment as fast as I could. A few minutes later I found myself outside the equine hospital and in front of the same security guy who'd told me a few hours earlier that I wasn't allowed inside. I showed him my competitor's ID and asked if I could please talk to the American veterinarian. After a quick nod he picked up his radio and called for Addie, who appeared at the door ten feet away.

She gestured for me to come over. "Hey. I just had a call from Mary. How're you?"

"I'm not sure." I tried to see around her into the hospital, hoping to catch a glimpse of Dew. "How's Dewey?"

"He's been trying to get hold of my shirt so I'd say he's feeling better. He's moving his neck grudgingly to get feed, but I'd be happier if he'd move it more freely." After a pause she added, "His vitals are normal. Now we just wait." She opened the door wider and pointed at the stall in the corner.

I could just see him, facing the door but still standing with his head low. My stomach lurched and I fought to keep my voice steady when I called, "Dewbles!"

He raised his head a little, eyes brightening as he spotted me. He nickered, far louder than the one he'd offered this morning. I stepped closer. "Can I come in?" I knew the answer but I had to ask anyway.

"I'm afraid not." She offered me an apologetic smile. "I promise I'll keep in touch, let you know every time he eats or takes a shit or goes down for a nap."

It took everything I had to not burst into tears and my response was a brusque, "Right. I guess I'll just leave you alone then."

"Caitlyn—"

I stepped away and Addie rushed to intercept me. She took my unresisting arm and led me along the side of the hospital to an area around the back away from eyes and ears. After a quick glance around, she took my hands in hers. They felt as strong, warm and dry as mine felt clammy and weak. Her eyebrows came together and after a few seconds she quietly asked, "What's goin' on? Can we just talk? Like adults?"

I didn't know if I could, as much as I wanted to. After an eternity trying to collect my thoughts I blurted, "I just don't know how to feel about this. I feel sick worrying about him, and then there's all the other stuff that I have to think about too."

"I know," she murmured. "And like I said, I'm going to do everything I can to get both of you into that arena, happy and healthy." She offered a fleeting smile. "Well, Dewey at least. I don't know the first thing about human health."

The tears I'd been trying to hold back made a valiant effort and broke free. "It's just…I've worked my whole life to get here, and over a decade with him. I know I sound like such a horrible person. And *of course* his health is the most important thing here. Of course it is." I swiped under both eyes. "It's just, I mean, I may never get the chance again. Maybe not with Dew. It's dumb, because I know I'll have horses who could easily be competitive at this level in a few years, but he's special. I just want the chance to get out there and do something great and if I miss it now who knows what's going to happen in the next four years. Maybe he'll break down, maybe something else will happen and then that's it—no more Olympic dream for us."

Addie kept quiet, as if sensing there was nothing she could say that would help me work through my mental gymnastics, or help me feel better with the guilt. I knew it wasn't my fault that he'd been stung. But I'd been late that morning because of being with Addie the night before. And a niggling thought persisted that maybe if I'd gotten there earlier, beat Wren even, and taken him out of his stall for a walk then it wouldn't have happened. I inhaled shakily. "And there's also everyone else I'm letting down. My coach, my sponsors, everyone who donated money or bought raffle tickets or a Dewey autograph and all that to help us get here." I gulped in air. "My family. And it may not even happen."

She cupped my cheeks in her hands, forcing me to look at her. "You're not letting anyone down, sweetheart. Equestrian sport can be fickle, everyone involved with it knows that."

After a sniff, I whispered, "I know. And I know how selfish and callous I must seem. Like my horse is sick and I'm here thinking about the fact that it might mean I don't get to ride in the Olympics and boo-hoo, woe is me. And we have a reserve combination so the team is fine, but it's not me and Dewey."

"It's not selfish or callous to have a dream and want to reach that." Her thumbs wiped gently at my cheeks. "I just need you to trust me, and that I'm doing all I can to help you reach it too."

I tried desperately to be neutral but couldn't find the ground. "Even with everything that's happened between us?"

Her eyes narrowed. "What d'you mean?"

"How can you possibly be objective about Dewey with everything you and I have done?"

Addie carefully withdrew her hands from where they'd been lovingly cupping my face and folded her arms over her breasts. "I can be objective because that's my job, Caitlyn. And I am *very* good at it, regardless of what's happening in my personal life."

"Are you sure?"

"Yes," she said flatly.

I stumbled over my response, trying to frame what was in my head the right way, and totally failing. "Maybe we shouldn't talk to each other unless it's absolutely necessary and about Dew."

Her mouth fell open and when she closed it again to speak, she spluttered for a few seconds. "Are you kidding me right now? Do you really think— Actually, you know what? I don't even know what to say to that, Caitlyn, except to ask you why? Why do you think that's a good idea?"

I had no idea how to tell her it was *me*, that I didn't know how to do this, how to set aside me and her when all of my emotional energy was being directed at Dewey. I didn't have the strength to compartmentalize my life right now. Knowing she had so much responsibility made me feel utterly powerless, and knowing the professional decision she had to make with the personal *us* in the way felt awful. So I'd step back and let her do her job without thinking about us. This had to be about Dewey and nothing else. I offered an ineffectual and evasive, "I just do."

"Right. Well the last thing I want is to get in the way." Her expression was admirably neutral. Her voice was anything but. "So, sure, whatever you think."

I swallowed the hard lump taking up most of the room in my throat. "I have to go watch Simone and Freddo and show my support, you know, in case they're competing instead of me and Dewey on Thursday." As soon as I'd said it, I wanted to pull the words back.

I knew Addie was doing everything she could to get Dew fit, and if the way she looked was any indication—it was taking its toll. Apparently it'd taken a bigger toll on me than I'd realized and my brain had lost its ability to control my emotions. But of all the bad timing, now really had to be the worst. She had done absolutely nothing to deserve me treating her like that, and even as my mouth had been saying the words my brain had been wondering what the hell I was doing.

Her jaw tightened. And that was the only response I got. To my face at least. As I walked off I heard her mutter, "Fuck my life."

Wandering numbly through the grounds I tried not to think about her anguished look. Tried not to think about the stupid things I'd said. And tried not to imagine how badly I might have just screwed up any possible future we could have once this was all over.

I dawdled on my way to the main stadium, stopping to grab a bottle of water and an ice cream from the Team USA cabin. Wren and Addie were deep in conversation in the stands beside the arena entrance and as I walked past each gave me a smile of varying friendliness. Okay then, probably not where I should sit. I moved to stand on the wide path by the entrance gate.

Freddo seemed to have taken serious offense to the arena setup, performing rodeo-bronc acrobatics and generally making his displeasure known. I leaned against the waist-high metal fencing and ate my ice cream. After a while Simone managed to settle Freddo and they did some solid work but by then, her timeslot was done. She brought him back to a walk and turned toward the exit where I stood.

She'd just left the stadium when a burst of extra-loud gunfire from the military echoed through the complex. Freddo spooked and shied violently sideways away from the sound. Simone brought him under control before he tangled himself in the fencing but he was piaffing, dancing around and doing small rears, then lunging forward, coming closer and closer to me. I slowly started backing away as Simone's exasperated, "Hey hey hey, cut it out!" was quickly followed by a wry smile and a look in my direction that clearly said *Horses*. I knew exactly what she meant and smiled back up at her.

Freddo abruptly stopped his piaffe, mini-rear and lunge routine and planted his feet. Simone was trying everything just to get him to move forward, and Freddo was trying his damnedest to ignore it. Eventually he did the most basic evasion to going forward. He reared. I pressed myself against the fence, not wanting to move quickly and startle him. The moment his front hooves landed again, Simone softened her hands and used a leg aid to move him forward. He ignored her. After a few seconds of asking nicely, she gave him a firm tap behind her leg with the whip.

Freddo reared again and this time, he was serious about it. He went almost vertical and Simone threw herself forward until her front pressed against his neck in a desperate attempt to not overbalance him. It didn't help. Freddo's rear hooves slipped on the thin surface of the path and the moment he started to go over backward Simone kicked out of the stirrups and bailed. It was almost six feet to the ground but jumping was always preferable to being crushed if the horse went over.

Simone cried out as she landed and lost her grip on the reins, leaving them flapping around Freddo's neck. I made a split-second decision to grab them to stop him from getting away. Him bolting around the complex would either cause serious damage to himself or start a riot which would have other horses doing serious damage to themselves.

I'd just managed to grab one rein when Freddo flipped fully over onto his back and wrenched the leather from my hand. He hit the ground with a loud crack. Having already thrown myself off balance to grab him, I tumbled forward and only just missed colliding with the fence and Freddo. I didn't miss hitting the back of my head on something and I scrambled onto my hands and knees to get away from the panicking horse. By the time I'd stood up, Freddo was flailing with all four legs in a desperate attempt to roll over and get up.

I looked at Simone, who had moved into a sitting position, and asked breathlessly, "You okay?"

"Think so." She went to stand then crumpled to the ground again. "My fucking ankle." When I went to go to her she gasped, "I'll be fine, hold him. *Please*."

My ears rang with shouting stewards and team staff as a crowd rushed in. I pulled both sets of reins over Freddo's head to keep him from tangling himself. The first person to reach us was a breathless Addie. She took me by both shoulders, her frantic gaze sweeping the length of me. "Are you all right?" she rasped out. Her face was a study in pure, raw panic.

"Yeah. But he's…I don't know what he is. I heard something go crack when he landed."

Addie glanced at Simone—who was muttering tearfully about her ankle while unzipping her boot—then let me go to attend to Freddo. I backed away, having been replaced by Freddo's groom who'd appeared from nowhere. She leaned over Freddo's back to avoid his still-flailing legs and fumbled to unfasten the girth. The moment she pulled the saddle off I realized the seat had broken in two, leather creasing over the break. "The saddle tree is broken. That could have been the sound I heard?"

Addie spared me a glance. "I sure fucking hope so."

Simone's sharp yell cut through the noise and when everyone looked at her she offered us all a wonky smile and held her boot up. "Twenty-two-hundred-dollar handmade boots. My favorites. No way am I letting doctors cut them off." She exhaled. "Is he—?"

Freddo tried one last flail, managed to get his hindlegs underneath himself, stretched his forelegs out and with a groan, stood. As he stumbled to his feet he staggered sideways, almost knocking Addie over, and I grabbed the back of her shirt to pull her away. Freddo struggled for balance and after a few seconds stood firmly on three legs, not weightbearing on the fourth—his left hind. He held the hoof six inches from the ground, dropping that leg and snatching it up again until he finally rested his toe on the ground. His posture was like a cat who'd had a fright, hunched over and standing almost on tip-toes.

Despite the crowd that had quickly gathered it was abundantly clear that Addie was in charge. With calm, quiet instructions she spoke into her radio, ordering the horse ambulance trailer brought around immediately and directing someone to notify the hospital that we were coming in with a horse that'd flipped over and landed hard. She did all of this while doing vitals and a physical assessment on Freddo and talking to those assembled about what was going to happen. Freddo had a quiet, unresisting shocked look to him.

Wren's first word when she arrived a minute later was a muttered, "Fuck." She took me by the shoulders and gently turned me to face her. "You okay? What happened? I ducked out to pee and came back just as hell was breaking loose."

I wiped away the gravel and fine sand sticking to my sweaty arms. I'd grazed my elbow as I'd fallen and had bits stuck in the ooze. "Gunfire and Freddo lost his shit. He did a massive rear, Simone bailed and fell over and lost the reins. I went to grab him to try to stop him getting away but he went over backward."

She looked me up and down then bent to brush my knees off. "He didn't land on you?"

"I tripped."

Wren noted, "You've got sand in your hair so you hit your head. Are you sure you're not hurt?"

"I'm fine, honestly. It wasn't a hard head crack." I glanced over at the horse who still stood in that same hunched position, and Simone who was hopping around him while leaning hard on Mary. The horse ambulance was making its way across the sand, and Addie was calmly directing the people around her and asking all nonessential people to leave.

Wren's arm closed around my shoulder. "Come on. There's nothing we can do here. I'm taking you to get checked by a medic."

Nonessential. Couldn't help Dewey. Couldn't help here. It seemed there was nothing I could do anywhere. I let her guide me away and as we walked I felt more useless and adrift than I ever had.

CHAPTER TWENTY-TWO

Addie

The mental and physical exhaustion of the past few days had left me feeling like a zombie, except even shambling and mumbling felt beyond my capabilities. After Freddo's accident the day before I'd been running on autopilot, antacids, and adrenaline. He had a non-displaced fracture of the iliac wing in his pelvis but was stable and comfortable and there was nothing to do except keep him quiet, restrict movement, administer pain relief and have the on-call Olympic PT work with him. Despite sounding serious, this injury was completely recoverable and with the right treatment and rehabilitation, he should be back in full work within twelve months.

Dewey's swelling had resolved, he had near-full range of neck movement and everything indicated he was feeling close to his usual self. With all that in mind, I would have to make a decision by tomorrow afternoon on his ability to compete. I hadn't administered anything after the initial injections, and I'd also cleared him for a light workout on the lunge coupled with fifteen minutes of riding in the air-conditioned indoor arena that morning. He'd been comfortable and shown no distress, but the rigors of a top-level dressage competition were far beyond just exercising on the end of a long rope with no rider aboard and some basic walk-trot-canter under saddle.

It was easy to pretend that the only consequences of my professional decisions would be professional. But I knew very well that they would have far-reaching implications for my personal life as well. Assuming there was even a personal life to look forward to after this, which seemed unlikely given Caitlyn's cool behavior the last few days.

I was trying very hard not to take it personally because I knew exactly how much stress she was under and that sometimes stressed people tended to react badly. And it wasn't as if I hadn't been short in response, as much as I'd hated it. It was easy to say that Caitlyn would respect my decision and that it wouldn't be personal. But it *was* personal, no matter how hard we tried to pretend otherwise.

I found James Parker, a UK vet who was part of the volunteer vet team whose job was to act as roving veterinary care for the facility, in the clinic vets' office. "Hey, James. You got a moment to go over my bee sting case?"

It was more than just a confirmation of my opinion. I had to be absolutely sure that my feelings for Caitlyn hadn't caused unintended bias. If there was any unconscious part of myself that had allowed feelings for her to influence my decision then I may as well hang my vetting hat up for good.

"Of course." He picked up his mug and stood, stretching his back. "He's up for clearance to compete isn't he?" There were few secrets around here.

"Mhmm. And you know about my fractured pelvis case, right?"

"I do. You must have some bad juju if you've had both a core team horse and the reserve horse go down."

"Thanks," I said dryly. As if I didn't know that not getting Dewey right would not only ruin Caitlyn's dream but the team's medal chances. Though up to four combinations were able to compete for a country, only the top three scores counted. Without Caitlyn's score—which would undoubtedly be the highest on the team—they would be unable to drop the lowest score from the team's combined Grand Prix and Grand Prix Special. And the average scores from the other riders wouldn't be good enough to put the USA in contention for a medal. "Based on everything I'm seeing, I'm going to declare Dewey fit. I discharged him back to his stall this morning and I just need to make sure I'm not missing anything. A second opinion is always helpful." I passed James my tablet. "I have to be absolutely sure before I sign off. And I want to test blood and urine for prohibited substances. We'll have results before competition starts."

Nervousness snaked through my body as I said those words. I held someone's dream in my hand, someone I was in love with, and it felt awful.

Shit. Someone I was in love with? Note to self: unpack that later.

James grinned. "Consider your buttocks covered." He took the iPad and skimmed through the latest results and vitals. "On paper he looks fine and you already know I agree with your treatment and the drug threshold times. It says here they worked him this morning under saddle?"

"Yeah. Fifteen minutes and he performed all the movements needed for a Grand Prix test, albeit not *quite* to his super-high usual standard, according to his groom. Both rider and groom were certain he looked and felt fine, if not a little sluggish, which I'd expect given the stress of the last few days. It's not something I'm concerned about at this stage. I checked him before and after and watched him work. Seemed bright, happy within himself and happy to work."

"Based on all that, I'd declare him fit. But let me examine him, and then we've covered every base."

"Good call. Thanks."

"When we're done today you need to go home and sleep. You look like shit and I'm sick of seeing you scuttling around here when you should be home." He held up both hands when I opened my mouth to protest. "I've watched you cuddling that horse and I know you're crazy about him, but we can handle anything that comes up. If I'm worried, I'll call you."

Crazy about both horse and rider was more like it.

Dewey's stall was occupied by both Caitlyn and Wren, grooming him and taking off his ice boots respectively. I knocked on the lower stall door, startling the humans but not the horse who vocalized how happy he was to see me. Wren stood from where she'd been crouching by Dewey's hind leg, rested a hand on his butt and offered a wave with the other. Caitlyn's face drained of color as she took in both me and James. "Hi," she managed, her voice barely audible.

Despite her aloofness over the last few days, my smile was automatic, as if my face couldn't help itself when I saw her. Stupid independent face. "Hey, this is Doctor James Parker. Mind if we check the patient?"

Caitlyn's nod was overly enthusiastic, as if she'd had to remind herself to be polite and had misjudged her intensity. "Sure thing."

James and I slipped into the stall and I offered Dewey first a carrot then a neck scratch before I checked his feed and water containers.

Eating and drinking as normal. Excellent start. Wren had unobtrusively removed the last of his ice boots and moved into the corner of the stall out of the way. Four people and a huge horse didn't leave much room for maneuvering.

Caitlyn hugged herself around the middle, and I had to force myself to keep my distance. Every cell in my body wanted to be near her, to touch her and comfort her and tell her it was all fine, just a checkup. Dewey snuffled my shirt pocket and I took his nose in my hands and kissed his little black dot. "Behave yourself."

Once James started his examination, I shuffled fractionally closer to Caitlyn. Wren was watching on, and I made sure to speak to both of them. "Everything looks normal, but I've asked James to confirm, okay? That's all this is, just a final check. I promise."

Wren nodded amicably.

Caitlyn exhaled, "Okay. Is he cleared?"

"Almost." My most reassuring smile didn't seem to reassure her.

While James checked Dewey over I studied every piece of the horse, trying to see anything that might be out of place. Swelling. A lump. A missed breath. If I screwed this up it would be a disaster on all levels.

After an eternity, James pulled his stethoscope from his ears. "Can't fault him. And if he's working well then I'm happy to cosign him as fit for competition."

Behind me, I heard Caitlyn's exhalation, and Wren's murmured, "Thank fuck."

Though I'd known deep-down that my assessment was correct, the relief of having another veterinarian confirm it made me feel like I'd just discovered a new periodic element. "Great." I turned to Caitlyn and Wren. "Excellent news. Looks like it's full steam ahead. I'm going to take blood and urine samples tomorrow morning to make sure everything is out of his system."

Caitlyn's expression had turned to a curious mix of relief and something that seemed a whole lot like embarrassment. She nodded, and eventually whispered a shaky, "Thank you."

I pulled James backward a step, away from Dewey's inquisitive mouth. "I'll get your signature on the clearance paperwork too if you don't mind? I'll come find you before I submit it."

"Sounds good." James patted Dewey and said his goodbyes.

I leaned my forehead against the horse's neck and he turned his head in his adorable way to press his cheek against my back, like an equine cuddle. When I felt his lips playing with the shirt at the small of my back, I laughed and disengaged myself. "I'll be here first thing tomorrow morning to get those samples, but if anything seems off from now on, let me know right away no matter the time of day or night."

"We will," Caitlyn and Wren answered together.

Caitlyn let out an indistinguishable sound as if a prelude to saying something and I gave her my attention. But she was silent. She looked like she wanted to speak but I had no idea if it was something she couldn't or wouldn't say in front of Wren, or if it she'd decided she didn't want to express it after all. I fought the urge to wilt. "Okay then. Catch you both later."

As I walked away I was pretty sure I heard Wren hiss, "You are such an idiot!"

By the time I'd filled in Dewey's paperwork, had James sign it and hand delivered it—because screw that super important thing being lost somewhere—it was almost seven p.m. I was beyond tired and hungry and should have been back at my apartment, showered and sitting at the tiny table eating whatever I'd managed to get delivered while going over the day to make sure I'd recorded everything from a temp check to extra electrolytes administered.

As I approached the gates to flag down a car, from behind me came Caitlyn's voice. "Addie!"

My heart sank and soared all at once. Thankfully she sounded far enough away that I had a few seconds to compose myself. I turned back and waited for her to approach. The moment I faced her, Caitlyn broke into a jog and the moment she was in my personal space, she blurted, "Hey. I've been waiting for you."

"Hey yourself."

"So…how are you?"

"Delightful."

"Great." She scratched the side of her neck. "I was just wondering if we could talk? Back at your apartment? Alone?"

"I thought we weren't allowed to talk unless it was about Dewey. And on that topic, there's nothin' more I can tell you."

"Addie…"

"What?" I snapped. The moment I dropped my guard and let my frustration free, the rest of it fell out in a tangled, angry mess. "What do you want? Because I honestly can't handle being your whippin' girl right now. I have been out here advocating for you and your horse from the moment he got sick. I've had more meetings with Mary and Ian than I'd care to, and I've been practically on hands and knees asking them to just let me do my job and get your horse well so that you can compete. I have spent hours beggin' them to give me the time to get Dewey right so you could hold your place in the team. Just a few more days, that I was confident he'd come good, that it'd go as planned. Because not only do I know how important you are to the team's medal chances but I know how important this is to you. And I did all that despite how you've been treatin' me because that is my fucking job, Caitlyn. I have put every ounce of professional and personal integrity on the line for you and you couldn't even extend me the courtesy of at least pretendin' to be nice. And you know the worst part of it? I don't even know what I did to deserve that reaction from you. I am completely fucking stumped."

She wilted. "You're right. I'm sorry. I've not handled this well at all."

"No you haven't," I agreed. "So what is it? Lookin' for a booty call? Happy that I cleared him so you're rewarding me?" I hadn't meant to think it, let alone say it, but after days of nonstop work and emotional stress, my filters had disappeared.

Her mouth fell open and after a long, silent pause, she muttered, "Ouch."

Ouch indeed. I hastened to verbalize my apologies. "I'm sorry. That was so far out of line it's practically back in the States. I'm sorry," I repeated. "Long and stressful few days as I'm sure you're aware. And in more ways than one." I raised a pointed eyebrow.

"I know. I'd just like to talk."

"Me too," I quietly admitted. My annoyance had left as quickly as it'd appeared. "Come on then, let's talk."

The twenty-minute ride to my apartment was silent and awkward which wasn't helped by the fact the driver was a rare one who didn't engage in conversation. With both of us in the backseat on our phones ignoring each other, it felt like the end of a bad first date. I had a clump of work emails, most of them patient updates. Then there was Eric's blunt email telling me that my septic premature foal from a few months back, who'd rallied and was doing great, had colicked badly and been euthanized. Things just got better and better.

The moment I'd locked the door behind us, I threw my things onto a chair. "I'm just going to shower. I've been living on coffee and adrenaline today and I'm sure I smell exactly like that."

"You smell great," she quietly said. "The same as you always do."

I pushed aside her compliment. "Have you eaten dinner?"

"Not yet."

"Sorry, I'm not cooking while I'm here so all I've got is limited snacks and alcohol. I'd kill for pizza if that's okay with you?"

"Sure."

"Great. There's a menu on the fridge for a great place that also speaks English. Any kind is fine with me."

I slipped into the bathroom and could hear her unintelligible words as I washed grime from my skin. After a minute or two there was a knock on the bathroom door before she called something that sounded like my name. I called back, "Yeah?"

Caitlyn's response was muffled by both water and a closed door.

"What was that? Sorry I can't hear you."

The door opened, then quickly closed partway again when Caitlyn seemed to register that from the doorway she had a direct line of sight to me in the shower. Her words floated through the crack in the door and sounded more than a little hoarse. "They're busy and delivery won't be for an hour. Is that okay or did you want to get something else? Or go out?"

Even if we hadn't been expressly warned to not go anywhere except our accommodation and the competition venue, the last thing I felt like doing was wandering the streets of a strange city at night, especially hungry and tired. "That's fine, I can wait. I might just have to eat a doorknob in the meantime."

A soft laugh. "Okay then."

I finished up in the shower and discovered midway through toweling myself dry that I hadn't brought in any clean clothes. I was really not used to company. Right. Mad towel dash it is. Caitlyn looked up from her phone screen. She didn't avert her gaze but she wasn't being a letch about my almost nudity either.

"This is not an intentional ploy, I promise, like oh my goodness whoops where *did* my clothes go," I said as I crab-walked to my room, trying to angle myself in such a way that all my bits were covered by the tiny bath towel. Not that I was worried about her seeing me naked, obviously, but right now didn't feel like a great time. "I'm used to it being only me here."

"It's fine," she said quickly. "I'll...leave you to it."

She tried to hide it, but the heat in her gaze was as bold as it had been the night we'd first slept together. I closed the bedroom door and dressed before I did something stupid. Feeling almost human for the first time all day, I took a few slow breaths to center myself before I left the bedroom. Caitlyn had settled at the small table with a bottle of Aura Lager, which she tilted toward me. "I stole one of your beers. Hope you don't mind."

"Not at all. My beers are your beers." I sat opposite. "We've got a little time before dinner. Do you want to talk now or wait 'til we've eaten?"

Caitlyn seemed to shrink in on herself, as if trying to hide from something or holding something in. She swallowed nervously, then swigged a mouthful of beer. After an eternity, she said, "Addie."

"Yes?"

It took her long moments before she spoke again, her voice tremulous and cracking. "I'm sorry. I've screwed up. And it's because of this thing between us. I'm a goddamned walking contradiction, say one thing and do the other. And I feel so guilty. I have one job, just one. I need to put Dewey's needs above mine and I didn't do that." She rubbed a hand over her face. "Everything is different here and I'm finding it so hard to get into my groove. I just feel like I'm handling everything wrong."

"How so?"

"I should have been there earlier that morning and maybe I would have seen he wasn't feeling well. And we could have done something sooner. But I was tired after spending the night with you, so I slept a little longer, and…"

The science of "If I'd only…" was one I knew well, and there was very little that helped with that awful feeling of having messed up, even if the feeling wasn't justified. "Caitlyn, being there a little earlier would have made no difference. What happened, just happened. It's nobody's fault."

"I know that deep down, I know. It's just—" The rest of the words tumbled over each other. "I'm so sorry for treating you like that. I didn't know how to act, I didn't know what to say and the whole time I kept asking myself why I was behaving like this. I'm so good at setting things aside, but no matter how I tried I couldn't do it this time. I kept thinking of how hard it must be for you to have both sides of the coin, Vet Addie and Slept-with-Me Addie. I think…I think I thought if I just backed away then maybe I might be able to get some clarity and maybe not having me around would make it easier for you too." Her hands worked nervously. "Because it was hard for me as rider and owner and person who's—" She broke off abruptly, and never resumed, leaving me to pick up the conversation.

I exhaled, trying to unravel what she'd just admitted. "Okay. Well that makes sense and honestly feels a whole lot better than just you freaking out about what we'd done and never wanting to talk to me outside of my job. But it still hurt. And while I appreciate the thought you obviously put into your approach, and the care that was behind your decision, it's not for you to decide how I'm going to respond, Caitlyn. I've spent my life compartmentalizing my job and my personal life. I'm pretty good at it now." I laughed dryly and added, "Except with you, as I discovered."

"What do you mean?"

"You said you have one job and you didn't do it? I did exactly the same thing. When Freddo flipped over backward all I saw was you right there and from where I was it looked like he'd knocked you over. And I freaked out. Do you know what my first thought was in that moment?"

"The horse is an idiot?"

Laughing I agreed, "Yeah he is. But that wasn't it. My first thought was you. The veterinarian whose sole purpose for being here is to look after the horses didn't think about the horse. She thought about you. And *then* my focus snapped to the horse. But when I got to you I forgot about him again, just for a few seconds, because I was so utterly horrified that you might have been hurt." I shrugged. "There you have it. I guess we're both not thinking straight."

She allowed herself a faint smile. "Not at all. Never have."

I poked her thigh. "Ha-ha. For the record, it *was* hard for me. The little part of me that's falling in love with you couldn't help thinkin' about your feelings every time I tried to come up with solutions."

Her eyebrows shot up so fast I would have laughed if not for the realization of why. "Falling in love?"

Shit to the power of infinity multiplied by a zillion. "Let's forget that came out of my mouth." What I'd said was true, as I'd realized earlier, but the timing could not be worse with everything swirling around us.

"I don't want to forget it," she whispered. She moved closer. "I want to have it in the back of my mind, like a little happy earworm."

"An earworm doesn't sound all that great, honestly."

"Usually not, but this one is going to be incredible." She kissed the tip of my nose then seemed to reconsider and moved lower to my lips. The kiss was gentle and slow and when we parted it seemed as if her tension had fallen away. "I'm sorry, and I admit maybe I took the *be neutral* too far into *be cool* territory."

I held my thumb and forefinger a quarter of an inch apart. "Lil bit. In future, why don't you talk to me about it? If you're not sure about something with us, then I'd prefer we discussed it, rather than either of us being uncertain and risking upset."

She paused. "In future?"

"Yes. I am *here* for a future. With you. Whatever that might look like and however we can make it work. And I'm still on board with waiting until after the Olympics. I'm on board with whatever you need right now."

The conflict danced across her face. "Okay. I think what I need right now is for you to be around, but…for there to be no pressure. I know it's kind of selfish, but—"

"I can do that." I held up both hands. "No pressure at all."

"Thank you. But even if I don't get much time to talk to you about anything other than Dewey, I'll be thinking about you. When I'm not thinking of the whole Olympics thing that is."

"And I'll be thinking about you too. I'm also here, you know? To talk about whatever you want if you need to. Please don't shut me out. Personal stuff aside, I need you to be talking with me so we can keep Dewey sound."

"I won't. I…think it keeps me sound too," she whispered.

CHAPTER TWENTY-THREE

Caitlyn

Olympic nerves, I discovered, were no worse than regular big-show nerves. The equestrian organizing committee had everything running so smoothly that there was no external stress. Just mild internal stress, which was normal. Dew had sailed through the trot-up, as had all the US Team horses, which meant we were all cleared to compete. Addie had watched us like a hawk, arms crossed and a thumbnail in her mouth as we'd run along the hard, flat surface to confirm the horses were sound. I'd spent the first day of competition watching Dakota and Jesse give solid performances, then had a light training session with Dew before dinner, social media, and bed.

I woke on my Grand Prix test day after a good sleep, had my usual quick workout to loosen up, ate breakfast, and took a car to Deodoro. Wren had texted me from the stalls at the buttcrack of dawn and I'd been getting steady updates all morning to let me know we were on track for our ride time of 2:24 p.m. All dressage competitions had precise scheduling but the Olympics organizers seemed to have dialed it up a notch, cutting down allocated times to the exact amount needed to enter the stadium, circle the arena, do a test and exit the stadium again.

Wren would have made sure Dew had breakfast, taken him for a walk, done some stretches with him and given him a solid grooming to make him feel good and get his blood moving. Then she'd wash and dry him, braid his mane, make him look even handsomer—if that were possible—give him a small lunch snack and have him tacked up ready for our warm-up forty minutes before my allocated start time. The air felt electrified when I walked through the grounds, as if everyone present was humming with the same excitement I was.

Addie had been flitting around the Team USA cabin, the stalls, the warm-up arenas and everywhere between. We'd managed a quick "Hi, how are you" exchange and even this simple short conversation was enough to settle my nerves.

I'd decided to take advantage of the air-conditioned indoor arena to try to keep Dew cool, before moving outside for some acclimatization before our test. I was joined by Wren, Mary, Ian, some other riders, journalists, and a dozen spectators who were filming me on their phones and would continue to do so while I rode. The warm-up arena held four other horses and I thanked the gate attendant who checked my credentials then let me in.

I caught Ian's nod, and his murmured encouragement. Wren, with Dew's halter and a bucket of assorted stuff in her arms, offered a sneaky thumbs-up. A few feet behind them, partially hidden by a post, stood Addie. She was in profile, expression hidden by sunglasses and the shadow of her ball cap. I took the few seconds I had before my mind blanked of everything except me and Dew to stare at her, absorb her.

If only we could make it work outside of this. We had so many obstacles and issues, but maybe… Maybe I should stop acting like a walking hormone on the day of my Olympic debut.

Ian's, "You set?" in my ear confirmed it was time to put everything aside except my ride.

I always felt sorry for Dewey in the communal warm-up arenas at shows, because I sensed how much he wanted to say hi to the other horses. Over the years we'd reached a compromise where during our initial walk he could look around at the other horses—but no touching—and the moment I took up the reins it was time for game face. There was a special kind of tunnel vision when riding but being in a shared arena meant I had to take some of my focus away from the ride to make sure we were obeying the arena rules and watching for those who inevitably didn't.

I played with some transitions within trot and loosened Dew's neck and back with changes of flexion and some long and forward neck stretching. When he was warm and loose I brought his head and neck back up again into a collected frame and added some pressure. Half-pass across the arena in both directions. Passage, piaffe. Canter, tempi changes, pirouettes. Ian was mostly silent in my ear, except for the occasional comments of, "More more, yes good, rhythm, rhythm." Dew felt forward and supple, attentive and enthused about working, but not explosive. Game on.

From outside the fence, a steward called, "Caitlyn Lloyd, USA. Ten minutes."

I raised my hand in acknowledgment, then rode out of the arena and halted outside the building. The heat hit me like a smothering blanket. Bah. Wren and Addie appeared as if they'd teleported. Addie studied Dew, her mouth turned down on the right side the way it always did when she was concentrating. Wren handed a bottle of water up to me. "How's he feel?"

I drank a few long gulps. "Good. Like himself."

Addie checked his gums, then pinched the skin on his neck and I saw her shoulders drop. She mumbled something to herself then peered up at me and Wren. "Hydrated, capillary reflex looks good." She turned to Wren. "He can have a mouthful of water if he wants it."

He didn't. Wren wiped Dew's coat where Addie had checked his skin, as if she'd messed up his perfection. They followed me to the ten-minute arena—the outdoor arena lined with eucalypts where we could have a final tune-up before entering the stadium. Now wasn't the time to fiddle. Dew didn't need to be settled or encouraged or trained, so I used the time for some walk and trot with him stretching his neck and back to stay loose. Another steward indicated that it was time for me to enter the arena. While Wren hastily pulled off Dew's protective boots I pulled out my earpiece and handed it down to Ian before double checking my coat buttons, my helmet strap, the fastenings on my gloves, and repositioning my tails behind the saddle.

Wren, unable to help herself, polished everything she could touch. "See you on the flipside," she said. "Kick some dressage-test ass."

I called over my shoulder, "Do dressage tests have asses?"

The steward walking at Dew's shoulder to escort me to the gate snickered.

Loudspeakers echoed through the stadium and Dew practically dragged me into the space, his trot so exuberant that his knees were almost up around his ears. He always knew when it was showtime and being the crowd-loving attention seeker he was, dialed up his exuberance to max levels. Despite his obvious excitement, he was still soft and attentive and I let him be because there was absolutely no reason for me to ever discipline a horse for wanting to try too much.

The stadium was a little over half-full and the announcer talking about me was a blur of white noise as we trotted around the outside of the competition arena laid out as usual with a foot-high white fence, and the arena letters around the outside marked with boxes containing decorative fauna. Dew's ears moved back and forth but he wasn't tense, just getting a feel for the atmosphere. The announcements quieted and the bell sounded to indicate I could start. I brought Dew back to a walk and did my superstitious and pointless, because they were already organized, rein organization.

Collected canter along the outside of the arena, small half circle to line up with the center line, and I entered the arena. I inhaled slowly as I saluted, gathered my reins again and then we were off. After consulting with Ian and Mary, we'd decided to throw everything at the test, and it was up to me to find the balance between big powerful movements, and the risk of breaking gaits. One of our strengths was accuracy, and I knew every movement would be exactly where it was supposed to be. All I had to do was be bold.

We had a small loss of consistency and elevation in our final piaffe, likely because Dew was tired and sapped by the heat. But when I asked him to give me just a little more, it was like he heaved a sigh, and said, "Okay, I'll do it." My final halt, salute was one of the best feelings I'd ever had and the moment I was done, I leaned down to thank Dew for giving me everything he had. I kept up my pats as we exited the arena at a walk, alternating with pats and waving to the roaring crowd.

I'd just ridden a dressage test at the Olympics. Holy shit. My throat tightened. I knew Dew was tired and hot—heck, I was tired and hot—but every time I'd asked, he'd answered. Masses of emotion hit me all at once. Relief and pride were the most dominant, followed closely by something I always experienced after riding a test, and had never managed to figure out, but that always made me feel like crying.

The same steward who'd escorted us to the gate took us to have my tack checked and confirmed as legal. She had to stretch her legs to keep up with Dewey's enthusiastic walk and had a hand raised to keep him from nuzzling her very interesting Panama hat. The moment we rounded the corner where my people were waiting, Dew stuck his nose out to greet Wren and her bucket of stuff. I had to remind him we weren't yet done and rode him into the shade cast by the trees.

Underneath me, Dewey was huffing to catch his breath as the official checked his noseband and bits and ensured that he hadn't bitten his tongue. Being out of breath didn't stop Dew trying to mouth the man's fingers. I offered the most contrite "Sorry" I could muster with my dry mouth. The early afternoon heat and humidity were horrible and I felt sorry for Dew who had to endure the checks before he was released for a cold shower.

I dismounted and at the sound of the announcer, turned back to check my score on the huge digital screen visible through the trees.

80.785%.

I blinked hard, trying desperately to keep the tears at bay. Not only had I scored damned well but my test, which was the last of our team's for the Grand Prix, had put us in third place overall which was a brilliant spot going into the Grand Prix Special which would decide the team medals. The small crowd around us erupted into cheers, applause, hugs, backslaps, and pats for Dew. I drew in a slow breath, trying to calm my emotion while Dewey searched for entertainment.

The video camera beside me was as intriguing as the official's fingers. Dew swung his nose and put it right in the lens. Hello, viewers, this is Dewey reporting live from the Olympics where I've just been a very good boy. I offered another "Sorry," this time to the laughing cameraman who was fumbling for a cloth to clean the camera.

"Happy?" Wren asked as she handed me a bottle of water.

Still aware I was being filmed, albeit by a probably fogged-up camera thanks to Dew's hello, I nodded and drank a polite mouthful when all I wanted to do was upend the bottle over myself. "Yeah, he felt really good. I was a bit worried by that final piaffe, he felt utterly beat but he picked up when I asked him to."

Wren grinned. "Superstar."

The official checked my spurs, then Dew's abdomen to make sure I hadn't spurred him to bleeding and declared all was fine. Not that I'd expected anything differently. I offered a smile and a genuine, "Thank you very much."

Wren took possession of Dew so I could hydrate before going to the press box. I drank half a bottle of water, removed my tails, then checked myself in the compact mirror she offered. "Right. I have to go answer some questions. You two okay here?"

"Absolutely perfect." Wren grabbed my coat and hung it over her forearm. "Go pretend to be extroverted."

"I'll do my best." I hugged Dew's neck then left him in Wren's capable hands so I could go face the firing squad. Uh, press.

After fifteen minutes of questions and confirming how pleased I was with our ride and the fact Team USA was in such a good position, and my relief that Dewey had overcome his bee encounter, a signal from the back of the room indicated this would be the final question before I had to vacate for the next rider. I paused for a moment after the journalist had finished, trying to phrase my response in a way that didn't sound like every other answer I'd given. "It sounds so clichéd, but I'm just so lucky to have such a willing and talented partner in Dewey, and a brilliant team surrounding me. I would never have enjoyed the successes I have without the unwavering support of my family. I'd be lying if I said it's been easy—nobody makes it this far in dressage without years of hard work and dedication." I laughed. "But I've been fortunate to have enjoyed a little luck as well."

I thanked everyone present then slipped out of the room to go check on my equine partner. I'd barely made it five steps outside before I was surrounded by people. After small talk, photos and signing a bunch of photos of me and Dew, I slipped through the crowds and made my way back to the stalls.

"How is he?" I asked Wren as I slipped into the stall.

"Nibbly," she said around the tool in her mouth that she used to unpick the thread holding Dew's braids together.

"Situation normal."

"He spent some time with the cooling fans after his hose-down and he's had a good drink." She undid the last braid and combed her fingers through the curly mane hair to straighten it. "I'm about to grab him a snack."

I gave Dew a few carrots and a kiss on his nose and knew immediately which of the two things he wanted more of. "Such a clever guy, yes you are." I got a face full of Dew breath. "Okay, I need to go get changed."

"And eat something. And maybe relax for five minutes?" Wren's eyebrow raise was pointed. "You know, those things you should have done before coming here."

"Right. That. I just wanted to check he was okay."

"If he breathes wrong, you'll know about it."

"I know. Thank you." I hugged my groom around the waist then left so I could deal with myself.

I'd just rounded the corner when the one person I never expected or wanted to see appeared.

"Caitlyn." My ex sounded as if I was the best thing she'd laid eyes on all week.

"Elin," I squeaked out. Elin wasn't part of the Danish team, so why was she here? After our breakup two years ago, Elin's Grand Prix horse had died tragically after a serious colic and she'd been away from the Big Tour circuit in Europe ever since. I'd thought that perhaps the universe was looking out for me.

"I was hoping to see you," Elin purred. Goddamn that stupid sexy accent.

"Given I'm competing it's not exactly a surprise."

"No, I suppose you're right." She touched my arm, lingering longer than was polite, even for someone I'd been naked with. "You look great. And such a brilliant first ride."

I had to give Elin one thing. Despite everything she'd done to break my heart, she knew how much I hated the me-versus-you atmosphere of the dressage scene. From the first time I'd mentioned it, she'd always given me honest feedback and never made me feel uncomfortable. Well, not in that regard anyway. Everything else was fair game.

"Thank you." I glanced down at the tag hanging from a lanyard around her neck. Not a spectator ticket, but one of the team family passes. "So why are you here?"

"My girlfriend is competing. Laura Richards," she supplied without me prompting. "For Great Britain."

"I know. Well I didn't know you two were dating, but I know who Laura is."

"Mmm. Listen, why don't we catch up for a drink later? And then…" She glanced around as if checking how alone we were and her voice lowered to a murmur. "Are you seeing anyone?"

I almost said yes, but at the last moment decided not to drag Addie into this, partly because she didn't deserve to be part of the Elin Shitshow and partly because I had no idea what she and I were doing. Aside from sleeping together and wondering what came after. So I evaded with, "You are."

"Semantics and nothing more."

My laugh felt like dust. "You really haven't changed at all."

Addie walked up behind Elin and when she spotted me with someone else started backing away. Elin, master of body language, turned around. I had no idea what she'd seen on my face but clearly something had given me away. Probably a mix of joy at seeing Addie and panic that Elin was there too. Addie offered an apologetic wave then disappeared around a corner.

Elin turned back slowly, as if using the time to think of what she was about to say. She raised a slow eyebrow. Damn her single eyebrow control. Before, it used to make me gooey inside. Now, it just annoyed me. After a dramatic pause, she asked, "A friend of yours?"

I almost brushed her question aside to point out that Addie was our veterinarian and the marvel who'd worked her butt off so Dew could compete and have that brilliant ride she'd just mentioned. But Addie was so much more than that. "She is, yes."

My ex rarely hid her emotions, and now was no different. Glee was written all over her. "And then some more than a friend I think. That look you just had on your face is the same one you used to show when seeing me for the first time after months apart."

I wasn't worried about Elin spilling her discovery to anyone because while she was many frustrating and upsetting things, she was always discreet. But having her know, having someone see that private part of myself felt weird and…wrong. And if Elin had seen it then surely Addie did. How embarrassing. "We're just seeing how it goes, or if it even *can* go."

"Well then, evidently you are seeing someone whether you choose to admit that or not." She squeezed my shoulder lightly. "I hope the rest of your rides are as good as today's. Take care of yourself and give Dewey a pat from me."

Elin wandered off in the same direction as Addie and I held my breath, hoping she didn't feel some sadistic need to stop and say something to her. But either Elin had moved past her toying-with-people stage, or she wasn't in the mood today because she strolled right past Addie's hiding corner without a sideways glance. I scuttled after her and almost collided with Addie who grabbed me by my arm to stop me from toppling. With the other hand she held an ice cream that she was twisting to stop its dripping.

A quick sweep of her tongue around the bottom stopped the drips but started my heart racing. After a sheepish grin, she said, "I'm sorry, this was actually for you but it was gettin' melty while I was waiting, so I had to take care of it."

"You got me an ice cream?"

"I did. Thought you might like one after that ride. Congrats by the way, it was brilliant."

"Thanks, and I would." I made a gimme motion.

"I've…licked it."

"And?" Leaning in, I reminded her, "We have swapped saliva before you know."

"I know but this is not that." Still she handed it over and I took a bite.

Bliss. I leaned against the fence and finished it off in a few more huge bites. "You're amazing."

"I know." After a quick inspection of my face, she quietly asked, "You okay?"

"Mhmm. Just someone I didn't expect to see here, someone I didn't want to see. And then she just *had* to talk to me so, yeah. Awkward."

She eyed me speculatively. "That was Elin Nygaard, right?"

"Yes. How'd you know?"

Addie's cheeks rapidly turned pink and she remained silent for a long moment before coming clean with, "I Googled her when Teresa mentioned you'd dated her."

That was so not what I'd expected her to say. "Why?"

"Because I wanted to see what kind of women you were into. I wouldn't have picked you for the Nordic goddess type." The statement was casual but her expression was anything but. Her face held interest but also surprisingly, resignation.

"I'm really not."

"Oh. She's very attractive," Addie said, still with that same casual tone.

"On the outside, yes. Inside, not so much."

"No?"

"No. Nordic goddess is actually Nordic cheater. I thought we had a relationship, but to her I was just a place for her to get sex she enjoyed. Orgasms are fantastic, don't get me wrong, but it's all of the other stuff that's important to me. Like the bread around an orgasm sandwich."

"Interesting analogy. You know how much I love…sandwiches. And yeah, Teresa mentioned that cheating was the rumor. Unsubstantiated."

"Consider it substantiated."

Addie nodded slowly. "My opinion, not that you asked for it, is that she's an idiot for doing that."

"She is, because I'm amazing."

"Can*not* argue at all." The grin faded to a serious expression. "Are you sure you're okay? I know it was a while ago, but shit like that lingers."

Her sweet concern had me melting like the ice cream. "I am. I mean of course it sucked and she hurt me, but also I'm grateful she did it. Not the cheating but showing me who she is."

"Why's that?"

"It forced me to move on from her, from that experience and it's left me open for other opportunities. Being tied down with that mess was not healthy and I didn't realize until we'd split how emotionally draining she was."

"New opportunities are always good," Addie said carefully. "So…if cheating Nordic goddesses aren't your type, what is?"

"Right now? It's cute veterinarians with adorable dimples and an odd sense of humor." The moment I'd said it I knew it was a bad thing to let out into the world. Admitting it to myself was one thing but to tell her that I was open to more than whatever this was felt like I was making a promise I might not be able to keep.

"Oh. Well that's not really my type at all, but whatever floats your boat." Addie had her teeth wedged in her lower lip, but the smile still twitched at the corners of her mouth.

"What's your type then?"

"Leggy, introverted dressage enthusiasts with brilliant smiles and the most incredible laugh I've ever heard."

I knew I was blushing when I managed a very articulate, "Ah."

Addie leaned in to whisper against my ear, "In case there's any uncertainty or ambiguity with that response, I mean you."

"I gathered that. I mean it was either me, or Donna Jameson who rides for Australia."

"There's no contest. It's all you." She smiled that heart-twisting smile at me. The one that made me forget everything that screamed this wasn't a good idea. "I was just on my way to check out your superstar partner. Wren called while she was hosing him down to say he'd come down well from the ride but I want to be sure."

"I just saw them before I had to do press stuff and yeah, he seems fine."

"Great. Care to join me?" She paused, and added a laughing, "To… see your own horse."

I squeezed her hand. "Love to."

CHAPTER TWENTY-FOUR

Addie

We'd get no downtime after the team's Grand Prix performance, with the Special scheduled for the day following the Grand Prix tests. I'd been run off my feet making sure all the horses were happy, that their limbs were cool and sound and that they were all eating, drinking, and crapping as they should. We'd been through more ice than I thought possible, using it to cool the horses and their legs and most of the riders were pouring it down their shirts as well.

Among the mayhem, Wren seemed to have appointed herself coordinator of the "Put Caitlyn and Addie together and alone as much as possible" cause, making herself scarce whenever I came by Dewey's stall. I'd been making a habit of leaving my evening visits to Dewey last so I could spend as much time with him to...uh, make sure he had no lingering effects from his bee sting. The fact that Caitlyn always seemed to be around then too was just a coincidence. The night of Caitlyn's Grand Prix test Wren spotted me walking down the laneway between the stalls and leaned over to open Dewey's lower stall door.

"Heading off?" I asked.

"Yep. I'm going to grab some dinner, hang out in the cabin with the other grooms and wait for final night checks." She lowered her voice. "How about you two don't be here when I get back at nine thirty? Maybe do something, I don't know...normal and romantic."

Caitlyn's voice from the back of the stall was dust-dry. "I can hear you too, you know. You are such a buttinsky."

Wren's answer was a shrug. She pulled her headphones over her ears and walked off.

I paused at the stall door. "Mind if I come in?"

"Not at all."

"Oh, I was actually asking Dewey if it was okay with him," I said as I stepped into the stall and locked the lower door.

The moment I came within reach, Caitlyn punched my arm. "Smartass." Then she rubbed up and down my bicep. "Are you okay?"

"Aside from my now-dead arm? Yes."

"I meant your leg. You've been limping all day."

I was so heart-melty over the fact she'd noticed something like that that I couldn't think of something sensible in response and instead blurted, "Caitlyn Lloyd, are you stalking me?"

"Do you want another arm punch?"

My answer was a facetious, "Yes please."

She leaned against the wall beside Dew's feeder. "Of course I'm stalking you. I've noticed the longer your days, the more you limp." She offered a helpless smile. "It worries me, that's all."

"You are the sweetest little cupcake I have ever met. I'm fine, really. It's just a lot of standing and walking and rushing and very little sitting. Tomorrow morning I'll start out good as new."

"And end up limping like you're missing a kneecap or something by tomorrow night?"

"Probably." I waved dismissively. "Part of the job. In other happy news, in case Mary hasn't told y'all, after the complaint we lodged and multiple attempts from the IOC who agreed what happened to Freddo was bullshit, the military have finally agreed to give up their live-fire exercises while the equestrian events are on." It'd been a nightmare of official complaints, IOC meetings and arguing with the military that no, just because elite competition horses should be desensitized to outside stimulus doesn't mean they should have to deal with gunfire.

"A miracle. I supposed nobody can complain because it was happening both days of the Grand Prix so the conditions were equal for all competitors."

"True. I assume they'll still be providing security for us."

"Undoubtedly." She shrugged. "I don't mind. Having more security around the horses makes me feel better, and they seem dedicated."

"That they do." I lightly touched her shoulder. "How're you feeling about tomorrow?"

She reached up and took my hand. "Ready. I mean the Grand Prix Special test doesn't cater to our strengths as much as the Grand Prix does, but I'm still sure we can go out there and kick some ass."

* * *

She really did kick ass.

Every one of the horse and rider competitors who'd made it to the Olympics absolutely deserved to be there—they'd put in the training, the money, the time and the dedication to reach the top of their discipline—and in such a sport where judging could be subjective, it could be hard to differentiate what separated the best from the others. I knew Caitlyn and Dewey had an intense bond, as silly and sappy as it sounded, and that's what set them apart.

Every time she threw a leg over him, it looked harmonious, as if they knew each other's thought processes, as if they would give their best for each other or die trying. It was easy to anthropomorphize Dewey, because he was always so engaged with people, but I truly felt how much he loved and trusted Caitlyn, and that elevated them to something beyond simply great.

When Caitlyn realized she'd scored 82.257% for her Special, she looked shellshocked, as if it didn't quite compute that she'd just sealed the bronze medal for the team and put herself comfortably in third place on the individual standings.

The crowd around us grew while I checked Dewey post-ride and prevented me from doing anything more than offering Caitlyn a quiet, "Congratulations." Wren, bless her heart, had tried to give us some privacy and ran interference but it seemed every time she managed to usher one group out to give Dew some space, another group came in. Eventually she threw her hands up and muttered, "I fucking tried."

Once the horses had been cooled down and readied for the medal ceremony, we were sent to hang around outside the stadium while the ground crew set up podiums and the like. Mary and Ian stood slightly apart from the group, studying some papers and conversing quietly. Dakota and her groom were having a heated argument, as much as they were trying to disguise it. Beau and Jesse were huddled together with their grooms, the two riders standing far closer than just friends would. Interesting. And good for them. Simone, with her broken ankle, had decided not to cause mayhem scaring horses with her crutches, and had managed to wrangle herself a place at the front of the stands from which to watch the ceremony.

But once I'd looked at Caitlyn, my attention stayed there. She and Wren were laughing together and trying to keep Dewey from nibbling things, which seemed to be causing more laughter. One of the ground stewards said something that spurred everyone into action, and a few minutes later the sound of the announcer introducing the medalists echoed across the grounds. The riders remained unmounted and as Caitlyn slotted into the last place of the four who filed past, she reached out to touch my hand.

Most of the horses stood fairly still, but a few squirmed and shifted. One of the German horses spooked and got herself worked up, and was being walked by her groom a safe distance behind the others. And then there was Dewey. Wren struggled to contain him as he tried to touch the medal podium, get hold of the fountains of greenery in pots on the ground and talk to all the other horses.

Wren moved him off to the side, where he kept straining toward the others, then eventually started bobbing his head as if trying to convey just how much he really *really* wanted to talk to the others. Three medal-winning teams of four horses meant there were eleven potential friends for him, but the other potential was that the horses might just tell him to "Fuck off" with teeth and legs.

My team stepped up onto the podium, waves and smiles aplenty. I gave each of them my attention for a few moments before my eyes went to Caitlyn. Before she stepped up, she yanked the front of her breeches down and I laughed, recalling her comment about camel-toe. She waved all around the stadium with both hands, smiling and laughing with the others.

I turned my attention to the huge screen. The moment the camera panned to show her face up there, I felt a sudden burst of pride and adoration and a million other emotions all bundled up. Oh God. I had so fallen for her. Caitlyn looked around the stadium, still waving, and her movement seemed to slow as her focus came to where I stood. Despite the distance between us, I swear she was looking right at me.

The riders had media commitments after the medal ceremony and I likely wouldn't see any of them for another few hours. I'd been to check Freddo who remained comfortable, awaiting another round of imaging tomorrow to confirm he was healing satisfactorily. I met up with a few of the other team vets, ate a sandwich and two ice creams then settled myself in my tiny office to do some of my seemingly never-ending paperwork. I'd been lost in the void of typing for who knows how long when a knock at the door took my attention from my screen. "Come in," I called.

Caitlyn peeked into the room and then slipped in. "Hey."

Pleasure at having her close spread through me as a slow trickle of heat. "Hey yourself. Where's everyone else?"

"Mingling and planning how to celebrate." She smiled wryly. "All that interaction was getting to me." She'd removed her tails and stock tie but still wore her sleeveless undershirt, breeches, and boots. Hanging around her neck was her bronze medal and she carried a small oddly shaped wooden box. "Medal box," she explained.

"Ah. I haven't had a chance to really tell you how amazing you guys were. Watching you was incredible."

"Thanks. It still feels kind of weird."

"I can imagine. What was it like out there?"

Her eyebrows scrunched together. "Um...hard to explain. Kind of surreal, like I'm not entirely sure it actually happened or that I was really present for it."

I leaned close to offer a conspiratorial, "You definitely were."

"Mmmm. Apparently so." Caitlyn turned around to check who was in view of the window—nobody, which I'd learned over the past few days was a benefit of being right at the end of the row—then closed the short gap between us and kissed me, one arm snaking around my waist. "My reward," she murmured before kissing me again.

My hands wandered to the small of her back, and we probably would have stayed like that for a while if not for my fear of someone coming to find me. Stupid brain.

With great reluctance, I pulled away and Caitlyn backed up and flopped down onto my spare chair, stretching out her booted legs. She looked like someone trying their best to appear casual. "We're doing it again, aren't we?" she said. "That thing we said we wouldn't do right now."

"We are. Dammit. We're hopeless." I sat down beside her, careful to keep some distance.

She laughed a quick, dry laugh. "Hopeless, or just really committed to doing whatever this thing is between us."

Bravely, or stupidly, I asked, "What exactly is this thing between us?"

"Something frightening. Something weird. I...don't really know how to explain it."

Despite her vagueness, I knew what she meant. "To me," I began carefully, "it feels like we're stuck between becoming more than, uh, lovers and moving into a relationship type thing, but stalled despite both of us clearly wanting to move forward."

Caitlyn bit her lower lip. "I think that sums it up." She paused and after half a minute's contemplation whispered, "Even though I want it, the moving forward part is scary for me, especially with everything else around it."

"Everything else like what?" I quietly asked.

"With Elin—" She paused. "Is this too awkward? Too much?"

"It's not too much. I want to know everything you feel like telling me."

She inhaled slowly, as if gaining courage. "I think what happened with Elin is maybe part of it. She said the main reason she cheated was because of the distance. And I know we've established Florida to Kentucky isn't exactly the same distance as the USA and Europe, but I guess I'm still gun-shy."

Judging by her expression there was obviously more to it than that, but now was not the time or place to delve deeply into the nuance of relationships and Caitlyn's fears. I forced a smile. "Well you won't have that problem with me. I can barely find time for one woman let alone another on the side." Wow. Just...wow. I could not believe I'd just let that come out of my mouth. I tried desperately to repair the damage. "Shit, that's such a stupid thing to say and this is so not the time for a joke. I wasn't even trying to joke. It just came out. What I mean is I'm *not* a cheater. If I have a problem with the woman I'm datin' then I either talk about it or we break up." My cheeks flamed with mortification and I felt like my eyes were the size of dinner plates. "Hell, that's not...I don't want to break up. Goddammit. Can you see why I'm single?"

Laughing she said, "Not really, no."

"Please go over what I just blurted and then it'll be clear." I exhaled a long breath and tried to find my intellect. "Caitlyn, I'm as monogamous as...as...a beaver. Shit, no. As a swan."

She gave me a double thumbs-up. "Keep going, darling. You're doing great." She wasn't even bothering to disguise her mirth, which made me feel slightly better about my clumsy attempt to show her I was a one-woman woman.

"Can I have a do-over?" I begged.

"Why? You're explaining yourself so perfectly."

I blew a raspberry. "Redirect, Your Honor. How do you feel about metaphors?"

"Depends if they're helpful or confusing."

"Probably a little of both, but hopefully more helpful."

Caitlyn made a sweeping gesture. "Then give me your helpful metaphor."

I took few moments to sort my thoughts. "Remember us learning that *pas de deux* together back in Pony Club?" Caitlyn nodded, and I went on, "I don't know about you, but I remember stuff like Buddy's trot strides were longer than Antoinette's so we had to work to keep in stride with me being slightly slower, you being slightly faster. Both of us learning the choreography, the music and how to ride as a team. We had to learn how to trust each other, like I knew that once I'd finished my circle left, you'd be done with your circle right and would be right there ready to meet me so we could ride forward together."

"I'm following."

"Good. Because I am on a roll, baby." I kissed her quickly. "Sorry, we promised we weren't going to do that 'til after the Freestyle."

"We did, didn't we," she mused. "But I think I've proven that my concentration when it comes to competing is on point, so a little kiss here and there won't hurt?"

"You are a terrible influence on me."

Her shrug was the epitome of nonchalance. "You were saying? With your wonderful metaphor?"

"Oh, right. I think you and me now is a lot like you and me back then with that ride. When the time comes, we just have to figure out how to be a team, how to adjust things so that we're in sync. We're gonna mess up choreography, be late or early or in the wrong spot entirely. But it doesn't matter because we'll keep working at it. And we've got plenty of time to smooth out those bumps 'til it's a first-place ride."

CHAPTER TWENTY-FIVE

Caitlyn

We'd had two full days to regroup and rest after the Special and medal ceremony before the top eighteen riders in the overall competition would advance to ride the Freestyle to determine the individual medals. The only other US Team member to secure a place was, surprisingly, Dakota, though realistically she'd have to perform far above her personal best or everyone else would have to seriously fumble their rides for her to medal.

I'd practiced my choreography, then checked and rechecked my *Frozen* soundtrack, which was specially arranged and edited with the tempo slightly altered in places to match Dew's paces, until it was burned into my brain. We had portions of "Let it Go" for my trot work, looped and mixed "Frozen Heart" for canter, "Love is an Open Door" for piaffe and passage and "In Summer" for walk.

I'd drawn seventeenth out of the eighteen competitors and the indoor arena was almost empty by the time I entered to warm-up. It was the hottest day yet, with the temperature hitting ninety-four by midday, and despite the aircon, sweat slid down my spine as I rode. All the movements, all Dew's buttons were in there. The only purpose of this was to get him listening and his muscles ready for our final test. Ian's sporadic interjections through the earpiece helped me tighten things up and make Dew even sharper until I felt like he was bursting at the seams ready to go out and show everyone what we had.

Wren fell behind us as I walked from the ten-minute arena to the stadium. The sun had a real bite to it that made my cheeks feel as if they were burning. I set aside my physical discomfort to focus on the next ten minutes. I had no idea of the scores of the previous riders. They didn't matter. It was all about Dew and me. Thanks to our two previous tests, Dew barely batted an eyelid as we entered the stadium. He held the same flamboyant excitement as our previous two rides, ears flicking around until I reminded him with a gentle finger pressure that we were here to do a job and he could look around once we'd finished our test.

I played with some micro transitions within the gaits to get him collected and really listening until the bell sounded to indicate it was time. I halted at the P marker on the long side close to the entry point at A and held up my hand to start the music for my Freestyle. The few butterflies in my stomach flitted away.

The instrumental of "Let it Go" filled the space and I moved Dewey into a collected trot, turned and entered the arena. Dew halted perfectly square at X in the center of the arena and I waited a beat before dropping my hand behind my thigh and nodding in salute. I regathered my reins as the music picked up, the underlying lyrical rhythm winding through the song. Straight up the centerline, turn left at C and then a huge extended trot across the diagonal. Dew's hoofbeats landed perfectly on each beat of the song and as we hit the long side I brought him back into a soft and elevated passage, continuing around the short side.

Then the music just…stopped.

Nothing.

No sound.

Dew's ears pivoted back and forth and I gave him a small rein reminder about attention. Probably just couldn't hear the music over— no there was no other sound drowning out the music. There was no music. The crowd was silent. An uncomfortable sensation fluttered in my chest. I rounded the corner and set up for the half-pass that would take us across the arena then back again. Still no music. The only sound was a collective murmuring from the stands around us.

For the first time in a very *very* long time, I got anxious while on a horse, and I felt Dew's reaction immediately. My anxiety was making him anxious. When I was on him, he trusted me to guide him, trusted me to keep him safe and now my body was telling him a sheep was about to eat him. His ears were swiveling in all directions and I could practically feel his eyes doing the same. Dew's jaw tensed, blocking the rein and his back tightened underneath me, which made sitting his huge trot very difficult as I rode the first part of our half-pass.

But I had to keep going until the head judge told me to stop.

As a kid I'd been taught the invaluable lesson of how to fake not being anxious on a horse. Because they always knew if you were afraid. I shut everything out, blocked the anxiety, made myself relax, and felt Dewey respond immediately.

Was it my CD?

The sound system?

Sabotage?

I almost laughed aloud at that last thought, which would have been disastrous. After an eternity, which thanks to my familiarity with my choreography I knew was really only ten seconds, the C judge Maribel Medina, stood and made her way down the stairs of her judging hut. She held up a hand, which gave me official permission to stop, and I deflated to a walk and made my way over to the top end of the arena where the judge was speaking into a walkie-talkie. A neck stroke seemed to settle Dew enough that he stopped looking for horse-eating sheep.

Halting Dewey far enough away that he couldn't reach the head judge and technical delegates who had joined her, I arranged my face into a polite smile though all I wanted to do was cry.

Maribel smiled up at me. "Hello, Ms. Lloyd. There appears to be a technical issue with your music."

Oh, I hadn't noticed. "Yes, ma'am, it would appear so."

"I assume the CDs you presented are in good order."

"Yes, ma'am, absolutely. We tested both discs this morning and there were no issues. At all."

Another smile, this one knowing. No rider would ever hand in a damaged CD for a Freestyle, especially not at an Olympics. "The sound engineer is just testing the music now."

"Thank you."

"As you know, if the issue is with your music CD then you will be disqualified." It looked like it hurt her to say it. I'd been judged by Maribel a number of times at national and international events and had always found her squarely on the side of fair competition and good sportsmanship.

"Yes, ma'am, I understand, thank you." I was well aware of the rules. It was my responsibility to provide a working copy of my music, as well as a backup copy. If something was wrong, then—I couldn't think about that.

I sat still, my pinkies scratching either side of Dew's neck. Though I wanted to look around, I forced myself to keep my eyes on the small group in front of me trying to figure out the issue. And I tried very hard not to think about the fact that if I was disqualified, then my Olympic individual medal chances just blew away in the wind. Deep down I knew medals didn't matter, but…they mattered. To come so close, after everything, and to not even get the chance to actually ride a full test was heartbreaking.

The walkie-talkie crackled and Maribel held the device to her ear. She smiled, nodding. My anxiety let go. Maribel clipped the radio to her belt. "A technical issue with the equipment, not your music. The staff have tested it and confirmed it won't happen again. You may continue."

I almost cried with relief. "Thank you very much."

She gestured to the arena. "You may start from the beginning of your test, or you may pick up from where the error occurred."

"I'll start from the beginning, thank you."

"Very well. As you know, the marks given for the movements the first time up to the technical issue will stand."

"Yes of course, thank you so much." Better to ride my first few movements again than set Dew up for a half-pass without the movements before. She indicated that I should reposition myself outside the arena, and as I walked down the centerline toward A, the ground staff opened the gap in the low fence. The announcer told everyone that due to a technical error I would restart my test and a slow round of applause echoed through the stadium.

"I'm sorry, pal. I'm sorry," I murmured to Dew. "I know it's so hot and I know you've already done this bit and you did it so well, but we're going to do it once more. Just for luck."

His snort told me what he thought of my pep talk.

I set him up again outside the arena next to the P marker and once the bell had sounded, paused for a few seconds, then raised my hand to indicate I was ready. The music started. Again. I entered the arena and began my test. Again.

His extended trot felt even better than the first time, dammit. Coming up to the spot where the music had stopped, I made sure I was relaxed and not anticipating that it might happen again. Passage around the short side and we still have music. Thank you, dressage gods.

The rest of the test, I could say without any ego, was absolutely fucking fabulous. We hit every music mark, the work was rhythmic, balanced, cadenced, and enthusiastic. The sound of the crowd clapping along with the music elevated Dew beyond his usual crowd-loving excitement and the moment we'd done our final salute I threw myself onto his neck and looped my arms around his neck to hug him. The crowd roared its approval, and I sat up again. If there was ever a time to throw both hands in the air for a celebration, this was it.

I threw both up, trusting Dew to just keep doing what he was doing, and waved enthusiastically in all directions at the cheering, clapping crowd. Dew started jogging and I picked up my reins again to bring him back to walk before he decided now was the time to get scared of noise and enthusiasm and dumped me in the arena. Leaning forward, I patted him on both sides of his neck. "You're magnificent. I love you."

So many emotions swirled, but the biggest one alongside relief was an overwhelming sense of pride and accomplishment. And those weird tears. I carefully dabbed my eyes on my sleeve. As I passed the next rider entering as I exited, I saw Addie behind the fence. Her smile was broad, and she offered me a thumbs-up and a wave before melting away. Standing in the stirrups I tried to find her from my position above the crowd, but she was gone.

The management team, minus Addie, met me at the entrance and they could have powered a small country with the brilliance of their smiles. "What happened?" was the first thing out of Mary's mouth. The second thing was, "Absolutely fantastic ride!"

"Equipment malfunction apparently. And thank you, it felt it." The adrenaline I'd been holding on to suddenly let itself go and my limbs went shaky. Dew, bless his heart, stopped dead at my wobble and I gently asked him to walk forward again.

Ian's pats on Dew's shoulder were rapid fire. "That could have gone very differently. Well done."

I barely had time to nod in agreement before Mary and Ian were swallowed by the crowd while I rode with Wren by my side to the gloriously shaded spot for my gear check. It felt like the number of television cameras had doubled and once I'd dismounted, I kept hold of Dew to make sure he didn't damage someone's expensive equipment. Wren, lover of social media and filterer of mean comments, had told me that Dew's camera snuffle had been the talk of the equestrian scene.

The announcer's words were muffled by the thudding of my heart in my ears.

I squinted over at the scoreboard. Squinted again to be sure I wasn't seeing things. 90.357%. Holy shit. I couldn't even make words in my head. Freestyles always had higher percentage scores because of the added artistic element, but that score was insane. It'd put me in second place, and was a personal best by a long margin. I didn't even bother trying to hold back my tears.

We passed our equipment checks and I leaned into my dual Olympic medal-winning horse, my cheek against his neck. With still one rider to go, I knew I was at least assured another bronze, but at that moment I didn't really care if I got bronze or silver. I'd taken the horse I'd bred and trained myself all the way to the Olympics and ridden well enough to get two medals. I fought down a full-on sobbing meltdown as I hugged him around the neck. Dew turned around and nuzzled my back. Frantic camera shutters sounded.

Wren lowered her voice so it couldn't be picked up by the video cameras. "Fuck me. I nearly had a heart attack. For real."

I took a moment to compose myself before moving away from Dew. "Me too."

The camera guy, the one I recognized from this spot after my first ride, gestured for us to come closer. I relaxed my grip on the reins and pushed Dewey toward the camera. He took the cue immediately and stuck his face in the lens as he had before. I laughed, waved to the camera—which always felt so weird—then got to work making Dew comfortable for the walk back to his stall to be cooled down.

Dew snuffled in Wren's equipment bucket for either a treat or his toy. I bit a peppermint in half, *yuck*, and offered him one half at a time to crunch around the two bits in his mouth. Despite his sweet treat, Dew kept snuffling in the bucket, eventually coming up with the cat chew toy Addie had bought for him in the Netherlands. When Wren went to take it from him, I intervened. "Oh, let him have his toy, he deserves it."

Midfields Adieu and I, Olympic medalists, walked back to the stalls with him holding a rubber toy cat in his mouth. The camera shutters going off all around added to the already deafening noise. So many people, so many congratulations and questions and chatter that I didn't know who to focus on, and the overwhelming emotion made my words catch in my throat.

I was called in to pee in a cup before my press conference, and when I came out of the bathroom was mobbed from all sides by people shouting that I'd won silver. My media commitments were a blur of noise and flashes until I was dragged out just in time for our final medal ceremony. Dew had stayed tacked up, but resting in the cool indoor arena and when I managed to get back to him he raised his head and let out a body-shaking whinny. Someone was pleased with himself.

"No more carrots," I told him. "I don't want orange chunks around your mouth in these photos."

I read a few text messages while shrugging back into my tails. Mom and Dad with autocorrect-laden congratulations. A major sponsor congratulating me. My other major sponsor with effusive praise and congratulations. Lotte with a simple *You did well*. Laughing, I turned the phone so Wren could see the message. "That's practically her throwing me a tickertape parade."

Another message pinged through as I was about to hand Wren my phone for safekeeping. This one was not for Wren's eyes. Addie. *I'm crying. I don't even know what to say. I don't think I will ever see anything as beautiful as that ride in my life. Except for you.*

CHAPTER TWENTY-SIX

Addie

Caitlyn being a dual Olympic medalist meant everyone wanted a piece of her. And as much as I wanted to barge into the crush, sweep her up into a hug and tell her how proud I was, how amazing she was and a million silly little things that basically amounted to *I love you*, I knew this wasn't my time. My time would be after. This moment was hers where she could bask in the fact everyone thought she was brilliant. Because she *was* brilliant.

After my final rounds for the afternoon and making sure all the horses were comfortable and healthy—and in Dewey's case, had been stuffed with carrots and licorice and smothered in nose kisses—I shut myself in my office to double-check my drug inventory ready to go home. Everything I'd brought in had to be accounted for and explained in what capacity I'd used it.

Thankfully everything was in order, because I did not feel like being dragged in front of the IOC and some official Brazilian narcotics unit to explain that in the fracas of one horse with a bee sting and another with a pelvic fracture that I'd just forgotten to pick up a used needle or empty vial and no, I hadn't sold a bottle of ketamine on the street. I'd finished locking everything back into its secure trunk when someone knocked. Mary had already been in twice, and I was hoping she had nothing else inane to tell me that I already knew.

On the narrow step was Caitlyn, now dressed in her casual team uniform shirt, wearing a huge smile and holding a small duffel. I leaned against the doorframe. "Well look who it is. All hail the Olympic conqueror."

She dipped her head. "Thank you. You may curtsey at any time."

I did the best curtsey I could, which wasn't very good, then took her hand and kissed the back of it. "M'lady, thou dost ridest dressage most excellently...est."

Caitlyn playfully slapped my shoulder. "You dork."

"Only for you." I straightened and ushered her though the door. "Come into the cool."

"Sorry I couldn't get here earlier." She flushed. "I got your text."

I felt myself flush too. "Yeah, sorry. Uh, you may have guessed I'm not much of a wordsmith."

"It was beautiful," Caitlyn murmured. "Thank you."

"You're welcome." I cleared my throat but it didn't clear away my embarrassment. "What's in the bag? You sneak in some Blow Pops and a Magnum of Cristal?"

"Close. It's clothes etcetera for an overnight stay. With you."

"Ah. A sleepover. Gettin' a little presumptuous there, aren't you?" I teased.

"Not at all." She grinned. "I told you I was going to see you after the Freestyle and I'd be in the mood to either celebrate or commiserate."

"That you did." I sat down and propped my feet up on the trunk of veterinary supplies. "How d'you want to mark this momentous occasion?"

Caitlyn took the other chair. "I'm not sure. Some of the other riders were talking about what they were doing. Champagne, visiting Christ the Redeemer with a tour group, partying. And when they asked what I was going to do I was just...blank."

"Glass of wine and early to bed?" I suggested. "That's my go-to whenever I want to pat myself on the back. As you can tell, I'm a real party animal."

"Close and tempting. I just know that I want to do something with you. I've never really celebrated my wins, big or small. There's no time after a competition because as soon as it's over we pack up and go home and then it's straight back into preparations for the next one or training another horse, or something else that's going to occupy my time."

"Ah. The price of excellence?"

A wry smile quirked her mouth. "Something like that. I mean it's never seemed all that important because there's always room to be better in dressage, so why celebrate?" The smile turned laughing. "Sorry, that sounds a bit 'harsh disciplinarian.' I'm thrilled." She fiddled with the strap on her duffel. "I've realized that I'd like some balance between horses and my personal life. Starting with wanting to celebrate my success this time. And I want you to help me do that."

"What did you have in mind?" I could think of plenty of ways to celebrate and congratulate her. My planning was interrupted by a message on my phone. "I'm so sorry, have to check this."

"No problem."

But it was. Caitlyn had just hinted at a personal life that seemed to involve a significant other. But this was my life, with work things intruding at inopportune times. "Every sample from the dressage competition returned clean results. The horses that is, I don't know what's going on with human pee." I laughed. "Congratulations, you get to keep your medals. And I might get to keep my USDF job."

She pretended to wipe fake sweat from her forehead. "Phew. We live to ride another day."

"I probably would have been fired if I'd gotten you banned from the Olympics on my first rotation as the team veterinarian."

"Probably. But you were an absolute rock star keeping everyone healthy this whole time. So I guess it's a double celebration tonight."

"True." I buffed my nails on my chest. "Now, how do you want spend the evening? I think I have some cheese and crackers. Do you want to go against all the advice and sneak out for a nice dinner? Or should we get something delivered?"

"Truth be told, I'm not huge on big fancy dinners. My idea of a great night is staying in with someone I…like very much, eating food I haven't cooked, drinking some wine, maybe a movie or a board game or something like that and then…" She didn't need to say what she was thinking—the implication that we'd fall into bed and have amazing sex until we fell asleep was clear.

"It's like you're looking into my brain. Let's go."

Calling from the car on the way to my place, we ordered dinner from the *churrascaria* that the Brazilian team vet had told me was a must-try. With the help of Google Translate supplementing my abysmal Portuguese, we'd asked the driver to stop by a liquor store and while we waited for our delivery of delicious barbequed meats I sneakily chilled the bottle of red. By the time we'd taken quick, separate showers dinner had been delivered. Once we'd set everything out and settled, I poured wine. "Are we toasting something?"

"We can. I always feel so weird about toasts, especially if they're directed toward me."

"Same." I picked up my glass. "Toastless it is. We know we're great."

"That we are." The *we* had a soft emphasis on it.

We ate dinner in a quiet, contemplative silence and once we'd tidied up, moved to the couch. She had an arm slung over my shoulders, and as I leaned into her, that hand softly stroked my skin. We didn't talk, just sat together. Caitlyn broke the silence first. "So, what's next? I mean after packing up and getting horses on a plane tomorrow." While some of the riders were staying on for the closing ceremony, my job was done.

I sighed at the sensation of her deft fingers sliding through my hair, gliding over the back of my neck and had to force myself to focus on what I wanted to say, not the fact her touch was turning me to mush. "Is this where we talk about what'll happen when we go home?"

"I think so." Caitlyn shifted slightly so we were facing each other. "You first or me first?"

"Well mine is pretty simple. I care about you. I care about Dewey. I love being with you and how I feel when I'm around you, like that niggling thing I've been looking for has suddenly just appeared. I want more of this, to build on what we've started here. And I can see something between us if we just give it a chance."

"Me too," she quietly said. "I love the way you've challenged me to look at what I really want, the way you make me think about things, make me want to do things. And not even in a scary way that makes little introvert me want to crumble." She inhaled shakily and when she spoke again it was tremulous. "I love how being with you makes me feel like I'm doing something right, something other than dressage. Before you, the only time I felt right was when I was on a horse."

I took her hand, pressing a kiss to her palm. "I feel like there's a *but* coming on."

"This is why I like you so much. You always seem to know just what I'm thinking." She held intense eye contact with me, as if willing me to really listen, to pay attention. "There is a but. Not a big one, or scary or—"

My kiss cut her off and Caitlyn let me cut her off for a little longer. With a quiet groan, I pulled away. "Tell me this *but*. It's just me, Caitlyn. I don't bite." My teeth raked my lower lip. "Except those times you asked me to…"

"That was an unfair distraction." She exhaled a long breath. "I keep thinking about it, wanting it, looking for ways, but I just don't see how this can work. Unless we both commit to long distance." She let the unspoken linger. It wasn't really unspoken because we'd been over this before.

I knew exactly what she wasn't saying. That she was afraid I would do what Elin had. I'd had such little time to chip away at her armor and it seemed I hadn't succeeded in showing her that I wasn't the past. Not our past as teenagers, but her more recent past where she'd been hurt. I'd just have to try harder and help her see that I wouldn't hurt her. "Do you want it to work?" I quietly asked, but I feared the answer because everything about her screamed that it was too much and she wanted to give it up.

"Yes," she said immediately. "I do, very much. But we just live such…incompatible lives, have incompatible lifestyles." The way she'd said it wasn't flat. Wasn't sarcastic. Wasn't cruel. It was musing, as if she was trying to work out how our differing lives could actually fit.

"Incompatible," I repeated. "You know, when I was a kid and trying to be your friend and trying to make you notice me, after a while I began to think maybe the reason you kept ignoring me was that we were too different—chalk and cheese. Now I know, after these past few months, that's not the reason. We are *not* incompatible, Caitlyn, not by a long shot. We are not our lifestyles."

Her eyebrows shot up. "Aren't we though? My life is dressage and that's basically it. I have no close friends, because I have no time. The thought of figuring out where you can fit in my life, and where I can fit in yours is terrifying."

"I agree. But I've always been one for facing terror head on, and I'm not saying we need to uproot our lives in order to try a new one together."

"What *are* you saying then?"

"That maybe we should just dig around a little and see what we can unearth. We don't have to change anything big right now, just maybe we think about how we can try and make our lives intersect. I know we can."

She exhaled. "I just don't know if you're really aware of how inflexible my life is. And me being the immovable object that you always have to come to isn't a fair way to have a relationship."

"Agreed, balance is always good, but isn't it for me to decide if I can handle being the one who's doing most of the travel? Because if it's a choice between that or nothing, then I choose travel. I will milk the shit out of some frequent flyer program. I choose emails and phone calls and texts. Video calls. Sexting and video sex. I choose all of that over giving up what feels like the start of something incredible. It's a no-brainer."

An unpleasant thought intruded. What about the future, when distance wasn't enough? One of us would have to be the moveable object. I knew it would have to be me and I fought to squash my anxiety at the thought of leaving my current workplace. Despite the numerous issues with Seth Ranger and Associates, the pay was excellent, and the small part of me that recalled scraping for every dollar as a kid feared losing that solid financial security. The financial security that'd paid a solid chunk of my college debt and kept me otherwise debt-free. Sure, all jobs came with salary, but…

My thoughts raced and I tried to center myself, to focus on the present, not the what-ifs, before I totally fucked up what I was trying to say. "My feeling of pride when watching you ride is indescribable. I want to keep havin' that feeling, keep being there with you when you have all those big moments. I can't believe I'm about to say this corniest thing ever but…I want to create moments with you."

After what felt like an eternity Caitlyn quietly agreed, "Okay. Okay, you're right. When we're both home, let's get settled in and start seeing if we can make some plans. No pressure, just seeing what we can do when we can do it."

"Sounds like a good plan." I paused. "I can't believe I'm about to ask this, but are you sure? I don't want you to agree to this just because you've been persuaded by my charm and rousing arguments for us taking this beyond here."

"I'm sure. One hundred percent." She blew out a long breath, followed up with a smile that was sweet and genuine. Her hand slid down my arm to my hand, and she entwined our fingers. "Now, what d'you say about a little not-gonna-see-you-for-a-month nookie?"

"I say…" I pulled my hands free to slip both under her tee. In one movement, I lifted it up and off over her head, leaving her torso deliciously bare. Her nipples were too tempting to resist, so I didn't, bending to take one in my mouth. Caitlyn cupped my face as I sucked one nipple then the other, and when I moved to glide my tongue between her breasts, she pulled my face up. Her kiss was fierce, needy, as if she feared this might be our last. No chance of that. I opened my mouth, sucked her tongue gently, lightly bit her lower lip.

Caitlyn's inhalation was quick, her breathing shallow and ragged. "I think what you're saying is yes please, make me come?"

I leaned in and traced the curve of her ear with my tongue. "Excellent translation."

CHAPTER TWENTY-SEVEN

Caitlyn

Though I would have loved to hang around Brazil to watch some other Olympic sports and attend the closing ceremony with my teammates—it was time to go home. After over three months away I needed to get everything back on track and start my horse training and financial balls rolling again. Odd-one-out Caitlyn strikes again.

Wren and I were on separate flights to the States where she would go to Miami to be with Dew during his seven-day quarantine while I went to Kentucky and straight back to work. Unlike my mess of connecting flights, the flights for equines were specially chartered nonstop adventures accompanied by grooms and a veterinarian. Knowing both Wren and Addie would be with Dew eased some of the usual anxiety I had about leaving him.

I'd given Dew a tight hug and wished him a nice flight before they loaded him into the pallet and began rolling him along the conveyor that would lift him into the plane. He'd made it about five feet in the air before he reached the limits of his attention span and I had to call for him to stop trying to bite his pallet-mate's halter. Dew swung his head in my direction and vocalized a huge whinny which shook the crane. I smiled at his adorable acknowledgment and then groaned when he seemed to take my direction to stop biting as meaning he should bite harder. Pierre had drawn the short straw of being next to Dew and mercifully seemed to have perfected the art of ignoring my idiot horse.

"Good luck with him," I murmured to Addie.

"I've got it under control," she assured me. She crouched to open one of the duffels at her feet, revealing bags of carrots, apples, and Life Savers. "When all else fails, bribery as a distraction."

"Smart. Just so you know, that also works with me."

"Good to know. I'll have to buy shares in Blow Pops." Addie stood again, shielding her eyes against the fading Rio sun. "Well, I guess this is where we say goodbye. You've got your own flights to catch and I have to get to work. I want to make sure everything is right and double check everyone's locked down tight."

"Of course." I fought to keep my voice and expression neutral instead of melting into a pile of upset. "Uh, have a good flight then I guess."

"You too." Her expression turned pained. "Stupid public goodbyes. I'll be thinkin' about you. When I have a free moment around keeping Dewey from chewing things."

Wincing, I said, "Sorry. Just growl at him if he's being annoying and biting things."

"It's fine. I like having him around. He reminds me of you."

"Because I'm…annoying?"

"Not so much. Just because he's yours. He makes me think about you. But I seem to recall you do like to bite things." Her teeth grazed her lower lip.

A rush of excitement filled my belly and my response was hoarse. "You're right. But only certain things." I tilted my head to the side, trying to see the faint mark from last night but it was hidden under her shirt collar.

Addie exhaled a long breath. "Right, okay. I really am going now. Otherwise I'll just stand here and stare dreamily at you for the rest of time. I—" Smiling, she shook her head. "Never mind. I'll just talk to you when I do. Soon. Safe travels, sweetheart."

"You too." If she kept calling me sweetheart, I was going to lose my heart. Fast.

I slept for most of the flights home and turned on my phone to another barrage of messages. Family, friends, sponsors, my coaches at home, journalists, Lotte, Mary. Then a few from Wren and Addie who had texted me at almost the same time with much the same message to let me know they'd landed and Dewey had traveled well. They'd also both included pictures of him in his travel stall on the plane and also being unloaded by the lift. He was stretched out trying to reach the lift arm with his nose. Typical.

As I waited for my bags I responded to the messages from friends and family, and those from Wren. Then there were Addie's texts. Everything I tried to say in response felt stupid and hollow, too deep for such a simple message to let me know my horse was safe. In the end, I typed out a simple and cowardly *Great! Glad he behaved himself for you.* If I said anything deeper then the ache of missing her would grow even more unbearable.

The first thing I noticed when I walked out of the airport was Brandon in the pick-up area. The second thing was that he wore a glitter-encrusted party hat and had a party horn in his mouth, which he started blowing obnoxiously the moment he spotted me. He skipped over to me and scooped me into a hug. "Welcome home, Olympic Badass!"

Laughing, I hugged him back as he lifted me up. "Thank you. It's so good to be home."

"I bet," he said as he lowered me to the ground. Grinning around the party horn in his mouth, he puffed out his cheeks and blew it until the damned thing unfurled and hit me in the forehead.

"Clown. You obviously spend too much time with Dewey."

"You say that like it's a bad thing." He pulled the horn from his mouth. "Have you spoken to Wren?" There was a hint of excitement in his question, and I didn't blame him. I couldn't imagine what it took for them to be physically separated for so long, and yet again felt a twinge of guilt. I knew it was part of their job and I accommodated as best I could. They never complained, and they reassured me constantly. But it was still a shitty situation, and one I was starting to understand more. I was missing Addie and we'd only been apart for a day. "Just before Dewey loaded, and then texts when they landed." I nudged him with my elbow. "A little over a week."

He grinned. "Yeah. Heart grown fonder and all that." Brandon grabbed the bigger of my two bags and one boot bag while I dealt with my smaller bag and the other boot bag, which I slung over my shoulder. There was still more gear to arrive with Wren and Dew next week.

On the drive home, Brandon filled me in on the goings-on while I'd been away. I already knew most of it from his emails. All the horses were sound and in good health, all were working well, nothing had broken or burned down. All in all, a successful time away. We made a quick stop for grocery essentials and were rolling through my double gates by three in the afternoon. As always when I saw the Midfields signs on the stone walls either side of my wrought iron gate, my chest swelled with pride.

Brandon paused at the intersection that split three ways to either the barn facilities, my three-bedroom cottage on the small hill or continued on to his and Wren's two-bedroom tucked behind some fields. "Do you want to take a look around now or in the morning?"

"Let me put my stuff in the house and take a shower to wash off these flights, then I'll meet you for a grand tour?"

On my kitchen table was a foot-high Jenga stack of mail. Something to attack later. I dropped my bags on the floor, flinched at the sharp thud that echoed through my quiet, empty house. The echo made me think how great it would be to have someone to share this moment with me.

It only took a half an hour to shower, partially unpack and put on a load of laundry and bag up my many pairs of competition breeches and uniform tails to be dry cleaned. In the bottom of my carry-on backpack was something I definitely hadn't put in there. I slid my finger under the flap of the envelope with my name written in now-familiar handwriting.

> *Caitlyn,*
>
> *I've thought of so many things I want to say to you but every time I try I worry that it's not the right time. But I'm not sure any time is right when we live the lives we do, so I've decided to just write this. These months have been amazing in a way I don't think I could ever explain. I'm so proud of you, and so proud to have been part of everything you accomplished here. If you'd asked me when we were fourteen what I most wanted in the world, it would have been what we shared these past few months, only I didn't know then that it could be as incredible as it has been. I can't wait to show you everything I have to offer you and I'm willing to take as much time as you need, and do whatever necessary to show you that I'm all in.*
>
> *I love you.*
> *Addie xo*

Oh, help.
Goodbye, heart.

I scooped up Rasputin, who'd sauntered into the house with his usual series of indignant mews and chirps about the fact I hadn't been around for a few months, and carried him down to the barn. As I walked across the neatly mown grass I contemplated doing a social media post about coming home. Later. Now was me time.

A banner with rainbow lettering proclaiming WELCOME HOME, OLYMPIC MEDALISTS! hung across the short side of the indoor arena. I snapped a photo, and smiling, sent it to Mom and a few friends. On a whim I sent it to Addie. "We'd better leave that up for Wren and Dewey when they get home."

"Planning on it," Brandon assured me. "Dirk already had a meltdown when he saw it during his ride this morning, so he should only spook at it ten times every ride 'til then instead of the fifteen he did with me."

"Goody. Can't wait."

All the horses were well conditioned and shone with health. The barn, fields and alfalfa pasture were immaculate. And Brandon, bless him, had been hard at work raising the height on the post-and-rail fences around two of my fields ready for our new stallion arrival. With the money I'd get from the US Olympic Committee for my two medals, plus my sponsors' bonuses for what they deemed "excellent performances," I'd decided to go all in and purchase Dougie on my own. That meant no stress of trying to manage anyone else's expectations about training and breeding, and I could bring the young stallion on as I wanted. He was due to leave the Netherlands in about ten days, once all his necessary inspections and tests had been completed.

So many pieces were slotting into place all at once, as if the gate on everything fabulous had opened to let greatness pour through. But something still felt hollow. I didn't need my mom's psychology degree to understand why. After all I'd shared with Addie, the possibilities she'd shown me, coming home felt great but not brilliant.

I wanted to call her, not because I wanted her to report on Dew, but because I just wanted to talk to her. But talking to her right now, feeling as lonely and flat as I did would only amplify those feelings when I had to end the call. Especially when it was nothing more than a selfish want that butted against everything my rational brain was telling me—that Addie plus Caitlyn wasn't going to equal an enemies-to-lovers fairytale. It would be a push and pull until she eventually tired of being the one who had to make all the effort for us to spend time together and broke up with me. The thought made me feel sick.

I'd just set my phone down to start grudgingly making dinner when a message landed. Saved by the bell. I was greeted by an Addie-Dewey selfie. Dew stretched toward the camera with Addie's face pressed to the side of his cheek. She held up her plastic baggie of Life Savers, her smile luminous, dimples deepening her cheeks. *Freshest breath in quarantine!*

Another message pinged through before I could think of something to convey just how much I loved the photo and that the most important thing in my life adored something I wanted to be important in my life. *We both miss you.*

My fingers acted without thinking. *I miss you both too.*

Hold on to that thought. Have to do official things, talk soon.

I'd just opened the refrigerator when another message alert sounded. Text from Wren. *Your girlfriend and I are taking excellent care of Dew.*

She's not my girlfriend. She really wasn't. Maybe pre-girlfriend?

Based on what I saw these past few months, I disagree. You're in lurve. Make it work, for everyone's sake. Dew adores her and I think she's pretty great too.

Operation: Set Caitlyn Up With The Hot Vet has recommenced. *Remind me why I don't fire you for being such a buttinsky?*

Huge smile emoji. *Because neither you or your horses could live without me.*

True.

Shit! I can't believe I forgot to tell you. Dakota fired Eleanor! Full marching orders, left quarantine staff to deal with Pierre. They are not impressed. Apparently groom's fault she didn't get an individual medal... something about loyalty blah blah. Eye roll emoji. *Addie is the most diplomatic person I've ever met. You should really marry her.*

My level of surprise is one out of ten. Poor Eleanor. Also not poor Eleanor being free of DT. See above re: buttinsky. And have you and my mother been colluding on the marriage front?

It's for your own good. Talk in the morning. Try to sleep. If you're cooking dinner, don't forget to preheat the pan before you start tossing shit in.

I turned on the gas under the pan and sent a final message. *Sure thing, boss.*

I cremated then ate dinner, started opening my massive pile of mail then abandoned it, and finally tried not to wander aimlessly around my empty house. I'd been told about Olympic Comedown Syndrome but I hadn't really expected to be affected. I'd spent so much time away at big important competitions, so why did I feel so blah now, as if

I'd forgotten to do something important. Gee, Caitlyn, I don't know. Could it have something to do with being maybe just a little in love with the woman you've only been apart from for…twenty-four hours?

Though it would be wonderful to stay awake thinking about Addie, it would also not kick jetlag in the ass. So I did the responsible adult thing and readied myself for bed. The moment I was in bed I got irresponsible and messaged Addie that I missed her and was about to go to bed alone.

Her response was almost immediate. *How much do you miss me?*

There's no real quantifiable measure for missing someone, but let's just say a lot.

Enough to practice our being apart sex? After a pause a winking emoji followed.

Her implication sent a wave of heat through my body. *Go on…*

Given I'm in a room with thin walls, what do you say to a little sexting? Then I won't give myself away.

I say I'm game if you are. I got your note, by the way.

It took almost five minutes for her response to land. *Oh. And?*

I didn't want to tell her I loved her for the first time over text, so I opened FaceTime and called her. The first thing she said was, "You could have warned me you were about to call and I would have brushed my hair or something."

Instead of a greeting or remark about her hair, which admittedly looked hilariously untidy, I blurted, "I love you too."

Her exhalation was loud. "I—I…good. I love you. I'm sorry the first time I told you was in a letter not in person but I wanted you to know."

"You're forgiven. It was an incredible thing to read."

"Phew." She settled back against the headboard. "Now, about that sexting…"

"Let's stay on this call and see what we can do. I think you could probably manage to be quiet enough."

And she was.

Knowing I'd be jetlagged and feeling generally meh, we'd kept the training board clear for my first day back, but when I woke a little after six after a slumber full of very explicit dreams about Addie, I decided to head to the barn anyway. I made my way to where Brandon would be in the middle of the morning feeding and stall-cleaning routine.

Rasputin sprinted over to me in the dawn light, chirping frantically. I picked him up, holding him against my chest as I walked into the brightly lit barn. "He'll be back in a few days, promise," I told the cat. All the stalls were empty and I could hear horses munching hay in the runs adjoining the building.

Brandon leaned out of stall eight at the far end of the barn. "Hey, mornin'. Didn't expect to see you."

"Morning." I dropped the cat to the barn floor. "Need a hand?"

"You know I'll never say no." He made a vague gesture. "Everyone's been turned out and they're eating breakfast so it's just the dirty stuff left."

"Fine with me." I collected a wheelbarrow and tools and got to work on stall two. Stall one of course belonged to the King of the Barn himself—Dewey. Currently bare of bedding and smelling faintly of disinfectant it seemed cavernous without his huge personality. No matter, he'd be home soon and lording his position over everyone, horse and human. It wasn't the first time we'd been separated because of quarantine, but it always made the barn feel weird when he wasn't around.

Rasputin wound around my feet and generally made a nuisance of himself as I sifted manure from the shavings and dropped it into the wheelbarrow. The mindless work helped settle my brain. A little.

"Hey, Caitlyn?"

"Yeah?" I turned around to find Brandon in the open stall door, holding up his phone to take a photo.

"Smile," he said and when I leaned on the fork and complied he snapped a few pics. "For ye olde social media accounts," he explained as he tapped his screen.

"Ah, thanks. This is why I keep you guys around. To make sure I'm hip with all the social stuff."

He grinned. "And here I was thinking you only kept me because I chill Wren out."

"That too." The pictures buzzed through to the phone in my pocket, and I uploaded them to Instagram, Twitter and Facebook with the caption:

Apparently silver and bronze medals in #Rio2016 don't make you exempt from cleaning stalls. We're all counting the seconds and keeping busy until #MidfieldsAdieu comes home from quarantine.

#MidfieldsTeamEffort #DirtOnMyFace #BFFRasputin

Within seconds I had my first reaction. Addie Gardner had *loved* my post. Well she had said she loved me...

CHAPTER TWENTY-EIGHT

Addie

Saying goodbye to Dewey felt like the final chapter in a book I wasn't ready to finish. During the week of quarantine, I'd spent most of my days with him and Wren and we'd become good friends. When I asked Wren why she hadn't flown home to see her fiancée, then come back to drive Dewey to Kentucky at the end of the week, she'd said casually, "I'll see Brandon soon enough." We'd made sure Dewey and Pierre were settled for the night and she'd invited me out for dinner. "Another week of being apart isn't going to kill us." Her voice dropped and took on a distinctly naughty tone. "And that's one more week of pent-up horniness to look forward to. You should think about that with Caitlyn and a possible long-distance thing."

Given Wren had been so involved in putting Caitlyn and me together, and Caitlyn had said Wren was more like a friend and sister, her comment didn't feel as icky as it could have. "So I've heard. But I'm still not one hundred percent sure there's going to be any *thing* with us, long distance or not."

Wren sighed. "I'm about to put my size eleven into this. Just between you and me? Caitlyn Lloyd is a certified Disney princess. Seriously. I'm talking some Snow-White purity-of-heart type shit."

I had to bite my tongue. Caitlyn certainly wasn't all pure. Not when she'd had me pinned to the bed and was— Not the time to think about that. Those thoughts were for tonight. And all the nights we'd be apart until we could figure this out.

"Part of her being like that is that she's naïve about some stuff. For example? Whatever's going on between you two. Give her a horse and she's like a Mensa-level genius with a touch of clairvoyant thrown in. But anything relationshippy or to do with her emotions? She's sitting in the corner wearing a dunce hat."

"I see."

Wren lowered the level of beer in her glass by half an inch. "Look, I adore her, I really do. She's not only a fabulous boss and rider, but she's a good person and all that being good encompasses. I want her to be happy. You make her happy. Simple."

Laughing at her no-nonsense explanation of how things were and how she thought they should be, I filled my wineglass from the bottle of red I'd sacrilegiously put into an ice bucket. "I wish it were that simple, but it's not. There's a lot of things we have to work out, work *through* before we even get to the startin' point of a relationship."

Nodding slowly, Wren murmured her agreement. "Right. Listen, I know you used to ride, so I know you're going to understand the well thought out, beer-inspired and very apt metaphor I'm about to impart upon you."

I sipped my wine. "Lay it on me."

"If you ask a horse to halt and it doesn't, are you just going to ignore it and let it keep moving for the rest of time until you've cantered to California? No. You're going to ask again. And maybe again. And sometimes you have to use a firmer aid if the horse doesn't listen to you. Then they get their reward of softness and support and trust. But! The reason they haven't listened the first time is the key." Wren paused, studying me intently and perhaps a little tipsily. "Did they not listen to your aid because they didn't understand what you said because you weren't clear? Are they distracted? Afraid? In pain?"

"I think I've been very clear," I murmured.

"Given the time I've spent in your company, I'm sure you have been," Wren agreed. "So why is she running from you? Running through you."

The answer required no thought. "Because she's afraid."

She pointed a forefinger at me "'Xactly! So what do we do with horses who are clear about what you've said, but aren't listening because they're afraid?"

I grinned. "I'd usually sedate them."

Wren laughed. "Ah. Yeah, that's not where I thought we would go with that. Let's move back to riding instead of vetting, yeah?"

"You show it that it can trust you. That you're a safe place for it to be." I peered into my glass. "You have to persist."

"Bingo. She wants to trust you, she wants to know you're going to be the safe place. Once she knows that you're there, that you're going to be a solid base for her, it'll all come tumbling into your lap." She lowered her voice to add, "Caitlyn would rather spend the rest of her life being miserable than think she might have made you unhappy in some way, because if that happens, then it means…" With both eyebrows raised, Wren left the words to hang.

I tried to pick up the words and failed. So we got drunk together.

I'd thought about that dinner conversation nearly every day for the rest of quarantine. I understood my fears about our future, but what was Caitlyn so afraid of? I knew she feared how our lives would rotate around each other like planets in opposing orbits, but aside from that I kept drawing blanks. Until it finally hit me while I was packing to go home, like an empty beer can doinked off someone's head at a football game.

After Elin's infidelity, aside from fearing more infidelity, Caitlyn feared not being enough. If I made the leap, made a big commitment, moved to Kentucky or whatever and it didn't work out then it would just exacerbate the feeling that she wasn't enough, in whatever ways she feared, to keep a partner. Goddammit. This was going to be a tough one to work around. But if I wanted a future with her, which I absolutely did, then I'd have to do everything I could to show her I was in it for real.

Walking back into the practice felt like someone had put a pin in my balloon. I'd driven back from Miami the night before, ignored all my bags, taken a shower and fallen into bed. I'd almost texted Caitlyn to let her know I'd seen Dewey off safely but figured Wren would have told her she was on her way home. Then I thought I might text her to see how she was doing. Maybe ask if she wanted to sext with me. In the end, I'd decided to just let her be while I consoled myself with memories of our time overseas together. That had lasted for about ten minutes before I opened up our text conversation and fell asleep reading her sweet words.

If only that could smother the annoyance that awaited me at work. As expected, Eric had sprawled until my space had been absorbed into his space. I dumped papers, folders, reference books and a plastic container of gummy bears back over to his side and booted up my computer.

My colleagues poked their heads in to welcome me home, ask about my time away, congratulate me on the team success and hype up my ego for how I'd dealt with Dew's bee sting. I'd sorted my emails and was confirming consults on the day's schedule when Diana waltzed in, stole Eric's chair and rolled across the floor toward me. "Just a heads-up, Seth's in a foul mood."

"Why?"

"The moon is waxing, someone looked at him, who the hell knows." She eyed me over the top of her glasses. "And...he's been complaining that since you left for your 'Special Little Olympic Adventure' caseloads have been off the charts and he's had to work on-call shifts to cover some of it."

Boo-fucking-hoo. "Hell. It's not like I've been loafing at home enjoying a nice break sleeping in every morning and doing sweet eff-all. I've been bustin' my ass." Mostly. "Look at the bags under my eyes."

Diana held up both hands. "I know, I know."

I forced a smile. "Great. Situation normal here while I've been gone, then?"

"Pretty much." She patted my knee. "It's good to see you. Come find me for a chat later. I want to hear all about it."

As usual, later never happened. I barely had a moment to breathe, and as the days blurred I spent my free moments thinking about Caitlyn. We texted every day, usually a disjointed conversation held at weird hours around our respective jobs. We managed to talk every few days, in the car on the way to a consult, or she was done for the day and I was usually still at work. At least once a day I checked equine vet job openings in Kentucky—just for interest's sake—then scared myself when I saw how little was on offer and closed the sites down again.

Most importantly we both discovered phone and video-call sex, which turned out to be a mutual kink neither of us had realized we'd had. In a strange way, it worked. But it wasn't great. I missed the physical. After eight days back at work, and fifteen away from her, we still hadn't made plans to meet up again. The prospects were murky. There was the possibility for a weekend visit early next month. In the meantime, I had plenty of work to catch up on. As Seth kept reminding me. No shit, Sherlock.

* * *

I pulled over on the road outside my client's place to double check messages, then set my phone onto the hands-free cradle and crossed my fingers as I dialed. Caitlyn answered after a few rings, her voice full of pleasure. "Hey. I was just thinking about you."

"What a coincidence because I'm usually thinking about you. What triggered this thought of yours?"

She laughed. "The vet just left. But also, you know, I love you so I think about you a lot."

"Nice save," I said dryly. "Everyone okay?"

"Yeah. Just a checkup for Antoinette's arthritis."

"Ah, good." I pulled out and started down the road on my way to my next consult.

"How's the day been?"

"Busy. I'm still trying to get to lunch." At three p.m.

"Oh, babe, that sucks. Try to eat something?"

"I will."

The sound of horse hooves on concrete echoed through the phone. "I'm just about to jump on Dew, but when we have some time maybe we could figure out when we can have our first visit?"

My stomach and chest did an excited flutter. "Absolutely. I'll call back tonight and we can set a firm date. I really miss you. This is great and fine, but you know."

"Yeah, I do know," she quietly agreed.

I could have easily spent a few more minutes having a gooey loved-up conversation but my work phone interrupted. "Okay, I gotta go too. Work call coming through. I love you."

"And I love you."

"I never get sick of hearing that."

"Good, because I never get sick of saying it."

With a quiet groan of frustration at our lack of time and not-lack of distance, I said, "Okay, I really gotta go before I combust of romance."

The call was for a colic emergency, which thankfully wasn't as much of an emergency as the client had made out. I arrived late to my next scheduled consult which was thankfully only a quick standard vaccination call, then headed back to the practice for my very late lunch. The moment I got out of the truck, Seth—who was an interesting shade of purply-red—bailed me up. "Where the fuck have you been?"

I only just managed to hold my tongue on a facetious response of, "Driving around, staring at the scenery, wasting time and getting paid for it." His face made it clear he was in no mood for jokes, so I went with the truth. "Out on consults?"

"For fuck's sake, Addie. I've got a colic coming in that looks surgical, the scheduled arthroscopy that's already been pushed back a day, and a mare who's about to abort if someone doesn't get their ass in there and stop it. Namely, you."

My temper, which had started sparking the moment he'd addressed me, flared. "Geez, Seth. I'm so fuckin' sorry I forgot to bring my clairvoyant hat this morning so I'd know all of that without anyone telling me." Given we all shit talked each other, griped at each other and let loose with tempers, I wasn't worried about talking back to him.

"Get your ass into stall five and deal with that mare. And so fucking help me God if she loses her foal, I'll—" Apparently nastiness had limits and whatever he'd been about to say was held back behind a clenched jaw.

"You'll what?" I raised my eyebrows. "Hmm?"

His answer was to stalk away, muttering under his breath, leaving me to calm down. I got that running a veterinary practice was stressful. I got that his wife was on him all the time about cutting back on the amount of work he did. I got that people sometimes let loose with emotion. But I didn't get why he thought it was okay to talk to his staff the way he did. And lately, I couldn't get why I was still hanging around taking it.

Unsurprisingly, my call with Caitlyn never eventuated. All I managed was a text around eight p.m. to let her know I was going to be stuck at work until who knew when, I was so sorry and I'd call as soon as I could tomorrow. Despite not being on call, I stayed until close to midnight with the mare until I was sure she wasn't going to lose the foal, and then skulked home to shower and sleep.

I was too tired to even be enraged about being treated like absolute dirt. I was the most senior vet on Seth's staff, and instead of respect I was treated like a first-year vet student. And I was just starting to realize that it didn't have to be like this. But that was a thought for another day.

Teresa called early the next morning while I was at my desk eating breakfast and typing up case notes. Her greeting was an indignant, "Addie, goddammit, why haven't you called me yet? You've been home forever. I need the Caitlyn gossip."

"I'm busy," I said around my mouthful of cereal.

"Right. You and every other vet on the planet. So listen, Emmett's decided instead of a locum he wants to add another fulltime vet to the roster. He's thinking a reasonably new graduate, someone looking for a place to settle long term who he can train up and invest in."

"Good plan."

"Right? He's getting ready to advertise but before he does that, he wants our word-of-mouth recommendations. I've got total baby-brain. You know any junior equine vets who want to work at the best vet practice around?"

"Not off the top of my head."

Seth leaned in the door. "You on a personal call?"

"Excuse me a moment," I told Teresa. Putting the phone down, I turned around. "No, Seth, I'm not." Dickhead.

His heavy footsteps echoed down the hall.

"Your boss is such an asshole," Teresa said when I'd raised the phone again.

"Don't I know it." I sighed. "I need to get back to paperwork. I'll call if I think of anyone."

"Don't be a stranger. And I won't forget you still owe me that gossip. I want all the details."

"Pervert."

Her laugh was her goodbye.

Around my morning consults I tried to think of anyone I could recommend to Teresa. I'd just made it back to the practice to restock my work truck before heading out again when I was intercepted by Pat, one of the staff from the café next to work. "Addie," she puffed, "I've been staring out the window for the last hour waiting to see you come back. We had a phone order come in for your lunch, from a… Caitlyn?"

"Oh?" I took the offered takeout container. "Thanks. What do I owe you?"

"All paid for. Catch you later." She jogged off before I could say another word.

I opened the cardboard box and found a thick sandwich and a Mars Bar. My stomach did a funny swirl of excitement at Caitlyn's sweet thoughtfulness and with one hand I texted her as I walked. *I just got your lunch. Thank you! Also, sneaky stalker figuring out which café is next to my work.*

Her answer came within a minute. *Glad you got it. I wish I could have delivered it in person. One day I will. I love you.*

I took my time reading the text again and by the time I was done, was struck with a sudden realization. I loved her and there was absolutely no reason I shouldn't be near her. I loved her sweetness.

Her compassion. Her tenderness. Her determination. And damn it all to hell I did *not* need to stay in Florida to work for a man who treated everyone like crap and fostered an unpleasant workplace, just for the sake of some extra money.

Hadn't Teresa said it herself, that her mental health was more important than a top-twenty-percent wage? And with my USDF work, it really didn't matter anyway. I was an adult now, I was financially secure, and I was such an idiot for letting childhood fears hold me back over something as meaningless as a small salary cut when what I'd gain personally was priceless.

I took my lunch and phone to my car, shut myself in and searched for a number. My call was answered with a cheerful, "Emmett Lake."

"Emmett, hi. It's Addie Gardner. Hope you're well."

"I am indeed. To what do I owe the pleasure of you calling me?"

"Teresa called me this morning and said you're hunting for a new equine vet." I ran my tongue around my dry mouth.

Emmett chuckled. "Addie, you're damned right I'm looking."

I tried to keep the shaky hopefulness out of my voice as I said, "I know you're thinking of hiring someone newly qualified, but would you consider someone with Olympic veterinary experience who's already licensed in Kentucky and wants to settle there?"

There was a long pause. "Are you about to make my day?"

"I might be, sir. Or it could be you're about to make mine…"

After hastily updating my résumé and a bunch of back-and-forth emails with Emmett in between consults, I strode back into my office and opened a fresh Word document. It took me ten minutes to write the letter and I did the very passive-aggressive thing of printing it at work and using an envelope from the stash at the reception desk. There was no point in waiting until the end of the day, or a better time, so I marched into Seth's office and held out the envelope. He eyed it like I'd just handed him a stick of dynamite. "What's this?"

"My letter of resignation, and my official two weeks' notice." He still hadn't taken the envelope so I placed it on his desk.

Seth leaned back in his chair, to the leather-creaking protest of the furniture. "I see. May I ask why?" The question was asked calmly but he couldn't disguise his irritation.

Though I wanted nothing more than to tell him exactly why I'd decided to quit and that it'd been coming for over a year but I'd been too scared to leave, I decided on the not-burning-bridges route. "After my time with the dressage team, I've realized I need to move my career in a different direction. And now that David West has officially retired, my position with the USDF is assured. My time with the dressage athletes made me realize that my passion really does lie with performance horse work. I'm so grateful for the opportunities you've given me and the things I've learned here in mixed equine practice." Like how not to treat employees. "But it's time for me to move on."

"If that's your only reason we can look at having you specialize." It sounded like desperate straws being grasped. I'd heard this promise before, and knew it started off great but after a few months I'd be back at square one.

"I appreciate that. But despite what you kept saying, I know you're unhappy with my position within the USDF. And I feel it's unfair to take myself out of the practice so frequently. It's disruptive to the workflow and puts unnecessary stresses on my colleagues." Because he wouldn't hire enough veterinarians.

I knew this was going to make things harder for the people I'd worked with for the past six years, but I also knew every one of them would sprint out the door at the first opportunity. We were all friendly enough when we weren't snarking at one another. But we weren't friends. Another reason I wanted out.

"You're going to do what, exactly?" It came out with a sneer, as if he didn't think me capable of changing course at this stage of my career.

"Move to a practice that's primarily geared toward elite performance horses."

He didn't bother disguising his annoyance. "Then I suppose that's it. There's nothing I can do or say to change your mind?"

"'Fraid not." No way, no how. I knew he didn't care that I was leaving. He cared that he'd have to figure out how to cover my position until he could find a new veterinarian or three, or shock and horror… have to work more himself. "I've already got a new job lined up."

"Where?"

"Kentucky." That was all I was going to give him. "Right, well I have to get home. I have no more consults this afternoon, and I'm owed hours for overtime. Already cleared it with Margot. I'll see you tomorrow."

All I got was a grunt. He'd picked up his phone and was scrolling through something on the screen. Thanks for making my decision so easy, Seth.

CHAPTER TWENTY-NINE

Caitlyn

The brief moments talking to Addie had quickly become the bright spot in my days, which were often mirrors of the one before. Sometimes we had a four-sentence conversation in between her consults and me swapping from one horse to the next. Other times it was hours at night when she'd finally finished work and we'd have conversations full of laughter, seriousness and intense connection before inevitably agreeing that yes, we should really practice our phone sex.

We'd finally managed to set a firm day for her to fly up this weekend but Addie seemed distracted. She wasn't exactly distant but I could tell she was busy, and not wanting to add to her work stress, which she'd started opening up about, I didn't push.

We'd found a comfortable space to exist in while being apart where it felt like we were really connecting and getting to know each other. Comfortable was fine but it was starting to feel a little stretched and I didn't know how I was going to say goodbye to her on Sunday. I'd been reminding myself that I would say goodbye because I had to, because this was how it was for us until we could find another way to be together.

Until then, I had my usual work. Dewey had settled right back in after quarantine and Wren, Brandon, and I all swore he was lording his position as Olympic Superstar over everyone. I'd picked up the training of my other horses where Brandon had left it, and others were trickling back in for me to train. And then there was Dougie who was acting like he'd lived here his whole life, and aside from a few expected issues which all related to him being a young stallion finding his place, I was thrilled with him.

On the schedule for ten this morning was Dougie's DNA testing for breeding purposes, along with a general checkup. I was untacking one of my clients' horses while Wren fetched Dirk, and decided I had enough time to call Addie. The call almost rang out before she answered with a breathless, "Hey, babe."

"Hey yourself. You going to a consult?"

"I certainly am." She paused. "Gotta cram in as much as I can before I come see you."

The thought made my stomach tighten with excitement. "I can't wait."

"Me either," she murmured. "I—" A ringing phone interrupted. "Honey, I have to go. Sorry. Work calls. I'll talk to you soon. Love you."

"Love you too."

Despite my manic excitement with Addie's call, I managed to ride Dirk without incident and had just enough time to rush up to the house to make myself a PB&J before the vet appointment. My first bite was interrupted by a knock on my screen door, which made it rattle against the frame. Wren was the only person I knew who never used doorbells, so I always knew when it was her at my door.

I leaned over the pony wall that made up one side of my kitchen and called, "Hey. Come on in."

She opened the screen door but didn't step inside. "Hey. Brandon has come down with some stomach flu thing, fluids coming out of him everywhere. Gross as hell. Sorry, but I need to head into town to grab him some things to uh, stop the flow. Will you be okay by yourself for the vet visit?"

Well that explained his absence this morning. I'd already planned to be there to talk to the vet about Dougie, so doing it by myself was no problem. "Of course I will, no worries, I'll take care of it. Hope Brandon feels better."

"Mhmm, great. I'm sure he'll be fine by tomorrow. Let me know how it goes with the vet." Wren flashed me an incongruous grin then jumped down the two steps off my front porch.

I slipped back into the kitchen and finished my sandwich and was just pulling on a pair of short boots when a white pickup with a canopy on the back rolled slowly through my gate. The vet was early. The truck paused at the intersection then turned off toward the barn. I wandered down the hill to meet them and noticed some lucky veterinarian at LakeVets had a brand-new work truck. Emmett and his staff generally kept their cars clean, but this one gleamed. The driver door opened and the last person in the world I'd expected to see stepped out of the truck.

Addie.

My whole body did a weird shudder as if I'd just plunged into an ice bath. Her smile, in person, was the best thing I'd seen in a month. Addie winked. "Howdy, darlin'." She laughed, shaking her head. "Wow that came out totally cowgirl and I have no idea why." Both her hands extended as if she was offering me something. "Surprise."

Seeing her right there, at my barn, sent a wave of emotion surging over me. Excitement, confusion, happiness, more confusion, a little bit of arousal, ecstasy and then a stack of emotions in between. I closed the space between us and flung my arms around her. Addie pulled me against her, snuggling her face into my neck. I felt her long exhalation against my skin, felt the relaxation sliding through her. She eased her grip to put a tiny bit of space between us, reached up to pull my face to hers and kissed me.

The kiss felt tentative, oddly so, and for a quick panicked moment I wondered if she wasn't pleased to see me. Then in the next heartbeat she seemed to relax and poured herself into me, and I felt her arms slide around my waist to hold me against her. Addie rested her forehead against mine. "I've missed you so much."

"Me too but I...what are you doing here? Did you get an earlier flight?" I asked dumbly. The answer seemed obvious given the truck and her uniform shirt—that she now worked at LakeVets. But the hows and whys were missing.

"I sure did. I'm working for Emmett Lake." Her smile was uncertain. "I bet you have a million questions, and I have a million answers for you. Teresa and Wren set this up."

"Ah, that explains Wren's departure and Brandon's absence." I smiled. "I guess he doesn't have a gross oozing stomach flu after all."

Addie's eyes widened. "I hope not."

My throat tightened and I felt an unexpected prickle of tears. "You're here."

"That I am." She dipped her head to catch my eye. "Are you happy?" The question was quiet, uncertain.

"I am," I blurted, meaning it absolutely. "Sorry, I'm just trying to process...this. My brain has been getting set for Friday not today and

I think it's melting down." I laughed. "I'm so happy to see you. I just don't know what to say." So I decided not to say anything and instead pulled her closer and kissed her again.

Addie's tongue skated along my lower lip before she made a sound of frustration and pulled away. "Ahhh, mercy. I'm technically working, and…" Smiling, she tugged her collar away from her neck, shaking it as if trying to cool off.

I took her hands, turned them over, studied them, ran my thumbs over her palms as I tried to sort my feelings. Layered alongside my overwhelming pleasure and unrestrained joy at seeing her was the fact that she hadn't shared this huge thing with me. "Why didn't you tell me that you'd taken this job? That you'd moved? When did you start?"

She glanced at her watch. "I started little over two hours ago. And as to why I didn't tell you…" Addie leaned back against the truck. "You know, I've asked myself that same question nearly every day for the past few weeks since I quit my job. And every time, I get a different answer." Her swallow was visible. "I wanted to surprise you and when Teresa suggested this it seemed like a good idea."

"You sure did surprise me."

"Good surprise or bad surprise?" she quietly asked.

"Very good, I promise."

"Phew. I really am sorry I didn't say anything. It's just…these last few weeks have been mayhem. I signed the contract for a new job a few hours after I handed Seth my resignation. I had to make sure my Kentucky vet registration was still in order and I spent every second I wasn't working packing up my tiny apartment. All my stuff, including my car, is on its way here so all I have is clothes and essentials. I took a red-eye last night after tidying up some last-minute things at work. I know I could have called or come around but it was so late, then I realized I didn't even know your address."

If not for how confused I felt, I would have laughed at the fact we'd never exchanged such basic information. "Where are you staying?"

"With Teresa and her husband until I can hopefully rent a place this weekend."

I was a few seconds away from going full U-Haul and suggesting she just stay with me, but thankfully caught myself. There was nothing about her that made me think she expected that either. I inhaled slowly. "Okay."

"Are you angry?" she quietly asked.

"Not at all."

"Then why do you have that face on?"

I smiled and indicated my face with a swirling forefinger. "This is not my angry face, Addie. Not at all. This is my I'm-so-happy-and-excited-but-trying-to-process face."

"Okay, good. I know none of that explains why I didn't mention it, and I know we've got a lot to talk about, but right now probably isn't the best time."

"So you're actually here for Dougie's consult?"

"Correct."

"Sorry, usually I have the horse ready to go but you're early."

She grinned. "Enjoy it, remember?"

"I will." I took her hand and pulled her toward the barn. "Come on, you can help me. Do you want a drink?"

"Maybe after, thanks." Addie laughed quietly. "Teresa said your hospitality was one of the best things about your consults." She leaned into me. "I think I'm going to find something even better about coming here than you giving me a drink…"

We collected Dougie's halter and Addie made a detour to say hi to Dewey, climbing through the fence to hug him, kiss the side of his nose and tell him, "I missed you. Yes I did." More kisses, which Dew tolerated because he knew kisses were always paired with treats. She gave him some licorice then left him to his grazing.

"Who'd you miss more?" I asked once she'd climbed back through the fence.

"Both equal." She side-eyed me and her expression was perfectly deadpan. "Okay, you a little more." After a long beat she said, "A lot more."

I nudged her, wrapping an arm around her waist. "Good answer."

She leaned into me. "For the record, I really did miss Dewey. He's such a loveable guy."

"Yeah." My other loveable guy, Dougie, came up to the fence and followed us along it to his gate. I picked up the long dressage whip and tapped him lightly on the shoulder to ask him to back off so I could enter. Given his stallion status, we were leading him with a bit attached to his leather halter for control and carrying a whip to remind him to keep his distance from whoever was leading him. He'd been so good but tended to forget his manners when he came within reach of other horses, and gentle reminders and clear calm guidelines would make him a productive member of society.

He fidgeted a little but was well-behaved for all the hair plucking, blood taking, and general standing around while Addie drew his markings and brands, photographed him and scanned him for his microchip. She squinted, lips moving soundlessly as she read the forms and wrote details on them. Since we'd been apart I'd totally forgotten that she mouthed when she read, and this tiny Addie-detail melted me.

She glanced up from the clipboard. "The notes said you were looking at having Lake—uh, us collecting semen from him and storing it with us? Just in case something happens to him?"

"Right."

"Has he ever had semen analysis done?"

"Before he left the Netherlands as part of the sale contract and seems he's as fertile as they get. For an unproven sire." No point in buying a stallion with the idea of breeding from him if he was a dud in the stud department. "I think it'll also help him focus on work more for the next few years if his only romantic interludes are sporadic ones with a padded barrel on legs and an artificial vagina instead of living, breathing mares."

Addie grinned. "True. Did they test any frozen or just do fresh?"

"Both." Laughing, I shook my head. "You know, this is really not a conversation I thought we'd be having the first time we saw each other in over a month."

Her answering laugh was rich. "No, I suppose not."

Rasputin meandered out of the feed room like a teenager emerging from sleep. He paused to stretch then wandered over to wind his way between our legs. Addie bent to stroke along his back. "Ah, the infamous Rasputin." The cat, having apparently recognized a kindred spirit, ignored me to focus on Addie who crouched to rub his face and under his chin. Once Rasputin had had enough petting, he wandered off without so much as a backward glance in search of a snack and a sun patch for a nap.

Addie brushed cat hair from her pants then sat down on the bench outside the tack room to check paperwork and the lab samples for Dougie's formal ID. "Right. I think we're done here. Is there anything else you needed me to go over with you?"

"Are you busy tonight?"

Her face relaxed. "Depends on whether you're going to ask me to come around after work or not."

"I am."

"Then yes, now I'm busy. I'll bring dinner with me if you just tell me where to get it. Or are you cooking?"

My anxiety spiked. "Uh. Remember those few mentions about me cooking? Or rather, how me and cooking are incompatible?"

"I do. I thought you were joking."

"I really wasn't. And boring, bland and shittily made food isn't particularly romantic."

Addie's eyebrows rocketed upward. "Romantic? Is that what this is?" The way she said it was sly, teasing, as if she knew that I'd meant to say it but obviously hadn't meant to say it. Her voice lowered to a conspiratorial whisper. "Is tonight…a date?"

Shit. "Can we just forget I said that and put all this weird expectation on us having dinner?"

Her dimples flashed. "Nope. Not a chance. I'm gonna think about it for the rest of the day."

I was too. "So just to be sure, I don't need to pick you up from the airport Friday?"

She laughed as she confirmed, "No, you don't." Addie offered Dougie a peppermint, which he took from the flat of her hand then promptly spat on the rubber mats underfoot, curling his top lip upward. Addie gasped. "Don't tell Dewey you just did that, young man." She stepped away from him and gave me her attention. "And I'll see you around seven after I've taken a quick shower. Emergencies pending of course but I'll let you know if I'll be late." She kissed me quickly but not gently, surprising me. I opened my mouth but before I could prolong the kiss, she pulled away. "I don't want to start something I can't finish."

"You'd better start something later."

Addie backed away from me, her mouth curved into a promising smile. "Count on it."

CHAPTER THIRTY

Addie

When Caitlyn had asked me to come back for dinner, I grew anxious at what exactly she meant by her invitation. I mean, she'd said romantic, but we hadn't had romance, not really. We'd had connection, great sex, getting to know one another. But not romance. Still, I was all for romance.

My first day at LakeVets had been comfortably busy with enough variation in consults to keep my brain engaged. Emmett and I agreed that I'd spend a few weeks getting to know my new colleagues, the area, and the clients, then I'd start moving into more specialized work with performance horses. When I'd popped my head into Teresa's office after lunch to tell her I wouldn't be around for dinner, she offered a sly smile and an even slyer, "Don't forget to take underwear and a clean uniform shirt over so you have something to wear to work tomorrow. I'll see you here in the morning."

And I'd blushed like a teenager getting ready for a first date as I'd thanked her for the reminder. Though I'd thought a lot about seeing Caitlyn for the first time since Rio, I'd kept blanking on the sleeping-together part. It made sense, with our regular and exciting sext and video sex sessions this past month that tonight would involve sex in one form or another but the idea of intimacy with her was overwhelming. Weirdly so.

Given we'd been to bed a few times already, I knew there was no expectation between us—which was one of the most refreshing things I'd discovered about our relationship. When things got odd or rocky we seemed to find a way to negotiate it together. Even if it took a bit of time and discomfort. So why was tonight any different? If I wasn't sure, I could just ask her and we could have a conversation like adults.

I finished work a little after my scheduled end-of-shift time, which was super early by my standards, then ducked back to Teresa's place to shower, change, and pack an overnight bag and my nerves. The small town of La Grange didn't seem huge on takeout options, so I stopped by a supermarket and picked up ingredients for beef tenderloin with my favorite mushroom sauce.

I parked behind a red SUV nestled in the carport, and was met on the front porch by Caitlyn, casual in faded jeans and a tee that might have been black once. I'd barely made it up the two steps before she'd nabbed me and pulled me in for a long, slow kiss that made me think maybe we should skip dinner and get right to the intimacy.

When she pulled back, she murmured a breathless, "Come on in."

Caitlyn's house was so…Caitlyn. Clean and modern, cozy and warm, and with evidence of horses lingering everywhere from the horse paintings and pictures of her and Dew, to the trophies and ribbons, including her two Olympic medals, on five shelves spanning the entire wall of her living room, to the brand new, still-had-tags bridle hooked over a chair.

I held up the grocery store bag and bottle of red. "I bring dinner. Deconstructed. I hope you're not starving because it'll take about half an hour to create my masterpiece."

"You're going to cook for me?" The way she said it was like no woman had ever cooked a romantic meal for her before.

"I am. I had no idea of where to get takeout so I went with Option B—woo you with cooking. I was thinking about our last meal in Rio, the *churrasco*, and how much you seemed to enjoy steak."

"Shit, I'm so sorry. I didn't even think about you being new around here. I do like steak and I'm always too scared to cook it for myself, so this is extra sweet." She blushed. "Thanks for remembering."

"I remember more than just that about our time together."

"Me too," she murmured. Caitlyn kissed me again then took my hand and led me through to her kitchen. "And no, I'm not starving. If you're not either we could relax, have a drink? Just so you're not sent straight to the kitchen the moment you get here, which feels a little like forced labor to me."

"Deal."

She left me to stash things in the refrigerator while she poured wine and made a small platter of nibbles for us. I fell into the butter-soft leather of her couch and set the platter on her coffee table, a single piece of unmilled but polished hardwood.

Caitlyn settled next to me and put her feet up against the edge of the table. "How was the rest of your first day working for Emmett?"

"Amazing. Peaceful. Interesting. Fun. Busy." I took the glass of red, noticing right away that it was cold, like she'd put a bottle in the fridge for me before I'd come over. "Thanks. It was everything I wanted. Busy without stress. Great facilities and equipment. My colleagues are like angels sent from heaven, everyone seems to like and respect each other. Totally different vibe. Like moving from a favela to the athlete's village."

Caitlyn's smile creased her eyes. "I'm so happy for you. I know how much Florida was wearing you down." She sipped a small mouthful of wine. "How'd you know about the job?"

"Teresa called and told me Emmett was looking for another vet, but it didn't really twig it could be me. Until a few hours later when a massive snowball of professional and personal dissatisfaction hit me and I just decided screw it, time to try a life change. Time to move my career and uh, maybe other stuff in the direction that I want."

"Why didn't you tell me?" she asked, and the question seemed calmer than it had that morning.

"Ah, yeah. We did say we were going to talk about that, didn't we?" I tried to find the words, and eventually came up with, "I just didn't know how. This whole time I was so excited for this move, to be closer to you and to start a great new job and then my excitement would tip over into this horrible uncertainty."

"Uncertainty about what?" she asked quietly.

"I'm embarrassed to admit that I was worried about money, which I guess is part of why I stayed so long in Florida. My old workplace was shitty but the pay wasn't, and that little kid beggin' for rides and wearing third-hand gear on her borrowed horse panicked a little that I would somehow spiral back into that if I didn't have the best-paying job I could. Totally irrational, but I kept thinking it."

"Addie," Caitlyn said gently. "I'm sorry." She took my hands and held them in her lap.

"Then I kept worrying if it was the right thing to do and thinking about everything that me moving here implied." I didn't give her a chance to ask what it implied, before I barreled on, "That I want a relationship with you. A real one. A long-term one. The kind where we share our lives like a couple. I mean, the long-distance stuff? It was fine, really. I feel like we'd kinda started figuring it out, and we would have kept refining it and figuring things out along the way. But I really missed the physical and the connection that comes with that. Me being here seemed like the logical step. I want to try making something permanent with you, Caitlyn. Something real and lasting. And it felt so good to think that, so…perfect and right, but then it'd fall into this panic that maybe it was pushing you into a situation you really didn't want and then I'd remember my panic about changing jobs, and then it just got all messed up in my head. So I didn't say anything. And the more I didn't say anything, the more it snowballed."

"Did you think I would tell you to go back to Florida or something? That I'd say no to something we'd already agreed to try on some level?"

"No it wasn't that. But let's be realistic. This is a big jump from us saying let's see how it all goes when we get home. But I couldn't stop thinking about being with you and I figured the first step is us being closer. And another upshot would be that I'd be happier professionally."

She nodded, slowly, as if trying to work through some mental gymnastics. "You being happier in your job makes me very happy. But, Addie," she sighed, "I spend a few months a year in Europe, and the rest of the year I'm training or competing horses. My free time is basically nonexistent. I'm not going to be able to give you the attention you'll want."

"Back 'atcha. Some days I'm out the door before dawn and not home until eight at night. Or later. When I'm on call I could leave our bed at ten p.m. and not come back until two a.m. or possibly not come back until the next night or leave multiple times and come back again." Laughing I added, "I'm really not selling myself very well, am I…"

"I've been sold on you for a little while now."

"Flatterer." I caressed the backs of her hands. "And as for Europe, I'd happily spend my vacation time bouncing around the circuit with you."

A dubious eyebrow went up. "Really? You'd use up all your free time to follow me around while I'm competing in the same places every year? It's not like you can skip off to check out the sights." She smiled wryly. "Well you can, but you'd be seeing them by yourself."

"Sure I would. I love familiarity and routine. When I was a kid I'd spend part of my summers at a friend's little cabin by the lake. I loved it, couldn't wait to sleep in my same vacation bed and see my same vacation friends and do my same vacation activities. One year my parents tried to change our summer plans and I lost my shit. You already know I like to eat the same breakfast, same lunch and something from my same rotation of dinners." Shrugging I added, "You're gonna have to do better than that if you're trying to get rid of me."

"What about the cold here and your leg? You're going to hate winter, especially if you're getting up in the middle of the night for after-hours calls."

"What about it? I've worked in Kentucky and cold places before. It's a compromise I'm willing to make." I sighed, feigning exasperation. "Geez, Caitlyn. What more do I have to do to prove to you that I want to try and make this work?"

"You've already proven it," she whispered. "It's just...I've been thinking about this all day and—"

"And what?" I gently prompted.

After a long silence she admitted, "I'm scared."

"Of what exactly?" I murmured.

I could sense how hard it was for her to verbalize, and I sat quietly until she was ready, stroking the backs of her hands with my thumbs. After an eternity, she whispered a tearful, "I don't want to mess this up. I don't want to be the one who's going to screw up this, this...gift."

"Why would a screw-up be entirely on your shoulders?"

"We talked about it, about...us," she uttered helplessly. "My life is not flexible. You're going to have to just fit in with the way I am."

"I'll fit in. I *want* to fit in. All relationships have give and take, compromise, flexibility. And given my excellent performance in Rio, my position as the USDF veterinarian is solid. Which means I'll get to come with you to all the big competitions anyway. Perfect solution. I'll make a witty encouragement sign to hold up in the stands, and everyone will know who I am because you'll talk about your girlfriend the team veterinarian and our story of childhood enemies, now equestrian lovers traveling the world together will make all the horse magazines and shit."

"Wow, you really haven't thought about this at all, have you," she deadpanned.

"Not at all."

Caitlyn's smile faded and her question came out so softly I had to strain to hear her. "You really moved here for me?"

"Absolutely, yes, without a doubt. But you're not the only reason and I think it's really important you know that." Her obvious confusion made me pause and think hard about how I should frame my words. "I figured out a few things during our time apart, or at least part of why you were so reluctant, and maybe a way I could help you with that."

"Oh? And what is this thing you figured out?" It came across light and teasing but her expression gave away her trepidation.

"Not to get all psychoanalytical on you, but I think after everything with Elin and other relationships you're worried that you're not enough to keep a woman interested, keep her happy, keep…I don't know, a spark or whatever going. Which is utter bullshit, by the way, because what Elin did was on her, not you."

"I know. And my knowing that was confirmed by the fact she's still doing it."

"Right." I shrugged. "I just thought if I showed you I'd moved here for you, but also for myself because of a great job that has the bonus of workin' with a close friend, then it might help you feel more comfortable, less pressured to make everything perfect because it's not just me here for you. Well it is, but also not. Argh." I rubbed my face. "You know what I mean, don't you? I just can't figure out how to say it."

"I do know what you mean. And it's incredible, really. But that scared part of me still wonders what if it doesn't work out?" Her eyes widened and she hastily amended, "Not that I don't want it to but in a hypothetical shit world where it doesn't, how are we supposed to work around each other if you get sent out for my consults or whatever?"

"If it doesn't work out in this gross hypothetical shitty world then I'm sure we could be mature enough to work together for regular vet consults or USDF stuff. If it doesn't work out then I'll still have a great job at LakeVets. One out of two ain't bad, though I'd prefer to keep both of the reasons I moved to Kentucky. Sweetheart, my job is the same regardless of whether or not we're sleeping together. And I mean, you managed not to kill me when we were kids and you hated me, right?"

Her answer was a quick and smiling, "For the millionth time, I didn't hate you."

"Okay, disliked and were confused by. Better?" I played my fingers over her thigh, delighting in the tightening of muscle and her quick inhalation.

"Yes, better."

I stroked higher and judging by her frustrated sound, it wasn't high enough. "I prefer to look on the bright side. We both want it to work, so we're going to do everything we can to make it happen." I stilled my hand. "Caitlyn, I fell in nerdy, hero-worshipping love with you when I was fourteen years old. Now, that feeling of being in love with you is so strong I feel like I can't exist without you in my life and I'm going to do everything I can to make sure you know that every day."

Caitlyn pushed me backward onto the couch and when she lay full length on top of me to straddle my thigh, the firm muscle of hers pressed between my legs. "Starting now?" she gasped.

"Yes. This very instant." I cupped the back of her neck to pull her down for a kiss.

The intensity of her response would have startled me if I hadn't felt so desperate myself. Caitlyn's tongue parted my lips and when I opened my mouth to her, I felt her quick intake of breath. I grabbed her ass, pulled her more firmly against me. Hands slid under my shirt and up my stomach to cup my breasts and when I sat up, she moved with me.

Clothing was an unwanted barrier and we quickly helped each other out of it. "Do you want to move to the bed?" she mumbled against my neck before she gently nipped under my jaw.

"No." Moving was the last thing I wanted. Losing the connection of skin on skin, the sensation of our hands and lips reconnecting was unfathomable. I felt as if I should say something, tell her just how much I'd missed this feeling. How I'd missed seeing her, touching her, listening to her. But I had no words that were adequate so I let my body speak for me and I knew she wouldn't mistake what it was saying.

Judging by her loud groans and gasps, Caitlyn's desire was as intense as mine. Every time we'd had sex before it'd been frantic, as if we'd both been desperate to absorb as much of each other as we could. This time, despite our hunger, we were slow and soft. No less passionate, but it felt like we'd both relaxed into one another, relaxed into knowing that we could have tomorrow, and all the tomorrows after. Our kisses were languid, our caresses careful and calculated. We took our time relearning each other, indulging until I felt I might shatter into a million pieces with the intensity of the sensations of being with her.

Even as we relearned things, there were those that needed no reminder. She knew how I loved that touch of teasing teeth on my nipple, the soft caress of tongue to follow. And every time I begged her to keep going, she'd chuckle as if it were the most obvious thing in the world and that she wouldn't stop until we were limp with satisfaction.

Without warning, Caitlyn abandoned her lavish attention to my breast and rolled off the couch. She knelt on the floor, then tugged and manipulated my legs until I sat up and leaned back. The anticipation of her mouth on me had my abdominals quivering and the wet heat of my arousal felt slick against my skin. She kissed her way slowly up the inside of one thigh, then the other as her fingernails traced patterns on my calves. After an eternity of torment she finally took me in her mouth. I arched against her, reached for her but Caitlyn took my hand and guided it to my breast, her fingers over mine teasing my nipple as her tongue played through my heat.

The silence between us felt intimate somehow. It wasn't an absolute silence—there were plenty of gasps…groans…low moans—but no words. We'd been unashamedly vocal every other time and afterward when I was alone, the exact tone of her "Fuck me, yes…harder, yes, please, there…right there…" would send a thrill of excitement through me. But now it felt as if we'd found another way to communicate. Caitlyn's mouth softened and the sensation of her lightly sucking my clit had me grinding myself into her, begging her for more.

Instead of more, she pushed herself up and straddled my thigh again, rocking herself forward against me. Despite the frantic movement of her hips, our kiss was slow and deep. She sucked my tongue and reached down to slide her fingers through my folds, pressing against my clit before slipping inside me. My head fell back against the couch as she teased and stroked, slicked and circled. She kissed me, sucked my neck, licked my collarbone, and the whole time she kept up that sweet torture on my clit, holding me right on the edge of climax. And when I thought I might come apart, Caitlyn just…stopped. Her touch withdrew and all that was left was the slow soft movement of her lips against mine.

In the wake of her attention I'd been dimly aware of her wet arousal against my thigh and now she'd stopped fingering me, the evidence of that arousal was plain. Her breasts rose and fell in long, slow breaths, almost as if she was forcibly trying to calm herself. When I reached between her legs to find what I most craved, she raised herself up before settling slowly onto my fingers. I groaned at the wet heat of her, leaning forward to bury my face in her neck. Her fingers came back to me and as we moved together, the heat spreading through my body had me pressing my mouth to her neck as I tried desperately to hold off until she was ready.

I wrapped my arm around her waist and surrendered, kissing her as I came, trying not to dislodge her from my thigh. Within moments Caitlyn's nails dug into my arm and she cried out her climax, a glorious unashamed sound of pleasure. I tightened my arm around her waist, steadying her. Steadying myself. Our bodies were slick with sweat, her hair disheveled and escaping from its loose ponytail. When I felt I could speak again, I carefully pushed hair back from her face. "So... you're happy I moved here?"

Caitlyn's smile was slow. "Insanely happy. Because now you're going to cook me dinner."

CHAPTER THIRTY-ONE

Caitlyn

In the three months Addie had been living with me, she'd slotted seamlessly into my life and I into hers. Somehow we'd found our shared ground—the place where I could do my things, she could do hers and we met comfortably in the middle on everything else.

If she was home while I was in the barn, she'd wander down from the house to either watch me ride or help Wren and Brandon with feeding horses or general maintenance around the place. And it never seemed like she had to have her veterinary hat on. She was just someone who loved horses, and if she spotted something vetty that she thought worth mentioning then she did. I'd learned to accept that sometimes she just had shit days and it was nothing to do with me, and that she needed some time alone to buffer work and home. Taking things personally had always felt like a sport for me, but Addie's love was helping me to change my perspective.

I woke just before my alarm, gratified to realize she was still in bed, and asleep. She'd left for a call just after midnight and slipped back in a little after four a.m., which I was starting to learn was actually a quiet on-call night. We'd reached an agreement fairly early on when she'd tried to sleep in the spare room on her on-call nights so I wouldn't be disturbed and I'd nixed the idea after one night—all-hours calls, her in and out of bed and then more calls were nothing compared to being in bed without her where I kept waking anyway because she wasn't there.

She had to go in at eight to complete a half-day of work after her two-night run on call, and wanting to let her absorb as much sleep as she could, I smothered my urge to snuggle up to her and kiss her bare shoulders. To suck the smooth, warm skin of her neck. To slide my hands down over her breasts and belly to give her a proper wake-up. That was something reserved for those weekends when she didn't have to work or I wasn't competing and we had the luxury of a slightly later start.

Addie always slept as if sleep was the most important thing she had to do that day, and having seen the hours she worked, I understood. I slid out of bed, dressed and left the house as quietly as I could. After about twenty minutes aboard Dimity I heard her truck leaving. So much for her sleep.

I'd worked three horses when she came back a little after twelve. The riding schedule had a very specific event on that afternoon, and after I'd finished up with Dougie, I jogged back up to the house to find Addie at the breakfast bar nursing a cup of coffee. Her smile was luminous. And exhausted. She offered a husky, "Hey, babe."

"Hey yourself." I checked the level of coffee in her mug—adequate—then leaned down to meet her for a kiss. "Did you eat breakfast?"

A headshake.

"Do you want to talk about your night?" Another thing I'd learned was that she liked to discuss her rough nights, her hard cases, her difficult clients. Though *discuss* was a loose term. Mostly it was just her rambling, unpacking things so that she could move on while I offered as much support as I could in the form of mhmm's, ahh's, I see's and a lot of kisses.

Another headshake, though this one had a knowing smile. "Later."

"Are you hungry?"

Addie often existed in the space between ravenous and too tired to cook, and as much as I could, I fed her. And she never declined my offerings which was perhaps not the smartest thing. She'd taught me how to make *huevos rancheros* and I'd almost perfected it. By perfected, I mean I could cook and assemble the ingredients in approximately the right way without burning the house down and she rarely grimaced while eating.

At her, "Starving" I pulled out a carton of eggs and jars of salsa, *pico de gallo* and bean mix that Addie made up in her free time. "We can change the ride for another day if you're not feeling up to it?"

She finally verbalized something more than a single word answer, her voice quiet and rough with fatigue. "I don't wanna change it." Addie smiled, apparently picking up on my *You look like your eyes are barely open* expression. "Babe, you've had this on the schedule for weeks, and you've moved your usual training around just trying to line up with my roster."

All true, but I'd still change it again if she asked me to. The stubborn set of her jaw told me she wasn't going to change her mind. "Okay then, if you're sure."

"I'm sure. Today I will ride a horse." She flashed her dimples. "I'm not gonna ride him very well, but that was a given regardless of how much sleep I'd had."

"You'll be amazing."

"Dubious," she rebutted, but she was still smiling. After a long silence, during which she watched me try not to screw up her first meal of the day, she moved to my side while I poured two eggs into the pan. Addie slid behind me, wrapping her arms around my waist. She pulled me against her, pressed herself to me. Teeth lightly raked my skin followed by soft, soothing lips. Her words were muffled against my shoulder. "Do you know how hard it is to leave you in bed, all naked and warm and enticing, while I go out into the cold night to save a colicky horse?"

I turned my head and was rewarded with a lingering cheek kiss. "Probably about as hard as it is for me to leave naked and warm you in bed so I can train some horses first thing in the morning."

She kept kissing my cheek, playfully pretending to nibble my jaw. I twisted around in the circle of her arms. "It's very hard to concentrate on your breakfast when you're doing that. And you know how much I need to concentrate when cooking."

"What do you mean?" She adopted a faux-surprised expression and drawled, "Baby, I love surprise pieces of eggshell in my food."

"Just for that, you're getting runny yolk."

"Well it's always fifty-fifty as to whether I'll be gettin' hard or runny so that's really an empty threat." Addie kissed the side of my neck and stepped away before I could swat her. She leaned against the counter, quietly drinking coffee while I finished making her breakfast. When I'd heated the tortillas, Addie set her mug down. "How were the children this morning?"

I glanced back over my shoulder. "Dimity was Bitchy McBitcherson, and Dougie was really good. He's starting to get the hang of trot poles and has some great elevation over them." A quick check of the pan told me her meal was ready. "Dew was very confused and a little indignant about the fact he was groomed then put out into his field without being worked."

Addie pulled a plate down from the cabinet above her head. "Did you tell him we were going on an adventure?"

"I did. His response was asking if he could have a carrot, so my guess is he's not as excited about it as we are." I assembled her meal and passed it to her. Once we'd both settled at the table, I asked, "Are you nervous?"

"About your cookin'?" she asked dryly as she began her breakfast-slash-lunch. "Always."

There was nothing I could throw so I settled for a muttered, "Smartass."

Addie's smile stretched around her food. "I am, yes. But it's Dewey and I trust him. Plus I figure if *you* can manage to ride him then surely I, with my superior equestrian skills, can pull it off."

"Wow, you're on fire this afternoon."

"It's delirium caused by lack of sleep. Makes me extra witty." She frowned, then turned away and discreetly spat the mouthful she'd just forked up into a paper napkin.

"Dammit, I even cracked the eggs into a bowl to check for shell. I swear there was none when I looked."

She ran her tongue around her molars. "Must have been hiding under the yolk. It's fine, I really don't mind a bit of texture, honey." It was her standard response every time she found something amiss with my cooking.

Addie held out her hand to me. When I slid mine into hers, she resumed eating her meal one-handed, the other still holding mine. She had incredible hands, delicate yet strong, and never without callouses or chunks of skin missing. I ran my thumb up and down the side of her forefinger. "I love you."

Her eyes widened comically. "Wow. Seriously? That is the weirdest coincidence, because I love you too. Good thing we're together then, huh?"

I kissed her, lingering until I felt satisfied. It took a while. "Good thing indeed." I checked her empty plate then the time. "Whenever you're ready, we can head out. Unless you need some chill time before we go?"

Addie downed the last of her coffee. "I'm good. I'll just go brush my teeth and change into my pro rider gear."

She emerged ten minutes later, dressed in brand-new breeches and boots and carrying a new helmet. Glancing down at herself, she said,

"Well if nothing else, at least I look authentic. Feels so weird to be back in this stuff."

I took my time to enjoy the sight of her in breeches. She was no stranger to yoga or running tights, but this was something else entirely. "If you decide after today that you never want to ride, you're still going to put that gear on for me again."

"Pervert."

"You can talk. Don't think I don't notice the way you stare at me while I'm dressed to ride."

"No comment."

Addie caught Dew while I nabbed Dirk, and we quickly got them ready together in the two sets of cross-ties that let them be close without touching. She asked me to double check everything once she'd saddled Dew then unclipped him and put her helmet on before leading him to the indoor arena. Wren and Brandon were conspicuously absent, though they were probably up in their house with binoculars watching Addie's reentry to the equestrian world. She mounted easily and shuffled to get into position. "This saddle is so comfortable."

"Only the best for my girl."

"And for you too, given it's one of your saddles."

Laughing I agreed, "True."

I was unsure if I should offer any tips or just sit back, but Addie thankfully solved my internal debate for me. "It's been a while. Gimme some pointers?"

As I shortened the stirrup leathers, I told her the same thing I told everyone who had ridden Dew. "Just think it, and he'll do it. He's the best body language expert I know." With a wink, I added, "But just in case he doesn't speak his stepmom's language, then don't be afraid to ask him more forcefully. He might be an Olympic superstar, but all his basics are the same. Leg for go, rein pressure and weight for slow, rein and opposite leg for steering. And despite what some people think, you're not going to ruin him or mess up his training."

"Mhmm, okay." She gathered the reins as Dew turned his head to smell her boot. He licked it, nibbled at it until she shooed him away. His expression was hilariously confused, and I could almost imagine his mental process as he tried to figure out what the hell Addie was doing up there instead of on the ground.

Once Addie was settled, I kissed her hand then left her to walk Dew around the arena and get comfortable while I fetched Dirk. Dew was utterly trustworthy and I knew they'd be fine for a few minutes. Dew was doing the very definition of amble—not putting in an ounce more effort than Addie was asking of him. I halted Dirk at the arena gate and leaned down to adjust my stirrups ready for the trail. "How're you doing, gorgeous?"

"He never seems this lazy for you," Addie called from the middle of the arena.

"Actually, I was asking Dew."

She gave me a middle finger.

Laughing, I said, "Not as easy as I make it look, is it?"

"You would make riding an unbroken mustang look easy. Come on, let's go."

I'd planned a short forty-five-minute loop, which would be more than enough for Addie's reentry to riding. The tree-lined trail had some small hills if she felt up to a little speed, and after fifteen minutes of walk with a few short sections of trot, she popped Dew into canter after a breathless, "I'm gonna try a canter. That okay?"

"Sure." Dirk startled at Dew cantering away and without my asking, began cantering too. He protested when I reminded him that he had to wait for aids, but eventually settled into a nice forward trot. Dew's canter was slow and collected which meant we were able to keep side by side and I could keep an eye on Addie. Not that I really needed to—she rode like a natural and as if she'd never taken a break.

Once we'd slowed back to walk, her neck patting was exuberant. "God, he's so good."

"It's all about the training, darling." I grinned. "And I suppose just a little of his natural amenability helps some."

"For someone who really doesn't have an ego, you sure have some ego."

I blew her a kiss and she responded with one of her own, then a question. "D'you think we could do this again?"

My answer was an immediate, "Of course. Means we're working two horses at once and also you riding Dew out means Wren or Brandon don't have to come out with me, and they can have a break."

"Maybe I'll have to get my own horse one day, some chill Quarter Horse or something to wander around the trails with once a month."

"If that's what you want, then let's do it. It's not like we don't have the space for more horses."

She stretched forward to softly tug Dew's ear and he responded with his happy grunty snort. "We'll see. I don't know if I'll be able to ride anything else after this one."

"I know the feeling."

Addie flashed me a wicked grin. "That's a kinda mean thing to say in front of Dirk." She gathered her reins. "Ready for some more canter?"

I shortened mine too. "Race ya." Dirk pigrooted. Dimwit.

We spent the rest of the ride alternating between walk, trot, and canter, talking and laughing and laying out plans for the fast-approaching competition season in Europe. My heart rate spiked when I noticed Dew happily passaging along the trail. A lazy passage, granted, but it was still passage and the slow, elevated, cadenced trot looked utterly ridiculous in such surroundings.

Addie glanced over at me. "Uh…why?" She didn't seem bothered, or in any danger of hitting the deck, so I relaxed.

"Did you ask him to do that?"

"I have no idea." Her eyes widened. "But I feel like we're not supposed to be passaging on a relaxing trail outing. And especially not when we're almost home and we should be cooling down."

I collapsed forward onto Dirk's neck, laughing so much I was almost crying. When I could finally breathe again, I offered a not entirely helpful, "Then just stop asking him to passage."

"If I don't know how I asked him to start passaging, then I don't know how to stop him, obviously." Her mouth set in a determined line and after a moment I saw her relax, then soften the rein contact. Dew deflated to a walk and I swear he looked pleased with himself, as if he'd just given Addie a gift. She stroked his neck, leaning forward to scratch up and down his mane. "Guess I was a little tense."

"Maybe a little. So now you know how to passage, would you mind riding my tests for me next weekend? I'm sure nobody would notice anything different."

She let both feet fall from the stirrups and pulled her leg away from Dew's sides. Groaning, she rubbed the inside of her thigh. "I'm pretty sure I'm not going to be able to walk next weekend, let alone embark on more riding."

"No riding?" I asked coyly. "Well that's a pity…"

"No riding horses," she quickly corrected me as she fumbled to get her feet back in the stirrups.

I moved Dirk closer and reached over to grasp the leather, twisting it so the stirrup sat perpendicular to Dew's belly and she could kick her toe in. "You know, the best thing for sore inner upper thigh muscles is massage."

"Are you offering?"

"Mhmm, I am. But my hands have a tendency to slip while I'm massaging upper thighs." I shrugged. "Sorry."

"I'm sure I'll forgive you."

I would have leaned over and kissed her if Dirk hadn't chosen that moment to spot a gremlin in the bushes right by the gate that opened onto my back field and execute a sideways twisty upward spook so violent I would have been tossed if I didn't spend every second aboard him readying myself for such a reaction to nothing at all. Dewey had no response to the incident except for something that looked an awful lot like an equine eyeroll. As if he'd never spooked at anything in his life, the big hypocrite.

Dirk fidgeted as I leaned down to unchain the gate connecting my property to the trails, which led to a mild argument about manners and appropriate responses to my aids. Dew looked on, bored, and with a definitely disapproving uncle vibe about him. Once we'd both made it through the gate, and Dirk had listened enough that I could close and latch it again, Addie and I rode at a walk toward the barn.

I let the reins out to the buckle so Dirk could stretch, and twisted toward Addie who'd done the same for Dew. "So I've been thinking, and I have a very serious question for you."

"I'm listening." She grinned. "I'm wary, but I'm listening."

"Do you want to make a baby with me?"

EPILOGUE

Addie

"Come on, honey, just push for me. You can do it, give me a push and we're going to have a beautiful baby."

Caitlyn sagged, wiping her face on her shirtsleeve. "God, I don't think I can do any more. I'm exhausted."

I glanced up and was instantly struck dumb, enraptured and awestruck by the sight of her. Muddy and wet from the rain, she was so damned beautiful that she made my heart quicken every time I looked at her. "Take a break then, babe. She'll be okay, you don't need to hold her head up. But she's not progressing the way I'd like so I'm going in to check what's going on in there." The white amniotic sack had appeared, but nothing else, and we'd just reached one of my most important foaling rules—if I didn't see part of a foal twenty minutes after the sack's appearance, it was time to investigate. "Can you grab the lube and a glove, please?"

I washed and dried my hands, put the shoulder-length glove on my right arm and knelt in the mud. Caitlyn pumped lube all along my arm and I carefully inserted my hand and felt around, trying to figure out what the actual hell was going on in there. After so many foalings, I knew what I *should* be feeling but it always took a minute to puzzle it out.

I shuffled into a more comfortable position on my stomach with my head resting on the mare's butt. I was exhausted, wet with not only rain and mud but birth fluids, which itched like crazy. *What have I got, what have I got?*

Caitlyn was trying hard to disguise her panic. "What's going on? Is she okay?"

"It's okay, darling. Just trying to work out the position of the foal."

I finally figured it out. Instead of both forelimbs outstretched for birth with its head resting on those legs as it should be, ready to dive down the birth canal, the foal had a leg hooked around the back of its neck. I needed to reposition it or it was not going to come out. A few days ago when I'd scanned the mare, the wretched foal had been in perfect position for delivery. Not anymore. "Can you grab the clenbuterol from my vet kit please? It's right on top, ready to go. I'm going to have to give her a shot to relax the uterus and give me some room to work."

Caitlyn grabbed the syringe. "I don't know how you do this day in, day out."

I grinned up at her. "To be fair, I don't have foalings every day, and certainly not overdue mares with a foal who's decided they just *had* to be in a stupid position." I poked Stella's stomach. "Are you listening in there?"

"If it's anything like its uncle, I'd say no, it isn't listening." Caitlyn had found Stella a year ago and snapped her up. She was technically a half-sister to Dewey—by the same stallion as Dew, and her dam shared half her bloodline with Dewey's dam, Antoinette. Caitlyn had joked that someone had been trying to make a Dewey two-point-oh. We'd used artificial insemination to put Stella in foal to Dougie and had both been waiting anxiously for the past eleven months for Dewey's niece or nephew. The waiting had been made slightly less anxious by the fact it'd been a near-perfect pregnancy. Miracle of miracles. Of course the flipside of a near-perfect pregnancy was an annoying birth with a foaling dystocia.

I huffed. "Of course, our foal couldn't have a straightforward birth, could it? And it couldn't be born inside, during the day instead of outside at night in the middle of heavy rain, could it?" Stella hated being confined and had a walk-in, walk-out stall adjoining her run. Still, the polite thing would have been to foal inside. "More lube please."

"What would be the fun in being warm and dry?" Caitlyn pumped more lube onto my arm. "At least out here we have a full audience." All the horses in their stalls had been watching on and off except for

Dewey who hadn't moved from staring out his back door since Caitlyn and I had first come out of the house at the sound of the foaling alarm. He seemed utterly transfixed. Caitlyn held out the syringe of clenbuterol. "Here."

"Darlin'. You probably didn't notice but I'm kinda stuck up to my shoulder in the birth canal so not exactly in a position to reach her neck to give her that injection. Can you please give it to her IV?"

Her sheepish smile was distorted in the rainy spotlight. "Sorry." As she crouched by Stella's neck she asked, "What about Delilah? Dillon?"

"Both sound good." She'd been throwing D-names at me since I'd confirmed Stella was in foal, because now naming her horses something that began with D was a superstition.

Seconds after Caitlyn had administered the injection, Stella apparently decided she was done with labor. She rolled back onto her stomach instead of the flat-on-her-side position she'd been in for the last fifteen minutes, and in the process just about torqued my arm out of its socket.

Thanks.

And because my arm hadn't taken enough punishment, she'd also decided it was time for more contractions, the first squeezing my arm so much it felt like she'd cut off blood flow. I lay flat on my stomach in the mud and pushed the foal back through the pelvic inlet so I'd have room to manipulate the leg. The extra room was a godsend and I could have cried in relief. "That's it, you little brat." To protect the uterus I cupped the gelatinous underside of the foal's hoof and carefully pushed the leg back, flexing it to get the leg over the neck. The moment I felt it pop over I extended the leg to get it into the right position with the foal's head resting on both forelimbs.

I kissed the wet horse hair under my cheek. "Thank you, Stella! And thank you, foal. Babe, watch out, it's about to get noisy. She's all slack in there so I'll have to help and pull this foal out. Can you get the resuscitation gear ready please just in case this doesn't go as smoothly as I'm hoping it will."

I waited to feel the next contraction and with my hands around the foal's fetlocks, pulled toward myself. Another contraction and I had a torso. This was the moment where I always held my breath, worried about hiplock and the foal getting stuck in the pelvic canal. Apparently, Stella was worried too and I hadn't had the next contraction I'd expected. I nudged her with my elbow. "Stella, can you fuckin' help me out here please?"

Stella, bless her heart, was agreeable to my suggestion. She heaved a few loud groans, I pulled, and within seconds the foal landed in my lap in a wet, slippery tangle of limbs. I tipped it to the ground and immediately propped it up to make sure its airways were clear. A few firm strokes down the foal's head to clear fluids out of its nose and it huffed a breath. Then another. And another. And then it exhaled a snorty little whinny.

Huffing a few relieved breaths of my own, I sank down and lowered the foal to the ground. Caitlyn dropped down beside me. "Is it okay?"

I was crying as I usually did during foalings—a mix of being exhausted and filthy and how everything was so beautiful and miracle of life shit. "Breathing and moving, so yes." I raised a hindleg to check the umbilical cord was still attached. "A gorgeous filly and lots of bling. Well there will be when that amniotic fluid is washed off and all the white is white instead of yellow."

Her laughter was part crying. "Similar markings to Dew."

I wiped my face with my sleeve, which was utterly useless given the rain. "It sure is." Dewey had lost his shit at the foal's arrival and had begun calling out, the deep sound of his whinny breaking through the hammer of rain on the roof. His vocalization was setting everyone else off, especially Dougie—fair enough, given it was his first kid—until it was like the scene in the *Lion King* of everyone welcoming the new baby.

I stood and pulled Caitlyn up with me to give the mare and foal room to move. The filly was moving in that jerky, just-born, oh-my-goodness, what-is-this-new-stimulus kind of way, so I deemed her okay for now. I checked Stella who'd rolled back onto her stomach and was looking around at her foal, nickering a huffy, soft I'm-in-love sound. Seemed all okay at that end too. First hurdle of foaling overcome. I leaned into Caitlyn, crossing my arms over my chest.

This was quite possibly my favorite part of being a veterinarian— the first moments when the mare realizes what has just happened and they get the dopey adoration thing going on. It was definitely more intense this time because I'd done the insemination, seen Stella every single day and been involved with the day-to-day stuff instead of just popping in and out to check and test and hand over medication and give directives.

Stella kept looking at the filly, still making little throaty noises which had the foal's ears jerking. After five minutes or so, with both of them starting to move, the umbilical cord broke away from the placenta. They lay like that for another few minutes, just staring at each other and talking mare and foal love language until Stella stretched her forelegs out and stood. The moment she was up, she spun around and nosed the filly. I disengaged from Caitlyn to take care of the birth membranes, tying them up so Stella wouldn't stand on them and tear them, because screw that sort of complication right now.

The moment I moved back to her side, Caitlyn slid her arm around my waist, pulling me closer against her. We were both soaked with rain and assorted grime and I was starting to come down from my adrenaline high which meant I was getting shaky. I shuddered. "We're gonna have to move them inside as soon as the foal gets up." I squinted into the rain. "Luckily it's not too cold but I'd be happier if they were both in out of the weather."

"Same."

The lights in Wren and Brandon's cottage flicked on and I knew we'd have company and another few sets of hands if needed. I sent up pleas to the universe that the foal would stand and move and suckle soon so we could get them into a stall and go back to bed. Thankfully the filly seemed to be thinking about standing, probably helped by Stella's nuzzling and licking.

There was nothing more for humans to do except wait. Caitlyn's hand slipped under my wet shirt to rest against my wet skin as we watched Stella and her foal bonding. Stella was acting like she'd just been given the world's greatest gift and she couldn't quite believe it.

I peered up at Caitlyn and murmured, "Someone's in love."

Her smile was brilliant in the rain-streaked spotlight beaming from the exterior of the building and she held my gaze for the longest time. That gaze said everything. We'd made the right choices. We were exactly where we were meant to be, even if it'd taken decades to find this place together.

She wiped mud off my cheek then kissed me softly. "Yes. Someone is."

GLOSSARY

Dressage, if you're not familiar with it, may seem like a foreign language. Honestly—sometimes it feels like that to me too. Below are some terms you'll find within the novel along with a few pronunciations to help you feel like a pro.

Dressage: The word is derived from a French term meaning "training." Dressage is training a horse in such a way that develops confidence, flexibility, balance, suppleness, and obedience. Think of it as gymnastics for horses where competitors ride set tests of movements according to training levels. In dressage, as with all equestrian sport, men and women compete directly against each other and under the same rules.

Grand Prix: The highest level of dressage competition with the most difficult movements. There are three possible Grand Prix tests – the Grand Prix, the Grand Prix Special and the Grand Prix Freestyle to Music. It generally takes a minimum of five years for a professional to train a horse to this level.

Walk: The horse's slowest gait, a four-beat movement.

Trot: The horse's middle gait, a two-beat movement equivalent to a human jogging.

Canter: The horse's third gait, a three-beat movement in which the horse "leads" with either the left or right foreleg.

Collected: Where the horse shortens its stride, shifting weight and balance to its hindquarters without changing the rhythm or tempo of the gait, or losing impulsion.

Extended: Where the horse lengthens its stride to cover more ground without changing the rhythm or tempo of the gait.

Piaffe (pee-ahhff): A highly collected trot which is cadenced and elevated, giving the impression of trotting on the spot.

Passage (pas-ahhge): A measured, very collected trot, elevated and cadenced where the horse is able to move forward.

(Canter) Pirouette: The horse pivots in a very small circle around its hind legs, which stay more or less in place, while maintaining the quality of the gait.

Half-pass: A movement in trot or canter where the horse moves forward and sideways across the arena while keeping its body almost parallel to the side. The legs appear to cross as the horse reaches sideways with each step.

Flying change (of leg): Where the horse changes the leading canter leg in the brief moment of suspension following the third beat in canter. One-time (tempi) changes are where the horse changes its leading leg every stride—and looks like skipping—and two-time (tempi) changes are where it changes its leading leg every second stride.

Aid: What the rider uses to communicate with their horse, e.g. hands/legs/seat/core.

Dressage arena: 20x60 meter space, with horse-appropriate footing, where dressage tests are performed. Letter markers are in set locations around the arena to indicate where each movement of the test is to be performed. The judges—seven at the Olympics—sit behind designated markers, giving them different vantage points to allocate scores out of a maximum of ten for each movement.

Bella Books, Inc.

Women. Books. Even Better Together.

P.O. Box 10543
Tallahassee, FL 32302

Phone: 800-729-4992
www.bellabooks.com

CPSIA information can be obtained
at www.ICGtesting.com
Printed in the USA
JSHW040453130421
13509JS00001B/1